Pirates of Aletharia

Pirates of Aletharia

LESBIANS, PIRATES, & DRAGONS
BOOK ONE

BRITNEY JACKSON

Noctem
Publishing

Contents

PIRATES OF ALETHARIA

Hardcover ISBN: 9798787510119

Paperback ISBN: 9798790135699

Published by Noctem Publishing

First Edition, December 2021

www.britneyjackson.com

Dedication

For every girl who wanted to be a pirate or kiss a pirate…

And for anyone who's ever longed for a place to belong…

Synopsis

Emilia Drakon was once the youngest and kindest of the dragon sorcerers, but she's now the last of her kind. Betrayed and angry, she trades her meekness for a sword and embarks on a quest for vengeance that will lead her straight into the arms of the legendary Captain Maria Welles.

Captain of the famed pirate ship, the *Wicked Fate*, Maria is every bit as treacherous and bloodthirsty as they say. She has her own vendetta and practically jumps at the chance to trick Emilia into joining her crew.

But when their animosity toward each other blossoms into a passionate romance, the two women will have to decide what they want most.

Vengeance?

Or love?

An award-winning sapphic fantasy romance for people who love dangerous women, magical worlds, and lesbian pirates.

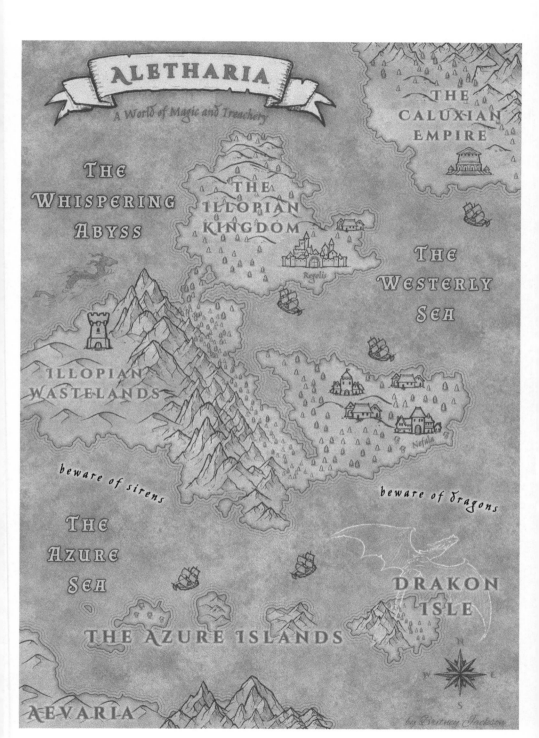

CHAPTER 1
A Villainous Descent

O n the day of her execution, Emilia Drakon decided that the only thing worse than being born an evil sorceress was being born a kind one.

If she'd been a little less kind, the woman Emilia loved would've never had the chance to betray her.

If she'd been a little less kind, Catherine Rochester would be dead—and not standing in front of Emilia, all proud and beautiful and…

Alive.

The guards tasked to escort Emilia to the gallows came to an abrupt halt at the sight of Emilia's ex-lover—which, unfortunately, meant that Emilia had to stop, as well.

The guards saluted Catherine, while Emilia—shackled at the wrists and ankles—simply glared.

"You're dismissed," Catherine told the guards.

That was the final insult, really—that Catherine assumed Emilia had learned nothing from the betrayal, that she assumed Emilia would walk to her death willingly.

Emilia Drakon was naïve once.

1

Not anymore.

"Admiral," one guard said, "with all due respect, she's—"

"I know what she is," Catherine said. "More so than you, I assure you."

"Yes, Admiral," the guard said. Even so, he hesitated. "But we were ordered to keep fourteen armed guards around her at all times."

Catherine folded her hands tightly behind her back and lifted her chin, her long, blonde hair glittering like gold in the sun. "And I, as your admiral, am belaying that order," she said. "Are you questioning my authority?"

"No, Admiral," the guard said quickly. "I would never."

Emilia narrowed her eyes at Catherine.

Only a few months earlier, she'd been enamored by the pride that glowed in Catherine's beautiful, light blue eyes.

Now, she despised it.

The guards, of course, followed Catherine's orders, like the mindless fools they were.

Alone with her traitorous lover, at last, Emilia trailed her gaze downward, taking in the sight of Catherine in uniform.

Perhaps, if Catherine had been dressed like this—and not injured and bleeding—when they'd brought her to Emilia, she would've known better.

In that pressed, blue waistcoat that made her blue eyes sparkle like the sea itself, it was obvious where Catherine's loyalties lay.

Though Emilia couldn't see the crowd from where she stood, their chants rung out, clear as a bell.

"Kill the witch!"

"Kill the witch!"

"Kill the witch!"

Almost as if she actually cared enough to *feel* uneasy about those chants, Catherine cleared her throat. "You've lost some weight."

Not that it was much in the grand scheme of things, but they had *at least* allowed Emilia to trade her rags from the dungeon for the clothing she'd worn before her arrest.

And those clothes hung loosely from Emilia's curves now, no longer fitted to her form.

"Yes," Emilia said, her voice like ice, "that tends to happen when you're not allowed to *eat*."

Catherine sighed. "They offered you food in exchange for information," she reminded Emilia. "It was your own choice to starve, instead."

Emilia forced a bitter smile. "Perhaps the *only* good choice I've made recently."

Catherine narrowed her eyes at that.

The clouds shifted in the sky, and Emilia cringed away from the sunlight. She hadn't left the dungeons in weeks, and the mid-afternoon sun burned her eyes.

Perhaps sensing weakness, Catherine stepped closer. "Emilia," she said, using that same gentle tone she'd used when they were lovers, "I have a lot of power now."

"So I've heard," Emilia sneered, "Admiral Rochester."

Again, Catherine sighed at her tone. "I don't want to see you hang."

Emilia lifted her wrists, the heavy shackles rattling in protest. "Then, maybe you shouldn't have put these on me."

The crowd roared louder, and Emilia realized the executioners had taken their places.

"To them, you're just another witch," Catherine said, as if that somehow justified the crowd's cruel excitement, "but I know better. You're different, Emilia. You're not like your mother."

Emilia scoffed at that. Did Catherine truly think the events of the last few months hadn't changed her?

Now, who was naïve?

"No, I'm not like her," Emilia agreed, "because she's dead, and I'm alive."

Catherine looked away. "It would upset a great deal of people," she said softly, "but with your cooperation, I can still save you."

Emilia lifted her eyebrows, as the gleeful chants of the crowd filled the silence between them.

"You got another witch for them to kill?" Emilia said.

"Like I said," Catherine said, "they'll be upset." She stepped closer. "But I'm still willing to do it—as long as you assure me that nothing has changed between us."

Emilia stared blankly at Catherine, stunned that those soft, perfect lips she'd kissed so many times were capable of such absurdity.

"You used and betrayed me. You slaughtered my people," Emilia said slowly. "You drugged me—used the secrets I'd shared with you against me." The acid in her voice grew thicker with each word. "You let them torture me, and now, you want me to tell you that nothing's changed?"

"I didn't do this to you, Emilia," Catherine told her. "I simply enforced the law. You're the one who—"

"Who what?" Emilia interrupted. "Was born? What terrible thing did I do—aside from saving your life?"

Catherine hesitated.

"And trusting *you*," Emilia snarled.

"Emilia," Catherine said with a sigh, "it's starting to sound like you have no intention of cooperating."

"I'm in shackles," Emilia reminded her. "How uncooperative can I be?"

Apparently, her sarcasm came through clearly enough to make Catherine think twice—because the woman Emilia had once loved suddenly looked down at the shackles, her eyes wide with alarm.

It was now or never.

Emilia shook off the shackles and lunged forward, snatching the sword from Catherine's sheath.

After so long with no food or rest, Emilia's arm ached at the weight of the sword, but she pressed through the pain and slashed it upward, as Catherine had once taught her to do.

Catherine froze, raising both hands, as the blade pressed against her throat.

"Emilia," she gasped.

Emilia looked up at the Illopian admiral, pressing the blade closer to her throat. "Where's my dagger?"

"Emilia," Catherine whispered, "give me my sword, and we can do this the right way."

"I've tried that already," Emilia reminded her. "I got my people killed, doing things the *right* way." She narrowed her eyes. "I think I'll try doing it the *wrong* way for a bit."

Catherine lowered one hand, reaching out toward Emilia's wrist, but Emilia swiftly shifted the sword, nearly sending the blade straight through Catherine's throat.

Both of her hands instantly went back up.

"My dagger," Emilia snarled. "I know you know where it is."

A slight flush darkened Catherine's porcelain-white skin.

"Emilia—"

Emilia was getting tired of hearing her name come out of that mouth—especially when the memories it triggered were *so* painful.

"Dagger!"

"You'll never make it past an entire armed guard with nothing but a dagger," Catherine warned, "especially not in the shape you're in right now."

"What armed guard? You sent them away," Emilia said with a sharp laugh. "Fortunately, the one thing I *can* count on is your pride. I knew you'd never let them see how you really defeated the dragon sorcerers." A bitter smile curled at her lips. "They wouldn't approve, would they?"

"No," Catherine admitted. Her brows creased. "I assumed you'd tell them. If you'd told them about us, they might've given you food in exchange for the information. But you didn't. I thought —" Catherine sighed. "I thought that meant you still loved me."

Emilia forced herself not to react to that. "Dagger, Catherine."

With a slow sigh, Catherine said, "I'll need to move my hands."

"Fine," Emilia said, "and I'll consider not slicing your throat open, when you do."

Catherine reached beneath her waistcoat and removed a long, sheathed dagger. She held it out, offering it to Emilia.

Emilia looked down at the dagger. "You've had it?" she said, blinking in shock. "All this time?"

Catherine nodded. "Emilia," she said softly, "I *do* love you."

Emilia knew she couldn't listen to that, lest her heart return to its softened state—the one Catherine had so easily taken advantage of.

"If you do this," Catherine said, "you'll only confirm what they already believe about you. You'll become the villain they think you are." She softened her voice, until it was nearly inaudible amidst the crowd's chants. "I don't want to watch you descend into villainy, Emilia."

Emilia's stare turned cold. "Then, close your eyes."

With that, she pulled the sword back and thrust it into Catherine's stomach.

Then, Emilia fled, leaving a blade inside the woman she'd once loved.

Emilia slid behind a tall, stone building and unsheathed the dagger her mother had given her.

Her mother hadn't given her much, but in that moment, this one gift was worth more than any other could've been.

Because it was her key to freedom—and her key to vengeance.

Only a few moments passed before the alarms were sounded, and then, boots pounded against the dirt, as the guards searched the city for her.

Like any form of creation accessible to mortals, magic didn't come from nothing.

Only gods could create from nothing.

Magic was more like transmutation than creation—taking from the sorcerer and creating something else in turn.

Emilia hadn't eaten well in weeks, and she'd used the last of her own energy to free herself from the shackles. If she wanted to create fire, she'd need to take from somewhere else.

Fortunately, her mother had crafted this enchanted dagger for that exact purpose.

Its magic had kept her alive, even through starvation, and now, its magic would give her the power to escape.

The sound of boots against dirt grew louder, and Emilia knew she didn't have much time left.

She closed her eyes and drew the magic from the blade, channeling it into a spell she'd pay dearly for.

In body and soul, she'd pay the price for this spell for months to come.

But it was her only chance.

She channeled the stored dragon magic into herself, and then, she cast a spell that her mother had once taught her—one she'd never intended to use.

As magical fire consumed the city of Regolis, their chants for her execution turned to screams.

With her own heart aching at the loss of her innocence, Emilia escaped in the ensuing chaos.

CHAPTER 2

A Pirate Port

After three months on the run, Emilia finally found a port city that *wasn't* swarming with the Royal Navy.

The inhabitants of this city seemed significantly less wealthy than the inhabitants of other port cities she'd seen. Fishing and merchant vessels filled the harbor, but the wealthier naval or passenger vessels were nowhere to be seen.

Even the sanitation of the city reflected less wealth and upkeep. Apparently, the great King Eldric only cared for the cities that put gold in his pockets.

What a strange coincidence, Emilia thought bitterly.

Though it was unfortunate for the city itself, Emilia was relieved by the navy's absence—because it meant she could finally rest for a while. For the first time since being captured, Emilia slept through the night.

She'd emerge the next morning to steal food, but for this one night, she'd rest.

It wasn't just for nutrients that she needed the food—though that was certainly a concern, as well. Emilia also needed food in order to use her magic. Magic required a sacrifice of energy, and if she had none to give, she'd either have to steal energy from someone else—through a blood sacrifice—or leave herself utterly defenseless.

And leaving herself utterly defenseless seemed like a bad idea, considering the entire Royal Navy was hunting her.

Emilia awoke the next morning feeling more rested than she'd felt in months. So, she slipped on her cloak, lifted the hood to hide her face, and ventured down to the water in search of food.

To her shock, however, she found the harbor empty. She blinked a few times, halfway convinced she was dreaming.

Wasn't it just the day before that she'd seen the merchant ships out here?

Emilia walked out onto the dock, carefully avoiding the loose planks of wood. This city desperately needed some repairs.

She passed several battered, wooden stands—where the merchants sold their wares, she assumed—but today, they were all empty. It was as if the city had evacuated in anticipation of a hurricane, and yet...the sky was a clear, cloudless blue.

Something had scared them all into hiding, but what could it have been?

Emilia noticed the wooden post with papers nailed to it. There was one in every town.

As discreetly as possible, she searched the Wanted Person notices for any depictions of herself. She saw image upon image of scraggly criminals—murderers, debtors, thieves—but she saw no drawings of herself.

One notice, in particular, drew Emilia's gaze. Listed beneath the drawing was a list of crimes so long that it required multiple papers. She didn't recognize the face of this criminal, but she recognized the name.

Captain Maria Welles.

She doubted there was anyone in Aletharia who didn't know that name.

The most dangerous villainess of the seas—a woman who sank ships without mercy and left no survivors.

Well…that was the story, anyway.

Emilia had healed some of her victims—the ones who'd washed ashore on Drakon Isle. So, though the pirate had clearly intended to leave no survivors, thanks to Emilia, some survived, anyway.

It was strange, after all of this time, to pair an image with the name.

Captain Maria Welles was more legend than person—a cautionary tale for sailors, a whispered horror story for children.

The stories had a way of distorting her into some sort of monster. So, to see her depicted as a normal woman—and an attractive one, at that—felt strange.

The name Maria Welles meant one more thing to Emilia, though.

She'd heard it often while she was with Catherine. Catherine never referred to Maria Welles as a captain, but she'd snarl the name *Maria* under her breath every time the subject came up. Catherine had loathed the pirate captain. She'd referred to her as a plague and a menace.

She'd told tales of how the pirate tricked and evaded her—and once, while drunk, she'd said she should've killed her while she had the chance.

Emilia gazed at the drawing, now, and wondered if the scars that marred the pirate's face were the result of that *chance*. Had Catherine left the scars?

Once, she would've thought the idea was absurd. Catherine had seemed so kind and gentle to her, but Emilia knew better now.

The woman in the drawing wore a tricornered hat and a black, leather doublet. In Illopian fashion, these clothing choices might've been considered masculine.

But, of course, these arbitrary lines were nonexistent in Emilia's culture—and less distinct in most others.

"I wouldn't get seen looking at that, if I were you."

Emilia spun around, startled by a voice behind her.

A man with dirty clothes and long, greasy, brown hair—tied behind his head with a frayed ribbon—leaned against a wooden stand behind her, watching her with a smile that struck her as arrogant.

Aside from that smile, she had no reason to distrust the man, and yet, already, she did. "What do you mean?"

With a dirty hand that was arrayed in ill-fitting, gold jewelry, the man pointed at the Wanted Person notice. "I'd bet my life whoever nailed that up there is already dead," he warned her. "Get caught looking at it like that, and they might kill you, too."

Emilia eyed him suspiciously. "*Who* might kill me?"

He waved a hand, and his loose, gold jewelry clanged. "She has eyes everywhere here."

"Who?" Emilia said again.

"The one you were studying so intently," he said. He offered her a tight smile. "Captain Maria Welles."

Emilia returned her attention to the notice. What was it about this woman that constantly drew her gaze? Was it curiosity? Attraction? Hope?

Even though the artist had drawn her in quite the severe manner, Captain Maria Welles was still lovely in her own way— with plump, curved lips and warm, alluring eyes. Was it simply attraction that Emilia was feeling? Or was it the hope that the enemy of her enemy might be her friend?

Or a temporary ally, at least.

"Captain Maria Welles practically owns Nefala—in everything but deed," the man added. "You can't do anything in this city without her finding out."

Emilia returned her gaze to him. "Well," she said, "I appreciate the warning, but I should be on my way."

Oddly enough, there'd been no depictions of Emilia on the post, but that didn't mean she was any less wary of being recognized.

Emilia tried to step past the man, but he stepped in front of her before she could. A nauseating twinge of suspicion swirled in her stomach.

"How?" the man asked. He made a show of looking around at the empty dock. "All the ships are gone."

Emilia narrowed her eyes at him. "What makes you think I need a ship? I never said where I was going."

"You're at the docks," the man pointed out. "Why else would you be here?" He gestured at the post, feigning concern. "Not worried about the notices, surely?"

Emilia clamped her mouth shut—to prevent herself from saying anything she'd regret. "Of course not," she said between clenched teeth. "Out of curiosity," she said, after a moment, "where *did* everyone go?"

The man chuckled, "You're new here, aren't you?"

Emilia sighed, imploring the goddess to grant her patience. Patronizing tones had never sat well with her. "I just got here," she confirmed. "So, where are they?"

He scowled, clearly not impressed with her tone.

Well…the feeling was mutual.

"You must realize what sort of city this is."

Emilia shrugged. "It's a port city—on the Azure Sea."

"Not just any port, miss," he corrected. "It's a *pirate* port." He waved his hand at the poorly maintained dock. "The Illopian king has all but forgotten about us—which makes Nefala the perfect port for pirates."

Emilia frowned. "Then, where have the pirates gone?"

"Word has it that someone spotted the *Wicked Fate* on the horizon," he explained. "They all scatter when the fearsome Captain Maria Welles comes to town."

Emilia's brows furrowed. "Wicked Fate? Is that the name of her ship?" She couldn't remember Catherine using that name. Catherine had called it the *Glorious Destiny*, she'd thought. Perhaps the pirates had renamed it.

It did sound like a twisted version of the same name. A glorious destiny became a wicked fate.

"I thought all Illopians knew Maria Welles captained the *Wicked Fate*," the man said.

Emilia hesitated at that. Perhaps it was just her anxiety, but she thought that 'all Illopians' remark had sounded a little…pointed. "Well, as I said before, I should be on my way." She tried, yet again, to walk around him.

But he followed her. "You look sick," he informed her. "Are you plagued? Will I need to see a physician?"

Emilia rolled her eyes. *The nerve of this man.* "No."

"Then, why do you look so sick?" he questioned.

Emilia strolled up a dirt path—not wanting to head back toward the forest with this man still following her. "I haven't eaten in a while."

"So, that's why you were at the docks!" he said, his voice a little breathless, after running to keep up with her. "You were looking for the merchants!"

Emilia froze—so suddenly that he almost ran into her. She turned. "Do you know where they went?"

"Hiding," the man told her, "like every other law-abiding person in Nefala." He laughed a little at that. "Not that there *are* many law-abiding people here."

Emilia's frown deepened. "So, that's it? They hear the most notorious pirate in Aletharia is in town, and they hide?" she asked. "Why don't they send word to the king? He could send his troops to capture her."

The man's hazel eyes widened. He stepped closer—his skin somehow pale, beneath all of that dirt. "You can't say that here!" he hissed. "I told you. She has eyes everywhere! There's nothing that goes on here that she doesn't hear about!"

Emilia scowled at him. Even if this man truly cared for her safety—which she highly doubted—she still didn't like being told what she could or couldn't say. "Right," she grumbled. "Then, I'll look for food in the next town."

"I said law abiding," he said, just as she was about to leave. "There's one place in Nefala that never closes—not even when Captain Maria Welles makes port."

If Emilia were any *less* hungry, she would've kept walking. "And what place is that?" she asked tiredly.

"The Shrieking Siren," the man told her.

Emilia turned toward him, a baffled frown twisting at her brows. "Sirens don't shriek. They sing."

The man blinked. "What?"

"And I hate to break it to you," Emilia added, "but if you ate food served by sirens, you might've eaten human flesh. They don't eat much else."

He stared blankly at her. *"The Shrieking Siren* is a tavern, miss," he said slowly. He pointed past Emilia—at a building that set at the top of the hill. "That tavern."

Emilia turned around, glancing up at it. Surprisingly enough, she did see a couple of women leave the place, as she watched.

"That tavern has all the gold in Nefala," he said.

Emilia turned back toward him. "Why is that?"

"Because it deals in a lot of criminal shit, for one," the man said with a laugh. He glanced back toward the sea, as if he thought the pirates were going to appear out of thin air. "It's the first place that Captain Maria Welles and her crew will go when they make port."

Emilia squinted skeptically. "Yet, you think I should go there?"

"It's empty right now," he explained. "It's the best time. You wouldn't want to wait until they arrived."

Emilia didn't want to admit that she didn't have the gold—because that would mean admitting that she'd planned to steal from the merchants at the dock. So, instead, she just mumbled, "It doesn't sound safe."

"I'll order your food!" he said—a little too eagerly.

Emilia pinned him with a suspicious glare. "Why?"

The man cringed, as if she'd just caught him in a lie. "In exchange for your help," he said. "Just a small favor, really."

Emilia didn't even wait to hear what it was. "No."

"I just need someone to come into the tavern with me," he tried to explain. "I'll draw less attention if I'm not alone."

Emilia glanced down at the gold rings that fit too loosely around his fingers. "And what would be so terrible about drawing attention to yourself?"

"I told you," he said, his eyebrows high. "There are few people in Nefala who follow the law."

Emilia nodded. "You're a thief?"

"It's almost a requirement," he said with a bitter smile, "if you want to eat, while in Nefala." His lip curled. "As I said, King Eldric doesn't care for us."

Emilia passed no judgement for that.

Stealing to survive was more a reflection of the greed and apathy of the king than the morality of the thief. "Your plan is to steal food from the tavern?" she assumed.

"No, my plan is to steal *gold*," the man corrected, "but if food is what you want, I'll get you some. In exchange for your help."

"Why not just steal the food?" Emilia asked.

He gave a short laugh. "Gold is worth more than food, miss."

"Not when you're hungry," Emilia said.

He spread out his hands. "Will you help or not?"

Emilia didn't trust him at all, but...food *would* give her the strength she needed to use her magic. And with magic, she could protect herself from whatever happened afterward. "I suppose so."

He flashed a sickeningly smug smile. "Perfect."

"Name's Paul."

Emilia followed him warily. She still wasn't sure about this. What was this Illopian obsession with gold, anyway? It made no sense to her. Leather was valuable because of its use in clothes. Steel was valuable because of its use in weapons. Food was valuable because people literally died without it.

But gold?

Its value was fabricated. It was useful only because Illopians said it was. Besides jewelry and spending, what use did it even have? To Emilia, it was a symbol of greed, and she distrusted anyone who clung to it so zealously.

When Emilia didn't respond with the response he'd expected, the thief prompted, "And your name is?"

"I'd rather not say," Emilia muttered.

He led her to a table in the darkest corner of the tavern, and she sat in the chair across from him.

With a disapproving scowl, the man said, "You're not very polite, are you, miss?"

That was another thing that annoyed her about the Kingdom of Illopia. Men were always telling women what was polite and what wasn't. She didn't know how Illopian women tolerated it.

On Drakon Isle, where Emilia was from, that sort of arrogant, patronizing bullshit would've gotten them nowhere.

Rather than fret over whether her facial expression was *polite* enough, Emilia averted her gaze. Instead of entertaining the thief, she watched a beautiful, red-haired woman wipe down the empty tables.

Emilia blushed, when the woman leaned forward enough for Emilia to see her soft, freckled breasts.

Was that the purpose of the corsets that so many Illopian women wore? To make their breasts look like...*that*?

So visible and so... well... umm...

Plump?

Suddenly embarrassed, Emilia returned her gaze to the thief. "Did you say something?"

Paul cast a curious glance at the woman Emilia had been ogling and, upon seeing her, lifted an eyebrow.

Emilia suddenly wanted to bury herself in the sand, like a hermit crab. Unfortunately, the sand was in the *other* direction.

Why had she followed this man again?

Her stomach grumbled over its emptiness, and Emilia sighed.

Right.

Food.

"Your name's Emilia Drakon."

Emilia glanced at Paul, her eyes wide. "What?"

He placed a folded sheet of parchment on the table and leaned back in his chair. "That was what you were looking for at the docks, wasn't it?"

Emilia picked up the paper and unfolded it. She sighed, as she found a quick sketch of herself and the list of her crimes underneath. "Why did you take it?"

Paul flashed a smug smile, his teeth yellowed by tobacco. "Let's call it a favor."

"Let's not," Emilia said.

His smile faded. "Fine," he said, leaning forward. "Then, let's call it insurance."

Emilia nodded in understanding. "What could you possibly want from me?"

"You mean, besides the bounty?" Paul said.

"Besides the bounty," Emilia confirmed.

Paul grabbed the Wanted notice and pulled it back toward himself. "I've lived in Nefala long enough to know better than to trek off in search of the Illopian Guard," he whispered. "It doesn't matter who I mean to turn in. She'd have me killed simply for speaking to them."

"She?" Emilia repeated. "You mean Maria Welles?"

"Shh!" Paul hissed. He cast a terrified glance around the empty tavern, and Emilia lifted her eyebrows in disbelief. He leaned toward her. "Are you trying to get us both killed? It's *Captain* Maria Welles." He widened his eyes. "Especially in here!"

Emilia shrugged. She hadn't eaten well in weeks, and now, a

gold-obsessed thief was blackmailing her. She really didn't have the energy to deal with it.

Shaking his head in disbelief, Paul continued with his explanation, "But just because *I* know better than to seek out the Guard, doesn't mean everyone does."

Emilia gave him another exhausted sigh. "Please, just tell me what you want before I starve to death."

Paul pointed a dirty, gold-arrayed finger at her. "That is very impolite, lady."

"So is blackmail," Emilia muttered.

"Anyway," Paul grumbled, growing more petulant by the moment, "I know of some people who are foolish enough to try to get that bounty. So, if you don't want me to show them this notice, you'll help me."

"Yes, yes, I got that part already," Emilia said with a roll of her eyes. "What do you *want* from me?"

Paul narrowed his hazel eyes at her. "You really do behave like a witch, don't you?"

Emilia's brows furrowed. What did that even mean? Witches behaved in all sorts of ways.

"Can I help you?"

Emilia looked up, blushing, as she found that beautiful, red-haired barmaid standing in front of her—with her breasts still... *very* visible.

Like any woman who loved women, Emilia could be quite distracted by them at times—the women, not the breasts—but she was floundering even more than usual today.

"Get us some bread," Paul said, waving her away.

Emilia scowled at him. And he called *her* impolite?

At least she wasn't barking orders at a barmaid, like some self-important asshole.

"Of course, sir," the barmaid replied.

Paul waited until the barmaid was out of sight to *finally* explain what he wanted. "I'm an excellent purse-snatcher. I don't need your help for that," he told her, "but in order to get to the woman who *holds* the purse, I'll need to sneak into the kitchen."

"Okay." Emilia glanced around the dark, empty tavern with a frown. "Do you need directions to the kitchen? Because…I don't even know where it is."

Paul rolled his eyes. "No. I know where the kitchen is," he assured her. "All I need from you is for you to sit here, keeping that tavern girl busy, until I have the gold."

"You want them to chase me, instead of you?" Emilia assumed.

"Possibly," Paul said—with no remorse. "What is it they say? You don't have to be faster than the bear, just faster than the person running with you?"

"Why would you run from a bear?" Emilia said with a frown. "Most of them are friendly, as long as you don't mess with their cubs."

Paul stared blankly at her. "You can't be serious."

"I've befriended a few bears, actually," Emilia said.

The thief's frown deepened.

Apparently, Illopians didn't have bear friends.

How odd.

"Here's your bread," the barmaid said. She bent to set the basket on the table, and again, Emilia found herself face-level with those soft, freckled breasts.

"Would you mind keeping an eye on my lady-friend for me?" Paul asked the barmaid. "She's sick."

Emilia scowled. She was no one's 'lady-friend.'

The barmaid glanced at Emilia, concern flickering in her blue eyes. "Oh! You *are* a bit pale, miss," she realized. "Do you need some water?"

"I'm fine," Emilia tried to say, but the thief interrupted.

"Yes! Water is exactly what she needs!" Paul said. He leaned forward. "Listen, I need to step out for a moment. Could I leave her in your care?"

The barmaid eyed them both suspiciously. "As long as she can pay…"

"She can," Paul lied, "of course."

The barmaid turned her attention toward Emilia, but Emilia averted her gaze. If only she had a bit of magic left, she could burn the notice and leave.

But without energy to channel into a spell, Emilia was as trapped as any nonmagical human would be.

"I'll get your water, then," she told Emilia.

Emilia kept her head down, but she murmured, "Thank you," when the barmaid turned to leave.

When the barmaid returned to the kitchen, Paul turned to Emilia. "Why are you thanking a server?" he muttered. "Are you trying to arouse suspicion?"

Emilia frowned at that. Once again, she was struck by how weird and complicated these Illopians were.

What kind of person wasn't grateful for water?

"Forget it. No time to waste," Paul said. He climbed to his feet and gave a cruel smile. "Good luck, witch."

Emilia grabbed a loaf of bread and took a bite of it.

In his hurry, the thief left the Wanted notice on the table, so as soon as he was out of sight, Emilia took it, rolled it into a ball, and tossed it into the fireplace.

The barmaid returned with a flagon of fresh water, and she glanced from Emilia to the fireplace. "What was that?"

"Nothing important," Emilia said. She took the knife from the basket of bread. "Tell me something. Can whoever it is that's in your kitchen…protect themselves?"

In the firelight, the barmaid's frizzy, red hair burned as bright as the flames themselves. "Why do you need to know that?" she asked nervously.

"Because," Emilia said, "the man who brought me in here didn't 'step out.' He went to the kitchen."

The barmaid's frown deepened. "Is he dangerous?"

"I have no idea," Emilia said honestly. She offered the knife to the barmaid. It wasn't terribly sharp, but it would still work. "But I'd rather not watch someone get hurt, so...take this with you, please."

The barmaid took the knife and nodded. "Don't go anywhere, miss."

Emilia sighed, as she watched the barmaid return to the kitchen. She couldn't just sit there and wait to get caught. So, she gathered up a few loaves of bread, hid them beneath her cloak, and headed toward the door.

The sun would set soon. If she hurried, perhaps she'd have her magic back by nightfall.

CHAPTER 3

Captain Maria Welles

E milia barely made it across the dirt road, before Paul came running out from behind the tavern. Although a small purse of gold coins jingled victoriously in his hand, he clearly hadn't gone unseen—if the woman chasing him was any indication.

Well, *chase* might've been the wrong word, actually.

A short, older woman followed him at a pace that was actually pretty leisurely. She looked more annoyed than victimized.

Emilia ducked into the shadows of a building on the other side of the road, hoping that the woman hadn't seen her. This must've been the tavern owner, Emilia realized.

Rather than a beautiful dress like the one the barmaid had worn, this woman wore a simple, brown dress, made with thick, sturdy fabric.

Thin strands of grey streaked through her brown curls, which she kept pinned back, out of her face. Aged wrinkles pulled at her soft, brown skin, and a fierce frown pulled at her lips.

At some point, while Emilia and Paul were inside, the ghost town had become a little less…ghostly.

Lots of people crowded the street now—men and women in tattered, salt-stained clothing with pistols or swords at their hips. Some walked in groups, traveling uphill, toward the tavern, while others stood around in small circles, talking and laughing.

Were these her pirates?

Captain Maria Welles?

The tavern owner stopped at the top of the hill and planted her hands on her hips, as if she were waiting for something. Still, the thief didn't slow down.

Paul barreled down the hill toward a group of sailors, gold still jingling in his hand, and a tall, lean woman with a dark, leather tricorn stepped out from the crowd. He must've recognized her—because he tried to turn and run the other way—but the woman in the tricornered hat caught him, before he could.

She spun him around to face the tavern owner, and she pressed her sword against his throat.

The tavern owner met the pirate in the middle of the street, and she held out a dark, wrinkled hand.

"Don't kill me!" Paul was sobbing. "Please, don't!"

Emilia squinted at the pirate. Was that her?

Was that Maria Welles?

Emilia couldn't tell from this distance.

The pirate kept her sword against him, crossed over his chest and pressed against his throat. "Return her gold."

"Yes, yes, of course," Paul said, and with trembling fingers, he dropped the purse into the tavern owner's hand. He waited for the pirate to release him, but she didn't.

"Is it all there?" the pirate asked the tavern owner.

The older woman opened the purse and peeked at the gold inside. "Yes, Captain. I think it is."

Captain.

She'd said *captain*.

Even with Paul between them, Emilia could still see some of the woman's clothes—faded, leather trousers and a black, leather doublet.

It wasn't much to go on, but that black, leather doublet *did* look awfully similar to the one Maria Welles had worn in the Wanted notice.

As did the tricorn.

Silence fell over the crowded street, as the pirates watched their merciless captain.

"You'll let me go now, right?" Paul said, his voice trembling. He tried to look over his shoulder at the pirate, but she pressed her sword closer. "Right?"

The pirate captain watched the tavern owner silently, as if she were waiting for some sort of signal.

And perhaps she was—because as soon as the tavern owner gave a small nod, the pirate slashed her sword across Paul, cutting him open from his neck to his hip. Emilia stepped back, stunned by the amount of blood that spilled out into the dirt.

The pirate dropped the thief into the dirt and wiped her sword across his back, cleaning off only a small sliver of the blood that now coated her blade.

She returned the sword to her scabbard, and Emilia realized, now, that the pirate carried two swords at her waist, not just one. Catherine had mentioned once that she'd fought an ambidextrous fighter who used two swords, but she'd never mentioned that it was the legendary Captain Maria Welles.

The leather tricorn cast a shadow over the pirate captain's face, so Emilia couldn't see her expression.

But there was a cold brutality in the way she killed that was totally unlike the fiery passion that Emilia was used to.

Every bit as vicious, though.

The woman wasn't *dressed* like a naval officer. She wore no bright colors, no deep blues, no fancy coats or wigs. Instead, she wore ratty linen and old leather. She wore dark colors, instead of bright—black leather pants and a black leather doublet, over a linen shirt.

She clearly wasn't part of the Royal Navy.

Yet, she'd acted as judge, jury, and executioner to a petty thief—one whose crimes *paled* in comparison to Emilia's.

Emilia couldn't let the pirate captain catch her, too—not when she was too starved and fatigued to use her magic—but she'd never reach the path that veered off toward the forest without them seeing her.

So, Emilia waited in the shadows, while the tavern owner spoke with the pirate captain who'd just murdered a thief for her. Eventually, the tavern owner moved along to speak with someone else, and as soon as she was out of sight, the pirate's dark brown eyes shifted toward Emilia.

Emilia froze, cold terror coursing through her veins.

How had she seen her?

Unless…she'd seen Emilia flee from the tavern.

Unless she'd known Emilia was there the entire time.

Unless she'd known Emilia was watching, when she killed Paul.

Could anyone *be* that shamelessly evil?

Emilia steeled herself, preparing to fight—knowing the woman would soon turn her swords on Emilia, as she had on the other thief. But she did no such thing.

A dizzying rush of shock poured through Emilia, as she watched the woman's mouth tilt into a sly smile.

The woman tipped her hat to Emilia—in this subtle, almost *taunting* way—and then strode down the hill.

She'd left Emilia in the shadows.

She'd kept her secret.

But for how long?

Emilia needed to move quickly, if she wanted to get away before the pirate captain returned.

But just as she tried to step out from the shadows, a group of sailors walked past, and in Emilia's struggle to avoid them, she walked straight into the short, older woman.

"Apologies, miss," the tavern owner said, as she turned to look at Emilia. Her dark brown gaze roamed Emilia's face, and her brows furrowed. "Have we met?"

Emilia held her breath, trying to contain the panic inside her chest. "No, I don't think so."

The tavern owner narrowed her eyes suspiciously. "What's with the cloak, child?"

Emilia stepped back, preparing to run. Even if she'd had the energy to defend herself with magic, she still wouldn't do it in the middle of the street.

"Evening, Adda."

Emilia frowned at the woman who'd suddenly joined them. She was dressed much like the other sailors—a linen shirt rolled up to her elbows and hemp breeches tied off at her knees.

But rather than wearing a hat or a headscarf, like the other sailors, she simply wore her wispy, brown hair short.

"Judith," the woman said warmly. "What can I do for you?"

The sailor smiled. "Captain has a question for you."

Behind her back, where the tavern owner couldn't see, the sailor brushed her fingers along Emilia's arm.

If it weren't for the shock, Emilia might've pushed her away—on sheer instinct.

The tavern owner planted both hands on her wide hips. "Well, you tell your captain that she isn't too good to come and talk to me herself."

The sailor chuckled at Adda's response. "It's about that old horse she loves."

Adda dropped her arms to her sides. "Shit," she sighed. "I better go deliver the bad news in person."

"Better hurry," the sailor said with a grin. "She's already gone to the stables."

Adda rolled her eyes. "That girl doesn't listen to shit I say, does she?"

The sailor waited until Adda left for the stables to wrap her fingers around Emilia's arm.

Emilia glanced at her, not sure how to react.

But the sailor leaned in close and whispered, "Captain says you're to follow me."

Emilia pulled her arm free. "What captain?"

"The one who might kill you, if you don't do what I say," the sailor warned. Again, she leaned in and whispered in Emilia's ear, "Do you want to get caught or not?"

Emilia's eyes widened. She didn't know whether to deny that she'd done anything wrong or ask how the sailor knew.

But when the sailor grasped Emilia's arm again and led her toward the tavern, Emilia stumbled along beside her, too shocked to do otherwise.

"Who are you?" she asked the sailor.

When they reached a narrow alleyway, beside the tavern, the sailor released Emilia.

"Name's Judith," she said. She turned to face Emilia and extended a hand. "Ship cook from the *Wicked Fate*."

Emilia glanced down at Judith's hand. The lack of food was making her increasingly disoriented, and between that and the shock, Emilia couldn't make sense of up or down.

The world reeled around her, as she thought about that name.

The *Wicked Fate*.

The dreaded pirate ship, captained by Maria Welles herself.

If Judith was from the *Wicked Fate*, then...

She was a pirate.

Emilia glanced down at the flintlock pistol that the sailor carried at her waist.

"What kind of cook needs a pistol?" Emilia said.

She'd expected an evasive answer, but Judith just dropped her arm and said, "One from a pirate ship."

Emilia blinked in surprise.

Judith just smiled. "We keep a smaller crew than a navy ship," she explained. "So, it's all hands on deck in a battle."

Emilia's brows furrowed. "Do you always announce your criminal status to strangers on the street?"

Judith snorted at that. "This is your first time in Nefala, isn't it?"

"Why do you ask?" Emilia said.

Judith curled a finger toward her, beckoning Emilia closer. She leaned in close, as if she were sharing a secret, and whispered, "The navy can't touch us here."

Emilia leaned back on her heels, blinking at the pirate. "Well, that's nice, but," she said uneasily, "I should, umm, go."

Judith stepped forward, when Emilia stepped back. "Yeah, see," she sighed, "the problem with that is…the captain didn't say you could do that."

Emilia frowned. "Do what?"

"Go," Judith provided.

"Again," Emilia said slowly, "she's not my captain." She shook her head in disbelief. "And how would you stop me, anyway?"

With absolutely no hesitation, Judith pulled the flintlock pistol from its holster and extended her arm, pointing the pistol directly at Emilia's head.

Emilia froze. "Oh."

Judith wrinkled her nose and gave Emilia a regretful nod.

Despite the rush of fear that poured through her veins, Emilia met the pirate's bright blue gaze boldly.

She didn't have any energy left for magic, but if it was the only way out, Emilia would just have to channel whatever she had into a spell.

She took a deep breath and made a desperate attempt to channel her energy.

But then, for seemingly no reason, the sailor began to laugh. Her scowl morphed into a wide grin, and the tension in her stance faded away.

Emilia stared at the pirate in stunned confusion, unsure of how to react to this abrupt change of mood.

Judith returned the pistol to its place on her hip. She tilted her head toward the stone wall beside them, and a lock of short, brown hair fell over her forehead. "Want to come in for a drink?" she said casually. "I'll get you whatever you like."

Emilia's frown deepened. Had she just *imagined* the woman aiming a pistol at her? "You're not going to shoot me?"

"I'd rather not," the pirate said, "if that's all right with you."

"It is," Emilia assured her.

"Good," Judith said with a friendly smile. "Drink, then?"

Emilia squinted suspiciously. "Why?"

The strange pirate shrugged. "I like having drinks with women."

Emilia squinted at the way she said that. Spending most of her time with fire-breathing beasts hadn't really prepared her for strange women who aimed pistols at her one minute and flirted with her the next. "No offense, but especially after the pistol, I..." She stepped back. "I think I'd rather just...go."

The woman gave her another shrug. "You can try."

Though the woman said it casually, the implied threat in that remark was enough to spur Emilia into action. She spun on her heels and quickly tried to leave—only to immediately collide with yet *another* pirate.

The pirate's boots were planted firmly on the ground—far more firmly than Emilia's own shoes had been—and because of that, she might as well have run into a solid wall.

The force of the collision nearly knocked her backward—and likely would have, if it hadn't been for the warm hand that curled around her shoulder.

"Easy there, love."

The soft, lilting voice that murmured in her ear sounded much too gentle for someone who was clearly quite strong.

It was like expecting a roar, only to hear a purr instead.

The lean, leather-clad form that pressed against her belonged to someone who was, at the very least, strong enough to have firm abdomen muscles.

Yet, the distinct softness of the pirate's chest alluded to loosely bound breasts.

She smelled a little like sweat, like you'd expect from a sailor, but there was another scent that clung to the woman's skin, too—a scent that was warm and sweet, like the tropics themselves.

The curved handle of the pirate's sword dug painfully into Emilia's hip.

Which was enough to remind Emilia of the danger she was in.

Emilia stepped backward, stumbling clumsily out of the pirate's grasp, and she froze, as she realized who she'd run into.

Beneath a faded leather, tricornered hat, mesmerizing, brown eyes stared down at Emilia. Those eyes—so warm and dark—reminded Emilia of the dragons she loved so much: fire burning within, waiting to burst forth at some unknown moment.

But what gave Emilia pause were those distinctive reddish-brown scars carved deeply into the pirate's brown skin.

If she'd had any doubt that the woman who'd killed Paul was Captain Maria Welles, she had none now.

The drawing on the Wanted Notice had depicted a crude carica-ture of the woman in front of her now. The artist might have known her features, but he clearly hadn't known her beauty.

Because the real Captain Maria Welles was as beautiful as she was fearsome.

But her scars—every single one of *those* had been drawn correctly.

"You're her," Emilia heard herself whisper.

"There are lots of 'hers' in the world," the pirate said with a taunting smile. "You're going to have to say my name."

The pirate captain was mocking Emilia's shock, toying with her fears, and that was enough to make Emilia hate her on sight.

"Maria Welles."

The pirate captain tilted her head slightly, as if she'd heard a sound she didn't quite like. She leaned closer to Emilia and said, "*Captain* Maria Welles."

Emilia narrowed her eyes at that. She wanted to tell the arrogant pirate captain to fuck off, but the woman's blood-stained swords made that idea *slightly* less appealing.

With as much venom as she could channel into one name, Emilia recited, "*Captain* Maria Welles."

Maria flashed a wide smile, her teeth shining in the evening sunlight. "Better."

Emilia took another step back, but she came to an abrupt halt, when she remembered Judith was still behind her.

She had nowhere to run.

Captain Maria Welles stepped forward, closing the space Emilia had just put between them. The belt at her waist held one of her swords—the one Emilia had felt just a moment before—but the other sword was in Maria's hand already.

Unsheathed and ready to use.

Maria leaned in close—close enough for Emilia to, once more, notice that sweet scent on the pirate's skin. Her breath warmed Emilia's ear, as she whispered, "You should've run while you had the chance."

Emilia's heart raced at the threat, but she lifted her chin, anyway, refusing to show fear. "Why would I run? I've done nothing wrong."

Emilia managed to flinch only slightly, when the pirate captain flicked open her cloak with her sword.

The captain glanced down at the stolen bread and then lifted her gaze to meet Emilia's. A spark of delight flashed vividly within those dark brown eyes of hers.

However Captain Maria Welles felt about Emilia's theft, the prospect of having leverage to blackmail Emilia clearly delighted her more.

With a smirk that was both infuriating and devastatingly gorgeous, all at once, the pirate captain said, "You were saying?"

Judith leaned forward to see what Maria was looking at. She let out a low whistle, when she saw the stolen food in Emilia's cloak.

Emilia looked away, her face warm.

Maria stepped closer to Emilia. "Should we drag you inside and ask the girls if you paid?"

Emilia could only assume that, by 'girls,' Maria meant the ladies who served the tables, and she knew at least one of them would recognize her as the person who'd come in with Paul.

"It's just bread," she muttered. "They won't even miss it."

The pirate captain pitched her voice low—too low for any passersby to hear. "You didn't answer me, thief."

Emilia glared at her. "You obviously already know I stole it," she said irritably. "So, are you going to kill me or not?"

Captain Maria Welles grinned wickedly at the question. "Join us."

Emilia blinked at that. "What?"

"In the tavern," Maria clarified. "I want you to come inside." Her smile widened. "Judith offered you a drink. I'm upping the offer to drinks *and* food. I know a thief desperate enough to steal stale bread couldn't possibly turn down the offer of a warm meal."

The pirate captain was taunting her. Again.

"You think I couldn't possibly turn you down?" Emilia scoffed. She leaned toward the captain and snarled, "Watch me."

Emilia tried to walk away, but the pirate captain caught her by the arm and pulled her back.

Emilia's backside collided with Maria's waist—only a few layers of leather and fabric between them.

Emilia tensed, half-expecting to feel Maria's blade plunge into her back.

Instead, she felt only Maria's lips, caressing her ear. "I'll keep your secret," the pirate said in an enticing whisper, "but only if you come inside."

Emilia's eyes widened, and an intense heat unfurled in her stomach—a heat she *swore* was fury and not lust. "You're blackmailing me?" she said breathlessly.

Really? Twice in one day?

This was getting ridiculous.

Maria laughed—and her laugh was far too pleasant in Emilia's ear. "Don't act surprised now," she taunted. "You've already said my name."

Emilia clenched her jaw, anger rising inside her. "Fine."

Maria released her arm, and the sudden loss of support nearly caused Emilia to stumble forward. The pirate captain slid her sword into the scabbard she wore around her waist.

Emilia spun toward Maria, her mouth open and ready to snarl out a retort, but the pirate captain stopped her with a single, tattooed finger.

That single finger gently lifted Emilia's chin, trapping Emilia's gaze with her own.

Emilia blinked. There was something about those large, brown eyes of Maria's. Like a tsunami, they drowned out Emilia's anger and decimated every thought in her mind.

Maria's deep, brown eyes bewitched Emilia more effectively than magic ever had.

With a sly smile, Maria murmured, "See you soon." She then dropped her hand and stepped toward the other pirate.

Before heading into the tavern, Maria stopped to whisper something in Judith's ear.

The short-haired pirate tilted her head, listening carefully to whatever Maria was telling her.

When she finished, Judith simply said, "Yes, Captain."

Maria patted a hand against Judith's shoulder and then strode into the tavern.

Judith waited until the pirate captain was inside and safely out of sight to turn to Emilia. "If you still want to run, this would be the time to do that."

Emilia frowned. "But she said—"

Judith offered her a friendly smile. "I know it might be hard to believe, but the Big Bad Pirate Captain of Legend *does* have a sense of humor."

Emilia scowled, irritation twisting in her stomach. "She thinks it's *funny* to threaten people?"

Judith scrunched up her nose in a way that was...honestly, much too adorable for a supposedly dangerous pirate. "I think that's covered in the 'Big Bad' part."

But even charming women couldn't squash Emilia's frustration, now. "Well, I don't find blackmail very funny."

Judith nodded. "No, I imagine someone being blackmailed wouldn't." She breathed out a long sigh. "Look, she went inside. If she intended to chase you down, she wouldn't have gone inside."

"And what about you?" Emilia said. "Will you chase me down?"

Judith shrugged one shoulder. "Only if the captain asks me to."

Emilia scowled at that. "That's not very reassuring."

"Sorry, mate," Judith said with another shrug. "Captain's orders are Captain's orders."

Emilia studied the pirate with a frown. Whether it was her honesty or her charm, Emilia couldn't have said, but something about this surprisingly friendly pirate made Emilia want to trust her.

Despite the fact that Judith must've known that Maria was standing behind Emilia and had chosen not to warn her, despite the fact that Judith had literally just confessed to having blind loyalty to her captain, somehow, still, Emilia wanted to trust her.

"So, there's no guarantee of my safety either way," Emilia said.

Judith gave her an apologetic smile. "You *really* shouldn't have stolen from Adda."

"Who's Adda?" Emilia asked.

Judith tilted her head toward the dirt road, where Paul's corpse still lay, abandoned in the dirt. "The woman who just got a man killed with a single look," she told Emilia.

So, there *had* been something communicated in that nod.

"You mean the tavern owner," Emilia assumed.

Judith chuckled. "Adda's a lot more than a tavern owner."

Emilia glanced out toward the harbor, where the sea shimmered beneath a red-orange sky. She couldn't stay in Illopia—not while her dragons might be in danger—but she couldn't cross the sea without a ship.

And the pirate captain inside that tavern just so happened to have a ship.

Catherine hated Maria Welles.

King Eldric hated Maria Welles.

Everyone who hated Emilia hated Maria Welles, too.

And the enemy of her enemy was her friend, right?

Emilia wasn't so naïve as to think that she wasn't in danger. She knew she was playing with fire by even being in the same city as Captain Maria Welles.

The pirate captain had killed someone in the middle of the street with no concern for who might be watching. She'd listened to his pleas for mercy and shown him none.

Clearly, Captain Maria Welles was just as bloodthirsty as the legends made her out to be.

But Emilia was a dragon sorceress. It was in her *blood* to play with fire.

"It's your choice," Judith said, while Emilia weighed her options. "You can run, or you can crawl further into her web. It's simply a question of how adventurous you are."

Emilia looked at the pirate. "Adventurous?"

Judith smiled. "Are you adventurous enough to dine with the most infamous pirates in all of Aletharia?" she asked. "Or would you prefer to run and hide with your stolen bread?"

Emilia easily rose to the challenge. "I accept your invitation."

Judith gave a surprised laugh. "I think I'm going to like you."

Emilia would never admit it, but she thought the feeling might be mutual.

∿

JUDITH LED EMILIA BACK TO A SMALL TABLE IN THE CORNER, WHERE they could wait for their food. She moved through the tavern as if she lived there, and when a short, blonde woman brought their drinks, Judith spoke and laughed with her as if they were old friends—or, more likely, lovers.

It didn't take Emilia long to spot the legendary Captain Maria Welles. Apparently, being the most wanted criminal in Aletharia meant nothing to her.

The pirate captain sat at the largest table in the room, visible to anyone who might enter the tavern.

She'd immediately made herself comfortable, stretching her legs out in front of her and leaning back in her chair. She didn't speak to the other pirates at the table. She just watched them in silence.

Emilia honestly wasn't *trying* to ignore Judith. Aside from, you know, aiming a pistol at her, Judith had been nothing but kind to Emilia.

In the last few minutes that they'd known each other, anyway.

But she couldn't bring herself to stop watching the pirate captain—for fear that, as soon as she looked away, Maria would reveal her secret. Sure, she'd *said* she'd keep Emilia's secret, but she was a pirate.

Could Emilia trust the word of a pirate?

"You recognized her awfully quick, didn't you?"

Emilia glanced at Judith, warmth flooding her cheeks, as she realized that Judith was watching her. "Who?"

Judith lifted her tankard to her mouth, taking a sip of ale. "The person you're watching," she said with a sly smile. She set her tankard on the table and leaned forward, folding her arms on the table. "My captain."

Emilia shrugged. "She killed someone in the middle of the street," she reminded the ship cook. "Fits her reputation."

Judith snorted at that. "Sure, but you recognized her on sight," she accused, "didn't you?"

Emilia hesitated. "There was a notice at the docks," she admitted. "It wasn't a perfect rendition of her, but it was close enough."

Judith glanced at Maria's table, her bright blue eyes sad and thoughtful. "It's the scars," she sighed. "No matter how long it's been since they've seen her, no one ever forgets the scars."

Emilia's brows furrowed at the pirate's suddenly sombre tone. Of course, there were lots of possible explanations for Maria's scars. Sailing was dangerous. Pirating, even more so. But something about Judith's tone made Emilia think Maria's scars had a more sinister origin.

"How did she get them?" Emilia asked.

Judith's bright blue gaze returned to Emilia, and she tsked playfully. "Much too soon to be asking questions like that, mate."

Emilia nodded. That was fair.

With a sigh, she cast one more glance in Maria's direction.

Maria hadn't moved since the last time Emilia had looked her way, but there was someone new at her table, now, and this *new* someone wasn't dressed like a sailor.

She might've been the prettiest woman Emilia had ever seen.

With a soft face and a softer smile, the barmaid circled the table, refilling the pirates' drinks. Her heavy, blue dress was nearly as nice as the ones Emilia had seen in Regolis, though the fabric was clearly cheaper.

A corset shaped her soft curves and wide hips, and her brown hair was pinned up, out of her face.

The beautiful barmaid must've told a joke—because hoots of laughter resounded from the table, as the barmaid turned her attention toward Maria Welles.

Maria, though—she didn't even *move*. She kept her hands

folded and her head tilted back, even as the pretty barmaid saun-tered toward her chair.

When the barmaid reached Maria, she hoisted up her skirts and straddled Maria's leather-clad thighs.

Emilia's mouth went dry.

The pirates at the table gave another round of laughter, but Maria barely moved a muscle—that is, unless you counted the slight twitch of her lips.

"That's Jane."

Emilia spun toward Judith. "What?" she said breathlessly.

Judith tilted her tankard in the direction of Maria's table, before taking another drink. "Barmaid. Her name's Jane."

"Oh." Emilia blushed, embarrassed that the cook had caught her staring.

Oddly enough, though, Judith didn't seem to care.

"She's simultaneously Adda's best barmaid and worst barmaid," Judith said, steadily drinking her ale. "The patrons love her, but erm…sometimes, she forgets to do her job for hours at a time." She laughed at her own joke. "Especially when the captain's around."

"Are they lovers?" Emilia asked. She glanced at them, noting that Maria still hadn't bothered to unfold her hands.

On one hand, Emilia couldn't think of a reason that the barmaid would be in Maria's lap, if they *weren't* lovers.

On the other hand, if they *were* lovers, Maria was an awfully inattentive one.

Judith chuckled at the question. "No," she assured Emilia. "No woman wants a pirate. For a night, perhaps, but not forever. We're never around. The only home we'll claim is the sea itself."

Emilia lifted her eyebrows at that. "So, it's not the crime and murder that turns them off?"

Judith snorted loudly, nearly spitting out her ale. "It might be a bit of that, too."

"Might be," Emilia repeated with a smile.

Judith finished her ale and waved for the blonde barmaid to bring her more.

Emilia had never seen anyone drink so much in such a brief span of time.

"Jane was about fourteen when the captain brought her here," Judith said. "She's been at the *Shrieking Siren* since. Which would be…what? Twelve years?" She squinted, as if she were already too drunk to do the math. She waved a hand. "Point is…yes, they're close—but more like friends that occasionally fuck than lovers."

Emilia blinked. "They let a child serve ale to pirates?"

"Fourteen is hardly a child," Judith said, "and if you saw the kind of people Jane worked for before the captain brought her here, you'd think pirates sounded like polite company."

Emilia wasn't sure what sort of people could make pirates sound polite.

Illopia's tyrannical king, perhaps.

Judith let out a delighted shriek, when the blonde barmaid dropped another flagon of ale on the table.

"You can drink as much of this as you like," Judith told Emilia —even as she proceeded to drink most of it herself.

Emilia wondered if all pirates drank like fish—or if this quirk was unique to Judith.

Maria did seem to have several flagons of ale at her table, as well.

Judith glanced past Emilia. "Ah," she said with a smile. "Here comes your food."

Right on cue, Emilia noticed the soft tap of a woman's heels behind her.

"Here you are, miss."

Emilia gaped at the overfilled platter of food that the server slid in front of her.

"Let us know if you need more," the woman told her.

"More?" Emilia said incredulously.

The platter in front of her now could feed an entire family.

"Ooh. *She's* new," Judith said, when another tavern lady walked by their table. She tilted her head to the side, blatantly watching the woman's backside. "And pretty."

Judith was clearly just as attracted to women as Emilia was, but poor Judith must not have been blessed with the ability to focus on anything *else*.

Or perhaps it was the two flagons of ale that had taken that ability from her.

"Where is Sarah?" Judith complained. "I haven't seen her tonight. Did anyone tell her I was here?"

Emilia frowned at the distracted ship cook. "I don't think I know a Sarah."

Judith blinked at her. "Oh, shit. Did I say that out loud?"

Emilia couldn't help but laugh.

Definitely the ale.

Judith smiled. "Eat your food, mate," she said gently, "before it gets cold."

Emilia picked at the roasted chicken with a frown. They didn't eat poultry on her island.

Eating winged animals seemed a bit inconsiderate, considering her closest friends were dragons.

Judith leaned forward and lowered her voice. "Better than stolen bread, right?"

Emilia scowled at her teasing. "Shhh."

Judith gave her an adorable wink, and Emilia blushed.

Judith didn't have the kind of bewitching magnetism that her captain did, but she had her own kind of charm that was quite lovely.

With a concerned look, Emilia whispered, "How much did this cost?"

Judith chuckled. "It didn't cost a thing."

Emilia frowned. "How is that possible?"

Judith tilted her head toward Maria's table. "The captain ordered it," she explained. "She doesn't pay here."

Captain Maria Welles owns Nefala, Paul had said.

Emilia looked down at the obscene amount of food, blinking in shock.

Judith tapped a finger against her second flagon of ale, giving it a look that was nothing short of *adoring*—and said, "She ordered this beauty, too."

Emilia cast another curious glance at the pirate captain—and froze, as she found those warm, brown eyes focused on her. The beautiful barmaid was still sitting in Maria's lap, but Maria's dark gaze was narrowed on Emilia.

Apparently, Judith noticed this, as well, because she said, "She's annoyed that you're not eating yet."

Emilia blinked. She looked at Judith, bewilderment twisting at her brows. "Did she...poison it?"

Judith snorted. "No, no. Poison isn't her style."

"What *is* her style?" Emilia said with a frown.

"Bloody," Judith said, as if it were obvious.

Emilia nodded. She remembered the way the pirate captain had sliced Paul open with her sword—and all of the blood that had soaked into the dirt after she dropped him. "She likes to kill with her swords."

"Always," Judith laughed. "Don't get me wrong. If the situation calls for it, she'll break your neck or strangle you, but she gets so cranky afterward." She shook her head sadly. "It's just not enough blood."

Emilia's eyes widened. "She sounds so pleasant."

Judith snorted. "Just eat—before she has us both whipped."

Emilia stared blankly at the cook. "Um, that's," she paused, "that's a joke, right?"

Judith laughed, but she didn't bother to assure Emilia that, no, this maddening pirate captain would *not* try to flog a complete stranger.

Emilia stabbed her fork into the chicken. They hadn't used forks on her island, so she just had to *hope* she looked natural enough, using one now.

"I'm not afraid of her," Emilia muttered, but she placed the fork in her mouth, anyway.

Her head spun at the taste of actual, *cooked* food. It'd been so long since she'd had anything other than berries or nuts.

Anything at *all*, really.

Eating that first bite of food seemed to remind her body that, oh yeah, eating was a good and necessary thing, and suddenly, Emilia felt as if she could empty the large platter in a matter of minutes.

She glanced across the table, at Judith, feeling self-conscious of her own hunger.

But Judith simply picked up her tankard and waved a hand. "Eat. I've seen hunger before. You won't get any judgement from me."

With a grateful smile, Emilia returned her attention to the food.

Judith lifted her tankard to her mouth and sipped her ale slowly. As Emilia attempted to eat everything in front of her, still a bit clumsy with her fork, Judith said, "You never told me your name."

Emilia was so enraptured by the taste of cooked food that she answered without thinking.

"Em—"

Emilia stopped midway through her name, her eyes widening.

She couldn't say her real name! What was she thinking?

Emilia glanced down at the chicken on her fork and answered her own question.

I was thinking I'm going to have to apologize to my dragons for enjoying the taste of a winged animal.

"Em?" Judith said with a curious smile. "Is that short for Emily, Emma, or Emilia?"

Emilia swallowed another bite of chicken. "Emily?"

Judith nodded. "Good answer."

Emilia's brows furrowed. What did the ship cook mean by that? Did she know Emilia was lying?

And if so, how?

Judith somehow managed to finish her second flagon of ale and waved for the barmaid to bring her another.

Emilia was nearly finished with her food, when the blonde barmaid set a third flagon of ale on their table.

Judith grabbed Emilia's empty tankard and dragged it toward herself. She carefully tipped the flagon of ale, filling Emilia's cup. "You need to drink something, love," she said, offering Emilia the drink. "You'll make yourself sick, if you don't."

Emilia hesitated, but then, she glanced at Judith's tankard and relaxed. If Judith was drinking the ale, it was clearly safe. Emilia accepted it. "Thank you."

Judith nodded, watching as Emilia drank deeply from the cup. "You like the food, I take it?"

Emilia glanced down at the platter, which was already mostly clean. "Yes," she said, blushing.

"Adda's kitchen girls are good," Judith said, but then, she leaned forward and flashed a wry grin. "But do you want to know a secret?"

Emilia leaned forward, too. "What?"

"I'm better," Judith whispered.

Emilia laughed. "Sure you are."

Emilia was mostly teasing, though, because the health of the sailors in the tavern, at the moment, attested to Judith's knowledge and skill in nutrition, all on its own.

Emilia had met many sailors in her life. None of them had been in as good of health as Maria's crew.

Judith took another drink of ale. "Sail with us, and you'll see."

Emilia frowned at the suggestion. "I'm not a sailor."

Judith drank her ale, smiling behind her cup. "Doesn't mean you can't become one."

Was she serious?

Emilia couldn't tell.

Emilia set down her fork. "How does one become," she said hesitantly, "what you are?"

Judith set her tankard on the table and leaned forward. "That depends on what you mean. A sailor?" she said. "You could talk to any ship captain to become one of those."

Emilia lifted her eyebrows. "And a pirate?"

Judith's smile widened. She tilted her head toward Maria's table. "Find a way to impress her," she whispered, "and she'll never let you go."

Emilia couldn't tell whether that was advice—or a warning.

With a nervous laugh, Emilia said, "How am I supposed to impress a woman who is so infamous that most people are afraid to whisper her name—as if she might somehow hear them?"

Judith chuckled. "Well, she might not hear them in the *literal* sense of the word, but she does usually get wind of it, eventually." She quirked an eyebrow. "She has a lot of eyes out there."

"Wait," Emilia said, stunned, "are you saying there's actually a reason for that superstition?"

Judith grinned, her bright blue eyes sparkling in the firelight. "There's a reason for everything."

Emilia's brows furrowed.

Judith sighed, "Look. I won't lie to you. It isn't easy to impress her." She glanced at Maria, perhaps checking to see if she was watching. "She's proud as hell and a bit of an asshole."

"You don't say," Emilia muttered.

The pirate captain had literally killed hundreds of sailors, and Judith said she was a *bit* of an asshole?

A bit?

"But," Judith continued, "it isn't impossible to impress her, either." She leaned forward, resting her deeply tanned arms on the table. "Don't run, and don't lie to her," she advised. "She wants respect, not cowardice. You could be the best sailor in the world, and she'd still think you weren't worth shit, if you ran."

PIRATES OF ALETHARIA

Emilia looked down, fidgeting uneasily with the clasp of her cloak. Her current predicament left her no options *but* to lie. "And if I'm not a sailor at all?"

Judith shrugged. "All that means is that you can't impress her with your sailing experience," she said easily. "Use a skill you *do* have."

Emilia smiled at the advice. "Why are you helping me?"

Judith leaned back in her chair and shrugged. "Honestly? Totally selfish reasons," she said with a shameless grin. "I could use a hand in the galley, and if she hired you, I'm sure I could convince her to lend you to me before meal times."

Emilia laughed. "Lend me?"

"Well, if she hires you, it'll be for her own reasons," Judith said. "She won't let me have you *all* the time."

Emilia laughed. She honestly wouldn't have minded that at all. She'd thoroughly enjoyed Judith's presence throughout her meal and would probably enjoy working alongside her.

But Emilia had bigger plans.

"What if I told you I don't want to be a pirate?" Emilia said.

"Then, I'd say you're in denial," Judith replied.

Emilia squinted at that. "Denial?" she repeated. "About what, exactly?"

"Em, you're practically a pirate already," Judith said, "and at the very least, you're a pirate at heart." She shrugged. "You're just short a ship, a bit of gold, and a few tattoos."

Emilia found herself laughing again. "Tattoos?"

Judith trailed her gaze downward. "No, you're right. I have no idea how many tattoos you're hiding under that cloak."

Emilia tried not to look *too* insulted by Judith comparing her to the seafaring murderers that were so hated in Aletharia.

After all, Judith seemed to mean it as a compliment.

Somehow.

"I don't understand you," Emilia said with a laugh. "What makes you think I'm a...pirate at heart?"

Judith leaned forward, her short, brown hair falling over her forehead. "The fact that," she said with a smile, "when I gave you the choice between safety and adventure, you chose adventure."

A hint of excitement fluttered in Emilia's stomach. "But I don't," she tried to explain. "I don't want to be a pirate. There is something I need to ask of her, but I don't want to work for her."

Judith scoffed at that. "You're going to ask the most dangerous pirate in all of Aletharia for a *favor*?"

"Not a favor," Emilia assured her. "I have something to offer, in exchange for her help."

Judith laughed, her bright blue eyes wide. "Oh, Em," she said regretfully. "Hasn't anyone ever told you not to make deals with pirates?"

"No," Emilia said honestly, "and—" She shrugged helplessly. "I don't have any other options."

Judith propped her face in her hand and gave a sympathetic sigh, "Oh, you poor thing. You actually think you know what you're doing, don't you?"

Emilia bristled. "What's that supposed to mean?"

"It means, my friend," Judith said, lowering her voice, "the captain'll take more than you *ever* intended to pay."

Emilia hesitated at the warning. She cast another glance toward Maria's table.

The barmaid was no longer in her lap, but Maria had barely moved a muscle, since the last time she looked.

Though she seemed to adore her captain, Judith spoke of Maria as if she were a dangerous predator—and as if Emilia were just some helpless prey animal, waiting to be snatched up in Maria's jaws.

But Emilia wasn't helpless.

She was a dragon sorceress.

The *last* dragon sorceress.

Yes, she'd lost everything, and she hadn't eaten well in months. It was possible that she wasn't thinking clearly.

But that didn't mean she was helpless.

Captain Maria Welles could *try* to take advantage of her, but she'd soon learn: she wasn't the only person capable of murder.

Emilia could kill just as easily.

"It's worth whatever she asks of me," Emilia told the cook. "I have no other options."

Judith nodded. "All right, mate," she sighed. "Finish your food, and I'll take you to her."

THOUGH MARIA GAVE THE IMPRESSION OF SOMEONE WHO COULDN'T care less about her surroundings, she was the first person to notice their approach.

Her dark brown eyes shifted toward Emilia with all the force and abruptness of a rogue wave.

And when that wave overtook her, Emilia stopped in her tracks.

Apparently, Judith noticed Emilia had stopped before *Emilia* noticed she'd stopped, and Judith returned to her. The ship cook took Emilia by the arm and tugged her along.

"Come on, love," Judith said. "There's no backing out now."

Maria didn't speak, as the two of them approached her table. She simply watched silently, her gaze dark and unyielding beneath that tricornered hat.

"Who's your friend, Judith?"

The question came from a man at the other side of the table.

He smiled at Judith, a whole set of gold teeth flashing in the firelight.

All pirates and merchant sailors wore some sort of gold—in their ears or around their necks.

Back on Drakon Isle, Emilia had once treated a wounded merchant sailor, who'd told her that his gold jewelry was his insurance in death.

47

But this particular pirate had apparently chosen to wear all of his gold in his mouth.

Perhaps, he'd lost his real teeth in an accident—because he'd clearly been in one.

He kept his long, brown hair tied back out of his face, leaving that vicious scar across his cheek unobscured.

Emilia studied that rough scar with a frown, noticing the perpendicular lines that crossed it. It looked like a terrible suture job—one that had most likely festered, before healing.

If he'd gotten that on Maria's ship, then Emilia could only conclude that Maria didn't have a very good healer.

Perhaps she had no healer at all.

Use a skill you do have, Judith had said.

"Found her at the docks," Judith told the scarred sailor.

Again, his gold teeth flashed. "Wait until Sarah hears that you're picking up women from the docks now."

Judith couldn't even suppress her grin. "She won't hear shit if you keep your mouth shut, Pelt."

Pelt?

Was that his actual name?

Judith turned her attention to Maria, making very careful eye-contact with the pirate captain.

The two of them shared a long look, as if there were some hidden meaning in their stares.

"She was looking for work," Judith said. She tilted her head and smiled. "So, I offered to introduce her to our good captain."

Maria narrowed her eyes at Judith, before shifting her gaze back toward Emilia.

A contemplative frown twisted at the pirate captain's scarred brows, and Emilia wondered if she and Judith had actually communicated something with that strange look they'd shared.

The man beside Pelt spoke up, next. "I didn't realize we were looking for new sailors."

This particular pirate looked a lot cleaner than the others.

Rather than faded leather or ratty fabrics, he wore a long, bright green coat, and he had his long, black hair slicked back into a neat ponytail.

Maria turned her narrowed gaze on the man in the green waist-coat. "Now, Zain," she said slowly, "you know better than anyone that there have been plenty of prizes I didn't *look* for." Her gaze cut toward Emilia, and her smile was as sharp as her swords. "That doesn't mean I won't take a look, if it's naïve enough to fall into my lap."

Emilia didn't know whether to feel more insulted by Maria calling her naïve or by Maria comparing her to a 'prize.'

Judith glanced back and forth, noticing the tension that settled between them. "Well," she said, turning to Emilia, "you're intro-duced. I've done my part."

Emilia blinked, as her newfound friend abandoned her to the wolves.

The pirate that Maria had referred to as *Zain* turned to Emilia. "Do you at least have sailing experience?"

Emilia cast a frantic glance in Judith's direction, but Judith was too busy stealing a chair from another table to notice.

Judith had told her not to lie to Maria, but she hadn't told her what to say to the man in the green coat.

Maria followed Emilia's gaze, and then, she turned back toward Emilia and lifted a scarred eyebrow.

It seemed that Captain Maria Welles wasn't very impressed with Emilia's subtlety.

"Judith?" Zain said, when the ship cook dragged a chair up to the table. "Can your friend not *speak*?"

Judith cast a puzzled glance at Emilia, before sitting across the table from the sailor she'd called *Pelt*.

"She speaks to me," Judith said with a shrug. "Maybe she just doesn't like you."

Emilia blanched under the pirates' scrutiny, stuck in this nervous silence that she'd accidentally fallen into.

Judith tapped the tabletop, as one of the pirates passed out cards. "Deal me in."

Maria continued to watch Emilia, even as the other pirates turned their attention toward the game. Without a woman in her lap, the casual looseness of her posture was even more apparent. She had both legs stretched out in front of her, the heels of her black boots resting against the floorboards. She'd folded both hands over her stomach and leaned back in her chair—as if she didn't have a care in the world.

Emilia refused to flinch beneath the captain's gaze, but to say that was easy...would've been a lie. Those deep, brown eyes—so warm and intense—seemed to unravel something inside of Emilia. Whatever control she *thought* she had seemed to slip away, as the pirate captain held her gaze.

"Sit," Maria said.

Emilia glanced around the table—at the lack of empty chairs.

Did Maria want her to steal a chair from another table, like Judith had done?

Were non-pirates even allowed to do that?

Her voice came out breathless, as she said, "Where?"

One of the pirates laughed. "She can sit on my—"

Maria looked at him, and he instantly fell silent. He shrank lower in his seat and said, "Sorry, Captain."

Maria's stare didn't waver. "Get up."

"Captain," he said uneasily, "it—it was just a joke."

"Up," the pirate captain snarled.

"Aye, Captain," he sighed. His long, brown hair—matted and dirty—fell into his face, as he stood up. "Where do you want me?"

Maria's voice was so cold Emilia nearly shivered. "Farthest table from me."

Despite the fact that the pirate was clearly quite drunk, he still managed to look absolutely ashamed.

"Aye, Captain," he said again. He immediately left, not even taking the time to grab his drink first.

To Emilia's surprise, none of the other pirates even looked up.

Apparently, this cold, unforgiving attitude of Maria's was normal for them.

The pirate captain's gaze returned to Emilia, its intensity as electric as a lightning bolt. "Sit," she said.

Emilia's stomach tightened. She glanced at the now empty chair, noticing how close it was to the captain.

She would be within arm's distance from the pirate.

This is what you wanted, Emilia reminded herself.

Yet, her chest fluttered faster, anyway—not because of fear. No matter how deadly this captain was with a sword, Emilia was far deadlier. No, it was something else. There was just…something else about this captain that unleashed a pleasant chaos inside her.

Emilia circled the table and sat in the vacated chair—far too aware of the way the captain watched her, as she did. Only when she was seated, did she meet the captain's gaze. Those intense, brown eyes never wavered—following every move that Emilia made.

"Hey, umm…Judith's friend," one of the men called to Emilia. "Could you pass me Nicholas's cards?"

"Cards?" Emilia said, unfamiliar with the term. She glanced down at the table, where several rectangular items lay face-down. Emilia assumed these were the cards, since the man who'd asked for them appeared to be holding an entire stack of them.

So, she carefully gathered them into her hand. They felt surprisingly thick and rough between her fingers—more like the canvas used for ship sails than the parchment paper that Emilia was used to. There were also unfamiliar symbols hand-painted on the canvas.

"Unless you'd like to play, too?" the pirate added.

Rather than admit that she knew nothing about this game, Emilia simply shook her head and handed the cards to the blonde pirate who was waiting for them.

"Is anyone going to drink Nick's ale?" Judith asked.

The pirate captain shrugged her lean shoulders and muttered, "Knock yourself out."

Judith stood and reached across the table, grabbing the forgotten tankard. By the time she returned to her seat, she'd already drunk at least a third of the ale.

The pirate in the green waistcoat, who'd questioned Emilia a few moments prior, frowned at Judith. "You realize you could've just waited until Jane came back and ordered one for yourself?"

The man with the gold teeth snorted. "Oh, she'll be ready for another one by then."

Judith lifted her tankard as if she were toasting him. "Of course," she agreed. She grinned at the one in the green coat. "See? Pelt gets it. Can't let perfectly good ale go to waste."

The well-dressed pirate rolled his eyes. "Just try not to pass out this time."

"You're no fun, Zain," Judith complained.

The pirate who had been passing out cards turned to the one Judith had called *Zain*. "Are you sure you don't want to play?" he said. "There's an extra spot now."

"I prefer to *keep* my gold, thank you," Zain said.

The one that Judith had referred to as *Pelt* taunted Zain, "Yeah, because you know you're going to lose."

"Aww. Is Zain scared of a little game?" Judith said.

Zain scowled at both of them, before turning to the pirate captain. "Are you just going to let your crew talk to their quartermaster like that?"

Maria shrugged, grinning at him. "If they're right."

"Oh, hell," Zain said with a groan. "Deal me in."

A collective cheer rang out around the table, as the card-dealing pirate passed several cards to Zain.

Judith and Pelt clanged their tankards together in celebration, splashing the table with frothy liquid.

Zain rolled his eyes at them. "You're all going to look *really* stupid, when I win."

Judith and Pelt couldn't even contain their laughter.

"Did you get enough to eat?"

Emilia spun in her chair, surprised by the question. The pirate captain had spoken quietly enough that no one else seemed to notice—but loudly enough that Emilia couldn't have missed it. "Yes," Emilia said, unsettled beneath Maria's dark gaze. "Thank you."

Maria's nod was so subtle that Emilia might not have noticed it, if it weren't for the slight twitch of her hat. "You'll eat once more, before you leave."

Emilia blinked. That certainly wasn't the *nicest* way to phrase that. "I appreciate the offer, but—"

"You'll eat," Maria said again.

Emilia glared at her. "And if I'm not hungry?"

A silence fell over the table, suddenly.

Judith cleared her throat, and when Emilia looked her way, she grimaced and drew her finger across her throat, warning Emilia to stop while she was ahead.

But Maria just said, "I'll wait all night, if I have to."

Emilia narrowed her eyes and opened her mouth to respond, but the barmaid returned before she could.

It was that same pretty, brunette tavern worker that Emilia had seen straddling Maria earlier. She slipped in between the captain and Emilia, her hips wide and lovely beneath her dress. Emilia felt those hips brush against her arm, as the barmaid refilled Maria's cup.

"Anyone else need more?" the barmaid called out.

"I'd bet Judith wants another one," Pelt laughed.

"Always," Judith said, holding out her tankard.

The tavern worker circled around the table, refilling Judith's tankard and a few others, as well. When she made it back to the captain's side, her blue-grey eyes settled on Emilia. "Well, hello! Who are you?"

Emilia panicked. Her mind raced, as she tried—and failed—to

come up with any response that wouldn't get her arrested. Luckily, Maria came to her rescue.

"She's with us," Maria said. "Get her a drink, Jane."

Jane's smile was genuinely the sweetest smile Emilia had ever seen. "Of course, Captain," she said.

Her stormy, grey eyes never left Emilia, even as she spoke to the captain. Jane curled her fingers around Emilia's shoulder and stepped closer. Her curvy hips slipped between the table and Emilia's chair, and her heavy gown pressed against Emilia's knee. While she wasn't *quite* close enough to straddle Emilia's thighs, she was plenty close enough to place her large, milky-white breasts directly in Emilia's line of sight.

"Is this your first time, miss?" Jane asked.

Emilia blushed, desperately trying to look at anything other than the very large breasts that were suddenly right in front of her face. "Uh, f-first time?"

"At the *Shrieking Siren*," Jane said. She slipped her fingers into Emilia's long, black hair, pushing it out of Emilia's face with the gentle sensuality of a lover. "I haven't seen you here before, have I?"

Jane wore some sort of perfumed oil that made her bosom smell exactly like freshly cut roses, and Emilia was extremely embarrassed that she was close enough to notice.

"I—" Emilia said, her cheeks hot. "I don't think so."

"How delightful!" Jane said. "I love the new ones."

Aside from Catherine and a beautiful siren named *Nerissa*, no woman had ever put her breasts this close to Emilia's face. And despite Emilia's best intentions to look *anywhere* else... well... they were breasts.

And very beautiful ones, at that.

The pirate captain reached out and lightly tapped her knuckles against Jane's hip, discreetly getting her attention. She was laughing, obviously amused, but when Jane turned to look at her, she shook her head.

"Ah," Jane whispered, as if Maria were speaking some silent language only understood by her. She let her hand fall away from Emilia's shoulder, and she took a step back. "Sorry if I made you uncomfortable, miss," Jane said with a smile. "I'll get your drink now."

Emilia could practically *feel* Maria's gaze on her, but she refused to look at the pirate captain until her face returned to a normal color—which, ironically, was not likely to happen while Maria was watching her.

Fortunately, the other pirates were too focused on their card game to notice Emilia's mortified distress.

*Un*fortunately, Maria didn't seem to miss a thing.

"Jane's used to pirates. She loves to tease," Maria said. She sipped her ale. "You can tell her if she comes on too strong. You're not going to offend her."

Emilia's flushed face refused to cool. "She didn't," she mumbled. "She was sweet. She just— She has—"

Maria glanced at her, grinning. "Breasts?"

Emilia glared at the pirate captain, her frustration finally catching up with her embarrassment. "Why aren't you playing that game with your crew?"

"Because I need to keep an eye on you," Maria said.

"Me?" Emilia sputtered.

Maria set down her cup and folded her hands over her stomach. "Yes, thief," she said, eyes dark. "You."

Emilia blanched. She glanced around, terrified that someone had overheard, but no one even looked her way. She returned her attention to the pirate captain. "You said you wouldn't tell anyone," she whispered.

"Have I?" Maria said. When Emilia didn't answer, she said, "The answer is no. You'd be dead, if I had."

Emilia cast a wary glance at the scabbard that Maria wore, knowing that those deadly swords of hers were only a quick draw away.

Maria planted her boots on the floor and leaned toward Emilia. "If you'd prefer to have this conversation *away* from listening ears," she said, "I'd suggest you get up and follow me outside."

Emilia narrowed her eyes. She cast a wary glance in Judith's direction and was grateful when the ship cook met her gaze. With an encouraging smile, Judith waved her on.

Emilia returned her attention to the pirate captain. She forced a smile and muttered, "Fine."

Maria snorted at her less than enthusiastic response. "Good choice."

CHAPTER 4
Deals with Pirates

E milia barely made it through the door, before she turned to
confront Maria.

"I am *not* naïve," she snarled.

Maria laughed. She closed the door, shutting off the light and
noise of the tavern, leaving them on a quiet, dark pier that overlooked the shallow, blue waves of the Azure Sea.

"You've been holding that back for a while, haven't you?" Maria
taunted.

"And I'm not falling into your lap, either," Emilia continued.

Maria stepped toward her and cast her gaze downward, as if
she were sizing Emilia up for a fight. Whatever she saw must not
have worried her. "You're loaded like a fucking pistol."

Emilia narrowed her eyes at the smug pirate captain. "You think
this is funny?"

"Lucky for you, yes," Maria said. She stepped closer and
lowered her voice. "But hey, at least you were smart enough to wait
until we were away from my crew." Her eyes darkened. "I'd be a
lot less amused, if you hadn't."

Emilia scowled at that. "I wasn't waiting. I was just—"

Maria didn't even wait for her to finish. "Keep walking." She gestured toward the blue water, which shimmered beneath the moonlight. "End of the pier."

Maria strode past her, and Emilia reluctantly followed. The pirate captain walked with heavy steps—the gait of a woman who just *knew* she could kill and get away with it.

She had such a persuasive power in her physique that even Emilia wasn't immune to it. It wasn't magic, but it was so enthralling that it might as well have been. It sent shivers of both intrigue and fear throughout Emilia's body, leaving her unsure of whether she was intimidated by the pirate or attracted to her.

The crisp, salt-scented air that rippled off the Azure Sea was soothing, in comparison to the warm, stuffy air of the tavern.

Nefala itself wasn't much to look at, but its view of the Azure Sea was breathtaking.

Whereas Regolis, the capital city of the Illopian Kingdom, overlooked the Westerly Sea, Nefala overlooked the Azure Sea.

And while the Westerly Sea was far safer and more suitable for fishing and sailing, the Azure Sea was the most beautiful—its waters crisp and blue, its currents powerful and untamable. The Azure Sea was Emilia's home, and the sight of it soothed her homesick spirit.

It must've soothed Maria, too, because when they reached the end of the pier, the pirate captain closed her eyes and inhaled deeply.

Maria turned and leaned against the rail. She tilted her head back, her tricorn tipping slightly, as she looked up at the second story of the large, stone tavern.

"Could've taken you upstairs," Maria said. "The rooms are private enough." She took another deep breath, and the muscles in her shoulders relaxed. "But I get a bit restless when I'm cut off from the sea."

Restless?

Emilia had never seen anyone look *less* restless than Captain Maria Welles.

"I imagine you also wouldn't want to give your," Emilia paused, as she recalled Judith's words, *"friend* the wrong idea."

Maria squinted at that. "What friend?"

"The...woman," Emilia said with a frown. *Surely,* the pirate knew what she meant. "The one who was...on top of you."

"Jane?" Maria scoffed. With a short, incredulous laugh, she said, "You think a tavern girl has say over me?"

Emilia scowled at the pirate's tone. "I just assumed she was more to you," she said with an irritated shrug, "than that."

"Why?" Maria said. "Because you saw her in my lap?" She laughed loudly. "She put her tits in your face. What would that make *you*? Her wife?"

Emilia blanched. "No, I just—" The crude reminder had left her barely able to string two thoughts together. "Where I'm from..." She shook her head in frustration. "Look, I'm sorry if I'm not familiar with all of your customs already."

Maria lifted a scarred eyebrow at that slip. "You're not from Illopia."

Emilia looked away. She hadn't meant to reveal so much, so soon, but the pirate captain had flustered her to the point that she hadn't realized what she was saying.

Had that been her goal all along?

As the wind picked up, the waves crashed harder against the pier's tall, wooden pilings, but the planks of wood beneath their feet barely even creaked.

Emilia returned her attention to Maria. Her stomach flipped, when she accidentally met the pirate captain's gaze.

The breeze gathered the soft, brown curls around Maria's neck, tousling and tangling them around the gold loops in her ears.

The blue headscarf beneath Maria's tricorn must've kept it secure around her head—because while the wind wreaked havoc on her hair and the loose sleeves of her shirt, it barely even affected that faded, leather hat.

"If it helps," Maria said with a wry smile, "I don't know if tavern life is as much an Illopian custom, as it is a pirate one."

Emilia didn't know why, but that *did* ease the tension a little.

She stepped closer, and in a soft tone she hoped no one would overhear, Emilia asked, "How did you know?"

"What?" Maria said. "That you're a thief?"

Though the poet's shirt that she wore beneath her doublet was already quite loose, Maria tugged at the loose laces of her collar, as if it were suffocating her.

Perhaps, she *had* been uncomfortable inside that tavern.

Emilia glanced around, breathing a sigh of relief only when she found the harbor as dark and deserted as before.

Maria gave her a careless shrug. "Nothing happens in Nefala that I don't know about."

Emilia returned her attention to the pirate captain. "You're lying," she accused.

A tight smile curled at Maria's lips. "Am I?"

"Yes," Emilia assured her. "There wasn't enough time. Even if someone saw me, they couldn't have told you that quickly."

Maria watched her curiously. "And if I said I just knew?"

Emilia scoffed at that. "I'd say that's not a real answer."

Maria chuckled. "Sounds like you're not getting a real answer, then."

Emilia narrowed her eyes.

The sun had set sometime while she ate, and the moon had risen high above the sea, casting a shimmery blue light over the surface of the sea.

Beyond the pier, a night heron picked its way among the shallow waves, searching for food.

Worry gripped Emilia's throat, as she wondered how her dragons were doing.

It'd been so long.

The soft brush of leather brought Emilia's attention back to the pirate captain.

Maria pulled a leather flask from her pocket and opened it. She held out the leather container, offering it to Emilia. "Rum?"

Emilia frowned at the hip flask.

"It'll loosen up those shoulders of yours," Maria said.

Suddenly aware of her own tension, Emilia tried to pry her tensed shoulders from her ears—just to prove she didn't need anything from Maria.

The unimpressed arch of Maria's scarred eyebrows let Emilia know that she'd failed to prove that.

"Might help if you take off the cloak," Maria pointed out.

Emilia scowled. "I prefer it on, thank you very much."

Maria shrugged and took a sip from her flask. "No one south of the Westerly Sea wears those heavy-ass cloaks," she said—between sips. "You know that, right?"

Emilia fiddled with the metal clasp of her cloak. It was a bit too thick for the warmer climate, but it offered anonymity that her own clothes didn't.

"I picked it up in Regolis," she admitted.

"Interesting choice of words," Maria said, tipping her flask. "You mean you stole it."

Emilia narrowed her eyes at the pirate. "You act like you're so much better."

Maria pressed the cork into the leather flask. "I *am* better."

Emilia stared blankly at her. "You're a pirate. You've broken hundreds of laws."

Maria returned the flask to her hip and smiled. "Which means I'm better at being bad."

Emilia pursed her lips. She would not laugh at this arrogant asshole of a pirate.

Nope.

Absolutely not.

Even if Emilia was a *tiny* bit amused, she would not laugh.

Maria's lips—full and dusky pink—curved into an even deeper smile. Her lips weren't without their own scars. There was a pale slash across the right side of her mouth, where her lips had likely been split once.

From a fall or a fist, Emilia couldn't have said.

But despite those scars, her mouth looked surprisingly soft.

Not that Emilia was concerned with Maria's...mouth.

In an effort to look...*anywhere* else, Emilia eyed the swords that Maria carried at her waist.

Maria's tattooed fingers curled idly around the curved handle of her right sword, but she made no move to unsheathe it.

"You keep watching my swords," Maria noted. "Afraid I'll use them on you?"

Emilia looked up, meeting her gaze. "I'm not afraid of you," she assured Maria. But then, she rolled her eyes and muttered, "You *did* lead me away from witnesses, though. I can't say the possibility hasn't crossed my mind."

Maria laughed at that. "You've got it all wrong, thief," she said. "I'd much prefer to kill you *with* witnesses than without." Her smile deepened. "More fun that way."

Emilia lifted her eyebrows in disbelief. "It's easy to see where you got *your* reputation."

"You sound surprised," Maria said. Amusement danced in those large, brown eyes of hers. "Were you expecting me to be different?"

Emilia shrugged her shoulders, suddenly aware of how much the cloak weighed them down.

"Well," she said bitterly, "there are *some* villains from Illopia's tales, who *didn't* earn their reputation."

"Hmm," Maria said, glancing out at the water, "how disappointing."

Behind Emilia, a heavy, wooden door creaked open, and someone stepped out onto the pier.

"Captain?" yelled a gruff, female voice that Emilia *vaguely* recognized. "Is that you out there?"

Maria didn't look at the person, but apparently, she didn't need to. "Yes, Adda," she called. "What'd you need?"

Emilia cast a curious glance over her shoulder, noticing the tavern owner's short, curvy silhouette, near the back door.

"Did you give my apples to that damn horse again?"

To Emilia's surprise, the pirate captain winced, as if she'd just gotten herself into some kind of trouble. "They're his favorite, Adda."

Adda planted her hands on her hips. "He's old!"

"All the more reason to give him what he wants," Maria countered.

The woman huffed in a way that made Emilia think the old woman had just rolled her eyes. "No more apples!"

"Yes, Adda," Maria said, but as soon as the woman returned to the tavern, she turned to Emilia and said, "I'll just give him some of mine. She'll never know."

Emilia *tried* to suppress her smile, but she didn't totally succeed. "So, you *were* at the stables earlier?"

Surprisingly enough, Maria's dark gaze seemed to soften at the sight of Emilia's smile. "Briefly."

While it certainly wasn't enough to make Emilia forgive the pirate captain for threatening her or blackmailing her, as a dragon sorceress with a particular affinity for animals, Emilia did find herself *slightly* endeared to anyone who would take the time to visit an animal.

Only slightly, though.

"You didn't answer the question my quartermaster asked you," Maria said—even though Emilia had no idea who her quartermaster was. "I assume that means you have no experience as a sailor."

Oh, Emilia realized. *The man in the green coat.*

Recalling Judith's warning, Emilia answered honestly, "None."

Maria rolled her eyes. "And yet, you thought I'd hire you?"

Any positive feelings that had briefly blossomed between them dissipated the moment Maria used that condescending tone.

"*I* didn't think anything," Emilia snarled. "That was Judith's idea." She narrowed her eyes at the pirate captain. "I don't want to work for *you*."

"No?" Maria said. She stepped toward Emilia. "Then, why the fuck are you wasting my time?"

Emilia couldn't believe she'd almost thought something *positive* about this self-obsessed pirate. "You were right. I'm not from here," she told Maria, "and I need to get home."

Maria arched those scarred eyebrows of hers, as if she were waiting for something. "And?" she said, when Emilia didn't continue. "What does that have to do with me?"

Emilia's confidence waned slightly. "Well, you have a ship, and—"

"Speak, thief," Maria snarled. "I don't have all night."

Emilia blew out a slow sigh, shoving down her frustration as well as she could. "I'd like passage on your ship."

Emilia thought she'd prepared herself for every possible reaction that Captain Maria Welles might have, but apparently, there was one she hadn't considered.

Maria didn't say yes. She didn't say no. She didn't even ask about payment.

Instead, the pirate captain burst into a fit of hysterical laughter.

Honestly, she had a lovely laugh—a bit loud for a silent pier, perhaps, but its lilting, melodic tone cascaded pleasantly across the waves.

"What's so funny?" Emilia said, after several moments of Maria's unexplained laughter.

Her laughter tapered into a sigh. "You." She shook her head, scoffing, "'*Not naïve*,' you said."

Emilia glared at the pirate captain. "You're mocking me?"

"Of course I'm mocking you," Maria said. "Passage? You can't be serious."

Emilia frowned. "But I am."

Everyone traveled by ship in Aletharia.

Why was Maria acting like it was such an absurd request?

"You should've gone along with Judith's idea," Maria told her. "I still would've said no, but at least *that* was plausible."

"I'm not asking you to do it for free," Emilia assured her. "I'd pay you. Obviously."

Maria stepped toward Emilia. The quickness of the movement caused the two swords at her waist to flop against her leather-clad thighs. Her curly, brown hair fell forward slightly—though held in place, for the most part, by her headscarf and hat. "You'll pay me with *what*?" she sneered. "Stolen bread?"

Emilia refused to step back, even as Maria closed the space between them.

"No. With gold," Emilia corrected. Since Maria had already invaded her space, Emilia hooked a finger through the long, gold chain that Maria wore around her neck and tugged lightly. "Pirates like gold, don't they?"

Rather than pull the chain from Emilia's grasp, Maria stepped closer and tilted her face toward Emilia's.

That enticing scent washed over Emilia again—warm and sweet, like small, silky flower petals and some sort of citrus.

It was something on Maria's skin.

An oil, perhaps?

The heat of Maria's body radiated into Emilia, and she stood close enough, now, that Emilia felt the gentle brush of Maria's swords against her stomach.

"If you have gold," Maria challenged, "why were you stealing food?"

Emilia dropped the chain. "I don't have it with me."

Again, Maria laughed at her.

"My homeland has more gold than you can imagine," Emilia

explained. "If you take me there, I can pay you whatever you want."

It wasn't a lie. The dragons of Drakon Isle hoarded plenty of gold.

Which was most likely the *real* reason King Eldric ordered an attack.

He pretended it was all about his war against magic, but the Illopian royals were as greedy as the god they worshipped.

"Name your price," Emilia said. "There's no debt I can't pay."

Maria shook her head. "You don't know the *meaning* of debt, until you've sailed with pirates."

'She'll take more than you ever intended to pay,' Judith had said.

"Name your price," Emilia said breathlessly.

Maria leaned closer to Emilia and whispered, "No."

Desperation gripped Emilia's throat so tightly that she couldn't force out even one word.

And at Emilia's silence, Maria turned to leave. "Good luck on your quest, thief."

Emilia followed her across the pier. "At least tell me why you won't!"

Maria spun around, her hand already resting on the hilt of her sword. "You really want to know?"

Emilia hesitated at the dark note in Maria's tone, but with as much boldness as she could muster, she said, "I do."

Maria stepped toward Emilia, gripping her sword tightly. "The *Wicked Fate* is a pirate ship, not a fucking passenger ship," she snarled. "You insult me by suggesting otherwise."

"No," Emilia said breathlessly. "I wasn't insulting you."

That didn't seem to extinguish Maria's rage whatsoever. "I decide what insults me," she growled. "Not you."

Emilia spread out her arms. "How is offering you gold an insult?"

Maria rolled her eyes. "Offer your gold to someone else."

"I can't," Emilia said softly. Memories of the dungeon came, unbidden, to her mind, and she squeezed the clasp of her cloak, letting the metal dig into her skin. The prick of pain grounded her. "Any other captain would turn me in."

"I kill for sport, darling," Maria said. "You'd really rather throw your lot in with me than with someone who would simply follow the law?"

"When the law would kill me, as well?" Emilia said. "Yes. At least, in sport, I might have a chance."

Maria chuckled at that. "I wouldn't be so sure."

Emilia stepped closer. "There must be some way to change your mind," she pleaded. "Just tell me what you want."

"I'm not the kind of person you want to barter with, love," Maria warned. "If you have access to as much gold as you say you do, you can pay a law-abiding captain *not* to turn you in." She turned to leave. "Try a merchant ship. The king pays them shitty wages, anyway."

"If they recognize me," Emilia told her, "they'll turn me in, no matter what I offer them."

Maria turned, quirking a brow at that. "Who are you?"

"I told you I wasn't naïve," Emilia reminded her. "I know better than to tell you that."

Maria shrugged. "Then, I won't help you." She turned to leave. "Try the merchants. Everyone has a price, love."

Again, Emilia followed. "Even you?"

Maria froze so suddenly that Emilia almost ran into her. "No."

Emilia smiled, elated to have finally trapped the legendary Captain Maria Welles. "One of those statements is a lie."

Maria apparently didn't take being outsmarted very well— because in one, quick, fluid movement, she drew her sword and spun toward Emilia.

Emilia stepped back, her back colliding with the wooden rail behind her, as the pirate captain placed the cold steel against her throat.

"This is your only warning," Maria said slowly. "Run—before you get yourself killed."

'Don't lie. Don't run,' Judith had said.

Emilia lifted her chin and met Maria's gaze with every bit of fire inside her. "I'm not the kind of person who runs from you," she said, "Captain Maria Welles."

Maria tilted her head to the side. Her eyebrows lifted, and her mouth twitched at the corners. She let her arm relax slightly, but she kept the sword against Emilia's throat.

"Who are you?" Maria asked again.

Emilia swallowed, wincing when that caused the blade to press into her throat. "I'm just someone who needs to get home."

Maria lowered her sword. "Darling," she scoffed, "sailing with me isn't how you get home." She grinned wickedly. "It's how you get to the gallows."

Emilia shrugged. "I've already been there once," she admitted. "I don't mind going again."

Maria blinked. She leaned back on her heels, both eyebrows raised. Her brown curls fell away from her face, as she tilted her head, considering Emilia with a frown. Then, one side of her mouth curved upward, and slowly but surely, an absolutely gorgeous smile spread across her face.

Every tensed muscle in the pirate's body seemed to unwind *with* that smile—beginning with her strong shoulders and ending with her locked knees.

Captain Maria Welles looked so much softer, all of the sudden—her skin smooth and dark, her smile bright and wide, her eyes warm and brown. "All right, thief," she said, sheathing her sword. "Let's talk."

Emilia squinted at that. "Weren't we...*already* talking?"

Maria snorted. She stepped forward, and Emilia watched curiously, as the pirate leaned against the rail beside her.

"You're not a sailor," Maria said, resting her elbow against the wooden rail. "So, why should I want you?"

Emilia could barely remember their conversation with the pirate standing so close to her. "You mean," she said with a frown, "besides the gold?"

"Besides the gold," Maria confirmed.

Emilia squeezed the clasp of her cloak, trying to ignore the way Maria's body heat radiated into her. "There must be others on your ship who weren't sailors before they met you."

"Why would there be?" Maria said. "I am the most renowned pirate captain in Aletharia. Any sailor willing to dip their toes into piracy for better wages *dreams* of working for me."

Emilia scowled at the devastatingly gorgeous pirate captain, who was also, obviously, quite full of herself. "Is there a point to all of this boasting you're doing?"

Maria laughed. She pressed her weight onto her left elbow, angling her body toward Emilia's. "The point is," she said lowly, "why would I settle for scraps, when I can have the whole damn meal?"

The spark of irritation and subtle burn of attraction that had been waging war in Emilia's head suddenly merged into full-blown, boiling-hot anger. "Scraps?"

Maria smiled, as if she were enjoying this reaction. "Surely, you don't think you're worth more than that. You have no experience."

"In *sailing*," Emilia said. "I have other skills."

Maria leaned closer, until her breath fell against Emilia's lips. "Name them," she challenged.

Emilia swallowed uneasily.

Above them, the clouds shifted in the night sky, allowing a stream of pale blue moonlight to fall across Maria's face, illuminating her deep scars.

"Who treated your wounds?" Emilia asked.

Maria leaned back, frowning at the question. "Why do you ask?"

Maria hadn't *once* tiptoed around Emilia's feelings. So, Emilia decided to stop tiptoeing around Maria's feelings, as well.

"It clearly wasn't a trained healer," Emilia said.

Maria lifted a scarred eyebrow, but she seemed merely surprised, rather than offended. "Bold assumption."

"Not really. I just know what I'm talking about," Emilia told her, "and your scars aren't even the worst of your crew. The man with the gold teeth—"

"I have multiple sailors with gold teeth," Maria interrupted, "but you're referring to Pelt, my boatswain. The scar on his cheek?" When Emilia nodded, Maria said, "He lost his teeth in the same accident that gave him the scar."

"A fall, right?" Emilia said. "Severe trauma to the face?"

"He fell from the rigging. Five years ago," Maria confirmed. Her brows furrowed. "How did you know that?"

"I told you," Emilia said. "I know what I'm talking about." She smiled. "Whoever it is you have treating your wounds, on the other hand, does not."

Maria's lips twitched at the corners. "Perhaps no one's told you, love, but medicine is a lucrative career in Illopia," she told Emilia. "Trained surgeons don't often resort to piracy."

"In that case," Emilia said—with an even brighter smile, "a person with experience in healing would be valuable, wouldn't she? You certainly wouldn't call her *scraps*."

Maria leaned closer. "Darling," she murmured, her breath warm against Emilia's lips, "are you trying to tell me you're a surgeon?"

"We're called healers where I'm from," Emilia said honestly, "but yes, I have plenty of experience in surgery, as well."

She neglected to mention that she used magic more often than surgery. The pirate captain didn't need to know that yet.

Maria inched closer. The wind rustled her curly, brown hair and her faded, leather clothes—bringing her scent into Emilia's space, once more. She smelled so enticing—like every alluring aspect of the ocean, bottled into one scent.

Much like she'd done before, Maria slipped a tattooed finger beneath Emilia's chin, urging Emilia to meet her gaze. "So, what you're telling me, thief, is that you aren't just a meal," she teased. "You're a delicacy."

Emilia shuddered. She told herself it was the breeze that made her shiver, but...well, Maria's closeness and that warm, tropical scent of hers certainly wasn't helping matters.

The fact that she was describing Emilia as if she were something to be eaten might have *also* been partially to blame.

"Does that mean..." Emilia trailed off, suddenly breathless. "Have I impressed you?"

Maria dropped her hand and laughed. "You think you've impressed me?" she scoffed. "With what? Your one skill?"

"No," Emilia said. Insecurity rose in her throat, making it harder to speak. "That's not what I meant. I just—"

Maria leaned closer. "I haven't even seen you in action yet."

Emilia swallowed. "Judith said I should impress you," she admitted. "That's all I meant."

Maria grinned at that. "Was she telling you *to* impress me," she whispered, "or was she warning you *not* to?"

Emilia hesitated at that. "I'm," she stammered, "not sure."

Maria chuckled. "What alias did you give her?"

"Alias?" Emilia repeated.

"By your own admission, you're a fugitive," Maria reminded her. "I assume you didn't give her your *real* name."

I almost did, Emilia thought sheepishly.

"Em."

Maria stared blankly at her. "Em?" she repeated. "That's it. Just...Em?"

"Yes," Emilia said, her unease increasing by the moment. "Just Em."

Maria glanced out at the sea, her brows high. She exhaled slowly, as if she were trying to hold in her anger—or laughter. Emilia wasn't sure which. "Please, tell me that isn't short for your real name."

Heat instantly rushed to Emilia's face. "It's not."

Maria cast a sidelong glance at Emilia—just in time to see her blush. "Fucking hell," she scoffed. She pulled out that leather flask again. "I'm going to need this."

Emilia watched the captain drink, anxiety churning in her stomach. "Do you want me to come up with a different name?" she asked. "I think Judith knew I was lying, anyway."

"Of course she did," Maria muttered. She lowered the flask and looked at Emilia. She waved her flask dismissively. "Nah. Don't worry about it, love," she said in a shockingly gentle tone. "We can work with Em." She studied Emilia with a curious frown. "Where are you from?"

Emilia glanced out at the sea, breathing out a heavy sigh, as she watched the steady roll of the waves.

Judith had told her not to lie to Maria, but this was one question Emilia couldn't answer honestly.

The people of this kingdom didn't know Emilia by appearance. They knew her by name. By *one* name.

Drakon.

Long before King Eldric declared them enemies of the Crown, long before Emilia's mother sent dragons to burn down their cities, long before their lifetimes, even, people throughout all of Aletharia knew the name *Drakon*. People throughout all of Aletharia feared the sorcerers who lived amongst dragons, the sorcerers who'd somehow tamed the godlike beasts.

And they knew where to find those sorcerers.

Drakon Isle.

It was an island that had belonged to dragons—and Emilia's ancestors—since the dawn of time. If Emilia were to tell anyone where she was from, they'd know who she was. They'd know she was a Drakon witch.

So, instead, Emilia just told her, "The Azure Sea."

Maria gestured toward the shallow, blue waves with her flask. "This *is* the Azure Sea, love."

"The islands," Emilia said. That was true, as well—technically. Misleading, perhaps. But still mostly true.

Drakon Isle was *an* island in the Azure Sea.

Just not one of the islands Maria would assume.

"You're from the Azure Islands?" Maria asked.

"Yes," Emilia lied.

One lie wasn't too bad, was it? Maria Welles *was* a pirate, after all. It wasn't like *she* could claim the moral high-ground.

"I assume Judith asked what 'Em' was short for," Maria said. "What did you tell her?"

"Emily," Emilia said.

At least she'd been able to tear her focus from the food long enough to lie about *that* part.

"Good choice," Maria said. "Emily is an Illopian name, and your accent's faint enough. You're less likely to get caught if people think you're from Illopia."

"Because they hate foreigners?" Emilia assumed.

"No," Maria laughed. "You're not in Regolis anymore, love. This is a pirate port. They're not like that here." She held out the flask—offering Emilia the rum, once more.

Again, Emilia politely refused.

"You don't like accepting drinks from people," Maria said, leaving no room for argument. "They drugged you, didn't they?"

Catherine drugged me, Emilia thought.

She looked away, her pulse spiking. "I'm just not thirsty."

Maria shrugged and tipped the flask back once more, drinking whatever was left.

When she finished, she turned the leather flask upside down, as if she wasn't sure that she'd drunk it all already.

The pirate captain scowled at the empty flask—as if it had emptied itself—and begrudgingly pocketed it.

"What I meant, love," she said, as she returned her attention to Emilia, "was that distancing your alias from your true identity will make it harder for them to guess who you are."

Emilia flashed a regretful smile at that. "Well, I already messed *that* up, didn't I?"

Maria chuckled. "A little, but we'll make it work."

For reasons Emilia didn't understand, something about the way Maria said *'we'* unleashed a pleasant, fluttery warmth inside Emilia's chest.

"May I see your wrists?"

Emilia looked up at her, blinking in shock. "What?"

"You can refuse me," Maria assured her. "I won't demand it of you, and I won't threaten you." Her dark brown eyes softened. "Not regarding this."

If she'd made the request with any less gentleness, Emilia might've refused.

But as it was, Emilia was so stunned by the abrupt change in tone that she decided to do as the pirate asked—if for no reason but curiosity.

Emilia offered her left wrist, and Maria reached out and took it.

Maria curled her fingers around Emilia's wrist, her touch stunningly gentle.

The tattoos on Maria's fingers were too small to see at a distance. Before, Emilia could only tell that there was black ink, etched into her brown skin.

But Emilia saw them clearly, now—small, nautical symbols, inked into each finger.

Maria pushed back the thick, black sleeve of Emilia's cloak and turned Emilia's wrist upward.

Emilia cringed the moment Maria saw the scars. "The shackles, they—"

Maria didn't wait for Emilia to finish. "I know," the pirate said softly.

Maria rubbed the pad of her thumb across the raised, reddened skin, and Emilia shuddered at the sensation.

Maria's light touch raised chill bumps on Emilia's skin and caused her stomach to flip in a delightfully pleasant way.

"Would you like to see mine?"

Emilia looked up. "What?" she said breathlessly.

"It's only fair," Maria said. "You let me see yours. I'll show you mine, if you ask."

Emilia blinked slowly. "May I?"

Maria let her hand fall away from Emilia's wrist. She rolled up the linen sleeves of her shirt and presented both arms to Emilia.

Much like the nautical tattoos on her fingers, tattoos covered Maria's forearms, as well—a siren on one arm, and a snake coiled around a sword on the other. But Maria wasn't showing Emilia her tattoos.

Maria was showing Emilia that she had them, too.

The scars.

With a soft intake of breath, Emilia reached out and brushed a fingertip along the discolored skin. "They look just like mine."

"Same dungeon," Maria said. "Same gallows."

Emilia lifted her gaze to meet Maria's. "But I never told you," she said, her chest fluttering, "where I was imprisoned."

"No, but like you said," Maria reminded her, "they look just like yours."

Emilia's brows creased. It was unsettling to have someone know what happened to her.

Especially someone as self-serving as Maria.

But at the same time, there was something comforting about being face-to-face with someone who knew her pain.

Maria dropped her arms to her sides. "Can you fight?"

Emilia nodded. "I've trained in sword-fighting."

With two fingers, Maria opened Emilia's cloak, peeking at Emilia's scabbard-less waist. "Where's your sword, then?"

"They took my weapons," Emilia told her.

The word *they* got caught in Emilia's throat—because what she really meant was *Catherine*.

Catherine gave the orders. Catherine did this.

Emilia reached into her cloak and pulled out the dagger she'd tucked into her belt. "I did manage to take this one back, though."

Maria lifted a scarred eyebrow. She reached out and took the weapon. She turned it over, watching as the moonlight reflected in the blade. Her brows furrowed, as she studied the design that Emilia's mother had carved into the handle. "I see why you wanted it back," she admitted. She handed it back to Emilia. "You'd get a bit of coin for that. You wouldn't need to steal to eat."

Emilia traced the design with her thumb—flames, bursting forth from the mouth of a dragon. A heavy sadness settled in her stomach at the thought of what the pirate captain was suggesting. "I can't sell this."

"Sentiment won't feed you, love," Maria said.

Emilia looked up. The pirate captain didn't know it was the last thing her mother had given her—nor did she know that the magic fused into the blade might just save her life, when nothing else would. So, even though her first instinct was to get defensive, Emilia just said, "It's more than sentiment. I can't lose this."

Maria's lean shoulders lifted in a languid shrug. "If you say so," she muttered. "Hypothetically, if I gave you a sword, could you wield it?"

"Yes," Emilia said.

Maria let the cloak fall closed. "What about a pistol?"

Emilia shook her head. "We don't have them on the islands."

"Hand-to-hand combat?" Maria said.

Emilia frowned at that. "I've never gotten into a fist-fight, no."

"Might want to avoid getting too drunk in the tavern, then," Maria muttered.

Emilia blinked at that. "What?"

"Any battle experience?" Maria said. "Or just sparring?"

Emilia's stomach turned at the memory. "There was a battle, but I ended up in shackles, so…" She looked away. "It probably won't impress you."

A gentle finger urged Emilia's face back toward Maria's. "I only care if you ran," she murmured, "and clearly, you didn't."

Emilia blinked, stunned by the kind words.

Was this the same pirate who'd mocked her and threatened her?

The same pirate who'd eviscerated Paul in the middle of the street?

Maria dropped her hand. "Who trained you?"

Emilia froze. She'd honestly tried to follow Judith's advice—and not lie to the pirate captain.

But there were some things Emilia couldn't tell the captain.

Like the fact that she'd been trained by Maria's worst enemy.

"Does it matter?" Emilia said. "All you need to know is that she was a great teacher."

The pirate captain scoffed at that. "You haven't seen great yet, love."

Emilia laughed at the pirate's arrogance. "I think she could take you."

As a matter of fact, if what Catherine told her was true, she'd already beaten Maria once.

Maria stepped closer—so close, now, that Emilia had to lift her chin to hold the pirate captain's gaze.

"Oh?" Maria said. Her smile widened, and an alluring spark of fire flashed in those dark brown eyes of hers. "Well, if she's as great as you say, her student should be able to take me, too."

Emilia's cheeks flushed. "I...could, yeah," she somehow managed to say, despite the roar of her own blood in her ears. "If you gave me a sword, I could."

Maria grinned wickedly at that. "You have *no* idea how tempted I am to take you up on that offer."

Emilia's breath caught at the way Maria said *'tempted.'* "Then, do it," she said. "If it gets me home, I'll fight you as many times as you want."

Maria chuckled. "Sounds like you're trying to get yourself killed, love."

Emilia narrowed her eyes at that. "I'm better than you think," she said. "Give me a chance to prove it."

"I'm sorry, Em," Maria said, and she actually sounded sincere, for once, "but the answer's no."

Emilia's stomach sank. "But—"

"I'll help you," Maria interrupted, "but not in the way you want."

Emilia's brows furrowed. "What do you mean?"

Maria stepped back. "Adda can hide you," she explained. "If I ask her to, she will. I've asked her to help fugitives before."

"You have?" Emilia said.

Maria nodded. "You remember Jane, don't you?" she said with a wry smile. "The woman who put her tits in your face?"

Emilia blanched. "Would you, *please*, stop bringing that up?"

Maria laughed. "Well, she was in a *lot* of trouble once," she told Emilia. "I brought her to Adda, and Adda's protected her since."

Emilia's frown deepened. Why would a pirate captain help a fugitive?

What could she possibly get out of it?

"Adda will hide you and give you work," Maria explained. "You won't need to steal to eat."

Emilia's stomach twisted with dread. "You're suggesting I work at the tavern?"

Maria leaned closer. "What's the matter?" she sneered. "Are you too good to pour some ale, surgeon?"

Emilia bristled at that. "That's not what I said." She narrowed her eyes. "I don't mind the work. It's the staying-in-Nefala part that I can't do."

"Everyone in Nefala knows that I will kill them, if they mess with any of Adda's girls," Maria told her. "You'd be safe."

Emilia shook her head. "You don't understand," she tried to explain. "I can't stay here. There are...people on my island, who need me."

Okay, so that was a bit of a lie.

78

There were *dragons* on her island, who needed her.

But those dragons were the closest thing Emilia had to family.

"That's your problem," Maria said. She gave a careless shrug. "Or theirs, I suppose."

Emilia frowned. How had Maria gone from speaking so kindly a moment ago to acting so coldly now?

What triggered this mood shift?

"I can't stay," Emilia said firmly. "I appreciate the offer of help, but I can't stay."

"Em," Maria said, leaning closer. "You'd be safe with Adda. You won't be safe with me. Do you understand that?"

"I can't stay," Emilia repeated.

"Em," Maria said again, as the sea breeze rustled her soft curls, "I need to know that you understand the choice you're making." She lifted a scarred eyebrow. "I'm offering you safety, and you're turning it down. Do you understand that?"

Emilia nodded, despair numbing her chest. "I don't want safety at the cost of theirs," she told the captain. "I'd rather get myself killed than not try to help them."

A deep, cruel smile curled at the corners of Maria's lips. "I warned you not to impress me."

Emilia's brows furrowed. "What does that mean?"

Maria cast a quick glance at the second story of the tavern and took another step back. "It means we'll continue this conversation later," she told Emilia. "I have a...*matter* to attend to."

The smirk that Maria shot Emilia's way was positively mischievous.

Emilia followed her when she took a step back. "Can't you give me an answer first?"

"Oh, no, love. That's not how this works," Maria said. Her smile deepened. "I am the most powerful pirate in Aletharia, and you are no one." She took another step back. "You don't get to make demands of me."

Emilia stared at her in disbelief. "You know, for a few moments there, you almost had me convinced that people were wrong about you," she snarled. "But now, you're back to acting like the power-hungry madwoman they say you are."

Maria laughed at the insult. "Well, that was your mistake, thief," she taunted. "You shouldn't let a moment of kindness change your opinion of someone."

Maria couldn't possibly have known how close to home that remark would hit for Emilia, but...oh, how it hurt.

Guilt turned her stomach with the strength of a hurricane.

If she'd only heeded that advice when she met Catherine, her family would still be alive.

Maria had already started toward the door, but she froze and spun toward Emilia, before she reached it. "Oh! And one more thing," she said, pointing a tattooed finger. "Don't leave."

With an incredulous stare, Emilia said, "You want me to stay on the pier until you're done...doing whatever you're doing?"

"No, no, of course not. There's no food out here." Maria's smile widened. "I told you you'd eat again, didn't I?"

Emilia scowled at that. "I'm not hungry."

Maria shrugged. "Then, you can sit at the table and stare at the food—until you are. It makes no difference to me."

Emilia glared murderously at the pirate captain. "I think you're forgetting something, *Maria Welles.*"

Maria's smile faded. "Captain," she snarled back.

Emilia stepped closer. "You might be a captain, but you're not mine," she told her. "Not yet, anyway."

Maria's eyes darkened. "Choose your next words carefully, thief."

Emilia didn't even flinch at the threat. "I don't work for you," she reminded Maria. "If you want to order me around, you're going to have to hire me first."

Maria grinned, a cruel delight flashing in her dark brown eyes. "Don't tempt me."

CHAPTER 5

A Part of the Crew

"I'm surprised you're still here."

The man in the green coat—the one Maria said was her quartermaster—took the seat across from Emilia.

Emilia didn't know where he'd gone, but he didn't look happy to see her upon his return.

The quartermaster dragged his hand along the front of his green waistcoat, as if he were smoothing out wrinkles—even though Emilia saw none.

Only when the quartermaster pinned her with a dark glare, did Emilia realize that his remark had been directed at her.

"Captain asked her to stay, Zain," Judith told him. She placed a card face-down on the table and then turned her attention toward Emilia. "Don't mind Zain. He'd interrogate his own mother."

"If she showed up here, I would," Zain muttered. "My mother wouldn't set foot in a place like this."

The pirate with the vicious scar—the one they'd called *Pelt*—placed his card on the table, as well. His deeply-tanned, calloused fingers lingered on the card for a moment, as he considered Judith's expression.

Emilia didn't understand the game they were playing, but she assumed it was some sort of Illopian gambling game—considering the heap of gold coins, steadily growing, on the table.

"Having second thoughts, Pelt?" Judith said.

Pelt released the card and leaned back in his chair.

"How long does she want you to stay?" Zain asked.

Emilia glanced at him, surprised he was still talking to her. "She didn't say. Until she gets back, I assume."

"Where is she?" Zain said. When Emilia shrugged, he glanced at Judith. "She's upstairs with Jane, isn't she?"

Judith frowned at the cards in her hands. "Yeah."

Zain rolled his eyes. He offered Emilia a sympathetic look. "You might as well get comfortable, then," he muttered. "She could be up there all night."

"Nah," Judith said. She placed another card on the table. "The captain doesn't linger. She'll fuck her once or twice and then come back down."

Emilia blinked.

That's where she'd gone?

Every moment Emilia spent in this tavern was another moment that someone could recognize her or arrest her, and that self-absorbed pirate captain had told her to wait—just so that she could have sex?

If Emilia hadn't already decided she disliked Maria, she certainly would've decided to dislike her now.

Enemy of my enemy, Emilia reminded herself.

She didn't have to like Maria. She just had to work with her for a little while—until Catherine was dead.

Zain rolled his eyes. "Do I even *want* to know why you know what the captain does or doesn't do, after sex?"

Judith snorted, "You'd know it, too, if you fucked women." When Zain frowned, she said, "They talk."

Pelt nodded in agreement. He took a large drink of ale and then said, "For example, I happen to know that Judith gets sentimental during sex."

Judith looked up at that, frowning. "I do not."

Pelt grinned, his gold teeth flashing. "Sarah says you do."

Judith grimaced. "I did tell her I loved her once."

Zain's brows furrowed. "Why would you do that?"

"I don't know, Zain," Judith said with a groan. "I was drunk. I love everyone when I'm drunk."

Zain lifted a dark eyebrow. "Is this the same Sarah who slapped you when she caught you kissing Jane?"

"Same Sarah," Pelt confirmed.

Judith set down another card. "I believe it was the location of my hand that she had an issue with."

Zain rolled his eyes. "See, even if I *did* sleep with women, I'd know better than to sleep with *all* of them."

"There are several I haven't slept with," Judith said defensively. She placed another card on the table.

Pelt snorted, "You mean the ones who prefer men?"

Judith chuckled. "Why don't you just focus on your cards, all right?"

Emilia glanced around the table, following their conversation with a strange curiosity.

Illopians *clearly* had some different relationship habits than islanders.

Or maybe this was a pirate thing, too.

Judith noticed Emilia watching her and smiled. "You better start eating," she teased. "Jane's probably on her second orgasm by now."

Emilia's face burned with embarrassment.

Was there anything these pirates wouldn't say?

Emilia picked up a piece of bread and took a small bite of it. She'd eaten plenty already, but if eating a little more would convince Captain Maria Welles to make a deal with her, she'd try it.

"Can I get you anything?"

Emilia froze. She'd heard that voice before—its high pitch and delicate lilt. She didn't dare turn to look at the tavern worker. Instead, she took a quick peek out of the corner of her eye. The tavern worker was a curvy woman with fair, freckled skin, and her frizzy, red hair fell around her shoulders.

Emilia recognized her easily. She was the woman who'd brought Emilia's water earlier—the one Emilia had warned about Paul, before attempting to flee.

"More ale," several pirates yelled, at once.

The barmaid laughed. "Should've known."

Emilia kept her head down, hoping that her long, black hair would hide her face from the tavern worker. But just when she'd thought she'd escaped the tavern worker's notice, the woman turned back.

"If you need any more food, miss, let me know," the woman said. "Captain Maria Welles says we're to keep bringing you food for as long as you're here."

I didn't even want this plate, Emilia wanted to say, but instead, she just said, "This is plenty. Thank you."

The tavern worker paused at the sound of Emilia's voice. She stepped closer. "Have we met, miss?"

Oh, no.

Judith's bright blue eyes shifted toward Emilia. She must've recognized Emilia's nervousness—because she suddenly turned toward the tavern worker. "Agnes, do you know if Sarah has come in yet?"

"Sarah *again*, Judith?" Pelt laughed.

"I'm not sure," Agnes said, "but I'll check for you."

"Lovely as always, Agnes," Judith said with a gracious smile.

Relief washed over Emilia, as soon as Agnes left, but it was short-lived.

Emilia desperately needed to get out of this tavern, before the worker returned.

Judith studied Emilia curiously. "You all right?"

Dread churned deep inside Emilia's stomach. The way Judith looked at her—she must've known.

She must've recognized the panic in Emilia's eyes.

Emilia set the bread on her plate and climbed to her feet. "I need to step outside for a moment," she lied.

Zain watched her with dark, narrowed eyes. "The captain won't like that. Not if she told you to stay."

Emilia was just about to inform the pirate that she didn't work for Maria—and therefore, didn't have to listen to her—but Judith spoke up, before she could.

"Leave her alone, Zain," Judith said. "The girl just needs a breath of fresh air. She'll come back." She lifted her eyebrows at Emilia. "Won't you?" Despite Judith's friendly attitude, there was an undertone in her question—that sounded an awful lot like a threat.

Emilia remembered the pistol that Judith carried at her waist and forced a smile. "Of course," she lied.

Judith put down another card. "Careful out there."

Emilia frowned at the warning, but she didn't have time to question it. The kitchen door opened, and the tavern worker returned with several more jugs of ale.

Collective cheers resounded throughout the tavern.

Emilia headed straight for the door. She berated herself for waiting so long. Clearly, Maria was only toying with her. She'd never intended to help Emilia.

Maria had made that clear, hadn't she? Sure, she'd *seemed* to change her mind, at the end, but she'd never said as much.

Emilia had been a fool to wait this long.

What were the chances that the most notorious pirate captain in all of Aletharia would help Emilia?

Emilia had risked her freedom—and for what?

One meal?

A fruitless conversation with a pirate captain who couldn't care less?

Emilia's hope wasn't just foolish. It was dangerous.

Though…to be honest, Emilia hadn't hated the time she'd spent in the tavern. She didn't want to admit it, even to herself, but there was something *about* these pirates—something that appealed to Emilia. It wasn't their line of work. It wasn't their appearance or their weapons or the state of their salt-stained clothing…

It was something else.

There was something in the atmosphere—as if the air itself tasted of rebellion. Emilia couldn't explain it, but she felt a sort of… kinship with these people she knew nothing about. Perhaps it was because the world feared them, too—just as it feared Emilia.

Emilia had almost made it to the door, when a voice stopped her. "You're still here?"

Emilia froze. Her hand tightened around the door's iron handle, but she didn't pull it open. Instead, she took a deep breath to calm her racing pulse, and then, she turned to face the person who'd questioned her.

Her pulse immediately returned to its former pace.

Because standing in front of her now, was the same, older woman who'd chased Paul out to his death.

Unlike the other women in the tavern, who wore corsets and heavy, high-waisted gowns, the tavern owner wore a simple, russet-brown, wool gown—with no flourishes and no corset. It looked a lot more comfortable than what the servers wore—and much more suited for outdoor work.

Adda rested a hand on her hip, as if she were tired. "I'm speaking to you, child." Her dark eyes narrowed. "What are you doing in my tavern?"

The tavern owner's hair was dark and curly, like Maria's, but she kept hers pinned up neatly, rather than leaving it loose and messy, like Maria did.

Emilia took a step back. "I was just leaving."

Adda stepped around her and pressed her hand against the

door. "Not until you answer my question," she demanded. "What were you doing here?"

Emilia turned toward her, eyeing the door that she could no longer use to escape. "I was just…eating."

Adda trailed her dark brown gaze over Emilia's long, black cloak. "What are you hiding under that cloak, child?"

Emilia swallowed, her throat tight. "I'm no child."

The older woman let out a short, amused scoff at that. "What are you, then?" she sneered. "A thief?"

Emilia held her breath. This was it. Either she used her magic to escape—or she opened her cloak and revealed to the tavern owner that she was a thief.

Either option required revealing a crime.

Either option would likely result in her death.

Unless…she killed them all, at once.

She could set fire to the tavern—leave no survivors.

That kind of magic came at a heavy price. Its most benign cost was the physical one. She'd be too tired to run or fight for weeks. But that didn't even *compare* to what it would cost her emotionally. She had paid that price in Regolis, though, and she could do it again.

"She's one of mine."

Emilia straightened at the sound of that familiar, lilting voice. She turned, her eyes widening, as she found Captain Maria Welles standing behind her.

With the exception of the thin sheen of sweat on her brown skin, the pirate captain looked no different than she had when they'd spoken earlier. Her tricorn hid any disarray in her hair, and her clothes were mostly in place—with the exception of her doublet, which she fastened, now, as she met Emilia's gaze.

The tavern owner looked up at Maria. "Captain?"

Maria glanced at her, flashing a wry smile. "Adda?"

Adda planted her hands on her hips. "There isn't a pirate who visits my tavern that I don't know," she reminded Maria, "and I know yours most of all."

"I hired her tonight," Maria said. "I hadn't had time to introduce you yet." There was no hesitation or anxiety in her lie. "I figured you'd be happy. You've been nagging me about hiring a surgeon for years."

Adda scowled at that. "Watch your tone, Captain," she muttered. She glanced at Emilia. "Surgeon?"

Emilia didn't want to contradict the pirate captain's story in any way. So, she just nodded.

"And I didn't even have to kidnap her," Maria bragged.

Emilia blinked. *Why was that even necessary to say?*

"She doesn't look like she's in the best of health herself," Adda said. "How's she going to take care of your crew's health, if she can't take care of her own?"

That was the second time that day that someone had suggested that Emilia looked sickly. She wished she had a mirror so she could see what they meant.

"I can always throw her in the sea, if she's bad at her job," Maria said with a shrug. "I already don't have a surgeon. It's not much of a risk on my part."

Despite her obvious suspicions of Emilia, Adda scowled at Maria. "Would you stop before you scare the girl off?" she scolded. Her dark gaze flickered toward Emilia again. "I do have some concerns I need to share with you, Captain."

"Of course," Maria said. Her voice took on a totally different tone, when she spoke to Adda. There was a gentle, affectionate quality to it. "I need to speak with my surgeon, but I'll come to your room afterward."

"Fine," Adda said with a disgruntled huff, "but you better not keep me waiting." She waved toward the stairs. "And tell Jane to get dressed and get back to work. I hired her to serve ale—not to sneak off with you!"

With an absolutely shameless smile, Maria said, "At least she'll be in a better mood now."

Adda shook her head. "I don't know why I put up with you," she grumbled, as she turned to leave.

Maria just laughed.

It wasn't long after Adda left that the pretty, brown-haired tavern worker came running down the stairs.

"She knows," Maria said, when Jane ran past her.

Jane froze and turned to look at Maria, her grey eyes wide. "Adda?" she said nervously. When Maria nodded, Jane complained, "Goddamn it, Captain!"

Maria chuckled—as Jane sprinted to the kitchen, nearly tripping over her own dress in her hurry.

Once Jane was out of sight, as well, Maria returned her attention to Emilia. She watched Emilia silently, as she finished fastening her black, leather doublet.

Emilia couldn't help but watch Maria's tattooed fingers, as they slowly and methodically tightened the last few leather thongs of the doublet. "Well," she said, breaking the silence, "did you enjoy yourself?"

A smirk pulled at the edges of Maria's lips. "I did."

Frustration twisted tightly in Emilia's stomach. She knew she should thank the pirate captain—for saving her from being discovered by Adda—but after the panic Emilia had just felt, having Maria stand here in front of her, smirking, as if she'd just done the world a favor by having sex with some woman, annoyed the hell out of Emilia. "I was just about to leave."

"You should've moved faster," Maria said. She let her arms fall to her sides. "Might've gotten away."

Why did she say things like that?

If Maria *wasn't* the villain they said she was, she certainly wasn't trying to change anyone's mind.

"You told her I was part of your crew," Emilia said. "Does that mean you've decided to help me?"

"Unfortunately for you, yes," Maria said. She tilted her head toward the door. "Go. We'll talk out there."

Emilia turned and led the way out of the tavern. As soon as the cool, salt-water air met Emilia's skin, her pulse slowed, and every muscle in her body relaxed.

Maria must have noticed. "You could've joined us," she teased, "if you were that scared of being alone."

Emilia turned, pinning Maria with a peeved glare.

But before she could spit out a retort, Maria said, "I'm sure Jane would have been happy to put her breasts in your face again."

Emilia grew more homicidal with every word that came out of this woman's mouth. She crossed her arms, caging in her anger as well as she could. "I wasn't afraid," she informed the pirate captain.

"No?" Maria said, lifting a scarred eyebrow. "In that case, perhaps I should've waited to see how you were going to handle that." Her smile was taunting. "I'm sure you had it all under control."

Anger boiled in Emilia's throat, threatening to spill out. "You wouldn't have liked the way I would have handled it."

Maria's brown eyes narrowed dangerously. "I see."

Emilia huddled deeper in her cloak. The sea-breeze wasn't cold, really, but it was cool enough to contrast with the heat currently burning underneath her skin.

Maria busied herself with rolling down her sleeves, tugging them back down to cover her scarred wrists and tattooed forearms.

"Adda suspects you, but she isn't sure," Maria told Emilia. "If she were sure, she would've accused you in front of me—and I, of course, would've had to kill you." She said that so casually, and she didn't even bother to look at Emilia, when she said it. "But since she isn't sure, I can dissuade her. I'll tell her that you were at the docks with Judith."

How was Emilia supposed to respond to that?

Thank you for the alibi, but it'd be even better if you weren't so willing to kill me?

Instead, Emilia just said, "Will she believe you?"

"Yes," Maria said. She adjusted her swords and belts, too—even though Emilia thought those looked aligned already. "Adda trusts me."

"But you're a pirate," Emilia said with a frown.

"I'm not just a pirate to her," Maria said. She left it at that—a note of finality in her voice that permitted no further questions.

Who is she to you? Emilia wanted to ask. *Your mother?*

They had a few minor physical similarities—just skin tone and hair, really. Not enough to actually guess they were related. But their attitude toward each other had definitely suggested familiarity.

"Well," Emilia said, suddenly unsure, "thank you."

For the first time since they'd walked outside, Maria met Emilia's gaze. "You might want to save your thanks," she murmured, her eyes dark. "You'll wish you could take it back soon enough."

Emilia frowned at the warning. "Why would I?"

"Everything comes at a price, Em," Maria told her, "and I'm not in the business of taking things fairly."

Apprehension settled in Emilia's stomach. "I offered you gold."

"A fair price, wouldn't you say?" Maria said. Her smile widened. "Again, love...I don't play fairly."

"You want more than gold," Emilia realized.

"Haven't you heard the tales?" Maria said. "They say my greed is insatiable, don't they?"

Catherine said that.

"What do you want from me, then?" Emilia asked.

Maria laughed at the question. "The question isn't what I want, love. It's what you're willing to give."

Emilia stared at the pirate, her stomach fluttering.

"I'm not finished here," Maria told her, "but I can't have you hanging around the tavern, where someone might recognize you." She stepped closer. "You see, love, now that I've claimed you as one of mine, that would reflect badly on *me*." She leaned in to whisper, "And I always look out for myself."

Emilia lifted her eyebrows. "Big surprise there."

Maria smiled at the remark, clearly not ashamed. She pulled out a small coin, holding it between two fingers. "If you want to leave on my ship, you'll have to follow these next instructions word-for-word. Do you think you can do that?"

Emilia frowned. "That depends on what they are."

"Yes or no, Em," Maria said. The moonlight cast a blue glow over her dark skin. "Can you do it?"

With a reluctant sigh, Emilia nodded.

"You're going to go inside, find Judith, and give her this coin," Maria said. "She'll know what it means."

Emilia squinted at the strange, silver coin. It didn't *look* like any of the coins she'd seen used in Illopia.

Or anywhere else, for that matter.

"Judith and Zain will take you to the *Wicked Fate*," Maria said. "You'll say exactly what Judith tells you to say—nothing more, nothing less. Zain is going to question you relentlessly. It's what he does. If you say only what Judith tells you to say, you'll be fine."

Agreeing to that, Emilia held out her hand.

Maria held the coin above Emilia's palm, but just when Emilia thought she'd drop it, she closed her fingers around it and pulled it back toward her. "This is the point of no return, thief," she warned. "If you want out, you're free to go—*if* you go now. But once this coin is in your possession, I will kill you before I let you disappear with it."

Emilia frowned at the threat. "Is it valuable?"

"It's absolutely worthless," Maria assured her, "but I refuse to lose it." Again, she dangled the silver coin above Emilia's palm. "Last chance to walk away."

Walking away wasn't an option for Emilia.

She had to return to her dragons—to protect them, to seek vengeance against Catherine… She had to return.

No matter the cost.

So, Emilia kept her hand out and waited.

Maria lifted a scarred eyebrow. "Don't say I didn't warn you," she murmured. She dropped the coin into Emilia's hand. "Straight to Judith. Speak to no one."

Emilia closed her fingers around the silver coin. For something that had come with such a heavy warning, it felt much too small and much too light in her hand.

Emilia looked up, meeting the pirate captain's gaze briefly. Emilia nearly drowned in those deep, brown eyes every time she looked at them, and it always took a few moments afterward for her to find ground again.

She hoped she'd find Judith at the table she'd just left, but the memory of Judith asking about one of the tavern ladies made her hesitate. "What if she's busy?"

"She'll do as her captain says, regardless," Maria said with a dark glare. "You might want to start learning that skill yourself."

Emilia met Maria's glare with her own. "Fine."

Emilia tried to step past Maria, but Maria reached out and grasped her arm, before she could. With her fingers tightly curled around Emilia's arm, she jerked Emilia against her.

"One more thing," the captain growled in her ear. "I'll see you later tonight. If you try any shit before I get there, you'll find that my sword is a lot harder to escape than a noose."

Between the anger coursing through her and the warmth of Maria's body, which was currently pressed against Emilia's side, heat consumed every cell in Emilia's body.

She narrowed her eyes. "Are you threatening me?"

"Yes," Maria said—without an ounce of regret. Her scent enticed Emilia's senses yet again—so sweet and warm—and her lean muscles pressed firmly against Emilia's side. With a sly smile, Maria said, "Welcome to the crew, thief."

Emilia jerked her arm out of the pirate's grasp and returned to the tavern, eager to get away from that absolutely infuriating pirate captain and her devastatingly beautiful eyes.

EMILIA DIDN'T SEE JUDITH AT THE TABLE WITH THE OTHER PIRATES, AND since Maria had so unreasonably demanded she speak to no one else, Emilia couldn't ask the others where Judith had gone.

So, she wandered the tavern, searching for her, instead.

It took her a while to find the ship cook—with her short, brown hair and those bright blue eyes—mostly because the aforementioned ship cook had her face hidden in a woman's bosom.

Emilia waited near the table, her face flushed.

"Umm…your captain told me to give this to you."

Judith pulled her mouth away from the lady's skin, just long enough to look at Emilia, but when she saw the coin in Emilia's hand, she cursed. She glanced up at the woman, who was straddling her lap. "Darling, I have to go," she said with a grimace. "I'm sorry."

With a peeved glare, the woman hoisted her gown up to her hips so that she could climb out of Judith's lap. "You said we'd have a whole night this time."

Judith raked a hand through her short, brown hair. "I know, I know," she sighed. "Next time, I promise."

The woman rolled her eyes. "That's what you said last time," she said, before heading toward the stairs.

"Ah, Sarah," Judith sighed, but the woman ignored her. She scrubbed her hand over her face. "Damn it."

Emilia watched awkwardly, unsure of whether she should apologize or pretend she hadn't seen anything.

Judith snatched the coin out of Emilia's hand and pocketed it. "It would seem she's your captain, too."

Emilia winced at that. "Well, yes. She did hire me."

Judith climbed to her feet and tucked her shirt back into her breeches. "You impressed her, then?"

"I don't know how impressed she was," Emilia said, "but she seemed more...interested, after I mentioned my experience in healing."

Judith looked at her. "You're a surgeon?"

Emilia hesitated at the flicker of worry she heard in Judith's tone. "Yes?"

Judith looked away, her bright blue eyes wide. "Shit," she whispered. "You never stood a chance, did you?"

Emilia frowned at that. "What do you mean?"

Judith shook her head. "Doesn't matter now," she said dismissively. She grabbed her pistol from the table and tucked it into her belt. "Follow me."

Emilia followed her toward the door. "I'm sorry, by the way."

Judith's brows furrowed. "For what?"

Emilia gave her an uneasy shrug. "Interrupting?"

Judith snorted. "Ah," she said. "Don't worry about that. I'd much rather irritate Sarah than the captain. The worst Sarah will do is slap me. The captain can make my life hell."

"What a comforting thing to hear," Emilia said, "just a few minutes after I agreed to work for her."

Judith laughed at her sarcasm. She led Emilia to the large, wooden doors. "She can be a bit...tough," she admitted—though Emilia suspected that was an understatement. "And she certainly has a penchant for murder." Judith pushed the doors open. "But she's still the best captain I've ever had."

"In that case," Emilia said with a frown, "I hope I never have to meet your other captains."

Judith laughed at that, too. "You're funny."

"It wasn't a joke," Emilia muttered.

Judith led her out into the dark, deserted street.

"This way," she said.

Judith took the torch from the sconce outside the tavern, and she held it in front of her, as she led Emilia down a dark alley.

Even at night, Emilia recognized the alley as the same one they'd used earlier that day.

But this time, they weren't alone.

The sounds of gasps and heavy breathing filled the otherwise silent alleyway.

"Judith," Emilia said with a worried frown. "I think this spot's taken."

"Not for long," Judith said. "Here. Take the torch."

Emilia grasped the burning wood, holding it out in front of her, as she squinted at the silhouettes in the distance.

It looked like a man and woman, and they were...

Emilia's eyes widened.

Oh.

Well...

That explained the heavy breathing, she supposed.

Judith took her pistol from its holster and pointed it toward the sky.

Emilia nearly jumped out of her skin, when Judith fired into the air.

Screams and gun smoke filled the alley, and the couple fled—not even bothering to adjust their clothes first.

Judith returned her pistol to its holster. "Nothing's taken when Captain Maria Welles is in town," she told a startled Emilia.

Emilia stared blankly at the pirate. "Convenient."

Judith chuckled. "It has its perks." She held out her hand. "Torch?"

Emilia gave the torch back to Judith. "So, does that kind of thing happen often in Illopia?"

"What?" Judith said. She snorted, "Oh, you mean public sex?" She shrugged a shoulder. "Technically, it's illegal, but this is Nefala. Illopian law doesn't mean much here."

"So it would seem," Emilia muttered.

"All right," Judith said, turning toward her. "Let me look at you."

Emilia couldn't see much of *anything* in that dark alley, but she still felt the urge to shrink back, under the pirate's scrutiny.

Judith lifted the torch between them, squinting at Emilia's long, black cloak. "I need you to take off the cloak, mate."

Emilia wrapped her fingers around the metal clasp, hesitating. "But someone might recognize me."

Judith shook her head. "There's no one here but you and me," she assured Emilia, "and if someone happens upon us, I'll just put out the fire."

Emilia glanced up at the torch. *She* could put it out, too—with a simple spell.

It wouldn't even take much out of her.

With a sigh, Emilia unfastened the clasp and slid the heavy cloak from her shoulders.

Judith trailed her gaze downward, lifting an eyebrow at Emilia's loose, black trousers. "No dress?" she said with a wide grin. "How scandalous."

Emilia smiled and shot a pointed look at Judith's breeches. "I don't think you have room to talk."

Judith snorted. "Fancy gowns aren't very practical at sea."

"They're not very practical for riding, either," Emilia countered.

She hoped Judith would assume she meant horseback riding, rather than…dragon-riding.

Though she most certainly *did* mean dragon-riding.

"Also," Emilia added, "my island doesn't have gendered clothing."

Her stomach sank, as a cruel voice in her mind corrected her.

It *didn't* have.

Past tense.

Judith nodded. "Neither does the Caluxian Empire," she said, "or so I've heard."

Emilia frowned at the mention of the northernmost empire. "I've never met a Caluxian."

After all, there was no reason for the northern people to brave the southern seas.

"You will," Judith said. "One of our sailors—Anuk? He served the Caluxian emperor before his banishment."

"Why was he banished?" Emilia asked.

Judith shrugged. "Didn't ask."

Emilia frowned. That...sort of seemed like an important thing to ask.

"What's this you're wearing over your shirt?" Judith asked. Her bright blue eyes widened. "Is that a cuirass?"

Emilia self-consciously brushed a hand over the dragon scales. "Would it be bad if it was?"

"Not bad," Judith said slowly, "but odd." Her brows furrowed. "Where did you even come from? An island full of warriors?"

In a sense, yes.

"It can be a dangerous place sometimes," Emilia admitted.

Judith nodded slowly. "And where is...*it*?"

Emilia chose to stick to the partial truth she'd given Maria. "The Azure Sea."

"Seriously?" Judith said. "Ever encountered a dragon?"

Emilia suppressed a laugh. "A few times."

"Shit," Judith said with raised eyebrows.

If she only knew.

"You'll probably want to lose the cuirass once you're on board," Judith suggested. "It looks heavy, and it might raise a few eyebrows."

"But it'll protect me in a battle," Emilia pointed out.

"You can keep it with you," Judith said. "But you probably don't want to wear it every day."

Emilia nodded.

With a playful grin, Judith said, "You always tuck your shirt in like a schoolboy?"

Emilia stared at the cook in confusion. She didn't think she'd ever met a 'schoolboy,' nor did she know how they dressed.

Emilia's mother had never asked her to dress any certain way during studies.

At Emilia's puzzled silence, Judith said, "I'm telling you to loosen up, love."

Emilia glanced down at her clothes, her confusion only growing.

She'd lost a bit of weight in those dungeons, and her trousers looked a little too loose already.

Judith waved a hand dismissively. "Forget it," she said. "I'll fix it later."

Emilia plucked absently at her black, linen shirt, still not sure what there was to *fix*.

"You wear a lot of black," Judith pointed out.

Emilia looked up, growing irritated with the constant scrutiny. "So does your captain."

Judith laughed. "Suppose she does," she said. "You sticking with Em?"

Emilia was still plucking at her shirt and hadn't totally caught that. "Hmm?"

"Your name—are you sticking with Em?" Judith asked.

Emilia nodded. "The captain said we could work with it."

Judith snorted at that. "And it's short for Emily?"

"That's the story," Emilia said.

Judith shook her head. "You're a pirate now, mate," she teased. "You'll have to learn to lie better than that."

"Sorry," Emilia said.

Judith waved her apology away. "Surname?"

Emilia blushed. "I hadn't gotten that far yet."

Judith laughed, "You've never done this before, have you?"

Emilia frowned at the strange question.

No, she had not, in fact, hidden her identity and joined a pirate crew before.

Did Judith think this was some sort of rite of passage that everyone engaged in?

First love, first betrayal, first imprisonment, first almost-execution, first mass murder, and now, first pirate crew.

Emilia supposed she *had* experienced a lot of firsts this year.

"Uh," was the only response Emilia came up with, "have *you*?"

Judith snorted. "No one pays attention to the cook," she said with a wink. "It's what makes me so useful to her."

Her?

Maria Welles.

She hadn't sent her quartermaster after Emilia. She hadn't sent her boatswain.

She'd sent Judith.

Maria *trusted* Judith.

"I've never needed an alias," Judith explained. "The bounty on *my* head wouldn't buy shit." She cast a thoughtful glance at the stone wall beside her. "But I've helped other fugitives before."

Emilia froze. "Wait," she said worriedly. "How did you know I was a fugitive? I didn't tell you, did I?"

"No, but you told the captain, didn't you?" Judith said.

Emilia's frown deepened.

Judith pulled that strange, silver coin from her pocket. "When you've known someone as long as I've known the captain, you learn to," she paused, turning the coin over in her hand, "speak without speaking."

Emilia remembered the look that Maria and Judith had shared in the tavern and wondered what they'd communicated then.

"Jane," Emilia said softly. "Mari—I mean *the captain*—said that Jane was a fugitive, too."

"'*Jane*' isn't her real name, either," Judith added.

"What is her real name?" Emilia asked curiously.

Judith shrugged. "No one knows—except the captain."

So, she can keep a secret, Emilia realized.

Judith pocketed the coin. "So, back to the matter at hand," she said. "You need a surname. An Illopian one, preferably."

Only one name came readily to Emilia's mind.

"Just give me the first one that pops into your head," Judith said with a snap of her fingers.

Emilia winced, before giving her honest answer, "Rochester?"

Judith frowned. "As in Commodore Rochester?"

"She's Admiral, now," Emilia told her.

Judith cringed. "The captain's not going to like that."

Emilia frowned curiously. So, the hatred between them *was* mutual, then.

"It was the only name I heard very often," Emilia admitted, "when I was imprisoned."

Emilia was careful to omit the *other* reason it was the only name on her mind.

Judith nodded. "We don't want anyone thinking you're related to...*her*, so," she sighed. "How about Northwood?" She looked at Emilia. "Can you answer to Emily Northwood?"

"Can I still be called *Em*?" Emilia asked.

"Of course," Judith assured her.

"It's a pretty name," Emilia said with a bit of insecurity. "Maybe a little too pretty for me."

"What?" Judith said with a small laugh. She shook her head and offered Emilia a gentle smile. "Nah."

Emilia blushed.

Judith was pretty—pretty enough to pull off those salt-stained clothes and that short, unevenly cut hair.

With those bright blue eyes of hers and that smooth, lightly tanned skin, the cook could dress however she wanted and still be pretty.

Emilia didn't think she had the same ability. "Why are you so nice to me?"

Judith snorted at that. "I pointed a pistol at you, love," she said with a baffled smile. "If that's your idea of nice, I'd hate to meet your other friends."

Emilia forced a smile at that.

She didn't have any other friends.

Not anymore.

"All right," Judith said after a moment. "Leave the cloak and the bread, and we'll head down to the water."

Emilia hesitated. "You want me to leave the bread?"

Judith cast a puzzled glance at the bread in the pocket of Emilia's cloak. "Well, what else would you do with it? Carry it in your arms?"

After starving for so long, Emilia's throat constricted at the thought of good food going to waste. "Well, no, but...it's food."

"We have food on the ship, Em," Judith said with a laugh. "We're not going to let you starve."

"But," Emilia said, "surely, there's someone who needs it."

Judith nodded, as she finally understood. "You don't want to see it wasted."

"I really don't," Emilia admitted.

Judith cast a thoughtful glance toward the end of the alley. "I know a place," she said slowly. "The drunks in town scavenge there. We'll leave it there."

With a relieved smile, Emilia said, "Thank you."

Judith glanced at her, frowning. "For what?"

"Understanding," Emilia said.

Judith smiled. "Anytime, mate."

Judith tilted her head toward the end of the alley. "Come on. I'll show you the way, and we can go over your story, as we walk."

Emilia clutched the folded cloak. "My story?"

"Zain will ask you a lot of questions. The whole crew will, honestly—but especially Zain," Judith said. "He's clever, Em. If we're not consistent, he'll see right through us."

Emilia followed the ship cook downhill. "But why do we need to lie in the first place?"

"Two reasons," Judith said. "First, because joining under a false name could be considered endangering the crew, which could get you killed."

Emilia frowned worriedly at that. "And the other reason?"

Judith sighed, "Do you know what makes Captain Maria Welles so powerful?"

Emilia shrugged. "Her ship?"

Judith laughed. "The *Wicked Fate* is one of the greatest warships in the sea," she bragged, "but no. That's not it."

"Her swords?" Emilia guessed.

It was said that Captain Maria Welles was the best swordsman in the Kingdom of Illopia *before* becoming a pirate.

Judith tilted her head slightly at that. "Closer," she said, "but let's go a little more abstract."

"Her reputation," Emilia realized.

"Exactly," Judith said. "A pirate captain's power is in her name, and the name *Captain Maria Welles* strikes fear into the hearts of all."

Emilia nodded, acknowledging that. Even the Drakon sorcerers weren't as feared as Maria.

"People say she's a madwoman," Emilia admitted. "Vengeful and merciless."

"And she is," Judith said, "sometimes."

Emilia lifted her eyebrows. "A madwoman?"

"Vengeful and merciless," Judith corrected.

Emilia nodded at that. Maria certainly hadn't shown any mercy to Paul.

Rocks crunched beneath their shoes, as they turned down a seldom-used path.

"The name Captain Maria Welles has power," Judith continued, "and situations like yours and Jane's don't...*fit* that name."

"Situations?" Emilia muttered.

Judith ignored the question. "Our story is that I found you at the docks and offered to introduce you to my captain."

Emilia nodded. She remembered Judith saying as much in the tavern. "You said I was looking for work."

Beneath the pale blue moonlight, Judith's reddish-brown hair looked almost purple. "Yes. Now, listen," she said, leaning closer, "when Zain asks about experience, tell him about your experience in surgery. That's why she hired you, after all." She held up a finger. "But—and this part's important, Em—don't lie about your experience as a sailor."

"You want me to tell them I've never sailed before?" Emilia asked.

"There's no point in lying about that," Judith said, waving a hand. "They'll know. Believe me, they'll know. An experienced sailor can practically *smell* the inexperience on you."

Emilia frowned. "Inexperience has a smell?"

Judith grasped the cloak in Emilia's arms and lifted it to her face, playfully sniffing it. "More like a lack of one."

Emilia couldn't help but laugh at that.

Judith's bright blue eyes sparkled in the moonlight, and when Emilia laughed at her joke, Judith gave her an adorable wink.

On the topic of smells, as they neared an old, abandoned well at the bottom of the hill, a terrible stench reached Emilia's nose.

"Rotting food," Judith said, when Emilia covered her face. "There's a reason only the drunks scavenge here."

Emilia wrinkled her nose. "Are they *trying* to get sick?"

"Possibly," Judith sighed.

Emilia knew the misery of starvation, but even when she was starving, she'd known not to eat rotten food. It's not really nourishment, if you're going to throw it up, anyway.

Down by an old, abandoned well—its wood long-rotted—an old man with filthy clothes and rotten teeth sat, with a dusty bottle of rum between his legs.

"I'll give it to him," Judith murmured to Emilia. "You just…stay back."

Back?

Did Judith think this feeble, old man was dangerous?

Emilia offered the cloak and bread to Judith, and Judith carried them to the well.

"Here," Judith said to the man.

The old man lifted his head, peering up at the pirate from beneath a curtain of dirty, grey hair.

"Judes?" he croaked out.

Judith stared at him tiredly. "Just take it."

The old man reached out with filthy hands and took the bread from Judith. She then tossed the cloak on the ground in front of him and turned to leave.

"Who's the girl?" the old man asked.

Judith turned back toward him, pinning him with a scowl.

Emilia didn't think she'd ever seen such an unfriendly expression on the ship cook's face.

Granted, she'd only known Judith for a few hours, but it still seemed so unlike her, somehow.

"She's our new surgeon," Judith told him. "The captain won't like it if you mess with her. So, I'd suggest you forget you saw us."

Emilia frowned at Judith's suddenly brusque tone.

Words slurred and belligerent, the old man said, "I'm not afraid of your glorified orphan girl."

Judith rolled her eyes. "Yes, you are."

Emilia wanted to ask what that meant, but Judith took her by the arm and led her away from the man, before she could.

As they walked away, Judith called back, "If you see James, tell him to get himself cleaned up before the captain pays him a visit."

"Do I look like I've talked to that boy?" the old man yelled after them.

Again, Judith rolled her eyes. "That's why I said '*if*,' Dad."

Emilia glanced at Judith, her eyes wide. "That's your father?"

Judith offered her a tight smile. "I told you I knew some drunks."

CHAPTER 6
The Wicked Fate

They didn't speak of Judith's father for the rest of the night. Emilia felt as if she'd seen something she wasn't meant to—even though Judith had been the one to take her there.

Somehow, despite the encounter, Judith was as jovial as ever—making jokes about a time she'd let a goat loose on the ship and terrified the quartermaster.

Apparently, Zain had insisted that Maria publicly rebuke Judith, but Maria had burst into hysterical laughter as soon as they were in front of the crew.

Zain had never forgiven her for that.

"So, what happened to the goat?" Emilia asked, as Judith swiped tears of laughter from her cheeks.

Judith waved a hand. "Ah, he was fine," she said. "Helen and Pelt found him in the hold, raiding our salt stores."

Emilia shook her head in amusement. As someone who'd grown up around dragons, she couldn't imagine being afraid of a little goat, but Illopians *were* a paranoid sort sometimes.

"The captain hasn't let me bring goats on the ship since," Judith said with a regretful sigh. "They're good for milk, you know."

"Well, that's not very fair of her," Emilia said. "She thought it was funny, too."

"Nah. Zain was right. It was irresponsible of me," Judith said dismissively. "So fucking funny, though."

There was no danger of awkward silence around Judith. The woman could talk for hours.

Judith pointed a finger at Emilia—and, in the process, somehow managed to get her feet crossed and nearly collapse.

Was she drunk?

"Every now and then, though," Judith whispered, "I catch Zain or one of the other sailors running from the cats, and that's just as funny."

"Illopians are scared of cats, too?" Emilia said.

"Well, not all of us," Judith assured her. "Zain grew up in the Illopian mountains. The mountain-dwellers are instilled, at an early age, with a healthy fear of mountain lions." She snorted, "Zain swears the tiny felines are just as vicious."

Emilia laughed at that.

"Captain just tells him to get over it, though," Judith added, "because she's not dealing with the rats."

Emilia had wondered a few times if Judith even knew where she was going. After all, she'd said they were headed to the water, but the docks were in the opposite direction.

But as they came to the end of the overgrown path they were on now, the trees and shrubbery opened up into a small inlet of sea.

Hidden in the overgrowth of trees, they found the longboats—and a man about three times the size of Judith and Emilia.

Emilia stopped a few steps behind Judith, staring up at the man, who could probably crush them both with one arm.

He didn't seem to have much hair, and whatever he did have was hidden beneath a stained, blue headscarf. His eyes were dark brown, and his skin was dark, too, like Maria's.

Though, whereas hers was a warm brown, his was more of a rich black.

"This is Fulke," Judith told her. "He doesn't talk much, but he's as friendly as a dolphin."

Emilia frowned at that analogy. Were dolphins friendly, really?

A shark would likely say no.

"Nice to meet you," Emilia said to the—*hopefully*—gentle giant.

Fulke smiled and touched his head in a sort of salute.

"I should clarify," Judith said, leaning toward her, "the reason he doesn't talk much is that his tongue was sort of…cut out."

Emilia turned to Judith, her eyes wide.

"Not by *our* captain," Judith assured her.

Emilia glanced back at the man, who simply chuckled. He didn't seem too traumatized. Was it rude to ask for details?

Leaning closer to Judith, Emilia whispered, "How does one lose their tongue in this…occupation?"

Judith snorted, "By offending the wrong captain, I assume."

Emilia blinked in shock.

"Though I'm not sure how," Judith continued, "Fulke's too nice to offend anyone, I'd think."

Fulke made a hand gesture that Emilia didn't recognize and then pointed one of his large fingers at Judith, and Judith laughed, as if he'd just told a joke.

At Emilia's curious frown, Judith said, "He said he's only nice to me."

Emilia cast another curious glance his way. On her island, when someone struggled with hearing or speaking, they used telepathic spells to make communication easier.

She'd never seen anyone speak with their hands before, but she liked the idea of it.

Again, Fulke signed something to Judith.

"He says to tell you not to worry," Judith translated. "This captain's much kinder than his old captain."

Emilia lifted her eyebrows at that. "Are you sure that's what he said?" she asked. "Because I've *met* this captain."

Fulke threw his head back and laughed loudly, his gleeful laughter echoing across the water.

Whatever they'd done to his tongue, they'd clearly left his vocal cords intact.

Judith laughed, too. "I think you've won over Fulke already."

Emilia smiled warily at that.

Fulke signed something else to Judith, and Judith snorted in amusement.

"The captain has a better chance with her than I do," she told him.

Fulke grinned and signed something else.

Judith chuckled. "No, no, she does, but you didn't see what *I* saw."

Emilia glanced back and forth between them. "What is he saying?" she whispered to Judith.

Judith threw an arm around Emilia, dragging her closer. The ship cook smelled of rum, sweat, and vanilla—a scent that was *mostly* saccharine.

"Don't worry about it, mate," Judith said with a smile. "You just worry about winning over Zain, like you did Fulke."

"Zain?" Emilia said.

Judith gestured toward the hill with a tilt of her head, and Emilia turned, just in time to see Maria's quartermaster making his way down the path.

Judith tilted her face closer to Emilia's. "And I regret to tell you," she whispered in Emilia's ear, "that you'll need more than a sense of humor to win *him* over."

Emilia glanced at Judith, noticing, for the second time that night, that Judith's balance seemed a bit off and that there was a slight glaze in her bright blue eyes. "Are you drunk?"

Judith held her thumb and forefinger an inch apart. "Little bit."

Emilia laughed.

While they waited for Zain, Fulke grabbed the launch boat with one, large hand and dragged it down to the water.

Zain walked toward them, weaving around trees and shrubbery and somehow managing *not* to get his long, green waistcoat caught on any limbs.

When he reached them, he offered Judith a bottle of rum. "The captain told me to give that to you."

Judith took the bottle without hesitation. "Ah! How does she always know exactly what I want?"

"By spending more than five minutes around you?" Zain muttered.

Judith uncorked the bottle and turned it up, drinking the rum as if it were mere water.

Zain turned to Emilia, pinning her with his dark brown gaze. "So, you convinced her to hire you, after all."

Emilia wasn't sure what she'd done to earn the quartermaster's disapproval, but he clearly wasn't happy to have her on the crew.

"She's a surgeon, Zain," Judith said. "You should've known the captain wasn't going to let a prize like that walk away."

Emilia might've objected to being called a prize—*again*—if she weren't so preoccupied with the way Judith had said that.

Because...that wasn't what had happened at all, was it?

Hiring Emilia wasn't *Maria's* idea...

Was it?

Maria hadn't even wanted to hire Emilia.

Right?

Zain eyed Emilia with a suspicious scowl, and his lip curled noticeably. The man could put more judgement into one expression than anyone she'd ever met.

"We don't even know if she's a *good* surgeon," he said. "And if she isn't? What use will she be to us, then?"

Emilia was getting tired of listening to the quartermaster talk about her as if she weren't there.

Though he was quite a few feet from them, his boots already

submerged in water, Fulke signed something with those dark, calloused fingers of his.

Judith laughed, and Zain muttered, "Oh, fuck off, Fulke."

The giant of a man gave a full, hearty laugh, and Judith leaned closer to Emilia to translate.

"He said 'about as useful as a pirate with a stick up his ass,' he figures," Judith told her.

With an amused smile, Emilia teased the giant, "That must be what you said to the captain who..." she trailed off, sticking out her own tongue for emphasis.

Fulke chuckled and signed something else.

"He says 'something like that,'" Judith said.

Zain rolled his eyes. "Oh, great," he said sarcastically. "Fulke likes you. How reassuring."

Judith kicked the quartermaster in the shin, causing him to yelp like a wolf pup.

"Your sour attitude is ruining my rum," she grumbled.

Zain grasped the hilt of his sword—perhaps instinctually—and glared at her.

If Judith were in any danger whatsoever, she clearly didn't care. "Ready, Fulke?"

The giant nodded and stepped into the launch boat. The small, wooden boat teetered precariously under his weight, but he sat down, anyway, and picked up both oars.

Judith pressed her hand against Emilia's back, urging her toward the water. "Your chariot awaits, surgeon."

Emilia reluctantly stepped into the water, the cool waves washing over her ankles. "No offense," she teased, "but it looks a little small for a pirate ship."

Judith and Fulke laughed, while Zain simply gave her an unimpressed arch of his eyebrows.

The water soaked through Emilia's shoes within moments, and Emilia immediately understood why so many of the pirates wore boots.

Emilia and Judith climbed into the boat, and Zain soon joined them.

The waves rocked the boat gently, and Fulke dipped the oars into the water, rowing the small boat toward the open sea.

Judith rested her right arm against the hull of the boat and leaned closer to Emilia. "Ready to see your new home?"

Temporary home, Emilia wanted to say, but she knew better than to say it, while Zain watched.

Instead, she simply said, "Where is it?"

The night grew late, but the yellow, waning moon was bright enough that Emilia was sure she'd have seen a large ship, if it were anchored anywhere near the shore.

"Believe me," Judith said with a grin. "You'll know it when you see it."

SHE WAS RIGHT, OF COURSE.

The *Wicked Fate* was anchored a good distance from shore, but as soon as they reached the open sea, Emilia couldn't have missed it if she were blindfolded.

The large pirate ship loomed in the distance—an ominous shadow on the dark horizon.

At this distance, the *Wicked Fate* was as dark as night and as daunting as the legends themselves.

The sails shone beneath the moonlight, pale as bone, and its single, black flag waved proudly in the wind.

"It's big," was Emilia's brilliant observation.

Zain snorted but, surprisingly enough, didn't give her a hard time about it.

Judith, on the other hand, apparently had her mind elsewhere.

"Nah," she said. She held up the rum bottle and tilted her head, as if she were reconsidering that. "For one person, perhaps, but it's the same size as any other bottle of rum."

Zain rolled his eyes. "She meant the ship, Judith," he muttered. "Not everyone thinks about rum as often as you do."

Judith squinted, as if she weren't sure if that were possible.

Not thinking about rum, that is.

"She was a first-rate ship-of-the-line before the captain took her," Zain said.

When Emilia didn't react to that, Judith whispered, "Means she's got a lot of cannons."

Emilia smiled at Judith, grateful for her constant commentary.

"I've seen pirate ships before," Emilia admitted, "but they were much smaller."

Zain nodded. "It's a lot easier to take a small, merchant ship and add cannons than to take a warship, like the *Wicked Fate*," he explained, "but you can't tell the captain that. Her ambitions are too wild to ever settle for something so *simple*."

For someone who worked so closely with Maria, Zain had an awful lot of negative things to say about her.

Almost as if she knew what Emilia was thinking, Judith said, "Zain's a grumpy sourpuss, but don't let him fool you. He's as loyal to the captain as the rest of us."

Zain rolled his eyes, but he didn't deny it, either.

Emilia blinked, as Judith suddenly thrust a half-empty bottle of rum right in front of her face.

"Thirsty?"

"Thank you," Emilia said, nudging the bottle back toward Judith, "but I'm all right."

Judith shrugged and lifted the bottle to her lips, taking another drink.

At least Judith didn't see through her as easily as Maria.

"You don't like to accept drinks from people," Maria had said, after only two refusals. *"They drugged you, didn't they?"*

Emilia looked away, hoping that no one else on the boat had the sort of uncanny perceptiveness that Maria seemed to have.

Water sloshed around the small boat with each stroke of the oars, and the boat rose and fell in a soothing, steady rhythm.

As a brief lull of silence stretched between them, Zain studied Judith with a frown.

"Sarah was a bit...incensed, after you left," Zain told her.

Judith groaned miserably. "Of course she was. You know," she said, waving the bottle of rum with enough vigor to spill it, "I'm no more unreliable than any other pirate."

Zain lifted a dark eyebrow.

"I mean, we're all shitty lovers, right?" Judith continued. "Our true love is the sea, and no matter how pretty the woman—or man—is, we'd never abandon the sea for them, would we?"

The longer Judith rambled, the more her syllables began to slur.

"And yet," Judith said, "I'm the only one who earns the ire of the ladies." She waved her arm wildly. "Pelt and Helen have both slept with Sarah, but I've never seen her angry at them, when *they* scurry off to follow the captain's orders."

Zain blew out a long sigh, clearly in no mood to discuss Judith's relationships—or lack thereof.

Fulke stopped rowing long enough to sign a response.

Judith squinted, as if she could barely see him through her drunken haze. "Women don't expect as much from men?" she translated. "Is that even true?"

He made a few more hand gestures that Emilia didn't understand.

Judith chuckled. "You're just guessing, aren't you?" She took another sip of rum. "Even if it *were* true, though, that only applies to Pelt. What about Helen? Or the captain?"

"The tavern girls have known the captain since before she *was* a captain," Zain reminded Judith. "They know what she's like."

Judith shook her head. "She wasn't always like this."

Emilia glanced at the cook, curious about that remark.

Zain narrowed his eyes at her. "You're not going to shut up until you get the truth, are you?"

Judith waved her bottle. "If you have something to say, Zain, say it."

"All right," Zain said, leaning toward her, "the truth is that it's your own fault."

Judith grimaced at that. "I've changed my mind, actually. Don't say it."

"No, no, you wanted the truth," Zain reminded her. "Everyone else is honest about what they want or don't want, but you," he sneered, "you're a sweet-talker. You make promises you can't keep, and then, you act like you have no idea why these girls are upset with you. You might have good intentions, Judith, but everything that comes out of your mouth is bullshit." He leaned back, apparently finished with his rant. "And you know it."

Judith stared blankly at him. "Goddamn it, Zain," she complained. "I take it back, all right? Just lie to me from now on."

Zain shrugged a shoulder. "Don't subject me to your incessant whining, if you can't handle my advice."

"See?" Judith whispered to Emilia. "Fucking sourpuss."

Definitely close enough to hear that remark, Zain rolled his eyes at the cook.

"What do you think, Em?" Judith said. "Is it my own fault?"

Emilia's lips quirked into a small smile. "Well, I'm the one who interrupted your...time with her," she admitted, "and I did so upon orders from your captain. So, I'd say it's more her fault than yours."

Zain shook his head, apparently just as disappointed in Emilia as he was with Judith.

Judith, on the other hand, beamed in delight. "I can't wait to tell the captain that you said *she's* to blame for my relationship problems."

Emilia shrugged. She hadn't hesitated to tell Maria what she thought, when they spoke earlier. She wasn't afraid to do so, now, either.

Fulke took up the oars again, and Judith tilted her head back, drinking the remaining rum even faster than she'd drank the first half.

The shadow of the pirate ship fell over them, as they drew up alongside it, and Emilia looked up at it, her eyes wide.

Anchored alone, in the Azure Sea, the impressively large pirate ship loomed over them, like a single, lonely mountain.

In the dark, Emilia couldn't have said if the ship were made of oak or mahogany, nor could she discern the color of the paint, but the figurehead on the bow of the ship—beneath the moonlight, at least—appeared to have been painted blue.

At first, Emilia thought it was meant to be a siren—with those womanly curves and fish-like features—but as they drew closer to the ship, Emilia recognized that wavy, blue hair, the blue skin, and those fin-like ears.

"Aletha," Emilia whispered.

Zain glanced at her. "It's supposed to be good luck," he explained. "They say the sea goddess is too vain to let a ship that bears her image sink."

Emilia sighed. Leave it to an Illopian to find a way to worship Aletha, while still blaspheming her.

"Did it ever occur to you that it might be kindness, rather than vanity?" Emilia said.

Zain scoffed at that. "Well, *your* inexperience is getting more obvious by the moment," he said with a derisive laugh. "No experienced sailor would ever call the Sea *kind*."

Emilia narrowed her eyes at the quartermaster. "You depend on her for your livelihood and then talk about her like this?"

"The sea goddess is evil," Zain said with a frown. "Everyone knows that."

Judith quickly interrupted, before the atmosphere could grow any more tense. "I'm running out of rum, and the ship is *right* there." She pointed at it. "What's the hold-up?"

When Zain continued to glare at Emilia, Judith shook her bottle for emphasis, causing the saffron-gold liquid inside to splash around the edges.

Zain eyed Emilia suspiciously. "I thought only islanders worshipped Aletha. Are you an islander, surgeon?"

"Who said I worshipped her?" Emilia countered.

Judith stood so suddenly that she nearly tipped the boat. With one hand around Emilia's arm, she dragged Emilia along with her. "No more talking. Only rum."

"You're not going to give her a tour of her new home?" Zain called out, as Judith dragged Emilia along by the arm.

Judith waved vaguely at their surroundings. "That's the ship. Your cabin's this way."

Emilia cast a quick glance over her shoulder. Zain stood, unmoving, on the deck, with his arms folded over his chest, and he watched them with a suspicious glare.

When they reached the cabin, Judith pushed Emilia inside and quickly closed the door.

Her bright blue eyes met Emilia's with surprising steadiness—considering how much rum she'd had.

"What the hell was that?" Judith hissed.

Emilia glanced around uneasily. The cabin was cramped and stuffy, and there was a metallic scent in the air—one that smelled alarmingly similar to blood.

Judith nodded toward a piece of furniture behind Emilia, and Emilia turned to find a table, stained with blood.

"Jonas used it for an amputation recently," Judith told her.

Emilia turned back toward Judith, her eyes wide. "That's too much blood for one person."

Judith nodded. "Yeah, the sailor, he, uh—he bled out."

Emilia's throat constricted with sympathy. She turned, glancing again at the blood-stained table. Her own blood ran cold at the realization that she was looking at someone's life-blood, spilled out and left to dry with no ceremony whatsoever.

Judith placed her hand on Emilia's shoulder, startling her. "You all right?"

Emilia's brows creased with pain. "Does this happen often?"

"Yes," Judith admitted. "Sailing's dangerous work, Em."

"I know, but," Emilia sighed, "I could've saved him."

Judith frowned. "A bit of confidence is a good thing to have, mate, but what makes you so sure?"

"I've never come across a person I couldn't save," Emilia told Judith.

Judith's frown deepened.

With a sigh, Emilia said, "I'm sorry I argued with the quartermaster." She shrugged sadly. "Aletha's important to me. It—it hit a nerve."

Judith offered a gentle smile. "Worship of Aletha is outlawed in Illopia," she explained. "Having her image on the ship *at all* is rebellion for an Illopian. Defending her, the way you did—"

"I know," Emilia sighed. "I'm sorry."

Judith patted her shoulder soothingly. "It's just a little suspicious, Em." She set the empty bottle of rum on the blood-stained table. "Nothing we can't handle."

Emilia looked up, surprised. "Really?"

"Of course," Judith said with a laugh. "The captain would kill me, if I gave up on you *that* easily."

Emilia frowned, as Judith strode toward a set of cabinets. She pulled out a bottle of rum and a couple of empty tankards.

"The captain wouldn't have sent Zain on ahead of her without instructions," Judith said, placing the tankards on the blood-stained table. "Which, luckily for us, will keep him busy for a while."

Emilia watched warily, as Judith filled both cups with rum.

"Which," Judith said again, "gives us plenty of time to practice your story." She held out a tankard of rum. "*And* get you drunk."

Emilia eyed the cup nervously. "Drunk?"

Judith laughed at her hesitation. "Sober people don't join pirate crews, love."

Emilia's frown deepened. "But I *am* sober," she pointed out, "and I *am* joining a pirate crew."

"Yes, and it's very unusual," Judith said with a laugh. She wiggled the tankard enticingly. "So, drink up."

Emilia hesitated, but ultimately, her choice was to either admit to Judith what Maria had so easily guessed—or to hide her anxiety.

And hiding her fears was far less vulnerable than admitting them.

Choosing the safest option, Emilia took the tankard and lifted it to her lips. The first taste made her wince in surprise.

"It's rum, not ale," Judith told her. "Bit different."

"So, aside from not being drunk enough for you," Emilia said, taking another sip, "have I done anything else wrong?"

Judith snorted. "Come here." She took a sip of her own rum, as she studied Emilia's clothing in the candlelight. "Take off the cuirass. You can keep it in that chest over there, until you need it."

Emilia set down the rum so that she could unfasten the cuirass. She folded the black, dragon-scale cuirass and stored it in the wooden chest, behind the table. Then, she turned to face Judith.

Judith set down her own cup of rum and reached out to tousle Emilia's wavy, black hair. "If you're going to keep it this long, you'll need something to keep it out of your face."

A memory came, unbidden, to Emilia's mind: caring for Catherine, while she recovered from her injuries—braiding Catherine's long, blonde hair.

Emilia closed her eyes, forcing the memory from her mind. "I can braid it."

Judith nodded. "Pelt does that," she admitted. "Zain does every now and then. And Helen, too."

Though Emilia had heard Judith mention Helen a few times, Emilia didn't think she'd met that particular pirate yet.

Emilia squeaked in surprise, as Judith grasped her black shirt and tugged it from her trousers.

"Better," Judith said, when the shirt was only halfway tucked in.

Emilia wasn't sure what was *better* about that.

Judith snapped her fingers in front of Emilia's face, as if breaking her from a trance. "More rum."

Emilia scowled—but picked up the tankard and drank from it, anyway.

Judith took her own tankard to the cot and sat down. She wrinkled her nose in distaste and bounced a little, testing the cot's pliancy—or lack thereof.

"Does she expect you to sleep on this?" Judith said. "You'd be better off sleeping below deck with the other sailors."

Emilia preferred privacy to comfort, especially with the nightmares she'd been having lately. So, she just muttered, "It's fine."

Judith gave her a skeptical look. "I'll talk to her. The captain's an asshole sometimes, but she's not cruel."

Emilia lifted her eyebrows in disbelief.

Slicing a man open in the middle of the street *wasn't* cruel?

"All right," Judith said, sipping her rum, "let's go over your story—so we can avoid any more…incidents with Zain."

Emilia winced at that. "Sorry," she said again.

Judith waved a hand. "It's as much on him as it is you," she said dismissively. "He's always been like this."

"Like what?" Emilia said.

Judith blew out a slow breath, clearly choosing her words wisely. "He takes his work *very* seriously."

Emilia offered her a playful smile. "You say that like it's a bad thing."

Judith grinned. "He's a fucking killjoy, Em."

Emilia laughed.

Judith rolled her eyes. "No, no. You're right," she sighed. "He's quartermaster for a reason. The captain needs someone like him."

"How so?" Emilia asked curiously.

"The captain has always had a bit of a temper," Judith said.

Another understatement.

The woman started a whole rebellion, for god's sake.

"We wouldn't survive storms or battles without the captain," Judith said, "but we wouldn't survive day-to-day life without Zain."

Emilia nodded. "He's the rational one."

Judith tilted her head a bit, her short, brown hair falling to the side. "I was going to say boring, but sure, let's go with your word."

Emilia suppressed a laugh. "I think he suspects I'm lying."

Judith gave a regretful nod to that. "He's good at what he does," she told Emilia, "and as it turns out, you *are* lying."

Emilia pursed her lips thoughtfully. "Is there any way to change his mind about me?"

"Usefulness will get you further with Zain than anything," Judith said. "We just have to keep him placated until you're able to prove how useful you are."

Emilia nodded. "So, until the first battle?"

"Aww, that's cute," Judith teased. "You think battles are the only time pirates get injured?"

With a worried frown, Emilia said, "They're not?"

Judith laughed. She waved her tankard toward the table, behind Emilia. "Avis was just climbing the rigging."

Emilia glanced at the blood-stained table. "He fell?"

Judith nodded. "Broke his leg in multiple places." She shuddered. "I swear I could hear his screams for weeks after he died."

Emilia's stomach twisted at the thought.

"Anyway," Judith said, pasting on a smile, "let's keep going over your story."

Emilia blinked.

"So," Judith said, as if they *weren't* just talking about something horribly tragic, "when Zain asks where I found you, what will you say?"

"The docks," Emilia said slowly.

"Perfect," Judith said, "and when he asks why you were there?"

"Looking for work," Emilia said with a frown.

Did Judith think she forgot things *that* quickly?

"And when he asks who you were hoping to sail under?" Judith said.

Emilia hesitated. "Maria Welles?"

"No," Judith said. She stood and returned to Emilia's side. "Absolutely not."

"*Not* Maria Welles?" Emilia tried again.

"Well, it is a bit ambitious," Judith said, "even for a surgeon." She shook her head. "But your real mistake was calling her Maria Welles."

"That's her name," Emilia said, "isn't it?"

Judith set her tankard aside, as if she were preparing for a long conversation. "It's *Captain* Maria Welles," she said, "or Captain Welles or Captain Maria. Use whatever variation you like—as long as it's always *Captain*."

Emilia resisted the urge to roll her eyes. She didn't want Judith to think she didn't appreciate the advice, but the distinction seemed awfully fastidious to her.

"But she wasn't even my captain then," Emilia said.

Judith pushed back that short, brown hair of hers. "Did she have a ship and a crew?"

"Yes?" Emilia said.

"Then, whether she was yours or not," Judith said, "she was still a captain, was she not?"

Emilia squinted at that. "Other people's mothers are still mothers, whether they're mine or not, but it'd still be strange if I called them all '*Mother*.'"

Judith snorted. "Islanders really *are* a different sort, aren't they?"

Emilia flashed a nervous smile.

As a witch, yes, she *would* say she was quite different.

With a sigh, Judith said, "The captain's enemies call her Maria

Welles." She raised an eyebrow. "You don't want to be associated with her enemies, do you?"

Emilia was beginning to feel like Judith was interrogating her, as well. "No," she said hesitantly, "but isn't Maria Welles just…her name?"

"It was. Once," Judith said, "but then, she became a captain." She sighed, "You haven't heard the stories?"

"I've heard some," Emilia assured her.

Judith held up a finger, motioning for her to hold that thought. "We need more rum for this."

Emilia was pretty sure *no* one needed as much rum as Judith thought they needed.

"All right," Judith said, as she refilled their cups. "Do you know how she became the notorious pirate captain she is today?"

Emilia remembered the story Catherine told her. "She stole from the Crown—and started a rebellion."

"Allegedly," Judith said.

Emilia's brows furrowed. "Did she not?"

Judith waved the bottle of rum. "Let's just say she did," she muttered. "The details of the crime aren't important. What's important is what happened afterward." She offered a tankard of rum to Emilia. "Do you *know* what happened afterward?"

Emilia took the tankard with a frown. "She was captured."

Judith sipped her rum. "Mmm-hmm," she murmured, "and do you know what they did to her?"

Emilia didn't know, but she could certainly guess.

She'd spent enough time in those dungeons herself.

Some of Maria's scars had clearly come from battle, but Emilia, unfortunately, knew all too well where she'd gotten the others.

She remembered the way Catherine had spoken so gleefully of the time she'd captured Maria Welles. At the time, Emilia had been bewildered by Catherine's obsession, but now…

Now, it turned her stomach.

"They tortured her," Emilia said.

"Yeah, that, too," Judith said, as if that were minor in comparison to whatever was on her mind. She took another drink of rum. "One of the many humiliations they subjected her to was publicly stripping her of rank and title."

Emilia thought that sounded insignificant, compared to torture, but Judith acted as if it were worse.

"Now," Judith said, setting down her tankard, "if your enemies had publicly stripped you of something that was rightfully yours, would it not feel like a slap in the face any time someone refused to acknowledge the title you were stripped of?"

Emilia shrugged. "I suppose?"

"She has a ship and a crew. She's a captain, whether King Eldric says she is or not," Judith said.

"Of course she is." On that, they agreed.

"And everyone who respects her makes it a point to acknowledge that fact," Judith added.

"By calling her captain," Emilia realized.

Judith nodded. "The women from the tavern aren't part of her crew, either, but did you notice that not one of them referred to her as anything other than *Captain* Maria Welles?"

Emilia did remember Jane calling Maria *Captain*.

Judith scoffed, "Hell, even Adda calls her Captain, and you should've heard the things Adda used to call her when we were kids!"

Emilia frowned curiously at that. "You knew her as a child?"

Judith froze, as if she'd only just realized what she'd said. "Everyone in Nefala knew Adda's orphan girl," she muttered. "Brilliant with a sword and an absolute nightmare in a fight." She shook her head. "Nearly killed my father once."

Orphan girl?

Emilia wanted to ask more, but the subject of Judith's father had come up again.

And Emilia didn't want to make Judith uncomfortable by dwelling too long on that subject.

"But we're talking about you, not her," Judith said.

Emilia gave her a skeptical smile. "I'm pretty sure we were talking about her, actually."

Judith chuckled. "We're talking about *you* calling *her* Captain," she amended. She grinned at Emilia. "Which is what you'll call her from now on, right?"

"Apparently, I'm an enemy, if I don't," Emilia said.

Judith snorted midway through a drink of rum. She dragged her hand across her mouth, wiping away the rum that had spilled out of her mouth.

She set down her cup, wiping her hands on her shirt. "Darling, I'm just trying to save *your* hide," she said with a grin. "The captain can be one terrifying asshole when she wants to be."

"I'm not afraid of her," Emilia assured her.

Judith lifted her eyebrows. "Gods," she muttered. "You're like every vice of hers, all rolled into one, aren't you?"

Emilia frowned at that. "What does that mean?"

A knock sounded at the door, and Judith was all too eager to answer it.

"That would be Zain," she said with a disarming smile. "Ready to be interrogated by the biggest killjoy in all of Aletharia?"

Emilia watched the ship cook suspiciously. "Sure."

CHAPTER 7
A First Impression

L ate into the night, while Emilia was scrubbing the filthy, blood-stained table that they expected her to use for surgery, a quiet knock sounded at her door.

Emilia froze, the wet, blood-stained cloth still in her hand. She didn't know any of the pirates well enough to discern who it was, based on their knock alone, but for whatever reason, it struck Emilia as just a bit too short of a knock to belong to Judith.

Please, don't be Zain.

He'd questioned her relentlessly already, and Emilia didn't think she could handle another round of questions—not after all the rum Judith had her drink.

She barely remembered her *real* background, at the moment, much less the one Judith had made up.

Her unknown visitor rapped their knuckles against the door a second time.

"Coming!" Emilia called.

She left her cleaning rag on the table and went to answer the door. She opened it, half-expecting to find Zain, returning with more questions, but instead, she found Captain Maria Welles herself outside her door.

Emilia blinked in surprise. "You."

The pirate captain leaned in the doorway, her elbow braced against the doorframe and her arm above her head. She held herself with such casual indifference, and yet, she tapped an impatient rhythm on the top of her tricorn, as if she'd been waiting for hours.

Maria leaned forward. "I prefer *'Captain,'*" she told Emilia. A wry smile curved at the corners of her lips. "Has a better ring to it than *'you,'* don't you think?"

With the captain so close, Emilia once again noticed that sweet scent on her skin—a sublime combination of floral and citrus. Those lovely, tropical flowers that Emilia often used for medicinal teas came to mind.

Hibiscus.

Maria smelled like hibiscus.

Hibiscus and oranges.

And rum.

There was *definitely* rum on her breath.

"You've been drinking," Emilia realized.

"As have you," Maria said. She chuckled, as Emilia tried to discreetly check her own breath. "Judith?"

Emilia dropped her hand. "She insisted."

Maria nodded. "Since you're still on your feet, I'm assuming she gave you the good rum."

"How many kinds of rum are there?" Emilia asked.

Maria looked over Emilia's shoulder, restlessness visible in those dark eyes of hers. "Invite me inside."

Emilia frowned at her abrupt tone. "Do I have to?"

Maria's gaze shifted back toward Emilia. "Well, I'd prefer that to picking you up and moving you out of my way." She shrugged. "My arms are a bit tired."

Even with just her forearms and collarbone visible, beneath that shirt and leather doublet, there was still enough muscle definition visible that Emilia didn't doubt the captain's strength.

What she *did* doubt, however, was that the captain could lift her.

Even after starving in a dungeon for weeks, Emilia was still on the curvier end of the spectrum.

She didn't really feel like calling the captain's bluff, though, so she stepped aside.

Emilia watched with a frown, as the pirate captain strolled into the room. Unable to think of anything better to say, she said, "Tired from what? Murder?"

Maria turned to look at her. "Carrying crates," she said, both eyebrows arched. "What kind of novice would be tired after one kill?"

Emilia blinked. She wanted to counter that question with her own: *What kind of person talked about murder like it was some insignificant errand?* But instead, she said, "Well, *my* arms get sore after sword fighting."

Maria cast a curious glance at Emilia's arms. "Your biceps are small. Was your sword made for you?"

Emilia looked down at her arms, not sure whether to feel insulted or not. "Umm...well, no. It was hers."

"Hers?" Maria repeated.

Emilia looked up. "The person who taught me."

Maria studied Emilia with an intensity that unnerved her. "Size difference?" she assumed.

Emilia shifted uneasily on her feet. She didn't want to describe Catherine in too much detail—lest Maria realize who she meant. So, she just said, "She's taller."

Maria nodded. "Stronger, too, I'd bet," she guessed, "if she's as good a swordsman as you say, anyway."

Emilia narrowed her eyes at that. "She is."

Maria turned away. "You need a lighter sword."

"Okay," Emilia said with a frown. "I'm trying not to take that as an insult." Her frown deepened, when she noticed Maria peering into her bucket of water. "It's sea water," she told her. "Not drinking water."

Maria picked up Emilia's cleaning rag. "What were you doing?" she asked. "Did Zain tell you to clean?"

Emilia snatched the rag from Maria's hand. "No, but if you want me to perform surgeries on this table, it needs to be clean." When Maria just stared at her, Emilia said, "You are *aware* of the dangers of treating wounds in an unclean environment, aren't you?"

"Yes," Maria said. She looked away. "Vaguely."

Emilia rolled her eyes. "No wonder you've lost so many sailors."

Maria's dark gaze returned to Emilia so abruptly that Emilia felt it as intensely as a crashing wave. "Piracy is a dangerous profession, Em," she snarled. "I'd argue that I lose very few, compared to most captains."

"Well, with me, you'll lose none," Emilia assured her. "As long as they're still alive when you bring them to me, I can save them."

Maria stepped closer. "I like your confidence, love," she said, "but bravado is seldom more than a facade to hide insecurities. I wonder what yours is hiding."

Emilia sighed. "I'm not saying I have no doubts," she assured her. "I'm only saying that I have enough experience in this to know that I can do it."

"Good to hear," Maria said. She took off her tricorn, leaving only her blue headscarf to hold back her dark curls. She set her hat on the table and gestured at the bed in the corner. "Have you tested out the bed yet?"

"Uh, no," Emilia said, baffled by the sudden change of subject. The bed that Maria referred to was more of a cot than a bed— totally bare of bedding and more suited for work than sleep. "What are you doing in here, anyway? Did you just come by to mock me?"

"Telling you to use a lighter sword is strategy, Em," Maria said, "not mocking." She stepped toward the bed, studying it with a frown. "And I told you I'd see you tonight, didn't I? Did you think I was bluffing?"

Emilia noticed another bloodstain on the table and scrubbed at it, too. "No. It's just been a long night."

The bed creaked behind her, and Emilia turned, just in time to see the pirate captain stretching out on her bed. Maria folded one arm behind her head, and she rested her other hand against her stomach, splaying her tattooed fingers over her black, leather doublet.

"Judith's right. This bed's shit," Maria muttered. "You'd be better off with a hammock. Would you like one?"

So, Judith *had* talked to her.

"I slept, chained to a wall, for months," Emilia said, without thinking. "I'm sure the bed will be fine."

A tense silence settled between them, and Emilia could practically *feel* the heat of Maria's gaze on her.

"I don't know why I said that," Emilia mumbled.

"I share your scars," Maria reminded her. Her voice lacked its usual humor and edge. There was an unexpected gentleness in her voice now—her lilt as smooth as rose petals. "That's why you said it."

Emilia couldn't bear to meet Maria's gaze, at the moment. So, she fixed her gaze on the table, instead.

She remembered the way Maria had held out her hands, showing Emilia her scars. Had Emilia taken some sort of false sense of security from that? Is that why she'd been so honest? Or was it simply the rum?

Instinctually, she reached for her cup, only to find it empty. "The bed's fine," she sighed. "That's all I meant."

"Here."

Emilia turned. Her brows furrowed, when she saw the leather flask that Maria was offering her. "No, I'm fine, really. I just—"

"You've seen me drink from it, Em. You know it's safe," Maria said. "Take it."

Maria spoke so casually of Emilia's deepest fears, as if Emilia were just walking around with a list of past traumas tattooed on her forehead.

Emilia stepped closer and took the proffered flask. As she took a sip of Maria's rum, she couldn't help but notice that, around her leather-clad waist, Maria still wore her scabbard and swords—even as she lounged in Emilia's bed.

Emilia was starting to wonder if Maria ever went anywhere *without* her weapons.

Did she sleep with them, as well?

Emilia didn't plan to find out.

"I assume Judith told you the cause of the blood stains," Maria said, as Emilia sipped from the flask.

The rum calmed Emilia's nerves and warmed her stomach. In moments like this, it was easy to see why Judith liked the drink so much. "Your carpenter attempted an amputation, but the person still died."

Maria nodded. "What would you have done differently?"

Emilia returned the flask. "Am I being tested?"

Maria's gaze didn't waver. "Answer the question."

Emilia shrugged. "I wouldn't have amputated."

Maria scowled. "The leg couldn't have been saved."

"Not by a *carpenter*, perhaps," Emilia said, "but I'm no carpenter. I assure you: I could've saved the leg."

Maria tilted her head, her curly, brown hair shifting beneath her. "You can't possibly know that," she said with a frown. "You didn't even see his injuries."

"I don't need to," Emilia told her. "Judith said he fell from the rigging and broke his leg in three places."

"There was bone protrusion, too," Maria said.

"I've treated injuries like that before," Emilia said. "I would need to set the bones with surgery, but I'd use salves and healing tinctures to treat the rest."

And a bit of magic.

She left that part out.

Maria gave her a skeptical look. "I'm to believe that you can save a critically injured sailor with…salves?"

"Not *just* salves," Emilia corrected. "But yes, with a few different forms of healing, I could've saved him."

Maria toyed with one of the thin, beaded braids she wore near the front of her hair, rolling the beads with her fingertips. "But," she said with a raised brow, "none of those forms are amputation?"

"I wouldn't have needed to amputate," Emilia told her. "I would have saved his leg *and* saved his life."

"That's quite the boast," Maria said. Her lips curled into a taunting smile. "I hope you can back it up."

"It's not just a boast," Emilia said. "It's experience. I've saved people from far worse injuries than that."

Maria didn't look convinced. "Have you?"

"Yes!" Emilia said. If Maria was trying to evoke a strong reaction in her, it was working. "I've helped people who were suffering from blood loss, infection, disease, sword wounds…" With a bitter smile, Emilia added, "I've treated people *you* left for dead."

Maria glanced at her, suddenly. "You've what?"

Emilia recognized the rage burning in Maria's deep, brown eyes, but it was too late to take it back now. "I treated your victims," she said boldly, "sailors you assumed were dead." She hesitated for just a moment, when Maria's eyes narrowed, but then, she continued, "Just hours before I was arrested, I treated a sailor they'd plucked from one of *your* shipwrecks. He'd lost multiple layers of skin in your cannon fire."

Maria sat up, her boots hitting the floor with a quiet thud. "You've helped my enemies?" she growled.

"Your victims," Emilia corrected.

Anger twisted at Maria's lips. She climbed to her feet and approached Emilia with slow, purposeful steps. "Do you have any idea who my *victims* are?"

The pirate captain sneered the word 'victims,' as if it were the slimiest, most repulsive thing she'd ever encountered.

Emilia tried to step back, when Maria cornered her, but her back collided with the table. "Sailors?"

"*Navy* sailors," Maria corrected. She stepped closer, leaving Emilia no escape from her intoxicating presence. "I sink navy ships, Em. If you treated *my* victims, you treated the king's men."

Emilia couldn't stop the memories from flooding her mind—of those first few weeks with Catherine, tending to her wounds, falling so foolishly in love with the person Catherine pretended to be. "And women."

Maria narrowed her eyes. "And you don't see how this would make me question your allegiance?"

Emilia looked up, meeting the pirate's gaze boldly. "Would you not question it more, if I'd lied about it?"

Maria laughed bitterly. "If I'd found out *after* you lied about it, I would have killed you first and asked questions later," she warned. "Consider the fact that I'm asking questions *before* I kill you…your reward."

"You're threatening me," Emilia realized, "again."

Maria leaned closer—so close that the sword at her waist brushed Emilia's hip. Emilia looked down at it, noticing how Maria's fingers curled around the hilt.

Was that just where her hand comfortably rested, or was she preparing to unsheathe it?

Emilia needed to prepare herself, in case the pirate captain *did* attack her. Maria's second sword brushed Emilia's right hand, when she leaned forward, and Emilia thought that, if she needed to, she could take the second sword easily—before Maria even noticed.

"I'm Captain Maria Welles," the pirate captain said, as Emilia weighed her options. "My presence alone is a threat."

Emilia resisted the urge to roll her eyes. "What are you looking for? An apology? For what? Doing my job?"

Maria gripped her sword tightly. "Careful, thief."

Emilia lifted her chin to hold the taller pirate's gaze. "Do you think I cared about you or your enemies?" she scoffed. "You might find this hard to believe, but some of us have better things to do than sit around, wringing our hands about some self-obsessed pirate captain with a vendetta."

Maria's gaze shifted downward, watching the small sliver of space between them disappear. A smile that hovered somewhere between mild amusement and murderous anger curved at the corners of her lips.

"The only thing you should assume, based on my past, is that I do my job, and that I'll help anyone you bring to me," Emilia told her. "I'm employed by you now. Until that changes, I obviously won't be helping any of your enemies."

Maria stared at Emilia, cruel amusement glinting in her dark eyes. "Perhaps I should keep you employed forever, then." Her smile widened. "Since you care so little about who you serve."

Emilia's brows furrowed. "You can't do that."

"Can't I?" Maria challenged. "Who's going to stop me?" She chuckled, as if the very idea that anyone *could* stop her was amusing. "Can't have my enemies gaining something I've lost, Em." She tilted her head, her brown curls falling to the side. "But then again, perhaps it'd be better just to kill you now—eliminate any possibility of your betrayal in the future."

Maria stepped closer, and yet again, her left sword bumped Emilia's right hand.

Emilia seized her opportunity. She reached for the sword, certain that she'd have it, but Maria moved faster than Emilia could've expected.

Maria caught Emilia's wrists and shoved her back, pinning Emilia's hands against the table. Her waist pressed against Emilia —her muscles warm and firm against Emilia's stomach.

The captain leaned forward, her large, brown eyes as lovely as they were furious. "First impressions really aren't your strong suit, are they?" Maria said.

Emilia stared up at the captain, her chest rising and falling with each ragged breath. Adrenaline coursed through her, quickening her pulse, but she couldn't move a muscle—not with Maria leaning against her.

Emilia tried, unsuccessfully, to pull her wrists free, but aside from the slight strain of muscle in her forearms and biceps, Maria showed no signs of struggle.

Okay. So, maybe Maria was right. Compared to *her*, Emilia didn't have much in the way of arm strength.

Maria watched her calmly, that scarred eyebrow of hers arching ever higher, as Emilia refused to speak.

When Emilia offered no explanation for her actions, Maria said, "If you're to sail on my ship, you better learn one thing very quickly." She leaned in close, her chest pressing against Emilia's. "You *never* draw your weapon outside of battle." The scent of rum lingered on her breath. "And you certainly don't draw *mine*."

Emilia continued to stare at Maria—mostly because she didn't know what to say. *Sorry I panicked?* Emilia couldn't admit that.

Not to Maria.

The woman had a big enough ego as it was.

Instead, Emilia said, "Am I not allowed to protect myself?"

"Of course you are," Maria said simply, "but you'll need your attacker to have drawn their sword first." Her next words came out in a soft growl. "And then, you better *pray* to whatever goddess you serve that there's a witness."

Emilia swallowed, her heart pounding in her chest.

"I don't like chaos on my ship, Em," Maria warned.

Despite the precariousness of her situation, Emilia's thoughts once again drifted toward that enticing scent on Maria's skin— warm and soothing, like hibiscus petals and oranges, with hints of sea-salt and leather underneath. She smelled of the tropics.

Emilia didn't *want* to like Maria's scent.

She didn't want to like the way Maria's long, lean body felt against her own. She didn't want to like the way Maria's fingers felt around her wrists.

And she certainly didn't want to *long* for Maria the way she longed for her now. She didn't want to feel this mix of fear and desire that swirled around inside her head each time the pirate captain was near.

"Do you understand, Em?" Maria said slowly.

With a defeated sigh, Emilia nodded.

Maria's eyes darkened. "Say it."

Emilia's brows furrowed.

She couldn't be serious.

But as the tense silence stretched between them, it became increasingly clear that she was.

"Yes!" Emilia said, finally. "Yes, I understand."

Maria leaned just a bit closer, which resulted in her strong, leather-clad thigh slipping between Emilia's legs. It was such a casual action that Emilia was sure Maria hadn't meant to do it, but the sudden pressure unleashed an overwhelming heat in Emilia's body, all the same. Emilia bit her lip, as she tried to hold back the embarrassing moan that tried to escape.

That was, *by far*, the last thing Emilia needed.

Maria's soft growl interrupted her internal struggle. "Yes, what?"

Emilia stared at Maria, her eyes wide. "C-captain?"

Maria immediately released Emilia's wrists. She set back on her heels and then took a step back, offering Emilia plenty of space to move.

Emilia straightened—hesitantly. Her back protested the movement, still a little sore from the roughness of the table. She avoided Maria's gaze, praying her face didn't *look* as flushed as it felt.

Emilia rubbed her wrists, her skin still tingling from Maria's touch. Then, she risked a glance at the pirate captain—only to find herself trapped by those dark, brown eyes, yet again. Clearing her throat, Emilia mumbled, "You drew *your* sword outside of battle."

"You mean when I killed the thief," Maria assumed.

Emilia nodded. "The rules don't apply to you?"

"I wrote them," Maria said with a wicked smile. "I can bend and break them as I please."

Emilia narrowed her eyes at that. "Then, how are you any different from King Eldric?"

"Well, now…you might be onto something, thief," Maria said. "King of the Seas does have a nice ring to it, doesn't it?" She flashed a taunting smile at Emilia. "Or better yet, *Queen* of the Seas."

Emilia was *really* starting to understand how this woman had become the most hated villain in Aletharia.

"Do you know what a mutiny is, Em?" Maria said.

Emilia might not have sailed before, but she'd met enough sailors to know that. "It's when your crew turns against you."

Maria stepped closer. "If I were to do something unforgivable— or just become too unpopular, even—I would lose my ship and my crew." Hatred burned in her deep, brown eyes. "King Eldric, however, does whatever he pleases, and no one can do a fucking thing about it." Vitriol dripped from every word. "*That*…is the difference in King Eldric and me."

As Emilia watched Maria turn away, as she noticed Maria clenching her fists at her sides, every muscle in her body vibrating with hatred, Emilia realized that she and the pirate captain had something in common, after all. They both hated Illopia's beloved king.

"They could kill him," Emilia suggested.

Maria turned back toward Emilia, her eyes wide.

"*We* could kill him," Emilia amended.

A slow smile spread across Maria's face. The pirate captain stepped closer to Emilia, wood creaking beneath her boots. "See?" she murmured. "Now, I know which side you're on." With two, tattooed fingers, she lifted Emilia's chin, urging Emilia to meet her dark, prideful gaze. "Glad to have you on mine."

A pleasant warmth unfurled in Emilia's stomach.

She told herself it had nothing to do with the warm, gentle fingers on her skin. She *swore* to herself that it did not—and *could* not—have anything to do with that glow of pride in Maria's gorgeous, brown eyes.

Clearly, she was just feeling all that rum she drank.

It had to be the rum.

Always blame the rum.

Maria dropped her hand. She reached past Emilia and grabbed her tricorn from the table. She placed it on her head and turned to leave. "Sleep well, thief."

"Wait," Emilia said—without thinking. She blushed when the pirate captain turned to look at her, though she wasn't sure why. It wasn't as if Maria could *hear* how fast Emilia's heart was beating, at the moment.

With a nervous shrug, Emilia asked, "Are there any other rules I should know about?"

Maria lifted her eyebrows at the question. "There's a Code," she told Emilia. "You'll sign it tomorrow."

Emilia squinted at that. "Pirates have a code?"

Maria snorted. "What's the matter?" she said with a grin. "Am I ruining your delusions of lawlessness?"

"No," Emilia said, "but I bet you'd ruin Illopia's."

Maria laughed softly at that. She took a ring of keys from the left side of her belt and removed a single, heavy, skeleton key— that, in Emilia's opinion, didn't look any different from the others.

"This is your key," Maria said, offering it to her. "I want you to keep your door locked at night. At least until I give you a sword," she advised. "You've got a sizable bounty on your head, and you know pirates love their gold."

Emilia took the key. "You knew about the bounty?"

"I assumed," Maria said. "You told me you escaped the

gallows." She sighed. "King Eldric isn't just going to sit back and *let* you make a fool of him, Em."

"You never thought of turning me in?" Emilia said.

Maria laughed, "Escaping the gallows is a feat, love—I'll give you that. But I don't care who you are." Her smile widened. "They'll never want you as badly as they want me."

Emilia couldn't argue with that.

Maria's head was worth more than most *countries*.

"Don't worry," Maria told her. "If you're as good a surgeon as you say, you'll be worth more than gold to me, and if *not*," she paused, lifting her eyebrows, "I'd still rather kill you than let my enemies have you back."

Emilia frowned at the threat. "That's supposed to make me *not* worry?"

Maria chuckled. "Welcome to the *Wicked Fate*, love." She opened the door. "Try not to get yourself killed."

CHAPTER 8

The First Day

Like most mornings these days, Emilia awoke in a state of panic—after yet another nightmare. Too anxious to stay in her small, stuffy cabin, Emilia wasted no time in fleeing to the open air of the deck.

Emilia closed her eyes and inhaled a lungful of crisp, salt-scented air. The fresh air eased the tightness in her chest and calmed her racing pulse.

Even after her panic subsided, she remained near the taffrail, gazing out at those majestic, blue waves.

They called it the Azure Sea for a reason. It had the bluest water in all of Aletharia. Unlike the Westerly Sea, which was often cold and grey, or the Whispering Abyss, which was so deep it was almost black, the Azure Sea was warm and intensely blue.

Emilia thought she saw a dolphin leaping in the distance, and she leaned closer to the rail, trying to get a better look. A few moments passed before it reappeared, its dark shape arching slightly above the horizon.

A sudden *crunch* interrupted Emilia's brief moment of calm.

Emilia nearly jumped out of her skin. She turned slowly, blinking, as she found none other than Captain Maria Welles herself standing next to her—with a bright red apple in her hand.

The pirate captain leaned against the rail, dressed in full gear already—leather-clad from head to toe and carrying two swords at her waist. She bit into an apple, apparently unaware of Emilia's presence.

Or so Emilia thought—until those large, brown eyes shifted her way.

Maria chewed her apple slowly, a smile playing at the corners of her lips. "Did I scare you?" she teased.

Emilia scoffed, "Not at all." She glanced out at the restless, blue waves, feigning indifference. "I guess you're not as imposing as you think you are."

Maria chuckled at that. "Careful, thief."

Emilia scowled at the warning. She tried to ignore the pirate captain, but every few moments, another *crunch* would cut through her thoughts. She turned to Maria, brows high. "Did you need something?"

Maria swallowed her bite of apple. With that smile that was both gorgeous and infuriating, at once, she held out her hand, offering the apple to Emilia. Her voice lilted sensually, as she murmured, "Want one?"

Emilia eyed the half-eaten apple with a frown. "Do I want an apple you've had your mouth all over?" she said incredulously. "No, actually. I do not."

Maria laughed. She took another bite of the apple, its crunch as crisp as ever. "Fortunately for you, my new pirate, there'll be plenty that I *haven't* had my mouth all over," she teased, "where I'm taking you."

Emilia scowled. "And where are you taking me?"

Maria rested her elbow against the taffrail, angling her body toward Emilia. "Somewhere *very* hot."

Emilia lifted her eyebrows at that. "Hell?"

Maria chuckled. "Well, there, too, most likely." A gleam of

amusement shone in her dark brown eyes. "But right now, I'm taking you to the galley." When Emilia frowned at that, Maria explained, "Judith says you agreed to be her new helper."

"Oh," Emilia said, nodding. "Well, I don't know if I ever agreed to anything, but I certainly don't mind."

Maria quirked a scarred eyebrow. "Don't mind?" she repeated. "I didn't ask if you *wanted* to do it. I said I'm taking you. You'll do what I tell you to, regardless."

Emilia stared up at the pirate captain, her eyes wide with disbelief. "Do you just go out of your way to make every interaction as frustrating as possible?"

Maria shrugged. "A *little* out of my way, perhaps."

Emilia narrowed her eyes. "Fine," she sighed, "but there's something I need to get from my cabin first."

Emilia turned on her heel—with every intention of returning to her cabin—but Maria stopped her.

"You mean this?"

Emilia spun around. Her eyes widened, as she saw what was in Maria's hand. "How did you—" Her confusion quickly turned to ire. She snatched her dagger from Maria's hand. "You dirty, little thief!"

Maria stepped closer to Emilia. She braced her free hand against the rail, trapping Emilia against it. Then, she leaned in and said, "I prefer *'filthy pirate.'*"

Maria was so close already—*too* close. The heat of her body radiated into Emilia, somehow even hotter than the tropic air itself. Emilia's entire body burned with a mystifying mixture of lust and anger. But she refused to let the infuriating pirate captain have the last word. So, Emilia leaned forward, onto her toes, closing the last bit of space between them, and snarled, "As long as we agree you need to bathe."

A quick, surprised laugh escaped Maria's lips, and the two of them were so close that Emilia felt that soft exhale of breath against her own lips. Maria's gaze lingered on Emilia's mouth just a moment too long, and her eyes dilated, growing even darker than usual.

Emilia told herself it was just the sun warming her skin, but she knew it was more than that.

Maria was as magnetic as she was maddening, and with her already so close, it was almost impossible to resist her pull.

"It's funny," Maria said, her breath warm against Emilia's lips, "that you'd call me a thief—considering how you found yourself in this…situation."

Emilia leaned back on her heels. "What situation?" she said with a puzzled frown. "I believe it was me who came to *you* and asked to join your crew."

"*Do* you believe that?" Maria said. She tilted her face closer and whispered, "How sure are you?"

Emilia's pulse quickened, and her blood roared in her veins. She tried to remember what, exactly, they'd said the night before, but her mind only wanted to replay memories of Maria's hands around her wrists.

Memories of Maria's hips against hers, of her thigh between Emilia's legs, of her eyes wide and dark…

Emilia cleared her throat, hoping that would clear her mind, as well. "Why were you in my cabin?"

Maria released the rail and leaned back on her heels. She lifted the apple to her mouth and bit into it. She watched Emilia silently, as she chewed. When she'd swallowed, she said, "Went to wake you up."

"Well," Emilia said with a bitter smile, "I'm sorry I took away your opportunity to order me around."

"It's all right," Maria said. "I'll have plenty more." She took another bite. "Like right now, for instance."

Emilia wished the pirate captain would leave that ridiculously loud apple alone for a few moments—because each time Maria chewed, Emilia found her gaze drifting toward Maria's soft, full lips, following every slight twitch and curve of them.

Maria swallowed. "What part of the warning that I gave you last night did you not understand?"

Emilia looked up, frowning. "What do you mean? I haven't drawn my weapon. *You* had my weapon."

"Not that warning," Maria said. "The other one."

Emilia's frown deepened, as she tried to remember what else Maria had said last night. "The bounty?"

Maria nodded. "Why are you roaming my ship unarmed, when I've already warned you that you might be in danger?"

Emilia winced. When she put it that way, it did sound a little foolish, but her nightmares had left her reeling that morning, and the only thing on her mind, at the time, had been a desperate need for fresh air.

Maria must've recognized something in Emilia's expression because those dark eyes of hers suddenly softened. "Just be more careful next time," she said softly. She tilted her head in what Emilia assumed was the general direction of the galley. "Let's go."

Emilia followed her, quickly recovering from her momentary distress. "If you're so worried about me being unarmed, why don't you give me a sword?"

"Who said I was worried?" Maria scoffed. "I'm not worried. *You* should be worried." She didn't slow her steps or turn to look at Emilia. She just continued with her relentlessly aggressive pace. "If someone kills you, I'll just throw your corpse overboard. There's no shortage of ocean, love."

Emilia nearly ran into a large, burly sailor, while struggling to keep up with Maria's brisk steps.

"Watch your fucking step, bitch," the sailor snarled.

Maria froze so suddenly that Emilia nearly ran into her, as well. She caught Emilia by the elbow, and then she turned toward the sailor who'd yelled at Emilia.

The sailor paled. "Oh! Captain, I—I didn't see you."

"Clearly," Maria said, her voice as cold as ice.

Maria was actually quite tall for a woman, but this man was

nearly twice her size. Yet, the antsy shift of his feet suggested he was fighting the urge to run.

With one glare, Maria had frightened the pirate.

The sailor gestured vaguely toward the sails. "I was just trying to work on the lines, and she ran into me."

Emilia might've apologized, if it hadn't been for Maria's grasp on her elbow. As it was, she was struggling to think of anything but Maria's touch.

Why were her hands always so warm?

When it became clear that Maria was waiting for something, the sailor mumbled, "I'm sorry, Captain."

Maria lifted her eyebrows, wordlessly urging him to continue.

The sailor's grey eyes shifted toward Emilia, and he breathed out a long sigh. "And sorry to the, erm—"

"The bitch?" Maria provided.

The sailor cringed. "I...didn't know her name."

"Well, I can assure you it's not that," Maria said.

"My apologies to the...woman," he amended.

Emilia thought *woman* was a strange word to settle on, too, considering there were currently two women standing in front of him.

"The 'woman' is my new surgeon," Maria told him. "Perhaps you'll fall the next time you're climbing the rigging, and she'll have the opportunity to show you the same courtesy you showed her."

The sailor's eyes widened at the implied threat.

"Get back to work," Maria snarled.

"Yes, Captain," the sailor said.

Emilia wasn't sure why Maria was still holding her arm, but there was something about that small point of contact—the gesture seemed almost...protective.

Emilia couldn't help but wonder if Maria needed a healer more than she said she did. After all, the table in Emilia's quarters was stained with the blood of sailors who'd died in Maria's service *without* a healer.

It wasn't until the sailor was out of sight that Maria released Emilia's arm. "That was Buchan," she told Emilia. "He'd shatter your jaw with one punch. So, don't go starting any more shit with him, all right?"

Emilia followed, as Maria took off at that ridiculously brisk pace again. "It's not like I meant to run into him!" she complained. "I was just trying to keep up with you, but you walk as if there's a fire."

"There *is* a fire," Maria said with a small smile. "How do you think Judith cooks our food?"

"Funny," Emilia muttered. "He had a sword. Have you considered the possibility that he may have seen me as an easy target because I wasn't wearing one?"

Maria stopped, catching Emilia by the arm, as she, once again, almost ran into her. With a virulent smile, Maria leaned in close and whispered, "Have you considered the possibility that I realized that, and that was precisely why I made him piss himself?"

Heat seared through Emilia's body, originating in the place Maria touched her, and unfurling outward.

Emilia swallowed uneasily. "I genuinely hope that's just an expression."

Maria laughed loudly at that. "Come on, islander."

Emilia followed her, but she hadn't yet given up on her pursuits. "Everyone on this ship has a sword."

"Well, that just isn't true," Maria said, as she walked. "Some of them carry pistols, instead."

"That's not...any better," Emilia said with a frown. "What good is a dagger against swords and pistols?"

"It's plenty good," Maria said, flashing a taunting smirk at her, "if you're as skilled as you say you are."

Maria slowed her steps as soon as they were past the bulk of the crew, and Emilia easily fell into step beside her. Maria kept Emilia between herself and the hull throughout the walk. Whether she did so purposely or just happened to take the inside path, Emilia didn't know.

"Yes," Emilia said, "I see you really proving that with those two swords you wear on you at all times."

Maria stopped near the hatch. She let her hand rest on her right sword, as she turned toward Emilia. "I once fought an entire armed guard with nothing but the clothes on my back." When Maria noticed Emilia eyeing her leather trousers and doublet, she clarified, "Not these clothes. No, they looked more like something I'm sure *you* wore not too long ago."

The dark note in that remark told Emilia all she needed to know. "You escaped the dungeons with no weapons?" she realized. Emilia frowned. "How?"

Maria stepped closer. "You had such a great teacher, remember?" She slipped a finger beneath Emilia's jaw, lifting her face. "Surely, you already know."

Emilia narrowed her eyes at that taunt. Without hesitating, she grasped Maria's fingers with her own. She pulled Maria's fingers downward, glancing at that deep scar in the middle of Maria's palm—the one she'd noticed the day before. "This was a sword wound," she said, tracing the scar with her thumb. "It looks like a pretty controlled cut. You must've closed your hand around the blade."

Maria jerked her hand out of Emilia's grasp. With a stunned frown, she said, "Why would I do that?"

"To catch your opponent by surprise," Emilia said. "I think—well, I *assume*—you let them think they'd caught you. You waited for the guards to attack you, and then, you took one of their swords."

Maria blinked slowly, her brown eyes wide and dark. "You know this from the shape of my scar?"

"No. I know this from the shape of your scar *and* my own knowledge of sword-fighting," Emilia said. "And because of my knowledge of *healing*, I also know that to let a blade slice so deeply into your palm would've been quite painful." Her stomach tightened in sympathy. "But after your time in the dungeons, I suppose you were conditioned to the pain. Which means they had only themselves to blame."

Maria stared at Emilia, her hand still suspended in mid-air, her brown eyes wide and mesmerizing. "All right," she said, after a moment. "I'll admit it." She leaned in, her lips curving. "I'm a little impressed."

Emilia smiled, warmed by the praise. "You are?"

Maria crossed her arms. "But you'll have to show me more than that, if you want a sword."

Emilia's smile instantly faded. "And...I can. I will!" she assured her. "Let's go. I'm ready to go now."

"Easy, love," Maria said with a raised eyebrow. "I didn't mean now. We'll fight later."

"But I want to fight now," Emilia said. "I'm ready."

Maria gave her a bemused look. "No, you're not."

"That's not your decision to make," Emilia argued.

"I'm your fucking captain. Of course it's my decision," Maria scoffed. She rolled her eyes. "And I'm not going to fight a half-starved, escaped fugitive. I have more self-respect than that."

"I'm not starved," Emilia said. "I ate yesterday."

"For the first time in how long?" Maria challenged.

Emilia frowned at that. "I traveled through the forest," she tried again. "There were...fruit trees."

"The forest is at least a week's journey from Nefala—and that's if you're traveling on horseback," Maria pointed out. "Unless you ate your horse, at some point, I assume you didn't have one."

Emilia recoiled in horror. "Illopians eat horses?"

Maria dropped her arms to her sides, frowning. "No. It was just a—" She shook her head. "My point was that it's been a while since you left the forest."

"Oh," Emilia said. "Well...there were rivers, too."

"You were on the run," Maria reminded her. "You didn't have

time to fish." When Emilia looked away, unable to argue with that, Maria said, "You can't lie to someone who's walked your footsteps before, love. There's nothing you've done that I didn't do first."

Emilia sighed, "It doesn't matter. I feel fine."

"Give yourself time to regain your health," Maria said, "and then, if you still want a sword, we'll talk."

"I don't need time," Emilia insisted. "I'm ready."

"Em," Maria said, stepping closer. "Do you see anyone else on this ship, challenging me the way you are? Of course you don't. Why do you think that is?"

Emilia stared up at the captain, her chest fluttering. "I suppose they're afraid of you."

"For good reason," Maria said. She narrowed those dark brown eyes of hers. "If you don't want to trust my judgement, you're welcome to jump ship. I'll throw you in the fucking ocean myself, if you want."

Emilia scowled at the threat. "No, thank you."

Maria didn't even react to Emilia's acidic tone. She stepped back, as if Emilia's reply had been absolutely genuine. "Then, you'll fight me when I ask you to. Not before." When Emilia didn't instantly agree, Maria said, "Besides, you haven't even signed my Code yet."

"Why would that matter?" Emilia asked.

"You're not getting anything from me until you sign my Code," Maria said.

"Well, when does that happen?" Emilia asked.

Maria shook her head in disbelief. "You're in *way* too much of a hurry to sign your own death sentence, love."

THE STEPS CREAKED BEHIND EMILIA, AS MARIA FOLLOWED HER DOWN. She felt a slight brush of heat, when Maria stepped past her and ventured into the dark space.

When Maria passed the unlit fire-hearth, she said, "Ah. Seems I lied." She shrugged. "No fire yet."

Judith looked up from the barrel of oranges that she was sorting through. "Why would I have a fire going already?" she said with a frown. "Sunrise was barely an hour ago. Are you trying to eat four hours early?"

Maria gave another careless shrug. "I don't know."

Judith laughed. She glanced at Emilia, her bright blue eyes sparkling with amusement. "What it is, Em," she teased, "is that the captain doesn't know the first thing about what goes on down here, but she likes to pretend she knows everything."

"That doesn't surprise me at all," Emilia said.

Maria glanced back at Emilia, both brows high. "You know I'm the one who decides whether you live or die, right?"

"Oh," Emilia said with a smile. "I'm sorry. I just assumed you were aware of your own arrogance."

Judith burst into laughter. "You know, Captain? I think Em and I are going to get along very well."

"You're going to get the girl killed," Maria said.

Behind Maria's back, Judith gave Emilia a sly wink.

Emilia couldn't help but laugh.

Maria turned. She reached out and plucked an orange from Judith's barrel. She turned it over in her hand, examining the brightly-colored fruit with interest. "If I knew how to cook," she teased, "I wouldn't need you, now would I?"

"Yes, you would," Judith scoffed. "What? You think you can cook and navigate a ship at the same time?"

Maria tossed the orange in the air and caught it. With a smirk, she said, "I can do whatever I want."

Judith rolled her eyes.

Maria extended her arm, offering the orange to Emilia. "Haven't had my mouth on this one."

"Which is a miracle, honestly," Judith said, "because I usually can't keep a piece of fruit in her general vicinity without her devouring it."

Despite Judith's assurance that poison was not the captain's preferred way of killing, Emilia hesitated to accept food offered to her.

She shook her head, politely refusing.

Maria studied Emilia with a curious frown. Then, rather than pressing her, the pirate captain sank into one of the chairs and unsheathed one of her swords.

Emilia watched with an incredulous look, as Maria began to peel the orange with the blade of her sword.

At this point, Emilia was almost positive that Maria did things like this simply to make sure no one forgot she *had* the swords— some sort of intimidation tactic.

After all, what else could it be?

Practice for peeling human skin?

"Adda can cook," Judith said. From a second barrel, the ship cook began to count out the potatoes she'd need that day. "I'm surprised she never taught you."

"She tried," Maria said, her blade slipping through the orange peel. "I almost burned down the tavern. So, she sent me to the stables to shovel horse shit."

Judith snorted. "And that didn't humble you any?"

Maria leaned back in her chair and propped her faded, leather boots on the table. "Why would it?"

Judith chuckled. "Suppose it wouldn't, Captain."

Emilia watched every careful shift of Maria's blade, and every precise turn of her wrist, half-expecting the strange pirate captain to scream out, at any moment, after slicing off a finger along with the orange peel.

It would serve her right, really.

"Wait," Judith said. Her brows furrowed. "That woman who was supposed to marry my uncle—she slept with Adda's stableboy, didn't she?"

Maria suppressed a smile. "Did she say it was a stable-*boy* or—"

"Captain," Judith said, her eyes wide. "You didn't."

Maria glanced at her. "You're referring to Alice?"

Judith's mouth fell open. "Captain!" she scolded. "You know he kicked her out for that, don't you?"

"Judith, your uncle once told me he'd give me one of his daughters, if I convinced the tavern girls to fuck him," Maria muttered. She sliced the remaining peel from the orange. "I'd say Alice dodged a bullet."

"Ugh," Judith said with a grimace. "What'd you tell him?"

"That the tavern girls wouldn't fuck him if he were the last person in all of Aletharia," Maria told her, "and that I'd already fucked his daughter, anyway."

"Elizabeth?" Judith said. "I thought she liked men."

"She did—before she met me," Maria said with a grin. When Judith scowled at her, Maria admitted, "She likes men and women."

Judith nodded. "Did you hear she married that farmer?"

"I don't keep up with your cousins, Judith," Maria said with a shrug. "Not even the ones I've fucked."

Judith shook her head. "I can't imagine what she sees in him," she sighed, "but my uncle likes him."

Emilia couldn't believe the two of them were just gossiping idly, while Maria sliced an orange with a *sword*, of all things. Was Judith really *that* used to Maria's antics? So much so, that she didn't even notice?

Maria turned to look at Emilia. She deliberately made eye-contact with her before popping an orange wedge in her mouth. At first, Emilia didn't catch on to what Maria was doing, but after the pirate captain chewed and swallowed the fruit, it dawned on her.

Maria was proving to Emilia that the food was safe.

"Shit," Judith muttered. "Forgot the damn carrots."

Maria waited until Judith disappeared behind a stack of crates to, once again, offer Emilia the orange.

But this time, rather than offer her the entire fruit, Maria speared a single orange wedge on the tip of her sword. She then extended her arm, holding the sword out toward Emilia. There was a challenge in Maria's smile—a taunt that Emilia could almost hear.

Still scared?

Emilia narrowed her eyes and plucked the orange wedge from the sword. She tossed the fruit in her mouth and chewed it, proving that she wasn't afraid.

Maria's smile widened. She turned back toward the table, rolling another wedge between her fingers. She disposed of a few seeds, before tossing that piece into her mouth, as well.

Emilia watched Maria chew the orange, her gaze drawn to the subtle movement of Maria's jaw. For someone with such scarred skin and such rugged clothing, Maria had a remarkably gentle jawline.

Judith returned with a barrel of vegetables. It was so large that Emilia could barely see Judith's short, brown hair above the top of the wooden barrel. Yet, when Judith finally dropped the barrel to the floor, she looked only barely winded. She shoved her hair out of her face, slicking back the short, brown strands with nothing but her own sweat, and then, she returned to the table to gather her tools.

"Does she need help?" Emilia mumbled to Maria.

Maria glanced at Emilia, before turning to Judith. "Need anything, Judes?" she said with a grin. "Your new mate, over here, wants you to put her to work."

Emilia narrowed her eyes at the pirate captain.

Judith looked up, blinking. "Nah. I got it," she said. "Appreciate the concern, though, love." Her bright blue gaze darted toward Maria. "I see you, Captain!"

Maria grinned—caught red-handed with her hand in the orange barrel. She pulled out a second orange, anyway. "Last one," she promised, before picking up her sword to slice the peel from this orange, as well.

Judith scowled. "I'm sure," she said sarcastically.

Judith returned to the barrel with her tools in hand, and she used a large hammer, along with a few tools that Emilia didn't recognize, to unseal the barrel.

Maria waited until Judith had her attention on her work to drag Emilia into her fruit-stealing exploits, yet again. She placed another orange wedge on the tip of her sword and lifted it, offering it to Emilia.

Emilia—who'd been watching Judith hammer at the barrel—blinked, as she, once again, found a piece of fruit in front of her face. It was on the tip of her tongue to ask Maria how thoroughly she had cleaned her sword, but when she looked at Maria, the words died on her lips.

Maria watched Emilia with the most enticing smile, eagerly waiting for Emilia to join her, yet again, in this absurd fruit-stealing adventure. Before Emilia could talk herself out of it, she plucked the orange slice from Maria's sword and tossed it in her mouth.

The juice that flooded Emilia's mouth was even sweeter than the previous orange, and it took all of her self-control to not moan at the taste.

Okay. So, perhaps the captain had a point.

It *had* been a while since Emilia had eaten well.

Despite her best attempts to hide it, the pleasure must've shown in Emilia's face—because the smile that Maria gave her was lascivious enough to bring a blush to Emilia's cheeks.

Maria leaned back in her chair, propping her boots on the table, much like she'd done before. She rolled the next piece of fruit between her fingers, but she never tore her gaze from Emilia's face.

The occasional hammering stopped, and Judith returned to the table to grab a tool she'd forgotten. "I'm not joking, Captain," she said, as she picked up a flat, metal object. "We have a long voyage ahead of us. You can't be eating all of the fruit on the first day. You'll have an entire crew riddled with scurvy."

As Emilia tried to swallow her orange as silently as possible, the captain continued to watch her with that enticing smile. A warmth unfurled through her body, a warmth that had less to do with her embarrassment and more to do with that absurdly gorgeous smile.

"There's plenty. I asked Adda for twice as much, this time," Maria said. She turned to Judith, flashing a proud smile. "You know she can't deny me."

Judith chuckled. "She spoils you."

Maria popped an orange wedge in her mouth. Her mouth remained curved, even as she chewed. "I have more than earned it —especially with those last spoils we brought in. She'll get a fortune out of that."

"She was quite impressed, wasn't she?" Judith said with a smile. She returned to the barrel. "Depending on how long we're at sea, our supplies might even outlast the voyage. That'd be a feat, wouldn't it?"

Maria cast a pointed look at Emilia. "Let's just hope everything goes smoothly, then."

Emilia looked away, her stomach sinking. She hated that it even bothered her. They were pirates, after all. What did it matter if she betrayed them? Was it not in their nature to do the same?

Judith looked at Maria. "Have you talked to Zain?"

Maria shrugged. "We discussed currents and wind patterns," she said, placing another orange wedge in her mouth. "Just your typical, first-day discussions."

"Well," Judith sighed, "he was poking around a bit about our new pirate." Her bright blue gaze shifted toward Emilia. "And I don't think he means to stop."

Maria nodded. "She has nothing to hide." She cast another pointed look at Emilia. "Do you, surgeon?"

With a forced smile, Emilia said, "Nothing at all."

Maria pointed at Emilia with her sword, wielding it as casually as a quill. "Nothing at all, *Captain*."

"Yes," Emilia said. "I'm aware you're the captain."

Maria turned to Judith—who looked even more concerned than before—and assured her, with a laugh, "We're working on it."

Judith nodded, her bright blue eyes wide. She slid one of the tools into the barrel, pushing downward. The barrel's lid came free a few moments later, and she carefully set aside her tools, before removing it.

"Besides, if we're lucky," Maria said, "one of the sailors will get injured soon, and she'll have a chance to prove her skill. Once she proves useful, Zain will find something else to fuss over."

"If we're lucky?" Emilia repeated. She scowled at the captain. "You call someone getting hurt '*lucky?*'"

"Lucky for *you*," Maria said, glancing at her. "If you want to survive, you need to prove your usefulness."

Judith must've realized that the next thing out of Emilia's mouth wouldn't have been pleasant—because she quickly interjected, "Even as just a cook's mate, she's useful." She wiped the sweat from her forehead. "How good are you with a knife, Em?"

"Oh, haven't you heard?" Maria said. She traced the blade in her lap with her fingertip, a smile curling at the corners of her lips. "She had a *great* teacher."

Emilia narrowed her eyes at the pirate captain.

Judith ignored the taunt. "Can you slice potatoes?"

Emilia looked up at her, blinking. "Of course."

Judith turned to Maria. "She'll cut my prep work in half, Captain. I, for one, see plenty of use in that."

An unfamiliar warmth unfurled in Emilia's chest. No one had ever defended her so readily. She didn't know how to respond—or if she even should.

Maria picked up another orange wedge, rolling it in her hand. "And I'm overjoyed for you, Judith," she sighed, "but I hired a surgeon, not a cook's mate. You know Zain will doubt me, if he doesn't see more."

"He *will* see more," Judith assured her. "I'll vouch for her for a few days, and by then…" She laughed. "Well, just think: it's been a few months since Helen blew anything up. We've got to be nearing her three-day countdown by now."

Maria dropped both feet to the floor and turned in her chair. "Judith, I swear to every god in Aletharia, if Helen blows up one more thing on this fucking ship—"

"You'll do what you've done every other time," Judith said with a smile. "You'll reduce her rum rations and increase her workload, which will discourage her for a few months." She held up a hand, when Maria tried to argue. "You won't kill her, and you know it—because she's too good at her job."

"Blowing up *my* ship is not her job," Maria said.

"You won't kill her," Judith said again, "because she's your best gunner. It's an idle threat that you make every time, and we all know it." She shrugged. "Reducing her rations discourages her for a few months. That's the best you can ask from her."

Maria turned back toward the table. "I can ask her not to blow up my ship," she muttered. She tossed an orange slice in her mouth, chewing irritably. "I swear that girl's going to make me bring back flogging."

Judith snorted. She returned to the table with an armful of carrots. "I wouldn't recommend it. Helen might get the wrong idea."

Maria continued to chew her orange. "Judith."

Judith suppressed a laugh. "Yes, Captain?"

Maria just shook her head and picked up another orange slice. She chewed silently, staring at the table with a wide-eyed expression that made Judith laugh.

"You've treated burns before?" Judith asked Emilia.

Emilia met Maria's gaze briefly, their conversation from the previous night replaying in her head. "Yes," she told Judith. "I've treated many burn victims."

A spark of irritation flashed in Maria's brown eyes, and Emilia knew the pirate captain wanted to argue with her use of the word *victim* again.

But she didn't.

Judith turned to Maria. "See? She'll treat Helen's burns, and Zain will shut up for a few days. Everyone wins."

"Except for Helen," Maria said, "who I'm going to kill—for damaging my ship again."

Judith rolled her eyes at the threat. She returned to the barrel to get more vegetables.

Maria tossed the last of the orange peel and seeds in a small bucket and climbed to her feet. "Well, I should get back to the helm, before Henry sinks us."

Judith shuffled through the vegetables with a frown. "Damn it! Tomatoes! I still need tomatoes." She disappeared behind the stacks of crates again, apparently searching for yet another barrel.

Maria sheathed her sword, staring in the direction that Judith had gone. "Keep an eye on her, Judes."

"Yes, Captain," Judith called out, from the back.

Confident that Judith wasn't watching them, Maria turned back toward Emilia. She stepped closer and held out her hand, revealing one, final slice of fruit.

"Saved you the last bite," Maria whispered.

Emilia glanced down at the small orange slice, which rested in the center of Maria's palm—and, consequently, in the middle of her scar. Emilia looked up at the pirate captain, her stomach flipping at the sight of those dark brown eyes. "I don't want it."

Maria's intense gaze didn't waver. "Take it."

Emilia's brows furrowed. This absurd, little game that Maria had dragged her into had started as a challenge, but there was something different about it, now—something about the dilation of Maria's eyes and the fascination that betrayed itself in her smile.

The pirate captain was enjoying this far too much.

"Take it," Maria repeated. "I know you want it."

Emilia stepped closer, lured in by the warmth of Maria's voice. She reached out, closing her fingers around the orange.

"Go on, love," Maria said, when Emilia hesitated.

Emilia placed the fruit in her mouth and bit into it. Its sweet juice flooded her mouth, yet again, and she closed her eyes, absolutely enraptured by the taste.

Where did they even *get* these oranges?

"Good?"

Emilia opened her eyes to find Maria watching her with arched brows. Heat rushed to her cheeks. She swallowed her food—and then mumbled, "It's fine."

Maria grinned, her eyes dark with lust. "Just fine?"

Emilia desperately wanted to hide in the back with Judith—at least until Maria was gone. "Just fine."

Maria laughed. She circled around Emilia—heading toward the steps, Emilia assumed—but her footsteps stopped too soon. Emilia straightened, as she felt the front of Maria's body brush against her back.

Maria leaned in and brushed her mouth against Emilia's ear. "Enjoy your first day," she whispered.

The rush of desire that coursed through Emilia's body, in response, was immediate and overpowering.

Emilia watched with a stunned frown, as the pirate captain ascended the steps without another word.

CHAPTER 9

A Pirate's Code

O nly a few hours had passed, when Emilia heard the
captain's footsteps on the steps again.

The late morning sunlight streamed in through the
portholes, illuminating the steps Maria now descended. At some
point that morning, Maria had loosened her shirt and rolled up her
sleeves. The nautical tattoos on her arms were now visible—along
with a thin layer of glistening sweat on her brown skin.

Maria braced her hands on the table and leaned forward,
watching as Judith sliced up some carrots.

Judith eventually set the knife aside and dumped the carrots
into the pot. "Need something, Captain?"

"It's time."

Judith glanced at her. "You gathered the officers?"

"Zain did," Maria said. "He wants her to sign it before we get
too far from land." Her dark gaze wandered toward Emilia, and a
wry grin played at the edges of her lips. "I told him we could just
throw her overboard if she refuses, but he didn't like that idea."

Emilia stopped slicing potatoes, for a moment, and looked up.
She blinked, as she met the captain's gaze.

Judith gave Maria a playful shove. "You're an ass."

Maria just grinned at her. "If you've already started cooking, you don't have to come," she told Judith. "Your new helper, on the other hand, has no choice."

Emilia frowned. "You *just* dragged me down here, and now, you want to take me somewhere else?"

"I'll take you wherever I want," Maria said.

A bit of warmth gathered in Emilia's cheeks.

Judith rolled her eyes at Maria's teasing. "Oh, I'm coming," she told Maria. "The girl needs a friendly presence in there. The rest of you are assholes."

Maria snorted at that. She circled the table, coming up alongside Emilia. She grasped Emilia's wrist—midway through slicing a potato—and plucked the knife from her hand. "Put that away. It's time to go."

Emilia scowled at Maria. "Where are we going?"

Maria leaned toward her. "The correct response is: *'Yes, Captain.'*"

Emilia narrowed her eyes at that. "And if I say no?"

Maria shrugged her lean shoulders. "I could drown you, stab you, have you whipped." Her lips curved. "There are plenty of options for me to choose from."

"Oh, gods," Judith said, rolling her eyes. "Would you stop before you scare her away?" She turned to Emilia. "You have to sign the captain's Code. If you choose not to, you'll go back to Nefala. That's all."

Maria just smiled. "Judith spoils all of my fun."

Emilia begrudgingly suppressed a smile. Why did Maria have to have such an amusing sense of humor? There was nothing quite as infuriating as finding herself amused by the person she intended to hate. "Should I be worried?"

"Only if the sight of blood makes you squeamish," Maria teased. She tapped her fingers against the hilt of her sword in a playfully menacing rhythm. "But if that's the case, you're on the wrong ship, anyway."

Emilia shot a puzzled look Judith's way. "Blood?"

Judith waved her hand. "The captain's just teasing you," she told Emilia. "It's barely any blood at all."

"Just a drop or two," Maria agreed.

Emilia's frown deepened. "But *why* is there blood?"

"Again," Maria said with that smile that was both beautiful and infuriating, "the correct response is: *'Yes, Captain.'*"

Emilia's answering glare could've melted steel.

"WELCOME TO THE CAPTAIN'S QUARTERS," JUDITH SAID.

Maria had entered ahead of them and was already seated by the time Judith and Emilia stepped inside.

Emilia spent the entirety of her time on Catherine's ship in the brig, so she had no frame of reference for what a ship captain's quarters usually looked like.

Maria's quarters were at least four times the size of every other cabin on the ship, but much of that space was filled with maps, unused rope, and weapons.

Besides that, there was a small bed against the left wall and a large table in the center of the room.

Maria sat behind that long, wooden table, now—relaxed, with her long legs stretched out in front of her. It was a similar posture to what she'd had in the tavern.

And there was something about that posture—the way Maria took up as much space as she wanted, the way she acted as if she didn't have a care in the world—it seemed to send a very particular message.

A message of: *This space is mine.*

That's what Paul had told Emilia, after all—only an hour before Maria killed him. He'd told Emilia that Maria owned Nefala—in every sense but the literal.

Nefala belonged to Maria, and so did this ship.

The law had stripped Maria Welles of all power, by declaring her a pirate, and yet, here she sat, declaring right back that she'd take whatever power she liked.

"She'll take the seas themselves, if I don't stop her," Catherine had once said.

Back then, Emilia had thought Catherine sounded absolutely paranoid, but looking at Maria, now—Emilia knew there wasn't much this woman *wouldn't* take control of.

Including you, if you're not careful.

Emilia shuddered at the thought.

There were only two chairs in the entire room—one on each side of the table. Maria sat in the one farthest from the door, while the other had been left empty.

Maria held out her hand, gesturing for Emilia to sit.

The other pirates stood around the table in a sort of haphazard circle. Aside from Judith, Emilia had only met two of them. Zain, the quartermaster who'd given her such a hard time, and Pelt, the boatswain with that vicious facial scar.

Zain stood behind Maria, and the two made a strange pair— Zain, with his flashy, red waistcoat, his combed, black hair, and his golden skin free of tattoos. And Maria, with her dark leather, messy curls, and dark skin covered in tattoos.

Emilia sat in the chair. Uncertainty fluttered in her stomach, but she forced herself to meet Maria's gaze.

Maria leaned back in her chair, resting her elbows on her thighs. "You've met Zain, our quartermaster."

Emilia nodded.

"And, obviously, you know Judith," Maria added.

Again, Emilia nodded.

Maria gestured toward her boatswain—with his familiar, long, brown hair and deeply tanned skin. "And you remember Pelt, I assume?"

Pelt smiled, his gold teeth flashing in the afternoon light.

When Emilia nodded at that, too, Maria said, "He's our boatswain." She then motioned toward a tall, muscular woman with braided, red hair. "And that's Helen. She's our master gunner."

Helen offered Emilia an easy smile and waved two fingers—two fingers that, Emilia realized, were actually quite filthy.

It looked as if the woman had dipped her hand in gunpowder, prior to the meeting.

Maria pointed to a man with sandy-brown hair and fair skin, who stood to the left of the table. "And that's Jonas," she said. "He's our carpenter."

Jonas stepped forward and held out a hand that was, fortunately, a little cleaner than Helen's. "I wasn't around yesterday, so I haven't had the pleasure of meeting you yet."

Calmed by his friendly tone, Emilia shook his hand.

At least there were *some* people on this ship who didn't distrust her on sight.

"Yes, I sent Jonas to a nearby farm town yesterday," Maria explained, "to collect some supplies." Her lips curled into a cruel smile. "My supplier in Nefala met an," she paused, licking her lips, "untimely end."

Emilia froze. "Farm town?"

Jonas gripped her hand with his calloused fingers, his friendly smile giving nothing away.

The only reason no one in Nefala saw the Wanted notice for Emilia was that Paul had gotten to it, first.

His blackmail very well might have saved her life.

But Emilia hadn't stopped in any farm towns. With no one to remove the notice, Jonas might've seen it.

Jonas released her hand and returned his attention to Maria. If he'd seen it, he gave no indication now.

"You met our master of arms last night," Maria continued. "Fulke? Big muscle. Doesn't talk much."

Emilia blinked.

Was this some sort of inside joke among the crew? Or did they just honestly think that 'doesn't-talk-much' was the best way to describe someone without a tongue?

Emilia glanced around, searching for the friendly giant—and unfortunately, not finding him.

"He's not here," Maria said, confirming what Emilia had already noticed. "Neither is Henry, my helmsman." She folded her hands against her lean stomach. "Someone had to take over the duties, while the rest of us were handling you."

Handling me?

Emilia wasn't sure she liked that phrase.

"New sailors are often surprised that we have so few officers," Zain said, "but that's the difference between pirates and soldiers, you see?" He waved a hand in explanation. "Things are more equal here."

Emilia didn't honestly understand the comparison. Not as well as an Illopian would've, anyway. Drakon Isle had been more democratic than anything she'd seen in Illopia, and as the leader's daughter, no one, besides her mother, had dared tell Emilia what to do.

From *her* standpoint, things were less equal here.

Maria must've recognized her confusion—because she explained, "The king's navy is all about structure and hierarchy. There, sailors are subordinate to many officers. Here, you're really only subordinate to me."

"Of course it's about hierarchy," Emilia said. "He can't let anyone get a taste of *non*-tyrannical rule."

A tense mixture of uneasy smiles and surprised laughter followed that remark.

Pelt, the boatswain, offered her a companionable grin. "You're a brave one, aren't you?"

"Did I say something wrong?" Emilia asked.

Maria chuckled at the question, and some of the other pirates laughed along with her. "Not at all," she told Emilia, "but in Illopia, they'd hang you for less."

"Insulting the king is a serious crime," Zain said.

"But don't worry," Pelt said. "We all hate him, too."

Maria's smile widened. "If anything, your hatred of him might just endear you to us more."

Well, Emilia thought, if hating King Eldric won her approval, just wait until they found out that Emilia wanted him dead.

Maria shuffled through a pile of maps and pulled out a single, rolled up parchment scroll. She removed the ribbon and unrolled it, smoothing the parchment with three, tattooed fingers. "Are you ready to sign?"

"Depends on what I'm signing," Emilia told her.

A smirk twitched at Maria's lips.

Zain narrowed his eyes at Maria. "I keep forgetting that you hired someone with no sailing experience."

Considering the number of times he'd mentioned it already, Emilia doubted the quartermaster had forgotten it even once.

Maria, for her part, looked totally unconcerned. She tilted her head back, meeting his gaze. "Bring me another surgeon, and I'll throw her out now." When Zain looked away, she said, "That's what I thought."

Emilia didn't know whether to be grateful that Maria had silenced the quartermaster's suspicions or alarmed by Maria's willingness to throw her out.

"Every ship, whether it's merchant, naval, or pirate, has an Articles of Agreement," Zain told Emilia. "You would know that, if you had ever sailed before."

"It's often called a Code," Maria said, "and it's a list of rights and responsibilities and general laws you're to follow, while under my command."

Emilia glanced down at the scroll, watching as Maria traced the parchment with her fingertips. "I'm allowed to read it before signing, I assume?"

"Of course," Maria agreed.

"And if you're illiterate," Zain added, "I can read the articles for you, and a witness will watch to ensure I don't skip anything."

"She's a surgeon, Zain," Judith reminded him. "I highly doubt she's illiterate."

"I can read and write in multiple languages," Emilia confirmed.

"Good," Maria said, pushing the parchment toward Emilia. "Then, if you miss something, it's on you."

Emilia reached out and took the scroll, realizing only afterward how impossibly long it was.

She quickly skimmed over the scroll, surprised by how meticulously detailed it was. It was divided into five general sections—or laws—but beneath those, it detailed hypothetical situations and consequences, as well.

She wanted Emilia to read *all* of this?

While they watched?

A sly smile graced Maria's lips, and—as if she knew exactly what Emilia was thinking—she said, "Be sure to read every word." Flecks of golden fire burned in her warm, brown eyes. "You don't want to sell me your soul without knowing what else I'll take."

Emilia looked up, her stomach flipping. It was still too soon for Emilia to know if Maria was the villain that the legends made her out to be, but if she wasn't, well...she certainly played the part well.

"This is your handwriting?" Emilia said. Somehow, her voice came out much quieter than her thoughts.

Maria's smile faded. "What makes you think that?"

Emilia glanced at the maps that lay between them. She scanned the scribbled notes in the margins.

Some of them were typical—notes on currents and wind direction, things that any ship captain might need to know. But some were a bit more distinctive.

For instance, the one that referred to the king's navy as *"fucking bastards."* Somehow, despite having just met her, this struck Emilia as *exactly* the sort of thing that her ever-so-polite captain would write.

"Because the handwriting is the same as what's on your maps," Emilia pointed out. "It's yours, isn't it?"

Maria crossed her arms. Apparently, she didn't find Emilia's perceptiveness as *endearing* as she'd found Emilia's hatred of the king.

But Judith, being the absolute gem she was, cut through the tension like a well-sharpened blade. "What she's trying to say, Captain," Judith teased, "is that the ugly scrawl you call writing is hard to miss."

And just like that, Maria's smile returned. "Well, if it's that bad, why don't I have you rewrite it for me," she said, turning to Judith, "in your own blood?"

"Without me, you'd have a hungry crew," Judith reminded her, "and we both know a hungry crew is a mutinous one."

Maria shrugged her lean shoulders. "There's been a lull in battle lately," she said with a grin. "Putting half a crew to death might cheer me up, actually."

Emilia blinked at that. She returned her attention to the scroll. Honestly, Judith's teasing wasn't too far off the mark. Maria wrote with a hasty carelessness that often made her writing difficult to read.

It was far from Catherine's perfect calligraphy.

Emilia's stomach lurched. She hated how easily her mind recalled memories of Catherine. She wished she could wipe them from her mind—or temporarily repress them, at least. Just until her heart stopped aching.

Zain cleared his throat. When Emilia's gaze shifted toward him, he said, "I've read the Code more times than I can count. I could summarize it, if you'd like."

Emilia cast a curious glance at Maria—and froze, as she caught the pirate captain's gaze. Maria was leaning back in her chair, like before, but her brown eyes had sharpened somehow.

She watched Emilia as if she were analyzing every subtle twitch of her body.

Emilia suddenly understood why Maria had looked so annoyed earlier. Being analyzed by someone was uncomfortable, when you had something to hide.

Which begged the question...

What was Maria hiding?

"Go ahead," Maria said.

"Yes, Captain," Zain said—before launching into a well-practiced speech. "The first law is simple..."

"You're mine until death," Maria interjected.

Emilia glanced at the pirate captain, her eyes wide.

"That's not exactly—" Zain shook his head, clearly not amused by Maria's humor. "Unfortunately, Em, it seems our good captain is not taking this seriously."

Was it a joke, though?

Because those dark eyes of Maria's looked capable of stealing a lot more than gold.

"That's a gross oversimplification of what the Code actually says," Zain muttered. "What it says is that you'll remain part of the crew until death or release," he told Emilia. "You can leave in one of three ways—your death or your captain's death. Or, if she chooses to, the captain can release you from your contract."

Maria grinned. "Which is, *essentially*, what I said."

Emilia turned to Maria, her heart racing. "Release?"

Maria *knew* Emilia planned to leave. Emilia had made that abundantly clear the night before, and yet, Maria hadn't bothered to mention this law, then.

Surely, Maria wasn't planning to force Emilia to stay?

But then again, this was Captain Maria Welles.

She wasn't exactly known for her kind heart.

"Yes, Em. Release," Maria said. "You can ask me to release you from your contract. Perhaps I'll say yes."

Just...perhaps?

"And if you don't?" Emilia asked.

Maria smiled. "Then, your death or mine."

So, I might have to kill her?

The realization sent a cold chill through Emilia's veins. Practically-speaking, it wouldn't be difficult.

She'd stay on good terms with the captain until she reached Drakon Isle, and then, she'd call her dragons.

They'd burn the entire ship and everyone on it, if Emilia asked them to.

Still, the thought of killing Maria chilled her.

"Desertion is, of course, discouraged," Zain said.

"But we're not the Royal Navy," Maria added. "We aren't going to hunt you down, if you desert."

Emilia breathed a small sigh of relief at that. So, she might not have to kill Maria, after all. "You won't?"

"No," Maria said. Her dark eyes narrowed. "But it's discouraged for a reason, Em." Flickering candlelight danced across her skin, highlighting those deep scars. "If you leave *with* my blessing, you'll remain part of my crew—no matter where you go. You'll always have a job with me, and you can come back whenever you like. If you leave *without* it, you're on your own."

Emilia's brows furrowed. "And that's a bad thing?"

Maria leaned forward. "It will be," she murmured, "when you're sitting in those dungeons, awaiting the noose, and thinking, 'Captain Maria Welles could've pulled some strings and gotten me free, if only I were still part of her crew.'"

Emilia tensed at the mention of the dungeons.

A fact that did not go unnoticed by Maria.

The alluring pirate captain tilted her head, quirking a scarred eyebrow. "There are benefits to being part of my crew, Em," she said softly. "I protect my own."

A stubborn surge of wounded pride filled Emilia's throat. She wanted to tell the arrogant pirate captain that she didn't *need* protection, that she could protect herself, but she couldn't make that argument without revealing her secrets. So, instead, she said, "How so?"

Maria settled back in her chair, her smile positively wicked. "There's more to piracy than meets the eye," she said in a low tone, "and I, my love, was born for it."

Emilia told herself that the heat that gathered in her cheeks was irritation, but the way Maria's voice dripped with sensuality every time she said the word *'love'* certainly wasn't helping matters.

Desperate to avoid those deep, brown eyes that pulled her in like a collapsing star, Emilia focused her attention on the scroll in her hands. "This second part is talking about an equal vote and an equal share," she noted. She looked up. "What does that mean?"

"It means what it says," Zain said. "We're equals on the *Wicked Fate*. My vote counts no more than yours, and the captain's vote counts no more than mine."

Maria gave a small nod to Pelt, and the boatswain dutifully took over.

"The only matters that aren't subject to a vote are the captain's orders during life-or-death situations, like battles or storms," Pelt explained. "During those moments, we obey the captain's orders regardless of how we feel about it—because not doing so would risk not only our own lives, but the lives of everyone on the ship."

"Besides," Helen said, "we all know there isn't a sailor in these waters who knows more about winning battles than Captain Maria Welles."

There was a soft murmur of agreement to that, and the other pirates gazed at Maria with the same sort of admiration that Helen's words had held.

No wonder the woman had an ego that burned like the sun. She had an entire crew fanning the flames.

Emilia scanned the next few sentences of the Code. "And equal share?" she said. "Equal share of what?"

Maria let out a low chuckle, her teeth shining in the candlelight. "We're pirates, love. What do *you* think?"

A few of the other pirates laughed along with her.

Emilia frowned. Captain Maria Welles was known for sinking ships and leaving no survivors, but she'd never asked what kind of cargo those ships had carried *before* Maria attacked them. "Gold?" she guessed.

Maria shrugged. "Eventually."

"After a successful plunder, we take the spoils to Nefala, where they're sold for gold," Zain told Emilia. "The costs for foodstuffs and ship repairs are taken out first, and then, whatever remains is divided equally among the crew."

"Everyone receives an equal share," Pelt added, "except for the captain, who receives two shares."

"But the captain uses most of hers to fund the operations in Nefala," Zain pointed out, "which benefit us all."

Emilia cast a curious glance at Maria. Catherine had told Emilia that Maria turned to piracy because of her own insatiable greed, but for someone supposedly driven by greed, Maria was awfully quick to part with her gold.

"Judith," Maria said. "Explain the rations to her."

"Yes, Captain," Judith said—as though they weren't just teasing each other moments before. She turned to Emilia. "Every member of the crew receives equal rations, as well," she told Emilia. "For the first part of the voyage, you'll receive a small, daily ration of water and a larger, daily ration of rum. If we're at sea long enough for the fresh water to spoil, at that point, you'll receive double rations of rum, instead."

"But hopefully, you'll have built up a tolerance for it, by then," Maria said with a taunting smile.

"At meal times, you'll be given ale," Judith said, "and the ale doesn't count against your rations."

Emilia nodded. She'd never needed to depend on anything other than water for hydration before, but if the rest of the crew could do it, Emilia was sure she could, too.

"That being said," Judith said, "if you need more than what we give you, let me know. I have my own stores of rum, and no one ever drinks mine, anyway."

"No one drinks it for a reason, Judith," Maria said.

Judith scoffed, "Just because you can't handle it—"

"No one can handle it, Judith," Maria argued. "The rat couldn't even handle it! It's fucking toxic."

Judith rolled her eyes. "The rat was fine."

"It was dead!" Maria said.

Emilia glanced back and forth between the pirates, not sure how to react to their strange argument.

Helen took one look at Emilia's face and laughed. "They argue about this like once a month," she told Emilia. "Apparently, back when they were in the navy together, Judith smuggled some of her brother's rum onto the ship and convinced the captain to drink with her. Somehow, this led to both of them blacking out and a lifetime of arguments about a dead rat."

Emilia blinked at the muscular redhead. "A dead rat?"

"The captain swears it was dead," Pelt interjected, "but Judith says that it was just drunk and *resting*."

Emilia squinted. "Did either of them...touch it?"

"No one knows," Helen whispered, "but we all secretly think the captain's story makes more sense."

Jonas and Pelt nodded eagerly, and—surprisingly enough— even *Zain* gave a small nod of agreement.

"Hey!" Judith said to all of them. "I saw that!"

"They believe me because they've all had your rum, Judith!" Maria told her. "That shit would kill a troll."

"Captain," Judith said, "are you suggesting my brother sold me something harmful?"

"I'm sure it wasn't intentional," Maria muttered. She turned to Emilia. "Just stay away from Judith's rum, all right? If the rest of us can't stomach it, you sure as hell can't."

Was she saying that because she knew, somehow, that Emilia

173

didn't drink much, or was she suggesting that Emilia looked so much *meeker* than the rest of them?

"You'll get plenty of rum with your rations," Zain added, "and we get that rum from Adda. It's safe."

"Don't listen to them," Judith told Emilia. "It gets hot down in the galley. You're going to want a little extra rum, and when you do, I've got you covered."

Maria—the powerful, ever-confident pirate captain—looked as if she were about to vomit. "Don't drink it," she warned Emilia. "Trust me. It's not worth it."

Emilia glanced back and forth between them, not sure who to listen to.

Out of the two of them, Judith insulted Emilia *much* less often, but Maria seemed to have the agreement of the others, as well, on this particular issue.

Before Judith could make any more arguments in favor of her supposedly poisonous substance, Maria said, "Continue with the third law, Zain."

"Yes, Captain," Zain said. "The third part says that the crew of the *Wicked Fate* is your family, and you should treat them as such. You should think of your crew as your brothers, your sisters, your—"

"Let's tone down the analogies a bit, Zain," Judith muttered. She shuddered in disgust. "Half of us have fucked each other."

Helen grinned at Judith, not even a slight blush in those fair, freckled cheeks of hers.

And Pelt—apparently privy to whatever secret the two of them shared—laughed freely, his gold teeth shining.

Zain, on the other hand, was less amused. "It's not my fault I'm the only person on this damn ship who can keep his pants on."

Maria folded her hands over her stomach and gave him a taunting smile. "Like you did with Edward?"

The golden skin of Zain's neck reddened. Helen might not have had any shame, but *he* certainly did. "I am not in the navy anymore, Captain," he said slowly. "You cannot blackmail me with that."

"Wait. Edward?" Judith said. She frowned at Maria, the wheels spinning in her head. "Not your lieutenant."

"No," Zain said, but Maria smiled and nodded.

Judith's blue eyes widened. "Lieutenant Ingelby?"

That name.

"I don't anticipate her fighting us anymore," Catherine had said— when Emilia had finally succumbed to her own grief. *"Put her in irons, Lieutenant Ingelby."*

Emilia looked away, her heart pounding at the memory. She'd had no idea that so many of these pirates had been in the navy. Catherine had always spoken as if the lines between pirates and naval sailors were stark and obvious, but the longer Emilia listened to these pirates, the more those lines seemed to blur.

"Zain Amari slept with an officer?" Judith said with a delighted smile. "And here I've spent all this time thinking that it was our captain who led you astray!"

"It was our captain!" Zain assured her. "She blackmailed me."

Maria shrugged those lean shoulders of hers. "It was for your own good," she assured him. "Ingelby was up Catherine's ass as much as he was up yours."

"Not funny, Captain," Zain grumbled.

Emilia's head spun at the mention of Catherine.

Different Catherine.

Please, be talking about a different Catherine.

"Could've been the other way around," Maria said, relentless in her teasing. "It's not like *I* ever watched."

"Captain, please," Zain groaned. "I do not want to think of that snake and Ed together."

"Ed?" Judith exclaimed. She threw out her arms in disbelief. "Ed!"

Emilia couldn't believe that these pirates were just sitting here, discussing Catherine with such nonchalance—as if she were their friend, rather than a mortal enemy.

Well...Zain had used some choice words to describe Catherine that, at least, clarified that she was not *his* friend. Who knew Emilia would end up relating most to the suspicious quartermaster, at the moment?

Emilia counted to ten, her head still spinning.

"Em?"

Maria's smooth, lilting voice cut through her fog.

Emilia looked up, meeting the pirate captain's gaze.

Maria tilted her head to the side, studying Emilia with those intense, brown eyes. "Are you all right?"

No, Emilia wanted to say.

But Zain saved her from having to respond. "No, she's not all right," he scoffed. "She's realizing that the officers on her new ship can't even make it through the damn Articles of Agreement without behaving like uncivilized ruffians."

Judith and Helen snickered, while Pelt and Jonas had the sense to look *slightly* rebuked.

Maria, on the other hand, didn't even react. She watched Emilia, still—a frown twisting at her scars.

Emilia swallowed uneasily. It made no sense, but she felt as if the captain could see straight through her. And the last thing she needed was this pirate captain figuring out her connection to Catherine.

Emilia cleared her throat. "The crew is like family?"

"Yes," Zain said with the first warm smile he'd ever given her. "Thank you, Em." Apparently, her desire to get away from the subject of Catherine had won her some approval points with him. "You're to treat the crew like family. Which means: you don't steal from your crew, you don't endanger your crew, and you don't betray your crew."

Emilia cringed. Her plan literally involved endangering *and* betraying the crew. "And, um," she said uneasily, "what happens if I break that rule?"

"You die," Maria said.

Her cold, unyielding stare sent chills down Emilia's spine. "Ah," Emilia said breathlessly. "Of course."

Maria's gaze followed Emilia's every move. "You'll want to pay *close* attention to the next law, surgeon."

Zain frowned at that. "The fourth part of the Code discusses violence and murder," he told her. "While all violence between crew mates is discouraged, there are only a few forms of violence that are punishable by death. Obviously, sexual violence and murder fall under that category."

"What else do you think I'd kill you for, Em?" Maria said, her gaze dark.

Emilia swallowed, as she remembered the captain's warning the night before. "Drawing a weapon?"

Maria smiled. "Exactly."

"That isn't to say you can't defend yourself. During battle, obviously, drawing your weapon is permitted. And...advised," Zain said with a frown, "but drawing a weapon against a crew mate—with no provocation—would result in your own death."

"Do you understand that rule, Em?" Maria said.

Emilia looked at her, and as soon as she met those fierce, brown eyes, she felt it all over again: Maria's hands around her wrists, Maria's waist against hers, Maria's thigh slipping between her legs...

With a—*hopefully* silent—gasp, Emilia averted her gaze. Her skin burned like a furnace, and she prayed to the goddess that Maria hadn't seen her blush.

She cleared her throat and muttered, "Of course."

When she heard Maria's soft, breathy laugh, Emilia thought her face might combust.

"A small altercation can devolve very quickly on a pirate ship," Zain added by way of explanation.

With a wink, Pelt added, "It's best to prevent the murders *before* they occur."

"And the only people who have reason to draw a sword outside of battle—that *doesn't* involve a fight and possible murder," Zain added, his brows high, "are the captain and myself."

Emilia glanced at Maria, her face still hot. "I see."

Maria watched her with a familiar smile—the same smile she'd worn earlier, while offering Emilia fruit.

"You do have the right to challenge someone to a duel," Pelt said, "as long as you seek approval from the captain or quarter-master first. Dueling without their knowledge is punishable by death."

"Death seems to be a common punishment here," Emilia muttered.

"Quite common," Maria assured her.

"I discourage duels when I can, because they will inevitably end in one of the duelist's death," Zain said, "and we would prefer to not lose any sailors." He sighed, "But it is your right to duel, if you choose to do so. I would oversee it, and if I saw that you were fighting unfairly, that would also result in your—"

"Death," Emilia assumed.

Zain flashed a tight smile. "Yes."

Emilia turned to Maria. "Is there anything I can do that *won't* somehow result in you killing me?"

Maria leaned further back in her chair, her eyes dark and unreadable. "You can do as you're told."

Emilia glared at that, and Maria grinned back.

Arrogant pirate, Emilia grumbled in her head.

She returned her attention to the parchment scroll in her hand, bottling up her irritation as she scanned the rest of the document. "Is that all?"

"Essentially," Zain muttered.

Emilia's frown deepened, as she read over the final law. "I, uh— I don't think I'm reading this correctly."

"Unfortunately," Zain said with a sigh, "you are."

The final law was so absurd that Emilia read over it at least five times to be sure, but each time, it said the same unbelievably ridiculous words as the first time.

"Don't fuck Helen."

Emilia cast a wary look Helen's way, wondering if the muscular redhead knew about this strange law.

Based on the shameless, gunpowdery wave that Helen gave her, in response, Emilia figured it was safe to assume that, yes, Helen did know.

Zain rolled his eyes. "I've tried to tell the captain so many times that it's not professional, but does she listen to me? No."

"We're fucking pirates, Zain," Maria scoffed.

Emphasis on the fucking.

Apparently.

Emilia stared blankly at the parchment, her brows furrowed in disbelief. "Can I, uhh— Can I ask *why*?"

"Of course," Maria said. She turned to Judith—who looked awfully uncomfortable, all of the sudden. "Would you like to explain to your new friend *why* I was forced to add this rule?"

Judith cast a sheepish look in Helen's direction, before mumbling, "Well, there was an accident…"

"Just a small mishap, really," Helen interjected.

"That resulted in some damage to the ship," Judith continued, "and unfortunately, a few…*costly* repairs."

"But no one was hurt!" Helen pointed out. "And I, for one, think we should get credit for that."

Emilia had never been so confused in her life.

"Credit?" Maria repeated, her eyes wide. "You blew a hole in the side of my goddamn ship, Helen!"

"Well," Helen said, "I think Judith is to blame."

Judith shot an incredulous look at her. "You didn't tell me you'd already loaded the cannons!"

With a blasé shrug, Helen said, "You didn't ask."

"I'm a cook!" Judith argued. "I've never worked with cannons! How was I supposed to know?"

Again, Helen shrugged those strong shoulders of hers. "We were in the middle of a battle. How could you *not* know?"

Pelt shook his head, clearly suppressing laughter. Zain and Maria, on the other hand, looked *much* less amused.

Judith sighed, "I just thought it'd be fun to—"

"Fuck her in the middle of a battle?" Maria asked.

Emilia didn't think she'd ever heard the word "fuck" used in so many ways before. She'd certainly never seen it in an official document.

Judith cringed. She spread out her hands in a sort of apology. "It was something I'd never tried before."

"For good reason!" Maria snapped.

Although Judith's friendliness often made Emilia want to side with her, even *Emilia* had to admit: it definitely didn't sound like Judith had thought that decision through.

"So," Emilia said with a wide-eyed look, "is Helen the *only* one not allowed to have sex? Or..."

Helen snorted. "If that were the rule, I'd break it even more."

Emilia's frown deepened.

"She can do whatever she wants when she's off my ship," Maria said, "but when she's here, I need her to focus on *not* blowing us up."

Helen laughed at Emilia's expression. "It's all right. We make port pretty often, actually. I take care of my own needs until we return to Nefala, and then..." She flashed a playful smile. "I indulge."

Emilia wasn't sure why the gunner thought she needed to know that.

"You must've indulged quite a bit last night," Judith said. "I didn't even see you come back."

"That's because she *didn't*," Maria said, "last night."

"I came back this morning," Helen admitted. She flashed a proud smile. "I wasn't late, though, was I?"

"We'd already pulled up the anchor," Maria said.

Helen pointed a gunpowder-covered finger at her exasperated captain. "But I still made it." She turned to Judith. "Oh, I almost forgot! Sarah wanted me to tell you that she hates you. Again."

"Yeah," Judith said, sighing, "I know."

Pelt shook his head at her. "You've got to stop going after Sarah, mate."

Maria's gaze shifted back toward Emilia. "All right. You've heard it all," she said. "Time for you to sign."

Emilia was so stunned by the rule about Helen that she'd forgotten that she still had to sign Maria's Code.

Noting her hesitation, Zain said, "It's not too late to say no. If it's too much for you, Fulke can take you back to shore. No harm done."

"Is it, surgeon?" Maria asked. "Too much for you?"

Emilia narrowed her eyes at the captain's taunting tone. "Of course not," she said. "I just need something to write with."

Maria's smile was as wicked as ever. She let her feet fall to the floor and leaned forward, grabbing the quill from the table. She reached across the table, holding the quill between two fingers. When Emilia accepted it, Maria grabbed a well of ink and slid that across the table, as well.

Emilia found the last page and read over the list of signatures. She recognized the names of the pirates in the room with her, and she noticed that some of the pirates had signed with an *x*, rather than a name.

But the strangest thing she noticed were the red marks beside all of the names. Was that red ink?

And if so, why?

Rather than ask about the red spots, Emilia asked, "Why are some of these signatures crossed out?"

"They're dead," Maria said simply.

Emilia looked up, stunned. "But there are so many."

Maria didn't even blink. "Yes."

Emilia couldn't believe the nonchalance in her tone. Had these signatures belonged to the pirates who'd died in battle? Or the ones Maria had murdered?

Just for breaking some arbitrary law.

Maria lifted that scarred eyebrow of hers. "Having second thoughts?"

"No," Emilia said. She'd already come too far in her villainous descent to back out now. She dipped the quill in black ink and then, on the parchment, she signed the alias that Judith had advised her to use.

Emily Northwood.

She placed the quill on the table. "There. It's done."

Maria's smile widened. "Oh, no, love. Not yet."

Emilia glanced back at the parchment, her stomach sinking, as she realized, "The red marks." She looked up. "That isn't red ink, is it?"

Maria shook her head slowly.

Emilia nodded. She should've known. "Of course not."

Maria pushed back her chair, and Zain stepped out of her way, as she climbed to her feet. She unsheathed her right sword and circled the table.

Emilia eyed the sword in Maria's hand warily. "What are you doing?"

Maria lifted the sword and pointed its dangerously sharp blade at Emilia's throat. She smiled, as Emilia instinctually straightened, pressing her back against the back of the chair. Maria carefully lifted the blade, letting the cold steel press against Emilia's chin.

Maria lifted Emilia's face. "Stand, surgeon."

Emilia gripped the arms of her chair and climbed to her feet. Maria's sword followed, and so did Emilia's heartbeat, fluttering in her throat, like the wings of a hummingbird. She met the pirate captain's gaze with as much boldness as she could muster, which wasn't easy, considering there was a blade on her throat.

A slow smile curled at the corners of Maria's lips. "Do you swear to serve the captain and crew of the *Wicked Fate* with diligence, courage, and devotion?"

"I signed your Code, didn't I?" Emilia pointed out.

Maria lowered her sword and stepped closer. With a sly smile, she pressed her mouth to Emilia's ear and whispered, "Say it."

Emilia suppressed a shudder. The slight flutter in her throat became a steady thrashing, and an intense heat spread beneath her skin, burning her from the inside out. The words tumbled out of her mouth before she could even think twice. "Yes, Captain."

What the hell was this pirate doing to her?

Maria stepped back, and her smile was, at once, the most enraging thing Emilia had ever seen *and* the most alluring. "Until your captain's death or your own?"

Emilia narrowed her eyes at that. *Be careful what you wish for, Captain.*

She reined in her anger as well as she could and forced out another, "Yes, Captain."

Maria held out her free hand. "Hand?"

Emilia offered her own, watching as Maria's fingers curled around her wrist. The pirate captain's grip on Emilia's wrist was soft but firm, holding Emilia in place—but without causing her pain. Emilia frowned worriedly, as Maria, once again, lifted her sword.

Don't you dare cut off my hand, you crazy asshole.

Maria obviously didn't hear Emilia's silent threat, but she must've noticed something in her expression—because she laughed. "Just a drop, remember?"

Emilia winced a little, when Maria sliced a shallow cut into Emilia's finger. "Did you really need a sword for that?" she said, when the blood surfaced on her fingertip. "A small knife would have sufficed."

Maria snorted at her snarky remark. "Don't worry," she whispered to Emilia. "I cleaned it this morning."

Emilia remembered the pirate captain's swords slicing Paul open the day before and was grateful.

Maria pressed Emilia's fingertip against the scroll, letting Emilia's blood soak into the parchment. "*Now*, it's done," she whispered. Her warm, brown eyes shifted to meet Emilia's, and her soft, full lips curved into a wicked smile. "You're officially mine."

Emilia swallowed. She felt the warmth of Maria's body all around her. Maria's fingers pressed against hers, still. The front of Maria's body pressed against her side. And Maria's face was so close to her own that she felt the warmth of Maria's breath on her lips.

Where Maria's muscles were hard and unyielding, her eyes were the opposite. They were deep pools of silky darkness that Emilia felt herself sinking into—the tether of reality slowly slipping from her hands.

Maria stepped backward. "You're dismissed."

The tether jerked Emilia back so suddenly that she nearly fell. She turned to leave, her head still reeling.

"Not you."

Maria's smooth, lilting voice cut through the haze in her mind. Emilia glanced at her, blinking slowly.

"You and I need to talk," Maria said, "alone."

Emilia nodded. She watched as Maria sheathed her sword and returned to her chair. Zain and Jonas left, first, with Pelt and Helen trailing not far behind.

Pelt slapped his hand against Emilia's shoulder—nearly hard enough to bruise. With a friendly smile, he said, "Welcome to the crew, Em."

"Thank you," Emilia said, her heart racing.

Why did one kind remark send her into a panic?

Pelt left, and Helen took his spot. The muscular redhead stopped in front of Emilia. "Remember," she said, pointing a *very* dirty finger at Emilia. "Captain doesn't care, as long as we're off the ship. If you've got the patience, lass, so do I." She winked at Emilia.

Maria rolled her eyes. "Get back to work, Helen."

"Yes, Captain," Helen said, waving as she left.

Emilia watched the master gunner with a puzzled frown, and when she turned back toward Judith, she found Judith's eyebrows raised. "Was she just—"

"Yes," Judith said, without waiting for Emilia to finish.

Maria lounged back in her chair. "That's Helen for you," she sighed. "You'll get used to her eventually."

"She's not a bad lay either," Judith said with a grin. "Probably want to avoid the gunpowder, though."

"Don't even think about it, Judith," Maria said.

Judith turned to Maria, her smile wide and guilty. "The advice was for Em," she said, "not for me."

Maria lifted a scarred eyebrow. "You're thinking about it."

Judith chuckled. "That last time *was* a lot of fun."

"The last time," Maria reminded her, "was when you blew a hole in the side of my goddamn ship."

Judith held up a finger. "The last time you *knew* about."

"Judith," Maria said slowly.

"Oh, come on," Judith laughed. "It's not a real law. You didn't even list a punishment!"

"You know what? You're right," Maria said. "I *do* need to list a punishment. Do you have any preferences, Judith?"

Judith snorted at the threat. "A few."

Maria rolled her eyes.

Judith was still laughing, when she turned to Emilia. "You did good, Em," she said, patting Emilia's arm. "I'm proud of you."

Emilia blushed. "I just signed my name," she said, "and bled." She held up her finger for emphasis.

Judith took Emilia's hand into her own, examining the small knick in Emilia's fingertip. "Hey, you cut me deeper than you cut her," she complained at Maria.

"Did not," Maria muttered, but then, she squinted, as if she couldn't quite remember.

Judith leaned closer to Emilia, and with a playful smile, she whispered, "It was ten years ago. I have no idea how deep it was."

Emilia laughed.

Judith's smile deepened. "You signed the fake name, right?"

Emilia nodded. "Emily Northwood."

"Perfect," Judith said. She released Emilia's hand and curled her fingers around Emilia's arm. "I know it's a lot to take in, but I promise you'll like it here."

Emilia's pulse spiked again. She couldn't afford to like it here. She couldn't afford to let down her guard.

Judith must've noticed her anxiety. "You all right?"

"Yeah," Emilia said breathlessly. "Thanks, Judith."

Judith smiled at her. "Welcome to the crew, Em."

Again, that unfamiliar warmth filled Emilia's chest.

"When you're done here, you and I are going to celebrate with drinks," Judith said. She cast a playful glance in Maria's direction. "But until then, I better get out of here before the captain has me whipped for *thinking* about breaking her sacred Helen rule."

Maria snorted at that.

"Bring her back in one piece, Captain," Judith said.

"No promises," Maria said.

Judith waved to Emilia on her way out of the cabin.

"Sit," Maria said, once the two of them were alone.

Clearly, the woman had never heard of a request.

Emilia returned to her seat, but she didn't bother to hide her irritation. "I signed your Code. What now?"

Maria lounged lazily in her chair, barely even lifting an eyebrow at Emilia's attitude. "I told you. We talk," she said. She took an apple from a bowl on her table, turning it over in her hand. "And *you*, thief, will eat."

Maria tossed the apple at Emilia, and with a squeak of surprise, she closed both hands around the apple—just in time to stop it from slamming into her chest.

A small cut on her finger, she could handle. Taking an apple to the breast, on the other hand, was a pain that Emilia would've found a little less forgivable.

"Eat," Maria repeated.

Emilia glanced down at the shiny, red apple in her hand. "Is this a test?" she said, frowning at the pirate captain. "Because I just signed about the...rations?"

Maria narrowed her dark, brown eyes. "If I tell you to eat, you eat," she growled. "No questions asked."

Emilia scowled. "Are you always so domineering?"

"I'm a captain," Maria said. "What do you think?"

Had Catherine been this pushy toward her crew?

"It doesn't count against your rations, if I give it to you," Maria told her. "It's from my personal stores—same as if Judith were to give you some of her rum."

"But I'm not supposed to drink that," Emilia said.

Maria waved a hand at that. "Drink whatever you like," she muttered. She tilted her head back. "Just don't say I didn't warn you when it fucks you up."

"If it's that bad," Emilia said with a curious frown, "why does Judith buy it?"

Maria sighed. "Because she loves her brother."

"Her brother?" Emilia thought about the old man at the well. He'd been alone, hadn't he?

There hadn't been any children with him.

"James," Maria muttered. "Too much like his father, if you ask me. But Judith loves him."

"Her father," Emilia said in a hollow tone.

Maria's dark gaze cut toward Emilia, as sharp and sudden as a dagger. "What do *you* know of her father?"

Emilia hesitated. Would Maria be angry, if she knew they'd taken a small detour on the way to the ship the night before?

It seemed like such a small thing, but still...

"Nothing," Emilia said, but when Maria's eyes narrowed suspiciously, Emilia quickly amended, "She mentioned you nearly killed him once."

Apparently, that worked—because Maria nodded and looked away.

"If you'd ever met him, you'd understand why," Maria said.

Emilia swallowed uneasily. She *really* wasn't cut out for this much deception.

"Her brother's a drunk, just like his father was, but," Maria sighed, "so far, he's been smart enough not to cross me."

Emilia frowned.

'The captain won't like it, if you mess with her,' Judith had told her father.

What exactly had Judith's father done?

"What, um—" Emilia stammered. "How does buying rum help her brother?"

"It lets him think he's done something successfully," Maria said, "rather than only surviving off his sister's pity."

"He brews rum," Emilia realized.

"Badly," Maria said.

Emilia traced the smooth skin of the apple with her thumb. The thought of Judith caring so much for her brother bewildered Emilia. She couldn't imagine her own family ever caring that much —even before their deaths. "How does he survive, then?"

"I told you," Maria said. "I take care of my own."

Emilia didn't know what that meant. Did Maria pay his living expenses? Did she pay for a caregiver? Did she pay for both? "He's part of your crew, too?"

"No," Maria said. She glanced at Emilia, her eyes dark and inscrutable. "But Judith is."

Emilia frowned, her pulse rattling in her head. This was completely contrary to everything Catherine told her. Maria didn't seem to be driven by greed at all.

It wasn't that she was surprised that Catherine had lied about it. Obviously, Emilia understood, by now, that Catherine was a liar— and a good one, too.

It was more that she was surprised that *Maria* was different. What kind of pirate gave away her gold?

"You're still not eating," Maria reminded her.

Emilia sighed at her. "Why do you care what I eat?"

Maria lifted a scarred eyebrow. "Why can't you just do as your captain says?" When Emilia *still* didn't eat the damn apple, Maria said, "You admitted earlier that you haven't eaten well since you escaped the gallows. How long has it been?"

Emilia stared at the apple in her hand, unable to meet the captain's dark, calculating gaze. "I traveled from Regolis to Nefala on foot."

"So, quite some time, then?" Maria assumed.

Emilia's chest tightened at the memories. "Yes."

"I know how things work in the dungeons," Maria said, her voice strangely calm, despite the subject. "You're only fed after torture—and the amount of food you're given is determined by how much information you give them." Her dark gaze traveled the length of Emilia's body. "From the looks of you, I'd say you didn't give them much."

Emilia frowned at that assumption. "I'm not thin."

"But you're thinner than when you went in," Maria said. Again, her gaze drifted downward. "Aren't you?"

Emilia looked down. She tugged at her loose, black trousers, knowing there was no point in denying it.

She heard the soft brush of leather—and saw, in her peripheral, Maria shift in her chair, propping one leg on top of the other. "You haven't seen your reflection, have you?" Maria said, her voice smooth and lilting.

Emilia let out a soft, bitter laugh. "How could I have?"

Maria nodded slowly. "Then, you don't know how sickly you look." It was a statement, not a question.

189

"Paul might've mentioned it," Emilia admitted.

Maria lifted that scarred eyebrow of hers. "Paul?"

"That was his name," Emilia said, her tone full of accusation. "The man you murdered yesterday?"

Maria watched her closely. "Was he your friend?"

"Far from it," Emilia said. "He blackmailed me."

The intrigue that burned in Maria's brown eyes told Emilia that the pirate captain wouldn't hesitate to do the same, given the opportunity. "With what?"

Without thinking, Emilia said, "My true identity."

Why had she told her that?

"So, the only person in Nefala who knew your true identity is dead?" Maria said. She leaned back in her chair. "It sounds like you should be thanking me."

With an incredulous stare, Emilia said, "I'm not going to thank you for slicing a man open and spilling his guts in the dirt."

There wasn't a shred of remorse in Maria's eyes. "Would you have preferred I'd given *you* his guts?"

Emilia frowned. "What? No. Why would I—"

Maria shrugged, her smile as self-satisfied as her posture. "Then, let's leave them to the dirt, shall we?"

Emilia stared at her. "You don't feel any remorse?"

Maria laughed in disbelief. "For killing a thief?"

"You're a pirate!" Emilia said. "Along with every other sort of criminal you are, you are also...a thief!"

Maria dropped both feet to the floor and leaned forward. "And there isn't a single person in all of Aletharia who would feel remorse for killing *me*."

Emilia blinked, her head reeling from the truth of that statement. She remembered the gleeful pride in Catherine's voice when she'd spoken of nearly killing Maria once before—the absolute joy at the prospect of seeing her hang one day. And more than that, she remembered how absolutely certain Catherine had been of the fact that she'd be hailed as a hero, if she were the one who finally killed Captain Maria Welles.

Maria knew how much the world hated her.

She knew the truth and was hardened by it.

Despite Emilia's anger and bitterness, she couldn't imagine ever knowing that and not being hurt by it.

It had certainly hurt *her*. In a small, pained voice, Emilia confessed the truth that she'd realized the first night in those dungeons: "I don't think anyone would feel remorse for killing me, either."

Maria gave a small nod. "Now, you're getting it."

Emilia looked away, her heart raw and aching.

"Eat the apple, thief," Maria said. "You're severely malnourished, and you're of no use to me if you die."

"I was never going to die," Emilia assured her. She could've kept herself alive indefinitely, if she needed to—thanks to a few incantations her mother taught her. More pain blossomed in her chest at the thought of her mother. "Besides, with as much as you keep insisting I eat, I doubt I'll starve anytime soon."

With a smirk, Maria said, "No need to thank me."

Emilia rolled her eyes and took a bite of the apple.

Maria's dark brown eyes seemed to follow every movement of Emilia's mouth. "You and Judith are behaving like close friends already," she remarked.

Emilia froze, a bite of apple still in her mouth. She swallowed it and replied, "Not as close as you two."

Maria leaned back in her chair, her eyebrows lifting. "Judith and I grew up in Nefala together. She's been my cook for nearly ten years—and my friend, long before that. We've been separated once —in all of that time."

Once?

When you got your scars, you mean?

But Emilia knew better than to ask that out loud.

"We're practically sisters," Maria admitted. "You, on the other hand, have only known her for a day."

Emilia nodded. "She's been really kind to me."

Maria's gaze softened at that. "Do you trust her?"

Emilia frowned suspiciously. "Why do you ask?"

Maria shrugged her lean shoulders. "Curiosity."

"I don't trust anyone," Emilia assured the pirate captain. *Especially not humans*, she added silently.

The smile that spread across Maria's face was full of pride. "Spoken like a true pirate."

Emilia bristled at that. "I'm not a pirate."

Maria leaned forward, like a lion, about to pounce. "Oh, but you are," she purred. "You're sailing under Captain Maria Welles. It doesn't get any more pirate than that, love." Her smile widened, and she pushed the Code that Emilia had just signed across the table. "And I have the proof, right here, in blood and ink."

Emilia stared at her own unfamiliar signature, the apple forgotten in her hand. "It's a fake name."

"But real blood," Maria said. "Still binding."

Emilia took a bite of her apple. She was grateful for the fruit, then, because it gave her something to do with her mouth, while her entire body surged with panic. It took her a few moments to muster up the courage to ask the one question she needed to ask.

"Are you going to release me?"

"Haven't decided yet," Maria said.

They weren't friends. They weren't even allies, really. But the cold dismissal in the pirate captain's voice stung like betrayal.

Emilia set down the apple, her appetite suddenly gone. "You knew I planned to leave," she said, her voice thick. "You knew, and you didn't even bother to warn me about your ridiculous Code."

"There's nothing ridiculous about my Code," Maria said. "What's ridiculous, thief, is that you asked a favor from me and are now surprised that it came at a cost." She laughed, her smile predatory as a shark's. "I'm a pirate, love. What did you expect?"

Judith's warning suddenly rang loudly in Emilia's head: *"Oh, you poor thing. The captain'll take more than you ever intended to pay."*

"I gave you so many chances to walk away," Maria said, her eyes dark. "I even offered to get you work with Adda, but that wasn't good enough for you. You trusted a pirate, Em. *That's* what's ridiculous."

Emilia looked away, humiliation churning in her stomach. She knew Maria was right, and that made her gloating that much harder to stomach.

"You can only dangle your naïveté in front of me so many times before I'll bite," Maria whispered.

Emilia shuddered. The last thing her overwhelmed brain needed, at the moment, was to think of Maria's bite—in *any* sense of the word. The heat of frustration turned to one of lust far too easily.

On the bright side, the anger Emilia felt over her own attraction cleared her mind enough to respond.

"I wasn't naïve," Emilia said.

"No?" Maria said with a cruel smile. "When you came to me, asking for help, you said you didn't *want* to be a pirate. You didn't *want* to work for me. So, I played around with you a little, and by the time I was done, you were thanking me for hiring you."

Emilia frowned, her blood cooling in her veins.

Maria laughed. "You said you didn't want to be a pirate," she said, tapping her finger against the Code that lay between them, "and now, what are you?"

Emilia didn't answer. She couldn't.

Maria grinned and whispered, "A fucking pirate."

In that moment, Emilia had never hated anyone more than she hated Captain Maria Welles. In another moment, she'd, of course, remember that she hated Catherine far more, but for this moment, at least, she let all of that hatred funnel toward the pirate captain who'd just confessed to tricking her.

Whatever reluctance Emilia had felt toward killing Maria was gone now.

Maria leaned back in her chair. "What's the matter, love? Have I hurt your pride?" She lowered her voice to a growl, "Like you hurt mine, when you asked me to carry you across the sea like a fucking ferry boat?"

Emilia glowered at the captain, red-hot fury searing through her. "I wasn't naïve," she said, once again.

"How did I play you so easily, then?" Maria asked.

"Because I let you," Emilia said. Pain and bitterness bled into her words. "I was naïve once. I trusted someone who was supposed to love me. I trusted someone who wasn't *supposed* to betray me. *That* was naïve, and I paid for that mistake. I paid dearly." She leaned forward, anger burning through every vein. "But you? I never trusted you. I knew the risk and chose to do it, anyway. I made a deal with you—not because I trusted you, but because, well… at least I know what you are."

Maria settled back in her chair, a smile turning up at the corners of her lips. If Emilia didn't know better, she might've thought the captain looked…impressed.

"Then, lie in the bed you made, thief," Maria said.

"You know I'll leave either way," Emilia warned.

Maria looked away, drumming her fingers against the hilt of her sword. "We'll see," she murmured.

Emilia narrowed her eyes, not satisfied with that answer. "You're not going to stop me from leaving."

When Maria's dark gaze shifted back toward her, any hint of amusement had vanished. "For fuck's sake, Em," she muttered. "I'm not going to tie you up and keep you against your will. If you desert, you desert. Just don't think you can come crawling back to me afterward. If you leave, you're dead to me."

"Oh, don't worry," Emilia snarled. "I'd never crawl back to anyone—let alone you."

"Finish eating, and get back to work," Maria said.

"Fine," Emilia said. She stood and turned to leave.

"Fine, what?" Maria called after her.

Emilia spun toward her. "Oh, I did say that wrong, didn't I?" She placed her hands on the table and leaned forward. "What I meant to say was: *'Fuck you, Captain.'*"

Maria tilted her head back and laughed, apparently enjoying Emilia's outburst. "Come on and try, then."

Emilia fell silent, instantly flushing at the invitation.

Maria's smile was smug. "Don't forget your apple."

CHAPTER 10
Picking Fights

"Whoa! Let's take it easy on the potato, all right?" Judith rounded the table and took Emilia's knife.

"What are you doing?" Emilia said with a frown.

"Confiscating this," Judith said. She held up Emilia's knife for emphasis. "For the sake of all of those poor potatoes you've been slaughtering."

"You asked me to slice them," Emilia reminded her.

"Em," Judith said, eyeing what was left of Emilia's most recent potato. "You've done a bit more than slice them." She looked up at Emilia, flashing a wry smile. "Whatever they did to you—I'm sure they're sorry."

Emilia glanced down at the potatoes and realized, with chagrin, that she *had* sliced them too thin. "I got a little carried away," she admitted, wincing. "Can you still use it?"

"Of course," Judith assured her. She leaned her hip against the table. "Want to talk about what's got you feeling so murderous today?" She offered Emilia a kind smile, sympathy shining in those bright blue eyes of hers. "Or should I say…whom?"

With the realization that Judith knew, already, what was bothering her, Emilia's frustration came spilling out much too easily. "How can you *stand* her?"

Judith lifted both eyebrows. She set the knife aside and crossed her arms. "That's a loaded question."

Whatever discomfort the heat caused was only intensified by the anger burning in Emilia's veins. It was enough to suffocate her. "Is it because you grew up in Nefala together? Was she different back then?"

"Of course she was different then," Judith said. "We were all different then." She shrugged. "But if you're assuming I'm only loyal to her now because of who she was then, you're wrong. She's a good captain."

"She's selfish and manipulative," Emilia argued.

Judith laughed softly at that. "She's a pirate."

Emilia looked away, the frustration churning in her stomach. "She gloated about it. It's bad enough that she tricked me. She didn't have to gloat about it."

Judith nodded. "She humiliated you."

"No," Emilia sighed, "it wasn't—" She stopped and glanced at Judith. She didn't know why it was so easy to talk to the ship cook. She didn't know why she felt like they were friends already. But in that brief moment, she'd almost blurted out the truth.

The truth was...no, Maria wasn't the person who'd humiliated her. It was Catherine who'd done that.

Maria had simply pricked the wound.

Judith dropped her arms to her sides. "Look," she said with a sympathetic smile, "why don't you go up and take a walk around the deck? You'll feel better."

"I'm fine," Emilia said.

"Em," Judith said. She placed a hand on Emilia's arm. "You look like you're about to pass out. It's hot. Get you some fresh air, and then, come back down."

Emilia shook her head. "You heard her this morning," she sighed. "I have to prove I'm useful."

"You are," Judith said. She waved a hand at the potatoes. "You've already sliced three times as many as I need. You've been plenty useful. Take a break."

Emilia's brows furrowed. "I sliced too many?"

"Don't worry about it," Judith reassured her. "I'll use them for the evening meal. You've been perfect."

Emilia smiled hesitantly at that. "Are you sure?"

"I am," Judith assured her. "You're angry. You're overheated. You're boiling on the inside and the outside, and that's not pleasant for anyone." She picked up an empty tankard. "Get some fresh air, and I'll have you some rum waiting, when you get back."

Emilia nodded reluctantly. "Thank you, Judith."

Judith nodded. "I only ask one thing," she said, holding up a finger. "Avoid the captain, if you can."

Emilia frowned. "Because I'm not supposed to be up there?" she assumed.

"No," Judith said. "Because I'm afraid you'll try to do to her what you did to my potatoes."

Emilia glanced at her bowl of potatoes and nodded. After what Maria had said to her earlier, slicing her into small pieces *would* make Emilia feel better.

Judith laughed. "I see that contemplative look, and let me just go ahead and tell you: it's not worth it."

An amused smile curved at the corners of Emilia's lips. "I think it would be cathartic, actually."

"She'd fucking kill you, Em," Judith said. She placed her hands on Emilia's arms. "Promise me you're not going to get yourself killed."

Emilia smiled, warmed by the concern. "I promise."

Judith patted her arm. "Perfect. Get out of here."

JUDITH WAS RIGHT ABOUT ONE THING.

It was much cooler above deck.

The sun still burned Emilia's fair skin, and the tropical heat still took her breath sometimes.

But the cool, salt-scented breeze made all the difference.

They didn't have that in the galley.

Emilia didn't walk far, before she caught sight of Maria—on the quarterdeck with Fulke.

Maria might've been tall next to most other people, but she looked like a child next to him.

Well…not a child, really.

No child would have such a lethal form.

Fulke must've been teasing her the way he had Judith—because after one particular hand gesture, Maria chucked an empty rum bottle in his direction.

Emilia could nearly hear their laughter over the deafening snapping of the sails.

Emilia turned away with a scoff. *Of course* Maria was still enjoying her day—as if she hadn't just sent Emilia into a murderous rage.

What had she expected?

Remorse?

Decency?

From Captain Maria Welles?

On second thought, perhaps some part of Emilia *was* still naïve.

Thanks to her blind rage, Emilia managed to walk straight into a large hulk of a man for the *second* time that day.

Unfortunately, the *gentle* giant was on the quarterdeck with Maria, which meant this particular, large, burly sailor was…the other one.

"You again," Buchan sneered.

Emilia avoided eye-contact with the bad-tempered pirate. "Unfortunately, yes."

Despite the light tan he'd already had, the sun had still reddened his skin a bit since their last collision.

And it certainly hadn't softened his mood any.

"I think you owe me an apology," the sailor demanded.

"Yeah, I—"

And honestly, she was just about to apologize to the asshole, before he opened his big mouth.

"Look at me when I'm talking to you, lady."

Emilia froze.

Honestly, she didn't like to make eye-contact much at all. It disrupted her thoughts and made her uneasy.

Perhaps that's why she loved her dragons so much.

They understood. Humans never had.

But she certainly wasn't about to make eye-contact with someone who spoke to her like that.

Considering what she *wanted* to do was slice him up like she had Judith's potatoes, Emilia thought she was showing a lot of restraint, when she said, "I think I'll just be going now."

But when she tried to step past the guy, he grabbed her arm.

"Did you not hear me, bitch?"

Emilia turned to glare at him. "Get your hand off of me."

Buchan narrowed those cold, grey eyes of his. "Or what?"

Some nearby hammering stopped, and within a few moments, a somewhat familiar face had entered Emilia's vision.

The man with sandy-blonde hair—*Jonas,* Maria had called him—approached them cautiously.

With a hammer still in his hand, the carpenter glanced back and forth between them.

With a wary smile, he said, "You making enemies already, Em?"

"Apparently," Emilia snarled.

Jonas leaned toward Buchan. "Look, I think the captain might be a bit...fond of her new surgeon, so..."

"Oh, is that it?" Buchan said to Emilia. "Is that why she humili-ated me earlier? Because you're fucking her?"

"What?" Emilia said. "No, I'm not—"

"I should've known," Buchan scoffed. "She's always so protective of her whores."

Jonas glanced toward the quarterdeck, where Maria was probably still having a carefree time with Fulke. "Buchan, it's not worth it," he hazarded. "Just let the girl go."

"She owes me an apology," Buchan said.

Jonas cast a hopeful look in Emilia's direction.

But Emilia snarled at the belligerent sailor, "You're not getting anything from me."

After everything Emilia had been through recently, she didn't have enough dignity *left* to sacrifice any for someone who spoke to her like this.

Spotting the quartermaster a few feet away, Jonas waved him down.

"Are you sure you want to pick a fight with me, little girl?" Buchan sneered.

Emilia stepped closer. "Are you sure you want to pick one with me?"

The tall, muscular mountain of a man laughed, as if she'd lost her mind.

But he had no idea what she was capable of.

The rage boiling between them must've been tangible—because Zain approached them just as cautiously as Jonas had.

"Is everything all right?" the quartermaster said.

When neither of them answered, Jonas said, "Get the captain."

With a sigh, Zain left to do just that.

Apparently, those were the magic words—because Buchan *finally* released her arm.

"You better sleep with one eye open, little girl," he said.

Not at all intimidated by the threat, Emilia rolled her eyes and turned to leave.

She only made it a total of one step, though, before she heard him mutter something to Jonas.

"She does have a nice ass, though. Maybe, before I kill her, I'll—"

The last ounce of patience that Emilia had managed to preserve snapped.

She didn't even wait for him to finish that before she turned and punched him.

Despite their size difference, Emilia still managed to hit him hard enough to unsettle his balance for a moment.

But when Buchan reached up to touch his nose and found it clean of blood, he laughed at her.

"Big mistake, little girl," Buchan said.

Jonas stepped back, clearly not wanting to get caught in the middle of the fight.

Emilia managed to dodge Buchan's first punch, but the second sent her head spinning and her body sprawling face-first onto the deck.

She pushed herself up onto her hands, waiting for the deck to stop spinning, before she climbed to her feet.

Warm blood spilled down her cheek—the skin split open after only one punch.

She climbed to her feet and ran toward him, but he grabbed her with just one arm and flung her back to the deck.

Her head still rattled from the first punch, she clumsily tried to climb back to her feet.

She only needed to use a bit of magic, and she'd subdue the man easily.

But with Jonas watching her so closely, Emilia knew she couldn't use her magic.

Buchan punched her before she even made it to her feet, and she hit the deck again.

Pain exploded throughout her entire body, as Buchan delivered a sharp kick to her left side.

On instinct, Emilia curled away from the blow, but Buchan continued to kick without mercy—whether his boot connected with her abdomen, her side, or her back.

Time passed in a blur of pain, as she fought her way back to her hands and knees.

The kicking stopped at some point—though Emilia was too disoriented to say when.

Emilia thought she heard laughter, muffled somewhere beneath the pounding in her head.

She coughed up a mouthful of blood, before lifting herself onto her knees.

The deck spun around her—Buchan's large form nothing more than a shadow at the edge of her blurred vision.

He was talking to Jonas, laughing and mocking her for going down so easily.

That's why, despite the pain throbbing in every muscle and vein in Emilia's body, she refused to stay down.

Emilia slowly, unsteadily, climbed to her feet, bracing herself for another attack.

When the pirate saw that she was on her feet again, he started toward her again.

Emilia didn't know how much more she could take, but she had no intention of letting someone who treated her like this win.

At some point, a crowd had gathered around them, dashing Emilia's last hope of using magic against her opponent.

As the large sailor approached her in what felt like slow motion, Emilia straightened her back and prepared for the onslaught of blows that would hit her next.

Buchan was just about to grab her, when someone stepped between them.

Even though her back was to Emilia, even though Emilia could barely see at all, she still recognized those lean muscles and slender, leather-clad hips.

Maria.

"Back the fuck off," the pirate captain snarled.

Buchan immediately raised both hands in surrender.

Maria held one sword in her hand—while the other hung at her waist, still. The pirate captain pressed the tip of her sword against Buchan's throat, forcing him back a step. "You better have a good fucking explanation, sailor."

"It was her, Captain," Buchan said. Fear flashed in his wide, grey eyes. "She punched me."

Maria turned, pointing her sword at Emilia's throat, instead.

Emilia wobbled slightly on her feet—but she stood as steady as possible, as the blade pressed against her throat.

Maria's eyes were even darker than usual, as alluring and mysterious as the darkest, deepest depths of the ocean. "Is that true, surgeon?"

Burning pain spread through Emilia's face, her cuts irritated by the salt air, but Emilia held her head high, anyway, refusing to cower. "Yes," she said, "but—"

"That's all, surgeon," Maria snarled. Beneath her black, leather doublet, her chest rose and fell quickly, and anger boiled visibly in her brown eyes. She kept her sword on Emilia—even as she addressed the witnesses. "Can you confirm this, quartermaster?"

Emilia cast a wary glance at Zain—who stood off to the side, watching. There was something positively chilling about the way Maria referred to each one of them by title, instead of name, when she was furious.

It was like an assurance that her personal feelings meant nothing to her, in that moment. She'd cut it off, instantly. Each growled title was a promise that she'd show you no mercy—no matter who you were to her.

She wasn't a companion or a lover, in that moment.

She was Captain Maria Welles, and she'd slice open her closest friend's throat, if the situation called for it.

"I didn't see enough to confirm it, Captain," Zain said regretfully. "I came to you the moment I realized that neither of them intended to back down."

Maria stepped closer, pressing the sharp tip of the sword against Emilia's throat. "Who else saw?"

"Jonas was here, Captain," Zain told her. His dark gaze shifted toward the blonde man who'd watched, as Buchan harassed her. "Perhaps he can confirm."

Frustration twisted in Emilia's chest. Of course the only witness would confirm Buchan's accusation.

They were friends—fellow crew mates.

And Emilia was just an outsider to them.

"Well?" Maria said to Jonas. "Tell us what you saw, carpenter."

Again, no name.

Just a cold, impersonal title.

Jonas stepped away from the rail, straightening. His gaze met Emilia's, briefly, before he said, "She isn't to blame, Captain." He ignored the shocked look that Buchan shot his way. "Buchan was harassing her. She asked him to stop. He didn't. I'm sure I'd punch someone, too, if they were treating me like that."

There was a quiet chuckle in the crowd of pirates, who'd gathered around to watch, but Maria didn't laugh. As a matter of fact, she, somehow, impossibly, looked even angrier than before. She spun, the heels of her boots grinding into the deck, as she pressed the tip of her sword against Buchan's throat. Again.

"You lied to me, sailor," Maria said in a low tone.

Buchan kept his hands up, but his fingers trembled now. "Captain, I—" he stammered, "I didn't lie. She *did* punch me first." Worry twisted at his brow. "I was only teasing. It's not my fault she can't take a joke."

Emilia narrowed her eyes at that.

A dangerous smirk tugged at one corner of Maria's lips. She lowered her sword, shrugging those strong shoulders of hers. "What are you so afraid of?" she said with a chilling laugh. "Fighting is barely even mentioned in the Code. It's not punishable by death."

Buchan blinked. "Oh," he said. He slowly lowered his hands, and a hesitant smile spread across his face.

"You didn't need to lie," Maria scoffed. "I would've given you a small reprimand or perhaps taken some rations." A cruel smile curled at the pirate captain's lips. "But there would've been no honor in killing you. Not without a clear crime."

A strange sense of dread unfurled in Emilia's stomach. She could almost feel the sinister fury radiating from Maria. She wondered if anyone else sensed it, too.

Considering the relief on Buchan's face, Emilia thought that, no, perhaps he hadn't recognized it.

"Of course, Captain," he said. "I understand."

Maria tilted her head. Her stance left much of her side and back to Emilia. Perhaps *that* was why Emilia was the only one who noticed the subtle twitch of her bicep and the shift of muscles in her back.

Emilia cringed, just a moment before she heard the soft *squelch* of Buchan's intestines, as Maria shoved her sword through him. Silence fell over the ship.

Maria curled her hand around Buchan's shoulder, holding him still, as he bled out around her sword. "But you don't care for honor, anyway, do you?"

Maria pulled the sword upward, slicing all the way to his sternum. Only when the life drained from his gray eyes, did she rip the blood-soaked blade from his body. She stood tall over him, as he collapsed.

She turned to the crew, and when the sunlight fell upon her, the thin spray of blood glistened on her dark skin. "If you don't have the nerve to tell me the truth, get off of my fucking ship!"

Her voice carried across the ship, the words ringing loudly in Emilia's head. Much like the night they met, Emilia was left asking herself: *How long until Maria turns her swords on me?*

When no one made a move to leave, Maria held out her blood-soaked arms and said, "Then, get back to work."

Emilia was more than happy to follow *that* order. After watching the captain slice someone open, yet again, for little to no reason, Judith's friendliness and *lack* of homicidal tendencies seemed preferable.

But Maria grasped her arm and wrenched her back, before she could. "Not you," Maria snarled in her ear.

Maria pushed Emilia against the rail and held her sword at an angle between them. The blood-soaked blade hovered near Emilia's throat—but didn't touch her. The contrast of the soft warmth of Maria's hips and the cold blood on her skin disoriented Emilia.

Or perhaps that was the concussion.

As the crew dispersed, Maria turned her rage on Emilia. "Didn't I tell you not to start any shit with him?"

Emilia met the captain's furious gaze with her own. "Didn't a witness just tell you that I *didn't* start it?"

"Lucky for you," Maria said, practically spitting the words in Emilia's face. That familiar fire burned in Maria's brown eyes, drawing Emilia in—even as everything else warned her to stay away.

The creaks and groans of the ship fell away—until all Emilia could hear was the sound of her own blood and the sound of the quick, shallow breaths falling from Maria's lips.

Maria lowered her sword—so that she could close the space between them. Her lean form pressed Emilia against the rail, and her eyes darkened. "At least have the sense to not look so fucking defiant when your captain addresses you."

Emilia held her gaze, refusing to flinch, even as her entire body tried to melt beneath those warm eyes.

Maria's gaze roamed Emilia's face for a moment, and then, she breathed out a slow sigh. Emilia nearly collapsed in relief, when Maria finally looked away.

Maria stepped back and slid her sword back into its scabbard. Her gaze strayed toward the blood-soaked corpse on the deck, and she ran her hand across the back of her neck.

Emilia watched Maria's tattooed fingers entangle in her curls, and she couldn't help but wonder how soft those curls might feel against her own fingers.

An odd thought to cross her mind, at the moment.

Emilia blamed *that* on the concussion, too.

Maria's gaze returned to Emilia. She stepped closer, and with surprising gentleness, Maria curled three fingers around Emilia's chin. She turned Emilia's face to the left and then to the right, studying the bruises.

All of the anger and arrogance that had previously radiated from Maria seemed to have washed away with the tide, leaving something softer in its wake.

"Well," Maria sighed, "you clearly weren't winning the fight." Her lips twitched slightly. "But you held your own. My crew respects that kind of thing." Her hand fell. "You've got nerve, Em. I'll give you that."

Emilia blinked, her stomach fluttering at the praise.

Was this the same Maria who'd just killed Buchan?

The same Maria who had looked more than ready to kill Emilia, too?

Maria stepped closer. That soft, tropical scent—both floral and citric—clung to her, still, mixing with the subtle scent of sweat and the metallic scent of blood.

Maria lifted her hand and gently swiped her thumb beneath a cut on Emilia's cheek. A drop of Emilia's blood lingered on the pad of her thumb, and Maria stared at it, as if it were somehow different from the rest of the blood that marred her skin.

Warm, brown eyes bore into Emilia. "If someone is harassing you, you come straight to me," Maria told her. "You're new. They'll give you a hard time. That's expected. But it sounds like this was beyond that. No one is going to mistreat you on my ship, Em. I don't tolerate that kind of behavior."

Emilia blinked slowly. She couldn't make sense of this side of

Maria. It seemed completely at odds with the vicious side that she'd seen only moments before.

"Do you understand, Em?" Maria murmured. She curled a finger beneath Emilia's chin, lifting her face. "Give me a name, and when I'm done with them, they'll be terrified to even *look* in your direction."

Emilia shuddered. So, the viciousness was still here, then. "I'm not a child, in need of protection."

Maria narrowed her eyes at the challenge. "It's not about protection, thief," she snarled. "It's about what I allow on my ship and what I don't."

Thief.

A jolting reminder of the *other* time Maria chose not to kill Emilia—which was, actually, only yesterday.

Was there any rhyme or reason to who Maria killed and who she didn't? Or was it just a daily routine she liked to keep?

Wash up, get dressed, check the maps, shove your sword through someone's guts, take the helm.

Yeah, that sounded about right.

"I won't let anyone mistreat you," Maria reiterated, "but I also can't have you picking fights you can't win." Her eyes narrowed. "So, you come to *me*. Understand?"

Emilia glared at her. "I could've won, if I'd just—"

"If you'd just *what*?" Maria said. "Fought unfairly? Drawn a weapon?" She leaned closer. "I hope that's not what you were going to say, thief, because then, it would be *your* corpse on my deck." The frown she wore now seemed to deepen her scars. "You signed my Code, Em," she said softly. "Don't break it."

For the first time since the fight, Emilia looked at Buchan—or what was left of him, anyway. He was a mangled mess of blood and spilled guts, at this point, but his face was still intact—still wearing that same, wide-eyed expression he'd had, when Maria plunged her sword through him. There were no bruises on his face, no gashes... Her punches had barely left a mark.

Emilia sighed, "Did he really look that much better off than me?"

Maria followed her gaze, lifting a scarred eyebrow at the corpse. "Well, he doesn't anymore," she teased. She grinned at Emilia. "Your organs still being intact gives you a small advantage."

Emilia tried not to laugh at that. It seemed cruel—considering she'd sort of gotten the guy killed.

Maria's smile deepened the moment she saw the twitch of Emilia's lips. "He's twice your size, Em," Maria said gently, "and he's not malnourished. You are." With a tattooed finger, she tilted Emilia's face toward her own. "You didn't stand a chance. Not in a brawl, anyway."

Emilia stared at her, transfixed by those dark eyes.

Maria breathed out a regretful sigh. "I need to clean this up," she told Emilia. She traced another gash on Emilia's cheek, wiping away the blood with the tip of her finger. "Clean your cuts, love."

Emilia couldn't exactly tell the pirate captain that she could heal herself anytime she wanted. So, she just nodded.

But apparently, that wasn't enough for Maria. She stepped forward. "Say it."

Emilia's pulse spiked, a strange mix of uncertainty and adrenaline filling her chest. "Yes, Captain?"

A smirk twitched at the corners of Maria's mouth—a smirk that Emilia instantly wanted to wipe away.

"Better," Maria said.

And then, she walked off—leaving Emilia to glare at the back of her arrogant head.

JUDITH NEARLY DROPPED AN ENTIRE POT OF WATER, WHEN EMILIA CAME down the steps. "I told you to take a *walk* around the deck, not beat your face against it," she said, her eyes wide. "What the hell happened?"

Emilia didn't know how she must've looked, after that fight, but based on the way Judith looked at her, she figured it was safe to assume it wasn't pretty.

She tried to shrug, but her right shoulder responded only with pain. "I'm not the best at making friends."

Judith snorted. She hung the pot over the fire and then walked toward Emilia. "Has the captain seen?"

"Yeah," Emilia said. "She wasn't very happy with me."

"I imagine not," Judith said with a laugh. She lifted her hand and touched Emilia's jaw, turning her face this way and that, much like Maria had done. She grimaced. "Fuck, Em. What did you fight? A troll?"

"You could say that," Emilia said. "He certainly behaved like one." She sighed, "His name was Buchan."

Judith dropped her hand. "No," she breathed. "You fought Buchan?"

"More like I punched him once," Emilia muttered, "and then, failed to get any other blows in."

Judith stared at her in disbelief. "I'm surprised you even survived."

Emilia looked away. "The captain intervened."

Judith nodded. "What did she say about your face?"

"She wants me to clean the cuts," Emilia said.

"Good advice," Judith said. She waved toward the table. "Have a seat. I'll help you get cleaned up."

Emilia frowned at the offer. "Why?"

Judith strolled toward a crate full of supplies and pulled out a few clean rags. "Because it's hard to clean cuts you can't see," she explained. "Go ahead, and sit down. I'll get the rum and the bandages."

Emilia winced at the thought of rum being poured over her cuts. "I'm a healer. I can do this myself."

Judith glanced back at her. "Surgeon or not, I can clean a cut," she assured her. "Who do you think the captain turned to every time she got *her* face fucked up in a fight?" She grinned.

Emilia lifted her eyebrows at that. "You mean to tell me that Captain Maria Welles has actually lost a fight?"

Judith winked at her. "Don't tell her I told you."

Emilia laughed softly at that—only to immediately clutch her side, as pain lashed through her middle.

Judith frowned worriedly. "He got you there, too?"

"Only a little," Emilia lied. "I'll be fine."

"Does the captain know he hit you in the stomach?" Judith asked. "I've seen people die from that, Em."

He'd kicked her, actually.

Many times.

But Emilia kept that to herself. "It's fine," she told Judith. "I'll make myself a healing tincture tonight."

Judith nodded. "If it gets any worse, let me know."

Emilia didn't know how to respond to Judith's concern. No one had ever cared for her like that before.

Her dragons, perhaps.

But no humans.

"Now, don't make me drag you to the table," Judith said, pointing at her. "Sit down, so I can help."

Emilia begrudgingly went to sit down at the table.

Judith joined her, only a few minutes later, with a bucket of water, a bottle of rum, and a few clean rags.

She knelt in front of Emilia, wincing, as she studied the gashes around Emilia's cheeks and eyes. "Well," she said, "your eyes are still attached. That's good."

"It doesn't *sound* good," Emilia said with a frown. "Not if that's the only thing you can say about them."

"Just don't look at your reflection for a few days," Judith said with a wave. "You'll be fine. Teeth?"

With a roll of her eyes, Emilia opened her mouth.

"Ooh, lucky," Judith said, apparently finding all of those

attached, as well. She dipped one of the rags in the bucket. "Try to keep those in next time, too."

"Next time?" Emilia repeated. "You're anticipating me getting beat up again?"

Judith wrung out the water. "What? With your amiability?" she said, blue eyes sparkling. "Nah."

Emilia laughed and then clutched her side again.

"Easy," Judith said. She leaned forward, crouching on one knee, as she cleaned the cuts on Emilia's face. "How did the captain react?" she asked curiously.

"Not…kindly," Emilia said, blinking at the memory. "She gutted him like a fish. While the crew watched."

Judith froze. "She killed Buchan? For fighting?"

"It wasn't for fighting," Emilia said with a baffled frown. "Honestly, I think he just…displeased her?"

"Ah," Judith said, as if she weren't the least bit alarmed by Maria's homicidal tendencies. She returned the blood-soaked rag to the bucket—and then flashed another one of those contagious grins of hers. "Told you she liked her kills bloody, didn't I?"

Emilia couldn't help but laugh. Clearly, nothing fazed Judith. "How does she manage to keep the loyalty of her crew, when she has no control over her anger?"

"She has plenty of control," Judith assured her.

"So much control that she randomly murders her own crew members?" Emilia challenged.

Judith picked up the bottle of rum and another rag. "The thing you have to understand about the captain is that just because it *looks* like anger, doesn't mean it is." She covered the bottle of rum with the rag and turned it upside down, letting it soak through. "The captain can't bear to look vulnerable. So, no matter what she's really feeling, all you'll ever see is anger."

Emilia's brows furrowed. "Are you trying to say he hurt her feelings?"

"Of course not," Judith laughed. "I'm only saying that she

might've been feeling a bit more than anger, when she saw what he'd done to her new surgeon."

Emilia laughed in disbelief. "Surely, you're joking," she said. "Judith, the captain doesn't care about me."

Judith stared at the rum-soaked cloth, her gaze distant, as she seemed to consider something. "Do you know *why* the captain hates my father?"

Emilia hesitated, surprised by the change of topic. "Why?"

"When we were about twelve, she and I went for a swim together," Judith said softly. "When I took off my shirt, she saw the bruises."

Emilia's stomach twisted with sympathy. "Oh, Judith. I'm so sorry."

Judith nodded, not meeting Emilia's gaze. "The captain went after my father in a blind rage," she sighed. "Most lethal twelve-year-old I'd ever seen."

Emilia frowned at the thought. Clearly, Maria was dangerous now, but as a child, too?

Judith folded the cloth in her hand. "Might've killed him, too, if my brother hadn't started crying."

Emilia's frown deepened. "Crying?"

Judith looked up at her. "James," she clarified. "He was only two at the time."

Emilia's stomach flipped at the thought of such a young child witnessing...*that*.

Emilia had witnessed some pretty gruesome murders when *she* was young, and to this day, she still had nightmares.

Judith leaned forward to wipe the cut beneath Emilia's eye. "I shouldn't have taken you around my father," she admitted. "He's not a good guy."

"It's fine," Emilia assured her. "I wanted to give the bread to someone who needed it. You were only doing what I asked."

"Still," Judith said, shaking her head, "if he'd hurt you..."

When Judith didn't finish that sentence, Emilia frowned, wondering what the rest of it might've been.

"Even if I hate him, I don't want to see him die, you know," Judith sighed.

"No, I get that," Emilia assured her.

Judith glanced up at her. "You do?"

Emilia tried to nod, but her head rattled at the movement. "My mother did some terrible things to me—and to others," she admitted, "but it still hurt when she died."

Judith's brows creased at that.

"Emotions are complicated," Emilia said.

Judith nodded. "My point is," she sighed, "you should never presume to know what the captain is feeling. More often than not, you're only seeing what she wants you to see."

With a skeptical smile, Emilia said, "And what she wants me to see is a ruthless murderer?"

"Better that than vulnerable," Judith said, "don't you think?"

Emilia frowned at that. On one hand, Maria *had* become infinitely angrier, after Jonas told her that Buchan had harassed Emilia. On the other hand, the idea that the same pirate captain who'd tricked her and gloated about it felt any sort of concern for her whatsoever was so far-fetched it was almost comical.

When Judith finished cleaning Emilia's cuts, she leaned back on her heels and said, "Now, tell me about that injured shoulder of yours."

Emilia blinked in shock. How had she known?

Almost as if she could hear Emilia's thoughts, Judith said, "You winced when you moved it."

"My shoulder's fine," Emilia assured her. Maybe it wasn't fine now, but it *would* be fine—as soon as she was able to use her magic without anyone noticing.

Judith's brows furrowed. "Does the captain know?"

No, and Emilia didn't want her to know, either.

"I'm sure she does," Emilia lied.

Judith gave her a skeptical look. "She knew you injured your shoulder and sent you back to work?"

"You think she cares about my shoulder?" Emilia scoffed.

Judith didn't answer that. "Let's have a look at it."

Emilia sighed, "Fine, but only if you promise not to make a big deal about it."

Judith chuckled. "I'm a pirate, Em. You shouldn't be trusting my promises, anyway."

Emilia nodded a little, acknowledging that.

CHAPTER 11
Scheming Ship Cats

K nowing Maria wouldn't be down for the first meal of the day, Judith set aside a bowl of food for her.

It wasn't for lack of appetite that Maria skipped meals on days like today. No, the woman could eat as much as anyone Judith had ever met.

It was shame.

Or fear, perhaps.

She'd been like this since the imprisonment. She always kept to herself after any sort of…emotional outburst?

Was that the right word for it?

Judith wasn't sure.

And so it was a few hours after Judith finished cleaning up that she heard the soft thud of Maria's boots coming down the steps.

"On the table," she called out—from behind a stack of crates.

Wood creaked softly, as Maria sat down to eat.

Judith emerged a few moments later with a crate of supplies. She left the crate on one of the back tables, and then, she took Maria a flagon of ale and an empty tankard.

Maria poured herself a cup. "Where is she?"

Judith didn't need to ask who Maria meant. "I sent her to bed," she said, returning to the other table, "like *you* should've done when you saw her injuries."

Maria sipped her ale. "It was just a few cuts and bruises," she muttered. "I sent her back to you because I knew you'd take care of her."

Judith lifted an eyebrow at that last part. Even when Maria was *trying* to be an asshole, little drops of the truth bled through. "It was more than a few."

Maria set down her tankard. "What do you mean?"

Judith glanced over her shoulder, smiling at Maria. "Is that concern I hear?"

Maria's eyes narrowed. "No."

Judith laughed.

She counted out the supplies she'd need for the evening meal, and Maria returned her attention to her food.

"Thought I was going to have to lock her in her cabin," Judith scoffed. "She's *way* too much like you."

Maria snorted. "Whatever you do, don't tell her that. I think she'd rather burn herself alive than find out she's anything like me."

Judith nodded at that. "She does *really* hate you."

Maria chuckled. "How much do you want to bet she's not in her cabin now?"

Judith cast a worried look in Maria's direction. "She needs rest, Captain. Those injuries of hers are bad."

She'd honestly assumed Maria knew—until she heard the captain's spoon clang against her bowl.

"What injuries?" Maria said.

Judith turned to face her. "She didn't tell you?"

"She didn't tell me any fucking thing," Maria said, tempestuous as ever. "*What* injuries?"

Judith winced at her tone. "Buchan didn't just hit her, Captain," she said. "He beat the shit out of her."

Maria looked down at her bowl and exhaled slowly, her nostrils flaring. She'd rolled her sleeves up to her elbows, but that had only hidden *some* of the blood stains. The blood splatter around her neck and upper arms was still visible, and a bit of blood had dried at the ends of her curly, brown hair, as well.

Buchan had certainly paid for his crimes, whether Maria knew them all or not.

"Where?" Maria said.

"Her shoulder," Judith told her. "She says it's fine, but she doesn't seem to be able to move it very well."

Maria nodded. "He must've grabbed her and slung her."

"I don't know how bad they are, but I think there are some internal injuries, as well," Judith added.

Worry twisted at Maria's brows. "Why would she hide that from me?"

Judith lifted her eyebrows at the inane question. "I don't know, Captain," she said. "Why did *you* always hide your injuries after the fights you lost?"

"That's different," Maria scoffed. "I was always a fighter. She's just a—"

"A woman who hates being underestimated?" Judith interrupted.

Maria hesitated. "Still," she said, with a little less certainty this time, "this was Buchan she fought. The only person on this ship big enough to even *consider* picking a fight with Buchan is Fulke."

"Never stopped *you*," Judith said.

Maria picked up her spoon, pointing it in Judith's direction. "You're starting to annoy me."

Judith smiled. "Only because you know I'm right."

Maria took another bite of her food. With a reluctant sigh, she said, "What's the crew saying?"

Judith abandoned the crate and went to sit in front of Maria. She poured herself a tankard of ale, as well. "Depends on who you ask," she said. "Some of them are warming up to Em already, and some of them are worried *you've* gone mad. The only thing the entire crew seems to agree on is that today was…exciting."

Maria snorted at that. "They do love a fight."

Judith nodded, sipping her ale. "Helen says she wants to set Em up in a fight with a new person every day," she said. "Pelt told her we couldn't afford to have you murder that many of our sailors."

Maria rolled her eyes. "It was *one* sailor."

"It was one *day*," Judith reminded her.

"Oh, save it," Maria scoffed, waving her tankard, "Zain's been lecturing me for the last three hours."

"Oh, I imagine so." Judith sipped her ale. "But you also know he's right," she assumed, "surely?"

Maria avoided her gaze. "Buchan lied to me."

"Yes—which calls for reduced rations, perhaps," Judith said. "Or if you're feeling especially violent, you could flog the skin off his back." She leaned toward Maria. "But it's not a cause for execution, Captain, and you know it." She hesitated, when Maria refused to look at her. "You *do* know it, right?"

"He was a coward," Maria muttered. "I have no use for cowards."

Judith sighed, "That's not why you killed him."

"He lied to me," Maria said again.

"That's not why you killed him, either," Judith said.

Maria set down her tankard. "Then, enlighten me, Judes," she snarled. "Why *did* I kill him?"

"For the same reason you nearly killed my father," Judith said quietly.

Maria flinched at the reminder.

Judith grabbed Maria's tankard and refilled it. She slid it across the table to Maria, and Maria, having a sudden need for it, tilted it up and drank every drop.

"The crew doesn't know that side of you," Judith said softly, "which, I know, in *your* mind, is a good thing, but Captain, it also means you look like a madwoman when you," she resisted the urge to say *overreact* and settled, instead, for, "act like...this."

Maria shrugged those strong shoulders of hers. "So, let them think I'm mad," she said. "Perhaps I am."

Judith shook her head at Maria's attitude. "You're the only captain I'd ever serve. So, I'd really like it, if you didn't get yourself removed any time soon."

With a soft sigh, Maria met her gaze. "You're worse than Zain sometimes, you know that?"

Judith leaned back, her face twisting in horror. She snatched up Maria's bowl and put it on another table.

"No more stew for you!"

Maria chuckled. "It was cold, anyway."

Judith spun toward Maria, pointing a finger in warning. "Keep it up, and I'll tell Adda that it was you who broke her water pot!"

Maria snorted at the threat. "That was twenty years ago, Judes."

"You don't think she'd still be cross?" Judith said.

"No, she would," Maria said. "I'm sure she would."

With a victorious grin, Judith said, "You're not the only one who knows how to blackmail someone, Captain."

Maria lifted her tankard to her mouth, hiding a smile. "Speaking of blackmail," she said, after a moment. "Do you have anything for me yet?"

Judith's smile faded. "You have to give her time to trust me first," she sighed. "It's been one day."

Maria tilted her head at that. "She's latching onto you faster than anyone else ever has."

Judith grimaced at that. Deciding she needed more alcohol for this conversation, she poured herself another tankard of ale. "I hope you've considered the fact that this might...backfire on you," she said worriedly. "I mean, the girl already hates you."

An amused smirk twitched at the corners of Maria's lips. "I don't need her to like me—as long as she likes you."

"Captain, I don't think you understand," Judith said, setting down her tankard. "Why do you think I sent her to get some air in the first place? You want to know the person she *really* wanted to fight, when she picked a fight with Buchan?" She gave Maria a pointed look. "She's sitting right in front of me."

Every ounce of arrogance in Maria's smirk vanished. "You're saying the fight was my fault?"

"No," Judith said, with a bit of hesitation. "I'm only saying that whatever it was you said to Em, before she left your quarters—it *really* hit a nerve."

Maria looked away, and Judith was shocked to see a hint of regret in those dark brown eyes of hers.

Maria set down her tankard. "I need to talk to her."

"Captain," Judith said, even though she knew she was fighting a losing battle, "I don't know if that's such a good idea."

"I'm her captain," Maria said, stubborn as ever. "I need to talk to her."

Judith nodded. "Do what you think is best," she said with a defeated sigh. "Just don't say I didn't warn you, when you push her too far."

Maria sighed at that. "Internal injuries, you said?"

"I think so, yes," Judith said.

Maria shook her head. "Perhaps I let Buchan off too easily."

Judith sat back, her brows high. "I'd love to know what sort of punishment you think is worse than murder."

"There are a few," Maria said. She climbed to her feet. "I need to speak with my—*apparently* injured—surgeon. Feel free to throw out my lukewarm stew."

Judith rolled her eyes. "You just want an excuse to steal more fruit."

"I'll do that regardless," Maria assured her.

Judith laughed at that. When Maria made it to the steps, Judith called out—reluctantly, "There *was* one, small detail she let slip."

Maria stopped. She turned back toward Judith, one hand on the rail already. "What was it?"

With a sigh, Judith said, "Her mother's dead."

Maria's lips parted in surprise.

Judith took another drink of ale. "It seems you two have even more in common than you thought."

MARIA WAS JUST ABOUT READY TO TURN HER ENTIRE SHIP UPSIDE-DOWN, by the time she ran into Helen.

Covered in a layer of gunpowder almost thick enough to hide her freckles, Helen said, "Need something, Captain?"

"Yes," Maria said with an agitated sigh. She'd already rolled up her sleeves and taken off her tricorn, and yet, still, the heat of the gun-deck was stifling. "I lost my fucking surgeon."

Helen laughed, her teeth strangely clean, compared to the rest of her. "Well, I can help you with that."

Maria crossed her arms and lifted her eyebrows.

Helen tilted her head, directing Maria's attention to the right—where Maria's very bruised surgeon was sitting, cross-legged, with a lap full of...*cats*.

Em looked up at Maria, her bright, green eyes innocent as ever. "You were looking for me?"

Maria spread out her arms, baffled by the sight in front of her. "What have you done to my cats?"

Em rubbed the chin of the solid grey cat, while the other six cats competed for her attention. "What do you mean, *'What have I done to them?'*" she said with a laugh. "They're fine."

"I warned her they like to scratch, but," Helen said with a shrug, "apparently, there was no need."

The largest cat in her lap—a silver-and-white tabby with frosty, blue eyes—nudged Em's jaw with his head, and Em, being the strange, little surgeon she was, curled an arm around the feral cat and hugged him, as if he were human.

"Is it true you haven't named them?" Em said with a disapproving glare. "That's awfully rude of you, Captain."

Maria wasn't sure *why* she felt the need to defend herself to this strange, cat-taming surgeon, but in a dumbfounded tone, she said, "They're feral."

"So am I," Em said with the cutest smile Maria had ever seen. "You still let me have a name."

Maria tried to focus on her impatience, rather than being utterly charmed by the sight in front of her, but...well, she'd never seen anything like it.

"Judith said she sent you to your cabin," Maria said.

Em scratched the ear of a small, white cat, while continuing to rub the chin of the grey one. "She did."

"So, why aren't you there now?" Maria asked.

Em lifted both eyebrows in disbelief. "You do see the cats, don't you?"

"Yes, I see them," Maria said with a frown.

Em shrugged. "Then, your question seems rather ridiculous, don't you think?"

"She's been talking to them for like an hour," Helen complained. "Didn't even say hi to me."

Em looked up at the gunner. "Oh," she said, blinking. "Hi, Helen."

Helen grinned and waved. "Hi, Em."

Maria shook her head at both of them. "Judith says you're injured."

"Of course she's injured," Helen scoffed. "She's like two feet tall and picked a fight with a giant."

"I'm well over five feet," Em assured her.

Helen shrugged. "Same difference."

Maria caught the small explosive that Helen was *juggling*, like a fucking apple, and held it out with a glare.

"Sorry, Captain," Helen mumbled.

"I have to let the healing tincture set for a few hours," Em told Maria, "but I'll be fine soon enough."

Maria gave her a skeptical look. "I need to see your injuries."

"Captain, they're on her face," Helen said. "I mean, unless blue and purple are her normal skin tones?"

Maria shot a peeved glare at Helen. "If you don't have enough work to do, I can give you more."

"Message received, Captain," Helen said with a playful salute.

Maria watched the master gunner rush off to...hopefully *not* blow anything up.

When they were finally alone, Maria said, "Come to my quarters, and let me take a look."

Em didn't even stop scratching the cat's ear long enough to *look* at Maria. "I'm fine."

Maria narrowed her eyes. "That's an order, surgeon."

Em breathed out a long sigh, as if Maria were being totally unreasonable. "Fine," she muttered, "but you have to give them names first."

Maria's brows furrowed. "What?"

"You can name one of them, at least," Em insisted.

Maria stared blankly at her. "One of...the cats?"

"Helen named this one Soot," Em said, patting the head of the large, grey cat. She tilted her head toward the little, white one. "And we named this one Winter." She then picked up the enormous, silver-and-white tabby and presented it to Maria. "This one still needs a name."

"Em, you're injured," Maria tried to tell her.

"He still needs a name, Captain," Em said.

It'd help if that smile of hers wasn't so damn adorable. "Rat-Slayer," Maria said. "Now, come on."

"She's not very good at this, is she?" Em whispered to the silver cat. "What do you say, Rat-Slayer? Will it suffice?"

Maria pinned her with a murderous glare. "*Now*, surgeon."

"He says he'll allow it," Em said, "but only on a trial basis."

Maria huffed out an exasperated sigh. "Em, if you don't get off your ass right now—"

"Told you she was rude," Em whispered to her lap-full of cats.

"How are they supposed to hunt rats if they're following you around like some sort of funeral procession?" Maria muttered.

Emilia rolled her eyes at the pirate captain's exaggeration. Only *one* cat was following her, currently, and he was following Maria, just as much as he was following Emilia.

"He's on his dinner break, Captain," Emilia said with a chiding tone. "Stop working him to death."

As Maria opened the door to her cabin, she gave Emilia a puzzled look. "Rats *are* his dinner."

Emilia suppressed a laugh. Laughter hurt far too much, at the moment, to be offering it up freely to her frustrating pirate captain.

As soon as they were in the captain's quarters—with no one but Emilia there to see—Maria knelt and offered her scarred hand to Rat-Slayer.

Already loving her unconditionally, the silver cat accepted her offer and immediately flopped over, displaying his well-fed belly for petting.

This time, Emilia couldn't even suppress her smile.

So, the murderous pirate captain *did* have a soft side.

Surprise sparked like fire in Maria's dark eyes, and one corner of her mouth twitched upward.

Maria happily obliged Rat-Slayer, rubbing his belly with those tattooed fingers of hers.

Unfortunately, her dark gaze flickered toward Emilia much too soon, and she immediately stood, as if Emilia had just caught her committing a crime.

Well, perhaps that was a bad analogy.

The pirate captain proudly committed crimes, whereas petting a cat, apparently, was something she did in secret.

"No, no. Don't let me interrupt," Emilia said. "Rat-Slayer was enjoying that."

Maria narrowed her eyes at Emilia and then stepped past her.

As Maria headed toward the table to light the candles, she said, "Why would you hide your injuries from me?"

"I didn't hide anything," Emilia argued. "*You* didn't ask."

Maria glanced at her, and the crease of her brows deepened. "I suppose you're right," she said with a sigh. "I didn't act too concerned for you, did I?"

Emilia blinked.

Was this some sort of trick?

Was Maria getting ready to kill Emilia and stuff her corpse under the floorboards?

Throw her into the ocean?

Feed her to the cat?

What was the plan here?

When she'd lit the final candle, Maria shook the wooden splint in her hand, extinguishing the small flame. "In the future, I expect you to tell me, if you're injured."

Emilia narrowed her eyes at that. "Out of the two of us, I'm the one who knows the most about injuries," she said. "So, why would I need to tell *you*?"

Maria turned to Emilia, and that familiar flash of anger was back in those dark brown eyes. "I'm your captain."

"For now," Emilia said.

Maria's glare turned murderous. "For the foreseeable future."

"Oh, no, Captain," Emilia said. After the day she'd had, she had no desire to cater to this arrogant pirate's temper. "I *definitely* foresee a future that doesn't involve you."

Maria's nostrils flared slightly at that. "Remove your shirt."

That shocked Emilia so thoroughly that she nearly choked on the air itself. "Excuse me?"

"Your shirt," Maria repeated, as if Emilia simply hadn't heard her. "Take it off."

Emilia balked at the demand. "No."

Maria rolled her eyes and strode toward the bed. She snatched a coarse, linen blanket from the bed and tossed it at Emilia.

"If you're uncomfortable, you can cover up with that," Maria said, "but I need to see your injuries."

Emilia clutched the blanket close, trying *not* to notice how it smelled like hibiscus and oranges, how it smelled like *her*.

"Well?" Maria said, crossing her arms.

"Fine," Emilia said, "but I'll need you to turn around first."

Maria nodded once. "As you wish."

Maria turned to face those floor-to-ceiling windows that set her quarters apart from every other part of the ship, and when only Maria's back was visible, Emilia began to undress.

Mildly offended by the sudden lack of attention, Rat-Slayer yawned, climbed to his feet, and went to join Maria. He circled her ankles, rubbing his fluffy, silver ears against her leather boots.

The captain looked down, lifting a scarred eyebrow at the supposedly 'feral' creature.

Emilia held back a cry of pain, when the shirt finally slipped past her shoulder.

She wrapped the blanket around her bare breasts and was just about to tell the captain she could turn around, when she noticed Maria shuffling her feet.

Maria was *playing* with the cat, letting him attack her boots, while she shuffled them back and forth.

And Emilia was absolutely enamored by the sight.

"You should try the rope," Emilia said, as she watched. "They love playing with rope."

Maria froze, her strong shoulders stiffer than ever.

Emilia rolled her eyes. Literally the only endearing thing the pirate captain had ever done, and she was ashamed of it.

How absurd.

"May I turn around now?" Maria said.

Emilia clutched the blanket closer to her breasts. "Yes."

Maria dropped her arms to her sides and turned to face Emilia.

Rat-Slayer pranced on ahead of Maria, reaching Emilia long before the pirate captain and claiming a spot against her leg.

Emilia smiled at the oversized kitten.

Maria watched with a curious frown. "I don't know what you did to them, but they've never been this friendly before."

"Well, first, I performed an ancient ritual on them," Emilia said. She leaned closer to the pirate captain and whispered, "I call it 'attention.'"

Maria laughed, and a surprising softness surfaced in those brown eyes that were usually so sharp.

Emilia hesitated at the sight, curling her fingers into the thick, beige blanket.

"Would you turn around for me," Maria said in a remarkably gentle tone, "Em?"

Emilia swallowed. When they fought, each insult and retort came so easily, but when Maria was like *this*, Emilia could barely remember her own name.

Maria must've misunderstood Emilia's hesitation. "I won't hurt you. I swear," she said. "I just need to see it."

The steady groans of the ship filled the silence between them, and yet, still, the harsh marcato of Emilia's heart seemed to echo throughout the room.

Emilia turned to face the door. She dug her fingers into the blanket, grateful that she had something to cling to, while her emotions whirled like a maelstrom.

Maria hissed in surprise. "Em…"

Maria's finger brushed lightly over Emilia's skin, and Emilia held her breath.

"It doesn't look good, love," Maria said softly. "There's a lot of bruising around your—"

"Kidneys," Emilia interrupted. "Yes, I know."

Maria traced one of the bruises with her thumb, likely discovering the feverish heat of Emilia's skin. "You're sure you can recover from this?"

"Yes," Emilia assured her. "I've made the healing tincture already. I'll drink it tonight."

"I hope you're right," Maria said, "but Em, I've seen sailors die from this."

Emilia couldn't help but shudder, when Maria's warm fingertip brushed her spine.

Maria jerked her hand back. "Have I hurt you?"

Emilia's cheeks flushed. "No, it was, umm," she paused, far too embarrassed to admit how nice Maria's fingers felt on her skin, "not pain."

Maria was quiet for a moment. Then, with no further comment, she returned to what she'd been doing before.

Emilia held tighter to the blanket, sure that, any moment now, she'd die of embarrassment.

Emilia knew the moment Maria noticed her dragon rune—because she felt Maria's fingertip trace the deep grooves of the mark.

"What the fuck?"

"It's just a mark," Emilia said. She hoped the pirate captain wouldn't recognize it too easily.

After all, it was a symbol all Drakon sorcerers wore.

"It looks like a damn *brand*," Maria snarled. "Who did this to you?"

Emilia frowned at Maria's reaction. "My mother?" she said in a confused tone. "It's a rite of passage on my island."

This particular rune strengthened her magic and helped her link telepathically with her dragons.

She had another on her ankle.

"Your *mother* burned a symbol into your skin?" Maria said. "At what age?"

It had less to do with age and more to do with mastery of magic.

"I received mine at twelve," Emilia said. "I was younger than most."

"You were a child?" Maria realized.

It was an honor, not an atrocity, but how could she make Maria understand that without confessing to witchcraft?

"It's no different from your tattoos," Emilia tried to explain.

But Maria wouldn't listen. "It's very different," she argued.

Emilia stepped forward, and Maria let her hand fall.

Holding tightly to the blanket, she turned to face the pirate captain. "You've seen my injuries," she said. "Am I *allowed* to leave now?"

"I've offended you," Maria realized.

Bright one, *she* was.

"It wasn't my intention," she added.

"Since when," Emilia said, "was it *not* your intention?"

Maria's dark gaze shifted downward, lingering on Emilia's sore shoulder. "I can help with that," she said, as if Emilia had never said anything. "I might not know what to do about the internal bleeding, but I've had that same shoulder injury before. I can help."

Emilia glanced down at her shoulder.

Was the swelling really so obvious?

Rat-Slayer nudged Emilia's ankle affectionately, and Emilia gave him a knowing look.

Scheming, little feline—trying to calm Emilia down so he could have twice the amount of attention.

Unfortunately, it worked.

"What do you have in mind, exactly?" Emilia asked Maria.

"It's something Jane taught me," Maria said with a sly smile. "You remember Jane, don't you? The woman who put her—"

Emilia didn't let her finish. "If you mention the breast incident one more time…"

Maria laughed loudly.

Suppressing a small smile, Emilia said, "I'm not sure how I feel about someone with no experience in healing 'helping me' with my injury."

"Well, I wasn't sure how I felt about having someone with no experience in *sailing* helping me on my ship," Maria countered. "I managed. I'm sure you will, as well."

Emilia scowled. "Just so you know, the only reason I'm even *willing* to let you do this is because I *know* I can undo any damage you do."

"Oh," Maria said with a smirk, "and here I thought you were only humoring me for the cat's sake."

Emilia laughed. "That, too."

Maria's smile deepened. "Go to my bed," she said, "and lie on your stomach."

Emilia squinted at that. "What exactly *did* Jane teach you?"

Maria snorted. "You'll see." She nodded toward the bed. "You can keep the blanket around you, if you like. I only need access to your shoulder."

Worry twisted at Emilia's brows. "Are you *sure* you know what you're doing?"

Maria strode toward that long, wooden table of hers. "I'm always sure."

Emilia lifted her eyebrows. She couldn't argue with *that*.

"And we absolutely cannot do this with my shirt *on*?" Emilia complained.

Maria picked up a small, glass bottle and examined it. "Are you that uncomfortable being topless around me?"

"I'm that uncomfortable being topless around *any* woman," Emilia said, but when Maria lifted a scarred eyebrow, Emilia immediately backtracked. "That...came out wrong."

Maria chuckled. "I think it came out exactly how you meant it."

Emilia glared at her. "I'm not attracted to you, if that's what you're thinking!"

Okay, so that was probably the biggest lie yet, but there was *no* way Emilia was going to let this arrogant pirate think she was into her.

Maria turned to face her, still holding that strange, glass bottle. "On the bed, love," she repeated. "You can bury your face in the pillow and pretend you're not blushing."

At that, Emilia's blush only deepened.

Careful to keep the blanket in her arms, Emilia went to the bed and sat down.

A surprised squeak escaped her lips, when the mattress sank beneath her.

No wonder Maria had complained about the cot in Emilia's quarters.

Maria's bed wasn't a cot or a hammock.

It was an actual *bed*.

Emilia slid her hand over the bedding beneath her, stunned by its softness. When she looked up to comment on it, she was stunned to find Maria unfastening her weapon belt.

"I didn't think I'd *ever* see you without your swords," Emilia muttered.

"You wouldn't have," Maria said, "if you were lying down, like I told you to."

Emilia narrowed her eyes at that. "I was marveling at your bed."

A smirk pulled at one corner of Maria's mouth. "Don't get used to it."

"Wasn't going to," Emilia assured her.

Maria set her swords on the table, still sheathed. "I know you're probably still wearing that dagger of yours," she murmured, "I won't ask you to remove it, but I will warn you not to get any ideas." Her dark eyes shifted toward Emilia. "I can kill you with my bare hands, if I need to."

Emilia rolled her eyes at the threat. "I would *never* try to kill you with the cat watching."

Maria cast a baffled look at Rat-Slayer, who was curled up in the middle of her floor, flicking his silver tail with interest.

Shaking her head, she turned to grab that strange bottle.

She removed the cork and sniffed the liquid inside, and a mischievous smile tugged at her lips.

"What is that?" Emilia asked.

Maria turned to Emilia, her brows high. "Lie...*down*," she repeated in an incredulous tone.

Emilia gave Rat-Slayer a peeved look. "I don't know why you want me to be friendly with her."

Maria jumped when the cat meowed back at her. She glanced back and forth between them, her brows furrowed.

She looked as if she wanted to ask Emilia a question—but thought it was too strange of an idea to entertain.

With an amused smile, Emilia turned, finally, to lie down.

When her face touched the captain's pillow, a familiar scent filled her lungs.

Maria's pillow smelled like the sweetest, most delightful aspects of the tropical seas.

Oh, there was a hint of sweat, too, but more than that, there was the scent of *Maria*.

Silky, hibiscus petals and juicy, mandarin oranges.

Convinced that the scent might somehow hypnotize her into *liking* Maria, Emilia turned her head to the side and tried not to breathe it in too deeply.

With her face toward the wall, it was easy to watch Maria's shadow move from one part of her quarters to the next. The candle-light flickered steadily, causing Maria's shadow to move and change, even when she was still, but it was still clear enough for Emilia to see Maria unfastening her doublet.

Maria removed the leather doublet and draped it over her chair, and then, she rolled the sleeves of her linen shirt even higher around her biceps.

The thin linen clung to Maria's muscles in a way the leather didn't, and even cast in shadow, Emilia could see her strength.

Though it had only been a day, Emilia had quickly grown used to the ambient creaking and groaning of the ship, and she found the sound relaxing now.

The soft thud of Maria's boots warned Emilia of the pirate captain's approach.

Emilia watched Maria's shadow grow larger and darker, and she considered turning to look at her.

"What are you doing?" Emilia asked.

"How many times are you going to ask me that question?" Maria said, her voice much closer, now.

"I don't know. How many times do I need to ask it before you answer?" Emilia countered.

Emilia could only assume the answer was 'a lot more,' since Maria didn't answer *that* question either.

"I won't touch the bruises," Maria assured her. "I don't want to worsen your injuries."

Emilia turned slightly and lifted her head so that she could see the captain.

"What *exactly* are you planning on doing to me?" she repeated.

But again, Maria just laughed. "Head down."

With a disgruntled huff, Emilia let her face fall into the pillow.

Damn it.

She'd forgotten about that hypnotizing scent.

She'd forever blame this day, if she ever found herself liking Maria.

Emilia's eyes popped open, when the mattress sank beneath Maria's weight.

"What are you—"

Her ability to form words fled her body the moment Maria slung a leather-clad thigh over her hips, and Emilia couldn't, for the life of her, remember how to finish that question.

Maria's weight pressed Emilia's hips deeper into the mattress, and Emilia stifled a gasp, when a deep ache opened up between her legs.

Maria stilled for a moment. "Are you all right?"

Emilia was sure she had vocal cords somewhere, but she couldn't seem to find them. "Mmm-hmm."

"Lovely," Maria murmured, and Emilia couldn't tell if she were referring to Emilia's response or something else.

Emilia thought she heard a soft, steady purr coming from somewhere nearby, and she internally rolled her eyes, knowing that the meddling feline was probably elated about this turn of events.

A soft breath fell from Emilia's lips the moment the captain's fingers met her skin.

It was just a brush—the briefest of touches—but it elicited a powerful reaction, all the same.

Maria's palm followed her fingers, pressing down on Emilia's shoulder, while her other hand curled beneath Emilia's arm, adjusting the position.

"This part might hurt," Maria said.

"I know," Emilia said, her voice strained.

She bit back another cry of pain, when Maria popped her shoulder back into place.

The searing pain, as sharp and painful as a burning dagger, eased slightly, after Maria released her.

But a slow ache rose to take its place.

"Talk to me, Em," Maria said softly. "Are you all right?"

"Yeah," Emilia said, her voice muffled by the pillow. "I guess you *did* know what you were doing."

Maria chuckled at that. "You haven't seen anything yet, love."

Emilia opened her eyes. "What?"

Maria's strong, leather-clad thighs seemed to clamp harder around Emilia's hips, as she reached down to grab that small bottle.

Maria then tipped the bottle in her hand and let the oil pour onto Emilia's back.

Emilia gasped the moment the cool oil cascaded over her bare skin, and then, within a moment, she could smell nothing but Maria.

It was as potent as it was pleasant—the scent of hibiscus and citrus—and Emilia realized that *this* was why Maria smelled the way she did.

This oil.

Another soft breath escaped Emilia's lips the second time that Maria's fingers met her skin.

Maria splayed her fingers, pressing the oil into Emilia's skin.

The scented oil warmed beneath Maria's touch, and any discomfort caused by its coolness melted into pleasure.

A soft moan spilled from Emilia's mouth.

If Maria heard, she gave no indication—though her breath *did* seem to quicken afterward.

Before Emilia had fallen in love with Catherine, she'd kept to herself—only ever allowing animals and dragons to invade her space.

Magical beasts and animals were far more trustworthy than humans—and a lot less complicated.

And so, even being touched by Catherine had been a new experience for her.

But this?

She'd never felt anything like this.

Touch meant for comfort—without sexual implications—was foreign to her.

Though...Emilia couldn't exactly say there was *nothing* sexual about the way Maria touched her.

Maria respectfully kept her hands near Emilia's shoulder—avoiding the bruises on Emilia's sides, and avoiding the bare skin of her back.

But still, her weight pressed Emilia into the mattress with each movement.

The pirate captain had to *know* what she was doing to Emilia.

She had to know how sensual each caress had become.

When Maria had finished massaging the tension from Emilia's aching shoulder, her fingers strayed toward Emilia's neck.

Emilia breathed steadily into the pillow, her muscles relaxing beneath Maria's touch.

Her encounters with Maria had always been so tense.

It was strange to feel her body relaxing under the same woman who'd wound her up.

Maria's right hand slid upward, tracing the back of Emilia's neck, and with her thumb, she brushed Emilia's long, black hair aside.

With her face now uncovered, Emilia turned.

Well…she turned as much as she could, anyway, with a woman as strong as Maria on top of her.

She glanced over her shoulder.

Her breath caught in her throat, when she met Maria's dark, lustful gaze.

Beneath that thin, linen shirt, Maria's breasts rose and fell quickly, as if she were out of breath, and a flush burned beneath her smooth, brown skin.

"Umm," Emilia stammered. "Are you done?"

It wasn't the most graceful response, but at least she'd found her vocal cords.

It was…progress.

Right?

Maria blinked, as if coming out of a trance. "Oh," she said with a frown. "Yes." She glanced toward the windows, where the moon had risen high in the night sky. "Yes, I am."

Maria climbed off of Emilia—and then, off the bed, too—and she wiped her hand against her thigh, clearly unconcerned with what the oil might do to her leather trousers.

Emilia sat up slowly, clutching the thick blanket against her bare breasts.

"Does your shoulder feel any better?" Maria asked.

Emilia nodded.

"Good," Maria said.

Behind Maria, Rat-Slayer gave a nettled meow, apparently unimpressed with their clumsy attempts at conversation.

Maria turned and walked to the table, keeping her gaze fixated on anything *but* Emilia.

Emilia still didn't understand what had just happened. She didn't know what to make of Maria's kindness—or whether she'd ever see it again.

"Captain?"

Maria turned, one corner of her mouth twitching upward. "Captain, is it?" she teased. "You're learning, love."

Emilia scowled at that. "I have a question."

Maria crossed her arms and leaned against the table, her shirt flattening against her muscles.

"Go ahead."

"Buchan seemed to think you were," Emilia began, "sleeping with me."

Maria lifted that scarred eyebrow of hers. "That's not a question."

"I suppose he thought that was the reason you defended me earlier," Emilia added.

"Again," Maria said coldly, "not a question."

Emilia sighed at her impatience. "There was a remark he made —I've wondered about it since."

Maria glanced toward the windows. "What did he say, Em?"

"He said you always protect your...whores," Emilia admitted.

Maria's dark gaze shifted back toward Emilia. "What's the matter?" Maria mocked. "They don't use that sort of language on your island?"

"No," Emilia said, but then, she had to clarify, "I mean, no, they don't, but also..." She shrugged—and winced afterward. "I just wondered what it meant."

Maria returned her attention to the window, gazing out at the moonlit waves. With a long sigh, she said, "He was referring to the woman you know as *'Jane.'*"

Emilia's brows furrowed. "But she's a barmaid, isn't she?"

"She is now," Maria said.

Emilia nodded in understanding.

"If you'd seen the people she worked for before," Judith had said, *"you'd think pirates sounded like polite company."*

"But you said she was just a fugitive you helped," Emilia said.

Maria looked at her. "I never said *'just.'*"

"Oh," Emilia said, her brows creased. "Judith said she was—"

"Too young," Maria interrupted, "yes."

Emilia squeezed the blanket in her hand. Maria might've been appalled at Emilia's runes, but at least nothing like *that* had ever happened on Drakon Isle.

"It's one thing if you choose that line of work," Maria said, "but no one should be forced into it."

Emilia paled. "They force people to do that in Illopia?"

"Sometimes," Maria told her. "It typically happens when you owe a debt to the wrong people."

Emilia frowned. "Jane owed a debt?"

"A big one," Maria said.

"But you rescued her?" Emilia said.

"I helped her," Maria corrected. "I didn't solve her problems for her. I just showed her a way out."

Emilia nodded. "And Buchan knew of her former...identity?"

"Unfortunately, yes," Maria sighed. "He'd had an...encounter with her, before she was Jane. He recognized her."

Emilia wrinkled her nose. "So, that's the kind of person he was."

"That's the kind of people who are drawn to piracy, Em," Maria said. "It's best to learn that now."

"But you're not like that," Emilia assumed, "are you?"

"You've seen me kill two people already," Maria reminded her. "Surely, you don't think I have any sort of moral compass?"

"Well," Emilia stammered, "no."

Maria flashed a tight smile. "My compass is for navigating the seas and nothing else."

"But what did you do," Emilia asked, "when he recognized her?"

Maria's eyes darkened. "I wouldn't have done anything—if he'd just kept his mouth shut."

"Based on the remark he made," Emilia said, "I assume he didn't?"

"He said something to her that upset her," Maria admitted, "something I refuse to repeat."

Emilia nodded. She preferred not to hear it, anyway. "So, what did you do?"

Without a trace of remorse, Maria said, "I had him beaten."

Emilia stared, her eyes wide. "Oh."

"He learned not to test me," Maria said, "but...I suppose he still held a grudge."

"It sounds like you held one, too," Emilia said.

"Does it?" Maria said darkly.

Emilia looked away. The part of her that usually fought with Maria hadn't quite recovered yet, and with her emotions still whirling from earlier, she found herself at a loss for words.

The soft thud of Maria's boots drew Emilia's attention, and she watched warily, as Maria returned to the bed.

Maria stopped in front of her, and with a gentle finger beneath Emilia's chin, she urged Emilia to look up. "Do you understand, now, why I needed to see your injuries?"

Emilia shook her head.

"Buchan's grudge wasn't against you, Em," Maria said. "It was against me."

Emilia's brows furrowed. "But I was the one who—"

"Yes, you hit him," Maria interrupted, "but who were you *really* upset with, at the time?"

Emilia hesitated.

"These injuries of yours," Maria said, "I'm responsible for them."

"No," Emilia argued. "I mean, I was upset with you, yes, but—"

"I'm responsible," Maria interrupted, leaving no room for argument, "but I swear to you, Em, it won't happen again."

Emilia blinked.

"I don't care if I have to kill every sailor on this goddamn ship. No one is going to hurt you." Her eyes flashed dangerously. "Not while I'm your captain."

Emilia stared, not sure how to respond to this strange declaration.

Maria dropped her hand to her side and went to grab her swords. "I have to go. I've wasted too much time with you, and the sun's already set."

Emilia's frown deepened at that.

"Take however much time you need, getting dressed," Maria said, "but I want you gone by the time I return."

Emilia couldn't keep up with the rapid turns in this conversation. Just a moment ago, Maria had sworn to protect her, and now, she was back to talking about Emilia as if she were nothing more than a nuisance?

It was impossible to follow.

Maria finished straightening her scabbard and then headed toward the door. "And take the cat with you. His dinner break is over."

When the captain closed the door behind her, Emilia looked at Rat-Slayer and said, "I'm holding you responsible for this entire, confusing night."

The silver-and-white tabby simply meowed, as if he were proud of the mess he'd made.

And Emilia couldn't help but smile in response. It was terribly difficult to stay angry at a cat—even when they coerced you into playing nice with women you'd rather kill.

Emilia dressed as quickly as she could and was just about to head toward the door, when she noticed the bottle by the bed.

She returned to the bed and picked up the small, glass bottle, expecting to find it half-full still, but it was empty.

Maria had used the last of her oil on Emilia?

Emilia's stomach fluttered uneasily. She could think of only one way to repay the pirate captain. So, she slipped the empty bottle into her pocket for later.

"Come on, Rat-Slayer. The rude pirate you like so much wants you out."

Rat-Slayer climbed to his feet and pranced happily after Emilia, apparently still pleased with himself.

CHAPTER 12

Swords and Kisses

E milia lay awake throughout the night.

She tried to sleep. She really did, and when she couldn't, she told herself it was simply the after-effects of the tincture she'd taken.

But like much of what she told herself lately, it was a lie.

Just like when she told herself that she'd never let her guard down again.

That's what she'd done, wasn't it? Let her guard down?

What other explanation was there for the warmth that fluttered in her stomach now?

What other explanation was there for the way Maria's touch consumed her every thought?

Maria's touch might've relaxed her, at the time, but the memory of it did the total opposite.

And though she did ache at the thought of Maria's touch, it wasn't arousal that kept her tossing and turning all night.

If it were just that, Emilia could've solved the problem hours ago—with her own fingers.

No, this was something far worse.

The longing that had flared up inside of her was deeper than a physical one—and far more dangerous.

"You never learn, do you?"

Alarmed by the familiar voice, Emilia shot up in her cot. "How?" she gasped.

Because standing in the corner of her cabin, was a woman who looked almost identical to Emilia—in all but age.

She had the same long, black hair as Emilia and the same bright green eyes.

And she wore that same long, black gown that she'd worn the day she died.

"This isn't real," Emilia said, denial twisting within her. "It's a dream. It must be."

Emilia's mother—the most powerful dragon sorceress of this century—tapped her long fingernails against the table.

"Are you certain of that?" she murmured. "Didn't I teach you, my dear Emilia, that witches are more susceptible to hauntings than humans?"

Emilia cringed at the way her mother said her name.

There was no *dearness* to it. Her mother hated her—and always had.

"I haven't slept," Emilia said, clinging to that last ounce of desperation. "This could be a hallucination."

Her mother gave her a cruel smile. "Keep telling yourself that, dear."

Emilia clutched her coarse blanket in her hands, feeling as though she might drown, if she let it go.

Emilia's mother stepped closer, and her translucent form flickered between light and shadow.

"How many times," the ghost snarled, "did I tell you not to trust humans?"

Emilia swallowed the lump of guilt welling in her throat. "But Aletha said—"

"The sea goddess is not your mother," the ghost interrupted, "no matter how much you might wish she was."

Emilia looked away. She wanted to argue that Aletha was more a mother to her than her real one, but she knew better than to push an angry spirit.

Her mother wasn't kind in life. She certainly wouldn't be kind in death.

It was always best to have a banishing spell ready, before antagonizing a spirit, and Emilia had prepared nothing of the sort.

"I warned you not to trust her, but you were *in love*," her mother sneered. "You might've mastered your healing magic at an early age, but even now, you still behave like a child."

Emilia glared at her mother. "I withstood torture to protect the dragons," she told her. "I escaped my own execution. I joined a pirate crew. How am I behaving like a child?"

Her mother's ghostly form flickered in time with the candlelight.

She cast a knowing look at the small, glass bottle Emilia had left on the table.

"What is that?"

"Nothing," Emilia said quickly. "An empty bottle."

"*Her* empty bottle," her mother corrected.

"She's not Catherine," Emilia said miserably.

"How is she different?" her mother said. "They're both human. You think this one's any more trustworthy than the ex-lover that you insisted was so *kind*?"

Emilia cringed at her mother's mocking tone. "She's *less* trustworthy," she admitted. "She's said as much herself."

Her mother stepped closer. "Then, why, my dear, are you falling for the same ploy all over again?"

"I'm not," Emilia lied. "I hate her, and if she tries to stop me from leaving, I've already decided to kill her."

"Have you?" her mother said. Her lip curled in disgust. "I'll believe it when I see it."

Emilia's stomach twisted with guilt. "If I could go back in time and kill Catherine, before she killed all of you, I would."

"But you can't," the ghost told her. "You chose a human over your own people, and we paid the price. You have to live with that, Emilia Drakon."

Emilia drew her knees up to her chest. Her heart ached as if it were being crushed, and she took deep breaths, hoping to alleviate the pressure.

It didn't work.

The ghost watched her without a shred of sympathy. "You'll make the same mistake again. One moment of kindness is all it takes for you to forget what they are."

"Please, go," Emilia whispered.

"Mark my words," Emilia's mother said. "Your foolishness will kill the dragons, too."

"No," Emilia whispered.

She closed her eyes, wishing she could wipe the images from her memory, but she couldn't.

With her mother there, she saw it even more clearly than usual: the burnt corpses of family and friends, an entire tribe burned to the ground by Catherine's fleet.

"Sleep well, daughter," her mother sneered.

A cool wind rushed through the room, and the candlelight extinguished.

Emilia didn't wait to find out if her mother had really gone. She simply pulled on her clothes and fled the room.

AN ORANGE SUN STILL HOVERED ABOVE THE HORIZON, WHEN EMILIA reached the main deck. Swatches of pink and orange light burned at the edges of the morning sky.

It would've been beautiful, had Emilia taken the time to look at it.

As it was, she barely made it to the taffrail, before puking up the contents of her stomach.

"Sea sickness?"

Emilia wiped her mouth with the back of her hand and turned to find Zain standing behind her.

He held out a beige handkerchief.

Emilia took it with an uneasy smile. "Thank you."

Emilia wanted to tell him that it *wasn't* sea sickness, that she was a healer and could easily deal with sea sickness, if that were all it was—but *then*, what would she say?

She couldn't exactly admit to the quartermaster that her dead mother had visited her and then purposely pushed her into a state of panic.

So, Emilia simply wiped her mouth and hands and then mumbled another thank you.

With an amused chuckle, Zain said, "Don't worry. Your body will adapt, eventually."

Emilia lifted her eyebrows. Somehow, she doubted her body would ever 'adapt' to her dead mother.

"Judith isn't up yet," Zain told her, "but you're welcome to join the captain and I at the helm. Sometimes, it helps to see the water."

Though Emilia appreciated the thought, the last thing her panicked mind needed, at the moment, was to be around Maria.

"No, thank you."

Zain's smile faded. "Fine. Let me rephrase," he sighed. "The captain sent me to fetch you. It's not a request."

Well, you sure made it sound like a request, Emilia thought bitterly.

With a forced smile, Emilia waved for him to lead the way.

The ship was quieter than usual this morning. Aside from the whipping of the sails and the groaning of the mast, Emilia heard only a male voice, above her, singing a sea shanty about a siren's kiss.

She looked up, watching as a sailor nimbly climbed the rigging.

"That's Nicholas," Zain said, noticing the direction of her gaze. "You might remember him from the tavern."

Emilia remembered the drunken sailor that Maria had forced to leave her table—and nodded.

With a dark look, Zain said, "He took on a extra shift—since Buchan can't pull his own shifts anymore."

Emilia felt the stab of accusation in the quartermaster's tone.

Clearly, he blamed her for Buchan's death.

And after that viciously protective remark Maria had made the night before, Emilia figured he was probably right.

Zain led her up to the quarterdeck, where Maria stood, her hands lightly gripping the wheel.

"Fetched your pet for you," Zain muttered.

Maria shot a quick glare in his direction, but whatever she had to say about it, she must've decided it was better said in private.

Maria returned her attention to the sea, tapping a tattooed finger against the wheel's wooden spoke.

"Are you all right?"

It took Emilia a moment to realize Maria was talking to her. "Oh," she sputtered. "Yes. Fine."

Maria must've heard the scratchiness of Emilia's voice—because she said, "Get her some water, Zain."

Zain rolled his eyes. "Aye, aye, Captain."

Maria waited until he was out of sight to mutter, "He hasn't forgiven me for killing Buchan yet."

Emilia's brows furrowed. "It's been less than a day."

"Which means he's had plenty of time," Maria said, "don't you think?"

Emilia squinted at the murderous pirate captain, not sure if she was joking or not.

Zain returned with a tankard, full of drinking water, and offered it to Emilia.

She glanced down at the cup, hesitating.

"Here," Maria said, holding out her hand.

Zain gave it to her, and Maria took a quick sip, before offering it to Emilia a second time.

Blushing, Emilia accepted the water.

Zain glanced back and forth between them, obviously confused by this interaction.

Emilia couldn't decide whether she was relieved that he didn't recognize her fear or concerned by what he must've thought of her sanity.

Emilia drank from the tankard, grateful, when the water soothed her sore throat and washed away the bitter, nauseating taste of fear.

Maria pulled out her compass, flicking it open. She turned the wheel slightly.

The early morning sun cast a golden glow over her smooth, dark skin, and the cool breeze rustled the sleeves of her shirt and tangled her soft, brown curls.

Was it too much to ask for the pirate captain to look a *little* less gorgeous on the day a ghost accused Emilia of feeling something for her?

Zain hopped onto a barrel, sitting atop it, as if it were a chair, and Emilia went to the rail, gazing out at anything *but* Maria.

By the time Emilia spotted the rocky shoreline, the activity on the ship had increased exponentially.

She turned to Maria—for the first time in nearly an hour. "Why are we so close to land?"

"Surely, you know of the dragons that fly over the Azure Sea?" Zain said with a skeptical frown.

Of course I know of them, Emilia thought. *I know them a lot better than any of you.*

But what she said, instead, was, "Surely, *you're* aware of the sirens who feed near the mountains."

"We'll avoid them," Maria assured her.

"Not if you keep sailing this close to the shore," Emilia said.

Maria glanced at her, lifting a scarred eyebrow. "I know what I'm doing, love."

On any other day, Emilia might've taken the hint, but on this particular morning, Emilia wasn't feeling herself at all.

"Yeah, well, it doesn't look like it," Emilia scoffed.

Maria's fingers tightened around the wheel, but for whatever reason, she let that one slide.

Zain, on the other hand, seethed at the breach of protocol. "How many ships have you captained, surgeon?"

"As many as you, quartermaster," Emilia countered.

Zain stared at her in disbelief. "You seem to have forgotten your place."

Maria blew out a heavy sigh. "Take the helm, Zain."

"Yes, Captain," Zain said, but he glared at Emilia, when he did.

Maria pocketed her compass and stepped toward Emilia. She grasped Emilia's arm and pulled her close. "Talk to me like this in private, and I *might* laugh it off," she hissed in Emilia's ear, "but we're in front of my crew right now. So, shut the fuck up."

Emilia glared at her. "It's not *my* job to make your crew respect you."

"Your job is whatever I say it is," Maria snarled.

Emilia suddenly understood why her mother had mocked her. She *had* given Maria too much power over her.

Maria took hold of Emilia's chin, turning her face with a surprising gentleness—especially considering how *not* gentle her words had been. "How are your bruises gone already?"

Emilia turned her face away, freeing herself from Maria's grasp. "I told you," she said irritably. "I made a healing tincture."

"That's some healing tincture," Maria murmured.

The sea shanty rang out louder over the ship, as more sailors joined in. They sang of human arrogance.

Appropriate, really.

"Healing tincture or not," Maria said quietly, "you don't look well. Did you sleep at all?"

The concern in Maria's voice unleashed a warm, fluttery sensation in her chest, and Emilia panicked at the realization that her mother was right. Again.

One moment of kindness *was* all it took for Emilia.

"What do you care how I slept?" Emilia lashed out. "Are you going to tell me how to do that, too?"

A hint of recognition flickered in Maria's dark brown eyes.

"Let me guess," Emilia said. "On my stomach?"

"What's got you in this state, Em?" Maria asked.

"What state do you mean, Captain?" Emilia sneered. "Honest?"

Maria watched her with an achingly sympathetic frown. "Terrified."

Emilia's blood ran cold.

Maria knew. She'd seen right through it all.

Again.

"I'm not afraid," Emilia said. When Maria's expression didn't change, Emilia added, "I'll prove it. Fight me."

Maria didn't blink. "No."

"You said you would," Emilia said, her voice rising in desperation. "I want you to fight me."

Maria cast a wary glance at Zain, who was watching Emilia with a suspicious glare. "Keep your voice down, love," she told Emilia. She stepped closer and lowered her voice, as well. "Em, you've been through a lot this week. I want you to take the day off. Get some sleep."

"Don't coddle me," Emilia snarled.

Maria's eyes darkened at that. "Careful what you wish for, surgeon."

Careful was the *last* thing Emilia felt, at the moment. "I want a sword," she said. Her heart beat so rapidly that she could barely breathe. "You said you'd give me one, if I proved I could wield one."

"I also told you that I would decide when you're ready to fight," Maria said. Every ounce of gentleness that had been in her warm, brown eyes had vanished. "Now, do as I said, and take the day off." When Emilia didn't scurry to follow her orders, Maria leaned closer and growled, "That's an order, surgeon."

But panic pounded so loudly in Emilia's chest, and anxiety buzzed so loudly in her veins that she could think of nothing else. In a blind state of panic, Emilia reached out and grasped one of the captain's swords.

Emilia jerked the sword from its sheath and pressed the tip of the blade against Maria's chest. "Fight me."

The jolly melody of the sea shanty faded away, as several sailors took notice of Emilia and Maria.

Zain released the wheel and stepped toward them, his hand already on his sword.

But Maria held one hand up, and Zain, as well as a few other sailors, immediately took a step back.

Maria's deep, brown gaze never left Emilia, even as she commanded them to stand down.

"You signed my Code, Em," Maria warned. "You have no excuse this time."

Emilia's chest ached with each beat.

Her mother was wrong.

Emilia had withstood torture for her dragons. She could withstand Maria, too.

"Fight me," Emilia said breathlessly.

"Em," Maria tried again, "you're crossing a line."

Emilia stepped forward, keeping the sword against Maria's chest. "Fight me," she insisted. And then, ensuring that the captain would have no choice *but* to fight back, she slashed the deadly blade at her.

Maria stepped back, easily dodging the sword, but the sword still caught her hat and flicked it off of her head. "I warned you," she growled.

When Emilia swung the blade a second time, Maria ripped her

other sword from its sheath and slashed it upward, easily deflecting Emilia's attack.

Emilia tried again, only to have Maria block that attack, as well.

As Emilia poured all of her pent-up adrenaline into each attack, Maria held her off with so much ease it was almost disheartening.

She'd thought Catherine had trained her well enough to hold her own against anyone, but apparently, *anyone* didn't include Maria.

It bothered Emilia that no matter how much energy she put into the fight, Maria seemed to respond with none whatsoever. She looked almost bored.

And she never fought back. She only blocked Emilia's attacks.

Emilia was exhausted by the time she gasped out, "Is this what you call fighting?"

"No, darling," Maria said, as she deflected one last attack. "*That*…was what I call *observing*."

Emilia froze. "Was?"

Maria tossed her sword lightly and caught it with her other hand, as she adjusted her position. She took a step back, twisting slightly at the waist.

Before, her posture had been lazy and casual—certainly not the stance Emilia would've expected from someone so renowned for her swordsmanship. But this stance, now, worried Emilia—because she was just starting to realize: for Maria, the fight hadn't even started.

Emilia stepped back, gripping the sword tightly.

She gasped, when Maria attacked her from an angle she didn't expect. She still managed to block Maria's sword with her own— but not before stumbling back.

With one attack, Maria had thrown her off-balance.

Emilia soon realized that this must've been Maria's intention— because Maria immediately launched into a flurry of swings and slashes that had Emilia nearly toppling over, as she struggled to block them all.

The pirate captain stepped and pivoted with each swing, attacking Emilia from new angles each time.

Emilia felt as if she were spinning in circles, as she tried to block every swing, and though she'd yet to miss one, she knew that she was quickly losing the fight.

Because every successful block sent Emilia another step backward, and with each one, the roar of the waves grew louder.

And while Emilia had begun to gasp for breath, Maria fought as if she were only warming up.

Her momentum fueled her—her speed and power increasing with each attack.

Emilia gasped—again—as her back hit the rail.

Maria showed her no mercy, refusing to slow her swings, even as they nearly threw Emilia overboard.

With one swing, Maria knocked the sword out of Emilia's hand, and with the next, she nearly sliced open Emilia's throat. She stilled the blade, her arm outstretched and rigid, just in time to stop it from slicing into Emilia's skin—but not in time to stop it from slicing through several strands of Emilia's hair.

Emilia stared at the captain, fully expecting to die.

"Yield," Maria growled.

Emilia opened her mouth, but no sound came out.

Maria stepped forward, causing the blade to press into Emilia's skin. Her soft, brown curls were loose around her shoulders, her headscarf partially untied, and there was one, tiny tear in the sleeve of her shirt, but aside from that, she looked no worse for wear.

Emilia, on the other hand, was already bleeding.

"I said," Maria snarled, stepping closer, "*yield.*"

Emilia watched Maria's mouth, as it formed that word. She watched the way Maria's full lips glistened, the way her teeth gleamed, when she growled.

With a sharp blade against her throat and a reckless sea behind her, for whatever reason, Emilia couldn't seem to look anywhere else.

Only a moment ago, Emilia had been the only one of them panting for breath, but now, Maria looked breathless, as well—her chest rising and falling with each breath. And a familiar flush unfurled beneath her golden-brown skin.

Maria took another step forward. This should have sent Emilia plummeting into the sea below—or just taken off her head completely—but Maria shifted the angle of the sword, holding it diagonally, instead.

Emilia stared up at the pirate captain, baffled by the *many* sensations swirling inside her, as Maria's body and sword pressed against Emilia, all at once.

Emilia had never known fear and desire to entangle themselves as closely as they did now. Maria was close enough to kill her or kiss her, and though Emilia was sure the captain intended to kill her, the thought of kissing her opened a desperate ache inside of her.

Emilia opened her mouth. But again…only silence.

Then, with a growl of frustration, Maria kissed her.

Emilia gasped, as Maria's mouth pressed into hers. The kiss took hold of every part of Emilia, possessing her in a way that no other kiss ever had. It burrowed into the wounds of her heart and aggravated them.

Maria's mouth felt so soft and warm against hers—even as it pressed hard enough to hurt. Maria kissed with enough anger and force that it might've thrown Emilia overboard, had she not grasped Emilia's hip with her free hand. Her tongue pressed into Emilia's mouth, caressing Emilia's tongue until she moaned.

Emilia tasted fruit and rum on Maria's tongue—and an intoxicating mix of anger and lust in her kiss. She leaned forward, clutching a thong of Maria's doublet, even as the sword pressed into her throat.

Maria seemed to realize the danger before Emilia—pulling away with a gasp. "Fuck." She licked her lips, and her brows furrowed, as she stared at Emilia.

"I," Emilia stammered, her lips still aching, "yield?"

Maria nodded. She dropped her sword to her side and stepped back. "If you want to survive what comes next," she whispered, "I need you to go to Judith, and don't leave her sight until I say." Her brown eyes were so dark, now, that they looked almost black. "Do you understand?"

Emilia couldn't even bear to meet Maria's gaze, as she mumbled, "Yes, Captain."

Maria stepped out of her way. "Go now," she said breathlessly. "I'll deal with Zain."

Emilia's lips still ached from that kiss, as she walked away.

She'd been desperate to put an end to her feelings for Maria, but instead, she'd only complicated them.

EMILIA SULKED INTO THE SHIP'S GALLEY, AS IF SHE WERE SULKING INTO her own funeral.

And for all she knew, she might've been.

Judith closed her book and sat up, her hammock swaying with the movement. "You're early."

Emilia just nodded and headed toward the barrels. "I need to work," she sighed. "What do you need?"

Judith climbed out of her hammock. She raked her fingers through her short, brown hair and then knelt to grab some shoes. It was so early that she'd barely even dressed yet—still in just a thin, beige undershirt and a pair of breeches. "What's your hurry, darling?"

Emilia didn't even look at her. "Just need to work."

Judith turned to look at Emilia, and her bright blue eyes widened, as she seemed to notice, for the first time, that Emilia didn't look so well.

Emilia honestly wasn't sure *what* she looked like, this time.

She knew she wasn't in as bad of shape as she'd been in after fighting Buchan, but Maria hadn't left her totally unharmed, either.

Warm blood trickled from stinging cuts on her face and arms, and though she had no idea what her formerly long, black hair looked like now, she knew Maria's sword had caught the left side of it.

Clearing her throat, Judith made her way over to Emilia. She touched a few strands of Emilia's hair, frowning at the uneven cut. "It's only day two, mate," she said warily. "What happened to you *this* time?"

Emilia avoided her gaze. "Nothing."

Judith let go of her hair. "Ah. Well," she said easily, "don't worry. I fucked up my hair the first time I cut it, too." She went to get a pair of sheers. "We'll fix it."

Emilia frowned, but she didn't bother to correct her.

"How short do you want it?" Judith said, when she returned with some sheers. She flashed a playful grin and flicked her own hair to the side. "Short as mine?"

Emilia's bright green eyes shifted upward, and she winced at the *very* short, brown hair. "No," she said quickly. "It looks great on you, but…I'd rather not."

Judith chuckled. "Understood, love," she assured her. She picked up a few strands of the longer side, comparing it to the side Maria had unintentionally chopped off. "I'll just even it out, if that sounds good to you?"

"That'd be great, Judith," Emilia said. "Thank you."

Concern twisted at Judith's brows. "You sure you're all right, mate?"

Emilia swallowed the lump of shame in her throat. "Yes."

"All right," Judith said, but she looked doubtful. She gestured toward the table with a tilt of her head. "Have a seat at the table, and I'll try to fix your, er, *situation*." Her eyes widened, just like they'd done the first time she'd seen it.

Emilia cracked a small smile at that. "Situation?"

"If you could see your hair, Em," Judith said, "you'd call it a situation, too."

Emilia laughed softly at that. She headed toward the table, and Judith followed her.

Judith circled behind Emilia and set the sheers on the table. She took both sides of Emilia's hair and pulled it back behind her shoulders.

Well, she pulled the *long* side behind Emilia's shoulders. The short side barely reached her *neck*.

"Now, while I have you here for a moment," Judith said, "how about you tell me why you're bleeding?"

Emilia sighed, "I'd rather not."

Judith picked up the sheers and began to cut the long side of Emilia's wavy, black hair—matching it with the short side. "I could always fuck up your hair worse," she said with a wry grin.

Emilia blinked at that. "You're blackmailing me?"

"I'm a pirate," Judith reminded her. "Are you really surprised?"

"I suppose not," Emilia said with a small, amused smile. "And you'll probably hear the story soon enough, anyway."

"Of course," Judith said. "Best to hear it from you."

"Just," Emilia said with a grimace, "try not to judge me too harshly." She sighed. "Even if I deserve it?"

"I'm a pirate, love," Judith said—yet again. "I like to leave the judging to those assholes in Illopia."

Emilia smiled warily at that.

She couldn't exactly tell Judith that her dead mother was haunting her. So, instead, she said, "I had a dream that, umm—well, I guess you could say it freaked me out a little?"

"And this *dream* resulted in your...erm...interesting haircut?"

"Sort of?" Emilia said. She sighed and began her tale, "I may have done something terribly rash."

Judith laughed. "Acting like a pirate already."

~

THE FIERY, EVENING SUNLIGHT STREAMED IN THROUGH THE PORTHOLES, as Emilia served dinner to the remaining sailors.

They were all exhausted and drenched with sweat, but apparently, even that wasn't enough to deter them from huddling together and whispering to each other every time they *thought* Emilia wasn't looking.

It'd been like this all day.

Being an outsider was nothing new for Emilia. Even on Drakon Isle, she'd always been too…*something* for everyone.

Too studious, too reclusive, too quiet, too unusual, too meek…

Only the dragons had accepted her as she was, which was why she'd spent most of her free time around them.

No one had ever denied her proclivity for healing.

They just hadn't found her very interesting, when they *weren't* injured.

And her mother's blatant disapproval of her certainly hadn't helped matters.

No, Emilia knew this feeling well, and she told herself that she could handle it.

Over and over.

Throughout the day.

"Don't let them bother you, little surgeon."

Emilia looked up, blinking, as she found Helen's smiling face directly in front of her own.

Well…she thought it was Helen's face, anyway. It was hard to see underneath that thick layer of gunpowder on her skin.

Did she work in that stuff *every* day?

"Little?" Emilia said with an incredulous look.

Helen's teasing was unending. "Well, you certainly aren't large."

As Emilia fixed Helen's bowl, she muttered under her breath, "Not compared to your biceps, maybe."

Helen snorted at that. "I like you," she said, taking the bowl from Emilia. "I hope she doesn't kill you."

Emilia didn't need to ask who Helen meant. She'd heard enough of the whispers to know that Maria was still furious—and that the majority of the crew wanted to see their murderous captain kill Emilia.

"I appreciate that," Emilia said with a pained smile.

Helen winked and then turned to leave, her long, red braid swinging behind her with each step. "Get her drunk, Judith!"

"Working on it!" Judith called—from behind a stack of barrels.

A few moments later, Judith came out and dropped a tankard full of rum in front of Emilia.

"Drink up, my friend who's in deep shit," Judith said. She held up her own tankard in a sort of toast.

Emilia picked up the tankard—and then hesitated, when she saw Judith cringe at the taste of her own rum.

Maria had warned her not to drink Judith's rum, but...well...if she was going to die anyway, she might as well, right?

Emilia turned up the tankard.

Judith nearly spit out her drink. With wide eyes, she reached out and put her hand on the tankard—stopping Emilia. "Slowly, Em," she said. "Slowly."

Emilia coughed at the pungent taste. "You said to drink up."

"Yes, well," Judith said, both eyebrows arched. "Didn't realize you were fucking fearless."

Emilia set down the cup. She cast another glance around the now empty galley, searching for the one person she hadn't seen since early that morning.

Maria hadn't come down for her afternoon meal, and at this point, Emilia figured it was safe to assume she wasn't coming down for the evening meal, either.

Would she really rather starve than look at me?

"How bad is it?" Emilia asked. "Do you know?"

Judith winced. Whether she was wincing at the question or the taste of that godawful rum, Emilia didn't know. "It's...bad."

Emilia nodded. She'd watched Judith mingle with the other

sailors throughout their meals, occasionally joining in on the whispers. The crew trusted Judith—which meant she'd heard a lot more than Emilia had.

Judith set down her own tankard. She leaned against the table and crossed her arms. "This is a ship, Em—smaller than any town, smaller than any island. News travels fast here," she sighed. "The entire crew is talking about what happened, and there are probably ten different versions of the tale."

"But they all agree on one thing, right?" Emilia said with a sad smile. "They all think she should've killed me."

"That *is* the general consensus, yes," Judith said.

Emilia nodded. "Do you think she's heard them? Most of them don't question the captain outright, do they?"

"No, but Em…" Judith trailed off with a sigh. She angled her body closer to Emilia's. "Captain Maria Welles has been a ship captain longer than the *legend* of Captain Maria Welles has existed, and before she was a captain, she was an officer. She joined the navy when she was practically a kid, and she soared through the ranks on pure skill." She lifted both eyebrows. "She has more experience, expertise, and skill than you know. That woman could take one look at you and know whether you respect her or not. Believe me. She knows."

Emilia's chest fluttered. "She didn't come down to eat," she told Judith. She hated that she knew that—that she'd watched so closely. But considering her predicament, it was just survival instinct, right?

It had *nothing* to do with that kiss.

"Be grateful for that," Judith said. "The longer she stays away from you, the longer you stay alive."

"So, you think she'll kill me," Emilia realized.

Judith lifted her narrow shoulders in a shrug. "It'd be the quickest way to shut down the rumors," she told Emilia. "She'd drag you up there in front of everyone and make a spectacle of it." With a wince, she said, "You'd wish she'd killed you earlier."

Emilia frowned worriedly at that. "What rumors?"

Judith shook her head. "She's a woman. What do you think?"

Emilia honestly had no idea. People didn't make a big deal about gender on *her* island.

"They're saying she's attracted to you," Judith said, "that she has a soft spot for you." She looked away. "The crew thinks her judgement is clouded."

Emilia's frown deepened. Had they seen the kiss? Was that the cause of these rumors?

Or was it simply that they couldn't think of any other reason that Maria would put up with Emilia's self-destructive behavior?

"And you think she'll try to prove them wrong," Emilia assumed.

Judith shrugged. "I don't know. I know Zain will advise it." She gave Emilia a sympathetic smile. "It's nothing personal, love. It's just his job."

Emilia picked up the tankard and took another drink.

"And I can't think of any reason she wouldn't take his advice," Judith continued, "unless…"

When she didn't finish her sentence, Emilia glanced at her.

Judith had that strange coin in her hand again—the same one Maria had told Emilia to give her. "Unless what?"

Judith turned the silver coin over in her hand, her expression one of contemplation. "The captain does have *one*…sentimental weakness."

Emilia found that hard to believe.

Before Judith could say any more, however, the wooden steps creaked beneath someone's feet.

Emilia and Judith cast a wary glance toward the entrance, as one of the sailors came down the steps.

Emilia frowned, as she met the gaze of that same blonde carpenter who'd vouched for her after her fight with Buchan.

"What is it, Jonas?" Judith asked.

"Pelt said you asked for a warning?" Jonas said. "Well, the captain's on her way down now."

"Shit," Judith said, her eyes wide. She grabbed Emilia's cup and poured Emilia's rum into her own. Then, she lifted the tankard and drank them both.

Emilia watched with an alarmed frown. "I thought you said *not* to drink it that quickly."

"Do as I say, not as I do," Judith said dismissively. She set down the empty cup and turned to Emilia. "Have you considered begging for forgiveness?"

Emilia scowled at that. "I won't beg for anything."

"Can't swallow your pride to save your life?" Judith muttered. "You're just fucking like her."

Jonas left before Emilia could thank him for the warning—apparently not wanting to stick around for whatever was about to happen.

"Okay, listen," Judith said, "I'll try to talk her down, if I can." She picked up a knife and offered it to Emilia. "Chop up some potatoes. It'll keep you busy so you don't open your mouth and make things worse."

Emilia rolled her eyes at that, but she took the knife, anyway. "Why would you want to help me, anyway? You know I brought this on myself."

Judith shrugged. "If you die, I have to go back to doing all of this work by myself," she said with a wry grin. She patted Emilia's arm. "Besides, we're friends, aren't we? You think I want to watch my friend die?"

Emilia dropped the knife. "Friend?"

Judith glanced down at the knife that had nearly sliced off Emilia's toes. "Umm. Are we *not* friends?"

"No, it's just—" Emilia shook her head bewilderedly. "No one's ever called me a friend before."

Judith leaned back on her heels, her blue eyes wide. "Well, that's fucked up."

The sound of creaking wood shut down any further conversation. Judith knelt and picked up the knife. She placed it in Emilia's hand and then hurried over to the steps, meeting Maria at the bottom step.

Emilia saw the boots descending each step—and knew, without a doubt, that they belonged to Maria.

Had she really paid that much attention to Maria's boots?

Or was it those self-assured steps that Emilia knew so well?

The dark, leather boots creased with each step, and the wood creaked softly beneath them. Emilia had always assumed that Maria's boots were black, but in the soft, evening light, they looked a bit more brown.

Emilia kept her head down, focusing on the potato in her hand. She internally thanked Judith for the excuse to look down—because she couldn't bear to look Maria in the eye.

Not after what she'd done.

Emilia sliced the potato so forcefully that she nearly sliced off a finger with it. The memory of Maria's kiss warmed her skin and quickened her pulse. The memory was so vivid that she could practically feel Maria's mouth on hers, still—the silky warmth of her lips.

So soft—yet, so angry and severe, all at once.

"Where is she?"

Emilia's stomach fluttered at the sound of Maria's voice. If she'd had any doubt that Maria was furious with her, it was gone now. Fury dripped from Maria's voice, like venom—just as thick and just as deadly.

"She's working," Judith said. She lowered her voice to a whisper. "She's sorry, all right? I know she is. I don't know if we're to the point where she'll actually say the words, but she regrets it. I can tell."

"Can you?" Maria said, her voice cold.

Judith hesitated, but then, she said, "Yes, Captain."

"Get out," Maria said.

"At least let me feed you first," Judith said. "You're twice as homicidal when you haven't eaten."

"I said," Maria snarled, "get out."

Judith made one last plea. "Don't kill her."

"Get. Out," Maria said. "Cook."

Judith sucked in her breath sharply. Then, with a note of resignation in her voice, she said, "Yes, Captain."

Another lump of guilt welled up in Emilia's throat. She'd never heard Maria refer to Judith by anything but her name. They were too close for that, she'd thought.

Practically sisters, Maria had said.

The familiar, quiet creaking of wood noted Judith's departure, and then, Emilia heard those familiar footsteps.

"She didn't deserve that," Emilia said—without looking up. "You're angry with me. Not her."

"Oh, don't worry," Maria said, her voice carrying across the galley. "I still have plenty left for you."

Emilia gripped the handle of the knife, chopping her already-sliced potato into even smaller slices.

Every muscle in Emilia's body tightened, and every quick, erratic beat of her heart ached, as the captain's footsteps grew louder. But she refused to lift her face, even as the captain closed in on her.

The shame she felt over her actions was just too much to bear.

"Look at me."

Emilia continued to chop the potato into impossibly thin slices. "Captain," she said, her face warm, "I—"

"Look at me," Maria interrupted.

Emilia shook her head, her pulse racing faster than ever. "What do you want from me?" she said. "Do you want me to cry? To beg for forgiveness? Because I won't."

Even as she *said* she wouldn't, her eyes burned with unshed tears.

Goddess, her mother would definitely mock her now.

Emilia froze, as cold, sharp steel pressed against her throat. Her rapid heartbeat came to a sudden halt.

Maria raised the sword, letting the cold metal press against Emilia's chin. She lifted Emilia's face with the tip of the sword, until Emilia's gaze met her own. "I want," she said in a softer tone, "you to look at me."

Emilia's breath caught in her throat the moment she made eye-contact with her captain. The maelstrom of fear and guilt that swirled inside Emilia quietened.

Staring into Maria's eyes was like being submerged in water. Every emotion felt muffled, every sensation dulled.

And as she stared into those warm, brown eyes, a steady warmth spread through her body, overtaking the previous emotions and leaving only...*desire*?

Was that really what she felt? With a sword against her throat? With her life so evidently in danger?

Yes, she did feel a bit of desire.

But she felt something else, too.

Though there wasn't much light in the ship's galley, and though Maria's tricorn cloaked part of her face in shadows, Emilia saw something unexpected in those lovely, brown eyes—something softer than usual.

Was that...*empathy*?

Maria sighed. She lowered the sword and flipped it, holding it by the blade. "Take it," she said, "before I decide to plunge it through your heart, instead."

Emilia set her knife on the table and reached up—wrapping her hand around the sword's hilt. She took the sword from Maria, stunned by how light it felt, in comparison to Maria's sword. "I don't understand."

"I said I'd give you a sword when you proved you could use one," Maria said. She crossed her arms, her leather doublet stretching tight around her muscles. "You proved that today." In a dangerously dark tone, she added, "Among other things."

Emilia's brows furrowed. "But I lost the fight."

"Of course you lost. You were fighting *me*," Maria scoffed. "That doesn't mean you aren't skilled."

Under any other circumstances, the pirate captain's over-whelming arrogance would've annoyed Emilia, but Emilia was a little too shocked to feel anything, at the moment.

Not only had Maria *not* come down to kill her, but she'd just given Emilia her own sword.

"There isn't anyone on this ship who could beat me in a sword fight," Maria told her, "but there are only about five who could beat you. You've trained well."

You mean Catherine trained me well, Emilia thought.

"I assumed you'd come to kill me," Emilia said.

"I should," Maria said, her eyes dark. "I should slit your throat in front of my entire crew—if for no other reason than to shut them up."

Emilia eyed the swords hanging at Maria's waist, wondering how close she actually *was* to that fate.

"Zain thinks I should let him put you on trial. The crew would find you guilty and force my hand," Maria told her. "But I don't think you *deserve* a trial."

Emilia's stomach lurched at her harsh words, but she didn't argue. "So, why haven't you killed me?"

Maria lifted her lean shoulders in a careless shrug.

Unsurprisingly, that answer didn't comfort Emilia.

"If you can manage to go a few weeks without giving me any *more* reasons to kill you," Maria said, "this will eventually blow over. Think you can do that?"

Emilia nodded.

"Say it," Maria said.

And just like that, a flicker of irritation returned. "Yes, Captain."

Maria lifted a scarred eyebrow at the anger beneath those words. With a small smile, she nodded toward Emilia's sword and said, "Do you have a scabbard?"

"No, but," Emilia said, "I'll figure something out."

Maria lifted her eyebrows. "You think I don't have extra?" she scoffed. She pulled a folded, brown leather belt from her pocket. "Come here."

You kissed me the last time we were that close, Captain, Emilia thought.

Swallowing uneasily, Emilia rounded the table, but Maria held up a hand, when she tried to approach.

Emilia froze.

"Put your sword on the table," Maria said, pointing at it. "I'm not having a repeat of this morning."

With a scowl, Emilia placed the sword on the table.

Maria curled her fingers toward herself, beckoning Emilia closer. Her eyes darkened, when Emilia closed the space between them.

Emilia stopped a few inches from Maria, assuming that was close enough, but Maria apparently felt otherwise—because she curled her fingers around Emilia's hip and jerked her closer.

Emilia gasped when Maria's hips collided with her own. Despite the cool leather that encased her body, Maria's waist felt warm and firm against Emilia.

Maria wrapped the leather strap around Emilia's waist and over her shoulder. She then pulled the strap tight, causing Emilia to gasp a second time.

"You can adjust it here," Maria said, tapping her finger against a small buckle, "if it's uncomfortable."

Emilia had every intention of looking at the buckle, but she couldn't seem to tear her gaze from Maria's lips.

Had Maria's mouth always looked so soft? Or did those full, dusky-pink lips look softer now, simply because Emilia now knew how they felt?

Gods, even that thin, pale scar that crossed the right side of Maria's mouth—even *that* had felt soft against Emilia's lips.

If Maria noticed the direction of Emilia's gaze, she didn't

comment on it.

"It'd be a waste to have a trained swordsman on my ship and not arm her," Maria said.

Emilia nodded.

But then, Maria hooked her fingers through the weapon strap and jerked it forward, dragging Emilia up onto her toes. "But you need to know," she warned, "if you *ever* draw a sword against me again, you're dead."

Emilia held her breath, afraid to breathe, for fear of accidentally giving into her desires. Maria's knuckles brushed against Emilia's stomach, igniting a slow-burning fire there, and Maria's lips were barely an inch away.

"Do you understand," Maria said, "surgeon?"

Again, Emilia nodded.

"Say it," Maria said.

Emilia narrowed her eyes at that. With each time Maria made that ridiculous demand, the flame of anger inside Emilia burned just a bit hotter.

And here Emilia had been feeling guilty about attacking her. The smug asshole deserved it.

Maria kept a tight grip on Emilia's weapon strap, lifting a scarred eyebrow, when Emilia glared.

"Yes, Captain," she recited bitterly.

One side of Maria's mouth twitched upward. "Perfect."

Maria loosened her grip on the scabbard, and Emilia fell back on her heels. Then, with one hand still on the weapon strap, Maria reached past her and grabbed the sword.

Her dark gaze was surprisingly gentle, as she slid the sword into its sheath. She took Emilia's hand and placed it on the hilt of the sword. "Is that comfortable?"

Too surprised to remember her irritation, Emilia simply nodded.

"Good," Maria murmured, releasing her hand. An amused smile pulled at her lips, and she ran a few fingers through Emilia's shortened, black hair. "Who cut your hair? Judith?"

Emilia froze the moment Maria touched her hair. Despite her best attempts to forget that kiss, it took only one touch from Maria to thrust the memory back to the forefront of her mind. "She evened it out for me," Emilia said. She hoped she sounded calmer than she felt. "Maybe you didn't notice, but you sliced through part of my hair with your sword."

Maria dropped her hand and shrugged, as frustratingly unrepentant as ever. "Could've been your throat."

"Yeah?" Emilia said. "Well, maybe next time, it'll be yours."

She tried to walk away. Unfortunately, she remembered just a little too late that Maria still held her scabbard, and the sudden jerk at her waist sent her falling into the woman she'd just tried to walk away from.

Maria caught her, laughing. That was the only consolation, really—that Maria's laughter sounded absolutely beautiful, compared to her anger.

With the brightest smile Emilia had seen all day, Maria said, "Would you like to try that again?"

"Not particularly," Emilia muttered.

Maria chuckled. She released the scabbard and lifted her hand.

Her knuckles trailed lightly along Emilia's soft jawline, and she lifted Emilia's face toward her own.

Maria's warm lips brushed lightly over Emilia's, and Emilia held her breath, her entire body aching at the thought of kissing Maria again.

Every rational cell in Emilia's brain begged her to pull away, to not let it happen again.

Her attraction to Maria was dangerous enough already.

Another kiss would only complicate things more.

And yet, as Maria drew closer, Emilia couldn't find the strength to resist.

Her muscles turned to gelatin beneath the captain's touch, and her pulse fluttered so quickly that it left her lightheaded.

Wood creaked above them, and Maria released her so fast that

Emilia nearly stumbled backward.

"Sorry," Maria said with a frown, as if she weren't quite sure what had happened. "I should go."

Emilia couldn't explain why, but every part of her protested the distance Maria tried to put between them.

She should've been relieved by the distance.

Instead, it...*ached.*

"But you haven't eaten yet," Emilia pointed out.

Maria glanced back at her. "I'll come back later."

The unspoken part of that rang clearly in the silence: *'when you're gone.'*

"Let me fix you a bowl," Emilia offered. "You can take it with you."

An unreadable emotion flickered in Maria's dark eyes.

She nodded once.

Emilia went to the table to get her a bowl. She noticed Maria watching the movement of Emilia's sword as she walked, and Emilia said, "It really is comfortable."

With a small smile, Maria said, "I'd hoped it would be."

Unsettled by the sudden tension between them, Emilia focused her gaze on the pot in front of her.

Emilia scooped some stew into the bowl and offered it to Maria.

"Thank you," Maria said—in a tone Emilia had never heard her use before. There was no longer a levity of humor in her voice or a growl of anger. There was only softness.

Emilia didn't know how to react.

"Just keep your head down for a few days, love," Maria said, "I'll handle the rest."

Emilia's pulse raced at the kindness, and before she could stop herself, she blurted out, "Why?"

A strange sort of anguish twisted at Maria's scars.

"I thought you'd kill me," Emilia said—for the second time that night. "Why didn't you?"

Maria didn't answer this time, either. "Enjoy your sword, Em."

CHAPTER 13
An Explanation

"What do you think, Rat-Slayer?" Emilia said, when the large, silver-and-white tabby curled up in her lap. "Will she like it?"

The silver cat nudged the glass bottle in Emilia's hand and purred.

"In that case, I *might* consider giving it to her," Emilia said.

Rat-Slayer meowed at that.

"Well, no. I'm not angry with her right now," Emilia admitted, "but how long do you think that'll last, really?"

His next meow was full of disapproval.

"You have a point," Emilia sighed. "It *is* a very nice sword."

She opened the bottle and inhaled the scent. Hibiscus and orange enticed her senses—stirring up memories of Maria's hands on her skin.

"I added a bit of magic," Emilia whispered to the cat. "I think she'll like it more than the original."

A knock at the door interrupted their conversation.

Emilia quickly sealed the glass bottle with a cork. The last thing she needed was for anyone on this ship to realize she'd just wasted half her night making some ridiculous gift for her captain.

Well, anyone besides Rat-Slayer, that is. The devious, silver tabby was *ecstatic* about it.

"Up, up," Emilia said to the large cat.

With a yawn, Rat-Slayer slowly climbed out of her lap, before curling up at the edge of her cot, instead.

Emilia placed the bottle on the table and dusted the silver cat hair from her trousers—before unlocking the door. She opened the door and froze.

"Captain."

Emilia could only assume that Maria's decision to visit her had been sudden—because she looked like she'd already gone to bed, prior to coming to Emilia's cabin. She wore her swords, still—because of course she did—but aside from those, she wore only a pair of faded, leather trousers and a thin, linen shirt.

"Hello, Em."

"Let me guess," Emilia said with a wary smile. "You changed your mind about slitting my throat."

An answering smile twitched at one side of Maria's mouth. "Not yet," she said. "Invite me in, love."

"Do you even need an invitation?" Emilia said. "It's your ship."

"Well, if that's how you feel," Maria said, a teasing glint in her eye, "step aside."

Emilia rolled her eyes—but stepped aside, anyway.

Maria eyed the sword at Emilia's waist, when she stepped past her. "How are you liking the sword?"

The truth was that Emilia loved it, but she'd never admit as much. "I'll need to stab you with it before I can say for sure."

Maria chuckled at that. "You'll have your chance."

"Is that a promise, Captain?" Emilia said playfully.

When Maria saw the large cat sleeping on Emilia's cot, she turned to Emilia. "Why is my fiercest ship cat lazing about in your cabin?"

Emilia waved her hand dismissively. "He was helping me with something."

Maria frowned. "Was that *'something'* a rat?"

"The cats deserve breaks, too, Captain," Emilia informed her.

"Fine," Maria said, "but the first rat I see—I'm blaming you."

Emilia winced. "Don't let me down, Rat-Slayer," she whispered to the sleeping cat.

Maria laughed softly at that.

Emilia cast a wary glance at the pirate captain, and her cheeks reddened.

Neither of them had spoken of that kiss since it happened, and to be perfectly honest, Emilia was fine with never mentioning it at all.

But…well…she would've been lying if she said she hadn't been thinking about it.

Constantly.

Every minute of this godforsaken day.

"So, if you haven't changed your mind about killing me," Emilia said, cursing how breathless she sounded, "why *are* you here?"

Maria tilted her head toward the door. "Close it."

Emilia closed the door—and locked it, too, just for safe measure. She turned to the captain, pinning her with an expectant look. "Now, will you tell me?"

Maria crossed her arms, her thin, linen shirt clinging to her muscles. "Perhaps."

Emilia frowned at the elusive answer. Spreading her hands in bewilderment, she muttered, "The suspense is killing me, Captain."

"You asked why I didn't kill you," Maria said.

Emilia dropped her hands to her sides. "Yes."

"I didn't give you an answer," Maria added.

"That's…also true," Emilia said with a frown.

Maria cast her gaze downward, narrowing her eyes on the floorboards beneath her boots. "But you deserve one."

Emilia's frown deepened. "I do?"

Maria's dark gaze flicked upward. "What you did today wasn't just foolish, Em. It was suicidal."

Emilia found herself staring at the floorboards, as well. The shame turned her stomach. "I know."

To her surprise, Maria slipped a finger beneath her chin and lifted her face. "Did you think you were the only one who'd ever made a mistake like this?"

Emilia's chest fluttered, as she met Maria's gaze. "Well," she admitted, "yes?"

"You're not," Maria assured her.

Emilia knew multiple languages, and she suddenly couldn't remember a single word of them.

Maria dropped her hand, and her gaze flickered toward the surgery table. She was quiet for a while, which gave Emilia time to find her voice again.

"How did you know?" she asked, her heart racing. "You looked at me and just...*knew* I was afraid."

Maria returned her attention to Emilia. "Disguising fear behind anger is a practice I know well."

Judith had told Emilia that, hadn't she? That Maria hid her most vulnerable emotions behind anger?

Had Emilia done the same thing?

She looked away, and her pulse raced ever faster.

"You've noticed the scar on my neck, I assume?" Maria said, after a few more moments of silence.

Her words sounded so much heavier than usual.

Emilia's gaze darted up toward the aforementioned scar. Of course she'd noticed it—the raised, pink line across Maria's throat. Maria hadn't exactly hidden it, and Emilia had spent a lot longer looking at Maria's slender throat than she *ever* wanted to admit. "Yes."

Maria slipped her fingers around the loosened lace of her poet's shirt and tugged the shirt downward—though there was no need.

"I'm curious, Em," she murmured. "You took one look at the scar on my hand and guessed its cause. Can you do the same with this one?"

Emilia swallowed. "Yes," she said hesitantly. "Your throat was cut with a sword. Attempted execution."

Maria let go of the shirt. She lifted her eyebrows, apparently surprised—or impressed. "You do know your shit, don't you?" she muttered.

Emilia blushed. "It's an important part of the job," she said dismissively. "If an injured person isn't able to speak, I have to figure it out on my own."

Maria nodded. "Do you know how it happened?"

Emilia shook her head. "Did they…attempt to execute you when you were imprisoned in Regolis?"

"No," Maria said, to her surprise. "They hadn't yet, anyway." She sighed heavily. "The preferred method of execution in Regolis is the gallows. I assumed you knew that as well as anyone."

"I do," Emilia admitted, "I suppose."

"Do you know *where* execution by sword," Maria asked, "is the standard?"

No, but it wasn't hard to guess.

"Ships," Emilia assumed.

Maria nodded.

The powerful and dangerous pirate captain who stood before Emilia, now, reminded her more of a baby bird, waiting for a push to begin her first flight.

So, Emilia pushed. "What happened?"

Maria waved a hand at the cot. "Mind if I sit?"

With an amused smile, Emilia said, "Actually, I think Rat-Slayer would *love* it, if you sat next to him."

Maria chuckled. She sat down next to the sleeping cat—and then, almost as an afterthought, she reached out and rubbed his head.

Emilia's smile deepened at the sight.

Maria tilted her head toward the empty side of the cot. "This thing's as hard as a rock. I'm sure it can handle the three of us."

"Oh, I don't know," Emilia said with a playful smile. "Rat-Slayer and I are a bit on the curvy side."

At that, Maria's large, brown eyes shifted toward Emilia's hips and darkened, but all she said was, "Sit. Please."

Emilia lifted both eyebrows. She'd never thought she'd hear the word *please* come out of Maria's mouth.

It was almost...*cute*.

You know, for a murderer.

Emilia sat on the end of the cot and folded one leg underneath her.

Maria held out her hand, and Emilia found herself taking it again—tracing the deep scar in her palm.

Those large, mesmerizing eyes of Maria's darkened.

"You said this wound would've been painful," Maria reminded Emilia. "What sort of person, do you think, would subject themselves to that sort of pain?"

"A person who was already suffering," Emilia said.

Maria must've been expecting her to say something else—because she suddenly frowned. "You wouldn't call that person mad?"

Emilia shook her head. "Insanity is subjective," she said. "What sounds mad in one instance is survival in another. I'd call it desperation, not madness."

Maria quirked that scarred eyebrow of hers. "Desperation?" She acted as if she'd never heard the word before, but perhaps, it was just that she'd never heard anyone apply it to her. Captain Maria Welles was supposed to be a villainous madwoman, not a desperate prisoner. "And if I told you it didn't end there? That even after I escaped, I continued to put myself in situations that no sane person would?"

"If you said *that*," Emilia said, looking down at her hand, "I'd say you sounded...a little like me."

278

Maria gave a subtle nod. "I lost a lot, prior to my decision to engage in piracy—if you can *call* it a decision," she muttered. "But I still had a crew—a small one, much smaller than before, but a crew, nonetheless."

Emilia listened curiously, surprised that Maria was offering up so much information.

"When I took the *Wicked Fate*, my goal was only to keep my crew alive. We'd engage in simple piracy to survive—steal from merchant vessels, sell to Adda." Maria shrugged. "I already had a fencer on my side. Nefala was already a pirate port. It made sense."

Emilia's brows furrowed. Maria had told her a few nights ago that her victims *weren't* merchants. She said she sunk navy ships, not merchant ships.

"What changed?" Emilia asked.

Maria gave another shrug. "I didn't *want* to steal from merchants. Merchants hadn't done shit to me," she explained. "King Eldric, on the other hand, had."

"So, you went after his naval ships, instead," Emilia assumed.

"The *Wicked Fate* was a warship, before I took her," Maria said. A cruel smile curled at her lips. "Why have cannons, if you're not going to use them?"

Emilia nodded. "How did your crew feel about it?"

With a sharp laugh, Maria said, "They thought I'd gone mad." She scratched the sleeping, silver tabby's ear with her left hand, as she spoke. "Zain told me he wouldn't follow me to my death. If I was determined to wage war against the world, I'd have to go at it alone." At Emilia's frown, Maria explained, "He was threatening mutiny."

Emilia's frown deepened. "And yet, you still have a ship."

Maria nodded. "I took him at his word. Rather than force my crew into a battle they didn't want, I took a longboat and went at it alone."

Emilia squinted at that. "Wait, you—" She shook her head in

confusion. "Captain, are you saying you attacked a warship? By yourself? In a longboat?"

Maria laughed, "In a fucking longboat."

An astonished smile twitched at the corners of Emilia's lips. "How did you even survive?"

"I almost didn't," Maria said, and then, she lifted her chin, directing Emilia's attention back to that scar.

Emilia nodded slowly. "You were captured."

"Easily," Maria said. "I never stood a chance." She glanced down at Rat-Slayer, and she continued to stroke those tattooed fingers of hers through his silver fur. "I was recognized immediately, of course, and my execution was set for the next morning."

Emilia remembered the sadness and loneliness she'd felt on the morning of her own execution, and empathy twisted deeper within her chest, as sharp as a knife. "How did you escape?"

Maria glanced at Emilia, and her smile suddenly deepened. "In the middle of my execution, my sweet surgeon, the *Wicked Fate* fired upon the navy ship."

"What?" Emilia breathed.

"Amazing, isn't it?" Maria murmured, and she leaned closer. "Despite my recklessness, despite my mistakes, my crew had come for me. They saved me, and I was able to watch my enemies burn, after all."

Emilia saw it again—those beautiful, little sparks of golden fire in Maria's dark, brown eyes.

That bloodthirsty fire of hers was, at once, a magnificent and dangerous thing to behold, and Emilia was as drawn to it as ever, just like a damn moth.

"There was no mutiny?" Emilia said, breathless with shock. "They just...*forgave* you?"

"Don't you get it, Em?" Maria said in a stunningly gentle tone. "That's what this *is*. Family." She lifted her hand and brushed her tattooed thumb against the softness of Emilia's cheek. "Very few of us on this ship have much in the way of blood-family, but we have each other."

Emilia held her breath, her skin tingling pleasantly beneath Maria's fingers.

"And that's what family does," Maria said softly. "They stand by you—even when you fuck up."

Emilia's throat constricted. "Not in my experience."

Maria tilted her head to the side, and her soft, brown curls fell against the collar of her shirt. She brushed her knuckles against Emilia's jaw, and Emilia shivered, again, at her touch. "Then, it's good that you came to me for a *new* experience, isn't it?"

Emilia licked her lips, her mouth suddenly dry. "That's not why I came to you."

"No?" Maria said with a skeptical smile. "You're telling me you *didn't* come to me for adventure?"

Emilia watched Maria's lips form that word, and a scorching rush of desire poured through her.

How did Maria do that? How did she make the word *adventure* sound so…enticing?

Maria tilted her face closer, and her breath—sweetened by rum and fruit—caressed Emilia's lips. "Why were you alone?" she whispered.

Emilia tried to remind her lungs to inflate and deflate, but all she seemed to be able to remember, at the moment, was how warm and soft Maria's lips were. "What do you mean?" she said breathlessly.

"When I went through what you're going through now, I had my crew," Maria said, "but you? You have no one." She leaned closer. "You came to me, all alone, practically begging me to fuck you over."

Emilia scowled at that. "There was no begging."

Maria ignored her objection. "You had no one to save you from yourself. Why is that, love?"

The grief expanded in Emilia's throat, suffocating her. But she couldn't let it show. "I—I don't know."

Maria leaned even closer, now, and her forehead, framed by the silkiest curls, brushed against Emilia's. "Stay with me," she whispered against Emilia's lips, "and you'll never be alone again."

An old proverb came to Emilia's mind, just then: *Words whispered by devils are sweet, indeed.*

Emilia didn't know if she believed in any sort of devils. Ghosts were as kind or cruel as humans, and gods came in all shades of good and evil, as well.

But Maria's words *were* sweet.

Far too sweet for Emilia to believe.

"I can't stay," Emilia sighed. "You know I can't."

Maria dropped her hand, and Emilia instantly missed the warmth of her touch. "We'll see."

Emilia swallowed, unnerved by the pirate captain's confidence.

Maria glanced off toward the surgery table. "You wanted to know why I didn't kill you," she said. "Well, now, you do."

"Do I, though?" Emilia said breathlessly.

Maria's intensely dark gaze returned to Emilia. "I know what it's like to spiral," she explained. "The difference was, when I did it, I had people to save me from myself, and *you*, my sweet surgeon, are alone."

When Emilia, in pure shock, failed to think of an adequate response, Maria dusted off her black, leather trousers and climbed to her feet. Heading toward the door, she murmured, "Goodnight."

"Wait," Emilia said, jumping to her feet, "Captain?"

Maria froze. She turned, and a devious smile curved at her lips. "I think that might be the first time you've called me captain without adding a bit of spite to it." A gleam of amusement shone in her dark, brown eyes. "I can't decide which way I like better."

The laugh that escaped Emilia's lips sounded a bit higher than usual, her voice strained with anxiety.

The subtle rise and fall of the ship—even tipping at a slight incline, at times—made it far too easy to close the space between them, and before Emilia even realized it, she was standing directly in front of Maria.

"What do you want, Em?" Maria murmured.

Perhaps it was the surprisingly intimate nature of their earlier conversation, or perhaps it was the slight drop in Maria's voice, when she asked what Emilia wanted. But the word *'you'* suddenly came to mind.

But the one question that had whirled around in her head all day was the one that spilled from her mouth. "Why did you kiss me?" Emilia whispered.

Maria stepped forward. Emilia's cabin was barely large enough for two people, as it was. With them both closing the space, Emilia felt as if there wasn't a bit of air left between them.

Emilia had promised herself she wouldn't mention the kiss. She wanted to forget it happened—to forget the warmth and pleasure she'd felt while Maria's lips were on hers.

It overcomplicated an already complicated issue.

Until that kiss, Emilia had been so sure that she hated Maria. But now, her thoughts were reeling, and she no longer knew *what* she felt toward the pirate.

Maybe she'd never known at all.

"You tell me, love," Maria said. She curled one hand around Emilia's hip and pushed her against the wall, and she pressed the other hand above Emilia's head. She leaned against Emilia, and every inch of her body—somehow both soft and firm, at once—pressed against Emilia. "Was it madness, do you think," she whispered against Emilia's mouth, "or desperation?"

Emilia's breath caught in her throat, and her eyes fluttered closed. Desire clenched throughout her entire body, and despite every negative feeling she'd ever had toward this pirate, she wanted nothing more, in that moment, than to kiss her again.

"I," she stammered. "I don't know what to think."

Maria tilted her face, and one of those thin braids she wore at the front of her curls fell forward. "Not such an expert now, are you?" She took her hand from the wall and brushed her fingertips along Emilia's jaw, lifting Emilia's face toward her own. Then, just as Emilia was sure they'd kiss again, Maria said, "What's in the bottle?"

Emilia opened her eyes. "What?"

"The bottle on your table," Maria said with a vicious smile. "Tell me what's in it."

Emilia glanced at the glass bottle and then back at Maria. "What does that matter?"

"It matters because I say it does," Maria said with a glare. "The fact that you seem so reluctant to tell me makes me think it matters a great deal."

Emilia matched Maria's glare with her own. "Well, it doesn't."

She couldn't believe she'd actually considered kissing this woman again.

One pleasant conversation, and she'd completely forgotten every good reason she'd had for hating the egocentric pirate.

Again!

Her mother's taunts were so, *painfully* right.

"Tell me what's in it," Maria said. "Is it poison?"

"Oh, for Aletha's sake!" Emilia said. She shoved the captain away from her and marched over to the table. She snatched up the bottle of oil and thrust it into Maria's hand. "Just take it and go!"

Confused by Emilia's reaction, Maria opened the bottle and sniffed. Her dark eyes widened. "How—"

"I made it, you self-obsessed imbecile," Emilia said. "What? You think I can make poisons but not oils?"

Maria stared at Emilia, her eyes wide. "Why?"

"I don't know!" Emilia said. What she'd done was humiliating enough as it was, and now, Maria wanted an explanation, too? "If you don't want it, I'll take it back."

Maria held it tightly. "I want it."

Emilia waved a hand at the door. "Then, take it and go," she snarled, "before I accidentally *poison* you."

"You won't even let me apologize?" Maria asked.

"Like you ever would," Emilia scoffed. She rolled her eyes. "Besides, it's me who should apologize—for forgetting what you're actually like for a moment!"

Maria looked away, nodding. "Goodnight, Em."

Emilia crossed her arms and fixed her gaze on the floorboards, too embarrassed to meet Maria's gaze.

Maria's departure was mostly silent, aside from the quiet creak of the door.

Rat-Slayer was awake again, and he expressed his disappointment with a meow and a flick of his tail.

"I know, I know," Emilia sighed. "You disapprove."

CHAPTER 14

Dine with Me

Despite living on a ship together, Maria somehow managed to avoid Emilia for the rest of the week. Whether that was because of the gift or the criticism she'd faced for sparing Emilia's life, Emilia wasn't sure.

"Hypothetically," Helen said, as Emilia cleaned her bowl, "if someone were to blow something up three days from now, about an hour before sunset..."

Emilia looked up at the master gunner, her brows high.

"And if—*also* hypothetically—she sustained some burns during the incident," Helen added, "would you be able to fix that?"

"Is your hypothetical person dead?" Emilia said.

Helen's thin, red eyebrows drew together in thought. "Not usually."

"Then, yes, I can fix it," Emilia assured her.

Helen grinned. "Perfect!"

Emilia suppressed a smile at her excitement. "Would you like me to make the burn salves ahead of time?"

"Yes!" Helen said. She pointed a gunpowdery finger, as if she thought Emilia were the brightest woman to ever exist. "That would be amazing!"

Emilia laughed. "I'll have it ready for you, then."

Helen clapped her hands on either side of Emilia's face and kissed her forehead in a strangely aggressive manner. "I'm so glad the captain didn't kill you!"

Blinking in shock, Emilia set down the bowl so that she could *attempt* to wipe the gunpowder off of her face. "Thank you, Helen," she muttered, even though the enthusiastic gunner was already gone. "I'll probably be flammable for the next three years."

Emilia set aside the bowl she'd already cleaned and picked up another bowl from the dirty pile.

Helen was a lot of fun, no doubt, but somehow, getting random baths in gunpowder just didn't seem like the best idea for a dragon sorceress.

It was only a few minutes later, when Emilia heard approaching footsteps—the soft thud of leather boots against wooden steps—and she knew, already, who it was. She didn't know *how* she knew. Was it the fact that everyone else on the ship had eaten already?

Had Emilia been subconsciously keeping count?

Or was it that strange heat that seemed to radiate between them whenever they were close?

Was that even real?

Or was it all in Emilia's head?

"If you hate me too much to serve me, you could at least tell me to fuck off."

Emilia felt her lips twitch into an involuntary smile. She briefly considered taking Maria up on that offer. Any excuse to throw a few expletives at the arrogant pirate captain was a good one, if you asked Emilia.

But instead, she tossed the cleaning rag aside and looked up. "My mistake, Captain," she said with a sassy smile, "I was cleaning your bowl. Next time, I'll just pour your stew into a filthy one."

Maria's soft chuckle caused Emilia's stomach to flip in delight.

For Aletha's sake, why did the pirate captain have to look so devastating tonight—leaning against the table, with that devilish grin and those dark, burning eyes?

Every inch of Maria's brown skin glistened with sweat, and her dark hair hung around her shoulders, drenched and longer than usual, beneath her equally soaked headscarf.

Emilia lifted her eyebrows. "Now, I know why I haven't seen you in four days," she muttered. "You've been spending all your time swimming."

Maria snorted, "It's sweat, love." Like her legs, her arms were long and lithe. So, even when she braced a hand on the table and leaned forward, she and Emilia were still practically at eye-level. "I'm sure you do it, too."

"Never," Emilia said sarcastically.

Maria watched, as Emilia dipped the ladle into a pot of stew. "So, you noticed when I wasn't around?"

Emilia froze. "No…"

A grin twitched at the corners of Maria's mouth. "But you just said—"

"Is this enough stew?" Emilia blurted out.

It was probably the worst attempt to change the subject in all of history, but desperate times called for desperate measures.

Maria glanced down, squinting at the mostly empty bowl of stew. "No."

"Right," Emilia said, her face warm. "I'll just…fill it up, then."

Maria's brows furrowed.

Emilia dipped the ladle into the pot and scooped out some more stew. "Pelt says this is one of Judith's best recipes," she said. "It does have a nice scent."

Maria just stared at her.

Emilia continued to fill the silence with non-Maria-related rambling. "Like tomato and hibiscus…"

"Hibiscus?" Maria repeated.

Nope, nope, nope. Hibiscus was Maria.

Focus, Em. Focus.

"I meant to say carrot," Emilia said, her cheeks growing hotter by the moment. "They're just so similar, you know."

Maria lifted a scarred eyebrow. "Hibiscus and...*carrots*?"

Emilia's blush deepened, but luckily, she'd already finished filling the bowl. She thrust it into Maria's direction and just *hoped* Maria would leave before noticing her reddened face. "Here," she muttered.

Maria took the bowl, but she didn't leave. "Now, fix another."

Emilia looked up, frowning. "You want two?"

"The second one's for you," Maria explained.

Emilia shrugged bewilderedly. "I'm working."

"Then, you'll take a break," Maria said, as if Emilia had no choice. "If the ship cats can take breaks, surely you can, too."

Emilia suppressed a laugh at that. "I will later."

Maria set down her bowl and placed both hands on the table, leaning toward Emilia. With an enticing smile, she murmured, "But I want you to do it now."

More heat gathered in Emilia's cheeks. "Why?"

"Well, first," Maria said, her smile widening, "because apparently, you're hungry enough to hallucinate similarities between hibiscus and carrots."

Emilia sighed at that. "And second?"

Maria's eyes darkened. "Second...if you can stand my presence for a bit longer today," she said with that devious smile, "I'd love for you to dine with me."

"That's a big '*if*,'" Emilia informed her.

Maria laughed. "What if I promise not to accuse you of trying to poison anyone tonight?"

Emilia's lips twitched. "All right, all right," she sighed, "but if Judith asks—"

"I'll take care of that now," Maria said, and before Emilia could stop her, Maria called out, "Judith!"

The chatter above them quietened, and Judith came down the steps, peering into the galley. "Yes, Captain?"

"Em's eating with me," Maria told her. "If you have more work for her, I'll send her back afterward."

Judith pushed her short, brown hair to the side, squinting at the pile of clean dishes. "Looks like she's done more than enough already."

"Good," Maria said, plucking a clean spoon from that same pile. "Then, I can keep her indefinitely."

Emilia blinked at that. She glanced at the captain—unsure of whether that had been a joke or not.

With Maria, she could never tell.

Maria grabbed another clean bowl and handed it to Emilia. "Fix yourself a bowl, and come with me."

Judith climbed up the steps again—and was soon laughing at a muffled remark someone had made.

Emilia would've argued—it was sheer principle, at this point—but the aching emptiness of her stomach was just too insistent to deny. So, she scooped some stew into her bowl and followed the captain. She expected the captain to take a seat at a table, but she strode straight toward the steps, instead.

"We're not eating down here?" Emilia asked.

Maria laughed. "No privacy down here, love," she explained. "You'll be dining in my quarters tonight."

Emilia frowned worriedly. "Why would we need privacy?"

Maria didn't answer that.

EMILIA WAITED, AS MARIA LIT THE CANDLES ON HER TABLE. THE windows behind her cast her lean figure in blue moonlight, and Emilia couldn't deny how gorgeous that figure was. There was such strength and power in every part of Captain Maria Welles.

"Have a seat," Maria said, when she'd lit the last candle. She turned to Emilia, her smooth, brown skin practically glowing in the candlelight. "Before your food gets cold." She sat in her own chair and waited for Emilia to join her.

Emilia ambled across the cabin and set her bowl on the table. She glimpsed a map, spread out on the far side of the table, illuminated in pale blue moonlight.

It was a map of the Azure Sea—with arrows drawn between Nefala and Drakon Isle. She panicked for a moment—before realizing that those arrows followed the flying patterns of the dragons.

The arrows had nothing to do with Emilia. They were simply warnings about which routes to avoid.

"Problem with my map?"

Emilia glanced at Maria, blinking, for a moment, at the question. Maria was staring at her with that familiar, inquisitive look—the one that made Emilia feel as if the pirate could see right through her. "Why would I have a problem with it?"

"You like to argue with me," Maria said. "I'm offering you the opportunity. Did I make a mistake?"

"I don't like to argue with—" Emilia pursed her lips, when she realized what Maria had just tricked her into saying.

Maria lifted her eyebrows in amusement.

"It looks fine," Emilia grumbled.

"That must be disappointing for you," Maria said, irritating Emilia even more. She tapped an impatient rhythm against her leather-clad thigh. "Sit down."

Emilia rolled her eyes at Maria's lack of patience—but took a seat, anyway. She was only one bite into her stew when she realized they had nothing to drink. She stood. "I forgot to grab a flagon of ale."

"Sit," Maria said again, as she set down her spoon. She climbed to her feet and went to her cabinet. She opened it and pulled out a bottle of wine. "This is better than anything we have in the galley, anyway."

Emilia watched, as Maria set two tankards on the table and filled them both with wine.

Emilia suspected it was an expensive drink—since she'd never seen ale or rum in such a nice bottle. "If it's so much better," she muttered, "why are you wasting it on me?"

Maria didn't answer until she'd finished fixing their drinks. She set the bottle on the table between them and returned to her seat. "I'll waste it on whomever I like."

Emilia rolled her eyes. "Of course you will."

Leave it to Maria to somehow take *that* as an insult.

Maria sipped her wine, her dark gaze never leaving Emilia. She set her tankard aside and picked up her spoon, the silence heavy between them. Then, finally, she murmured, "How was your first week?"

Emilia swallowed her stew. "It was…eventful."

A smile tugged at one corner of Maria's lips. "Yes. It was."

Emilia held her spoon still, her food forgotten, as she watched that gorgeous half-smile spread across the pirate captain's face. "You seem to be in a better mood today."

Maria tilted her head, acknowledging that. She set her spoon down. "I meant what I said the other night, Em. I like the oil."

"Oh," Emilia said with a nervous smile. "You've tried it already?"

"I have," Maria said, "and I didn't die either. So, I suppose it wasn't poison."

"I suppose not," Emilia said pointedly.

Maria chuckled. "I did appreciate the gift, Em."

Emilia blushed. "Oh," she said. "Well, if you want more, I'll need more hibiscus." She scooped some stew into her spoon—but didn't eat it just yet. "Judith had some for teas that she let me use, but I don't want to deplete her stores."

"You'd make more," Maria asked, "for the pirate who nearly killed you a few days ago?"

"Well, when you put it that way," Emilia muttered.

"I don't understand it, Em," Maria said. "Why *did* you make that oil for me?"

Emilia swallowed. "Rat-Slayer thought it was a good idea."

Maria stared at her in clear disbelief. "You're blaming the cat?"

"More like crediting him," Emilia said. "If you want to thank someone, you should thank him."

"And if I *don't* want to thank anyone?" Maria asked.

Emilia shrugged. "Then, I'll just tell him you're being rude again."

Maria laughed at that. She scooped up a spoonful of stew and put it in her mouth, chewing silently.

"So," Maria said, when she'd swallowed that bite, "are you telling me that it *wasn't* a product of your own kindness?"

"No," Emilia said—a bit too forcefully. When Maria lifted a scarred eyebrow, Emilia said, "I was that sort of person once. I'm not that person anymore."

Maria frowned. "A kind person?"

"An easily manipulated person," Emilia said bitterly.

"Ah," Maria said. She lifted her tankard to her lips and took another sip. "You think people can change that much?"

Emilia's stomach twisted with fear. "Well, I hope so," she said. "I don't think I could live with myself, if I made the same mistakes twice."

Something that looked almost like empathy flickered in Maria's brown eyes.

But surely, that wasn't what it was.

Right?

Maria set down her tankard. "Well, if you were looking for a villainous descent, you certainly came to the right person."

Emilia's lips quirked up a little at that. "Are you going to teach me to be evil, Captain Maria Welles?"

A gleam of delight flashed in Maria's dark eyes, when Emilia spoke her full name. "Yes." She leaned back in her chair, resting her hand on the hilt of her sword. "For our first lesson, you should pretend you're going to kiss the girl who just made you a gift and then, really, *truly* ruin the night by accusing her of trying to poison someone, instead."

Emilia set her spoon in her bowl and made a show of searching the table. "Do you have a quill? I need to take notes."

Maria tilted her head back, laughing loudly at that.

"Do I get extra points for attacking you earlier this week?" Emilia asked.

"Hmm, no," Maria said with a thoughtful smile. "Perhaps if you'd attacked an Illopian guard, instead…"

Whether it was the wine that loosened her tongue or that lovely laugh of Maria's, Emilia didn't know, but she just couldn't seem to stop. "And what if I've attacked—*and* killed—multiple Illopian guards?"

Maria's smile faded. She leaned forward, a dark sort of intrigue burning in her eyes. "Tell me more."

Emilia swallowed uneasily. She pushed the wine away from her, not willing to risk any more. "I think I should go."

"But we were having so much fun," Maria said, a hint of venom in her voice.

"Not anymore," Emilia muttered.

"Em, sit," Maria said, when Emilia pushed back her chair and stood. "Finish your food."

"Why?" Emilia snapped. "So you can trick me into saying more?"

"You wanted me to teach you how to be evil," Maria said. She spread out her arms proudly. "Watch and learn, darling."

Emilia narrowed her eyes. "Goodnight, Captain. Please, feel free to avoid me for another four days."

"Em! Em, please," Maria said, when Emilia turned to leave, "finish your food."

Emilia hesitated at the strange plea.

Had the captain had a sudden lapse in arrogance, or was this just another trick?

"Why?" Emilia said.

"I'm not going to be the reason my most malnourished sailor didn't eat," Maria said.

Emilia rolled her eyes. "I've been eating for a week now. I'm fine."

"Finish your food," Maria said. "Then, you can continue with your dramatic exit, and I'll pretend to be surprised."

Emilia didn't appreciate the implication. She sat back down and muttered, "It wasn't dramatic."

Maria watched her curiously, her brown eyes softening with concern. "Believe it or not," she said, "I'm trying to help you."

Emilia gave her a skeptical look. "By tricking me at every opportunity?"

"If you'd volunteer the information on your own," Maria said, "I wouldn't need to."

"I nearly starved to death, rather than give information to my captors," Emilia snarled, "and you think I'm going to voluntarily give it to you?"

"I'm not your captors," Maria said.

"Then, stop acting like them," Emilia said.

For the first time since she'd *met* Maria, Emilia saw a flicker of regret in Maria's eyes.

A tense silence settled between them, and Emilia had no interest in breaking it.

They'd been eating in silence for several moments, when Maria said, "No one's bothered you about it, have they?"

Emilia looked up, her brows furrowing. "About what?"

"Your...*mistake*," Maria said, leaning back in her chair.

Another wave of guilt washed over Emilia. "You mean when I attacked you?"

"I thought 'mistake' was a clear enough description," Maria said. "Have you made any *other* colossal mistakes I should know of?"

"You mean...aside from joining a pirate crew and punching Buchan?" Emilia said.

Maria lifted a scarred eyebrow at the ever-lengthening list. "Yes."

Emilia shrugged. "I may have promised three different cats that they could sleep in my cabin tonight."

Maria frowned at that. "There's no room in your cabin for three cats."

Emilia scooped up another bite of stew. "Yeah, that's why I called it a mistake," she said. "I should've alternated the days or something."

When Emilia opened her mouth to say something else, Maria held up a tattooed finger. "Before you go confessing that you fucked Helen or something," she interjected, "*yes*, I do mean the attack."

"I have not had sex with your forbidden gunner," Emilia assured her. "I did promise her some burn salves, though."

Maria sighed heavily. "Please, stop confessing things to me."

Emilia shrugged and scooped up a spoonful of stew. "You asked."

Maria snorted, "So, has anyone said anything out of the way to you or not?"

Emilia shook her head. "There were whispers, but no one said anything to my face."

Maria nodded. "The whispers should die down soon." She sipped her wine. "Zain says they're losing interest."

Emilia hesitated at the mention of Zain. "I'm sorry if I," she mumbled, "caused any problems for you."

Maria's dark gaze shifted toward her. "You're sorry?"

"Yes," Emilia said. She looked down, her stomach churning with shame. "I—I thought that was obvious. After."

"After, yes," Maria told her, "but why are you still holding onto the shame? If I still had any ill feelings about it, you'd know." She returned her attention to her food. "It's over now, love."

Emilia stared at her in disbelief. Out of all the people she'd ever known, the pirate with the deadliest vendetta of all was the *last* person she'd ever expected to let go of her anger that quickly.

"But your crew's still talking about it."

"I'm not concerned with that," Maria said. "If anyone says anything out of the way to you, you tell me, but as long as it's just whispers..." She shrugged. "That's just the nature of leadership, love. They'll be questioning my judgement for a totally different reason by next week."

Emilia looked down at her stew. "Let's just hope I'm not at fault for that one, too."

Maria smiled. "Yes. Let's hope."

"Oh, good, I'm almost done," Emilia said, as she scooped up her last spoonful of stew, "which means I can leave soon."

As if she hadn't even heard Emilia, Maria grabbed both tankards and refilled them. "Em, I need to know who you are."

"You know I'm an islander and a fugitive," Emilia said. "I think that's more than enough."

Maria slid the full tankard of wine toward Emilia. "I'm not saying I've given you much reason to trust me—"

"Much?" Emilia scoffed. "You haven't given me any."

"Perhaps not," Maria admitted, "but you must realize, by now, that I'm willing to risk a good deal in order to keep you on my ship."

Emilia looked up from her stew, her mouth half-open in surprise. "Me?"

"Yes, you," Maria sighed. "You're a surgeon, Em. That alone makes you a valuable asset to me."

Emilia's frown deepened. "It does?"

Maria crossed her arms, her black, leather doublet stretching over her muscles. "Yes, Em. If you must know, yes," she said irritably. "You're also good with a sword, and you have some bizarre power over my cats."

Emilia suppressed a laugh at that.

"If I'd wanted you dead, you'd be dead by now," Maria pointed out. "I've had multiple opportunities to kill you."

"No, you don't want me dead," Emilia admitted. "You just want me trapped here." She flashed a bitter smile. "Still not a reason to trust you."

Maria drained her tankard of wine, as if she couldn't care less about Emilia's anger. "I'm your captain," she muttered. "I don't have to explain myself to you."

"No, you don't," Emilia agreed, "but it would be nice if you did something—*just once*—without an ulterior motive."

Maria offered her an uncaring shrug. "I'm a pirate."

"Right," Emilia said. Why did she keep falling for Maria's lies? She pushed her empty bowl aside and climbed to her feet. "Sorry for thinking you were anything more."

Somehow, *that* was the part that earned the pirate captain's attention.

"You signed my Code, surgeon," Maria said in warning. "You must realize what will happen, if a crew mate learns your secrets before I do."

"I'll be arrested, right?" Emilia assumed. "By whom? You or Zain?"

"It doesn't matter," Maria told her. "The results are the same. You remember the law about equal power, don't you?" She set down her tankard and leaned forward, as if she were sharing a secret. "I have one vote—just like every other person on this ship. Even if I *wanted* to save you, I couldn't. Once you're on trial, there's very little I can do."

Emilia shrugged. "I didn't ask for your help."

"No?" Maria said, and then, she was on her feet, too, circling the table to confront Emilia. It took only a few of her long strides before they were face-to-face. "And when they force you to your knees and put a sword against your throat?" She leaned in close, her sweet, fruit-scented breath falling against Emilia's lips. "Will you ask, then?"

Emilia's stomach flipped at Maria's closeness, a traitorous warmth unfurling inside her. "No."

Maria's eyes dilated, growing wide and dark with both lust and anger. "We'll see."

Emilia scoffed, "I don't need your help, and even if I did, I don't trust you enough to accept it." She leaned forward, onto her toes, closing any space left between them. "And why should I? Like you said, you're a pirate."

"As are you," Maria reminded her, "whether you like it or not." A dangerous growl reverberated beneath her words. "You've yet to share your true identity—even with me. Yet, I brought you onto my ship, anyway. Why should I trust *you*?"

"For the only reason you've ever done anything, Captain," Emilia said. The air between them burned like dragon fire. "Because there's something in it for you."

Maria's mouth curved slowly, forming a cruel smile that cut like steel. "Were those Catherine's exact words, or are you paraphrasing?"

Emilia flinched at the mention of Catherine. "What are you talking about?" she said breathlessly.

"Oh, I think you know," Maria said. Her dark gaze trailed downward. "Which were you, Em? A friend or a lover?"

Fear lurched inside Emilia's stomach. "I—I don't know what you're talking about."

"Liar," Maria snarled. She lifted Emilia's chin, examining her face with a cold scrutiny. "Lover, I'd bet. You're her type. Lovely curves, lovely eyes. Fair skin that reddens *so* easily. Too sweet to see the danger right in front of you..."

"Fuck you," Emilia snarled.

"Did she?" Maria said with that dark smile of hers. "Fuck you?"

Emilia gripped the hilt of her sword, as her entire body surged with panic.

Maria glanced at her hand. "Don't do it, Em," she warned. "I never show mercy twice."

Emilia's voice shook, as she whispered, "Then, get out of my way."

Maria stepped back, lifting both hands.

Emilia stepped past her, heading straight for the door.

"You didn't finish your wine," Maria called after her.

Emilia stopped and turned back toward her. "I'm not falling for the same trick twice, Captain."

Maria picked up the tankard and held it out. "I wasn't asking you to stay," she assured her. "I just meant for you to take it with you."

Why did *that* matter?

With a roll of her eyes, Emilia returned to take the cup. She tried to gather up the used bowls and spoons, as well, but Maria waved her away.

"I'll take care of it," Maria said. "I need to speak with Judith, anyway, and it'll be easier to avoid you, if you're not down there."

"Fine," Emilia said. That was the only word that came readily, at the moment. With a bemused wave of her hand, she muttered, "And thank you for the wine."

Maria watched her leave with a frown. "You can take the whole bottle if you'll stop being such a—"

Emilia slammed the door closed before Maria could finish that.

EMILIA FLED AS FAR FROM THE CAPTAIN'S QUARTERS AS HER FEET would take her—which, since she was on a ship, was only to the main deck.

In a dire situation, perhaps she could've summoned the sea goddess for a bit of water magic, but it'd be awfully hard to convince the pirates that she wasn't a witch, if she started walking on water.

Emilia fell against the taffrail, gasping for breath.

She couldn't have said what had suffocated her so severely—only that something had.

Was it how easily Maria had figured it out?

Was it simply the memory of Catherine herself?

The fear of having her identity known?

The ever-present tension between herself and the captain?

Emilia wasn't sure, but whatever it was—it gripped her throat, not allowing a single breath. It compressed her lungs and burned her from the inside out. It made her feel as if she'd die, if she didn't flee from it as fast as she could.

Emilia leaned against the rail, inhaling the salt-scented air. The dark, moonlit waves lapped recklessly at the sides of the ship, rocking it slightly.

She watched the waves lift and fall—letting their steady rhythm ground her.

She tried to match her pulse to that steady rhythm, but slowing her erratic pulse in the middle of a panic attack was easier said than done.

The sound of nearby voices made her hesitate. She turned, breathing heavily still, as she glanced around the mostly deserted deck.

Only those on night watch still worked, and the night crew was far sparser than the day crew.

Maria's helmsman, Henry, stood on the quarterdeck, and above her, a limber sailor climbed the rigging—tightening knots or repairing tears, Emilia assumed.

But neither of *them* were close enough for Emilia to have heard over the roar of the sea itself.

She followed the sound of the voices, and behind a stack of crates, she found two familiar faces.

The boatswain, Pelt—with his easily distinguishable facial scar —leaned against a stack of crates with his deeply-tanned arms folded over his chest.

Jonas—the shorter, sandy-haired carpenter, who'd testified in Emilia's defense that first day—stood next to him, laughing.

"There's no way she didn't notice that, mate."

Pelt laughed, too. "Well, if she did, she didn't mention it."

Still dizzy with panic, Emilia braced her hand against a wooden crate, which promptly shifted beneath her touch.

Pelt and Jonas both turned at the sound.

Pelt squinted in an effort to see through the darkness. "Em? Is that you?" he called. "Are you all right?"

"Yes," she said, still breathless. "I just needed some air."

"Mm, it's a good night for it," Pelt said, nodding. "The breeze is perfect."

Was it?

Emilia still hadn't caught her breath enough to notice.

Jonas watched her with a curious frown. "What's in the cup? You look sick."

Emilia hesitated at the question. If there'd been rumors about Maria and her before, she could only imagine how quickly those rumors would spread, if word got out that she'd dined with the captain.

Emilia braced herself for what she was about to do, and then, with a slight shrug, she tilted the tankard back and drained it of wine.

The two pirates lifted their eyebrows.

It wasn't as bad as she'd expected, really.

More like ale than rum, the wine lacked that intense burn that often made rum hard to drink as quickly, and its taste was both bitter and sweet.

Like revenge.

When Emilia finished the wine, she showed them the empty tankard. "Rum," she lied.

Emilia figured rum couldn't be traced back to Maria as easily as wine.

After all, every pirate on the ship had their own rations of rum.

"Do you need me to get the captain?" Pelt said. At her worried frown, he added, "I mean, if you're feeling unwell?"

"I feel fine," Emilia assured him. "I don't need the captain."

"You don't look fine," Jonas muttered. "No offense."

Pelt smiled, his gold teeth flashing in the moonlight. "He just means you look a bit pale. That's all."

Anxiety churned in her stomach, but she tried to keep her voice steady, despite it. "You're both on night watch?"

"Jonas is. I'm not," Pelt said. He slapped the carpenter's shoulder. "I'm just keeping him company."

Jonas rolled his eyes. "He makes it sound like he's out here for my benefit, but really, he just couldn't find anyone else who'd listen to all of his ridiculous gambling tales."

Pelt flashed that sparkling, golden smile, yet again. "That, too."

Emilia nodded. The wine warmed her blood and soothed her anxiety. "Well, I think I'll get another look at the water, before I turn in."

"Try the starboard side," Pelt suggested. "Moon's reflecting nicely over there."

"Oh," Emilia said, glancing toward the starboard side. "Thank you."

Pelt waved two fingers, and Jonas said, "Goodnight."

Pelt was right. The view *was* better on the starboard side.

The moon wasn't quite full yet, but it still shone brightly in the night sky. It cast a gorgeous, silver light over the surface of the water that rippled like dragon-scale.

Emilia breathed out a wistful sigh, missing her dragons more than ever.

Almost as if he'd sensed her sorrow, Rat-Slayer suddenly came slinking across the deck.

"Well, hello," Emilia said in the happiest tone she could muster.

The cat meowed and brushed his oversized, silver-and-white body against her leg.

"Can't fool you, can I?" Emilia sighed.

She crouched low and brushed her fingers through Rat-Slayer's striped fur.

"I hate that her memory still has this kind of power over me," Emilia confessed. "Perhaps, one day, when I've had my vengeance, the name *Catherine Rochester* will mean nothing to me."

Rat-Slayer's blue eyes shifted beyond Emilia, suddenly, and his soft, silver-and-white fur rose.

Emilia followed his gaze toward the stack of crates. She leaned closer to the cat and whispered, "What is it?"

Rat-Slayer hissed in warning.

Worry fluttered inside Emilia's chest. "I'll check it out," she promised the cat, "but I need you to find somewhere safe to hide."

Rat-Slayer didn't move a muscle. Nor did he lower his hackles —even for a moment.

Instead, the silver tabby stepped toward the stack of crates, letting out another dangerous hiss.

"Rat-Slayer," Emilia whispered worriedly.

Emilia tried to catch him in her arms, but the cat sprinted forward with a speed she couldn't match.

With just three leaps, he cleared the crates and, with a loud yowl, hit his target.

A low, pained grunt followed the attack.

It was a human.

Determined to protect the cat, Emilia ran to look behind the crates.

But the human was gone. She found only Rat-Slayer—and a few drops of blood, already seeping into the deck.

"Where did he go?" Emilia whispered.

The cat growled at someone behind Emilia, but it was too late. A cold, wet blade sunk into Emilia's hip, before she had time to react.

Acting almost on instinct, Emilia lashed out with a wave of magic, sending the crates toppling onto the person who had stabbed her.

Again, the human grunted in pain.

The crates shuffled loudly across the deck, and then, Emilia heard footsteps, as her attacker fled.

Emilia reached down to touch the wound in her hip, and the cat meowed worriedly. "I'm fine," she lied. Her vision blackened at the edges, as she lifted her hand to her face and sniffed. "Oh, no."

Emilia tried to walk toward her cabin, but she made it only one step before the drug took effect.

She collapsed on the deck, her eyes fluttering closed.

Rat-Slayer nudged her arm, and though Emilia tried her best to reassure him, her body simply wouldn't move.

"Get help," she whispered—only a moment before she lost consciousness.

With a frightened yowl, the brave, silver tabby cat bolted toward the captain's quarters.

～

MARIA HAD JUST STOPPED TO LOCK HER DOOR, WHEN SHE HEARD A *meow* behind her.

She turned around, frowning at the large, silver cat. She knelt in front of him and slid her fingers behind his fluffy, silver ear.

"Since when do you wander around here at night?" Maria said with an affectionate smile. "The rats are in the bilge, love."

The cat meowed and flicked his tail impatiently.

Maria hesitated, studying the feline with a curious frown.

She couldn't explain it, but something about the cat's behavior set her on edge.

A meow was just a meow, right? It wasn't like Maria spoke *cat*.

And yet, even Maria recognized the alarm in that meow.

"Is something wrong?" Maria said.

The cat let out a sound that was so full of alarm that it was practically a wail.

"Show me," Maria murmured.

And then, as if the cat had understood her somehow, he turned and sprinted toward the deck.

Maria followed.

Even though she was truly puzzled by this strange turn of events, Maria curled her fingers around the hilt of her sword, expecting a fight.

The deck was quiet, and at first, Maria didn't see anything out of place, but as the cat led her toward the starboard side of the ship, she noticed a scattered stack of crates.

She hurried toward the crates, noticing a familiar shape, lying on the deck.

"Em," she breathed.

In the pale blue moonlight, Em's fair skin held a bluish tint, and Maria feared the worst.

She knelt beside the unconscious surgeon and pressed a finger against her neck.

Maria breathed a small sigh of relief, when she felt the steady pulse, beating against her fingertip.

"She's alive," Maria told the cat—even though she didn't think the animal could understand her.

The large cat continued to prowl around Em, as if he were protecting her.

Maria noticed the small puddle of blood, steadily growing beneath Em, and she lifted the surgeon's shirt slightly.

Both fear and fury lashed through Maria, at once, when she saw the wound. "Who did this?" she snarled under her breath.

She'd said the question more to herself than to anyone else, but the way the silver tabby looked at her, when she said it—she wondered if the cat knew the answer.

Maria studied the feline's intelligent, blue eyes—and identified with the emotions she saw behind them. "I swear to every god in Aletharia," she told the cat. "I'll find whoever hurt her, and I'll kill them."

The ship cat, who was obviously quite fond of Maria's new surgeon, seemed to approve of that.

Vengeful, little animal, wasn't he?

Maria gathered Em's unconscious body into her arms and stood.

"Boatswain!" Maria yelled, when she saw Pelt heading toward his cabin.

The boatswain turned toward her. His brows furrowed, when he noticed the woman in her arms.

"Is that—"

Maria didn't let him finish. "I need a list of everyone who was on night watch tonight," she growled. "Immediately."

Pelt nodded. "Aye, Captain."

CHAPTER 15
An Exchange of Power

E milia awoke to the most dreadful feeling. Her stomach lurched violently, and she rolled over in an arduous effort to miss the bedclothes.

Her head spun too fiercely for her to see the floor, but to her relief, a warm hand curled around her shoulder and gently guided her.

"Into the bucket," said a familiar, lilting voice.

Again, Emilia couldn't *see* the bucket. She just had to trust the hand on her shoulder to move her to where she needed to be.

She must've vomited four times the amount of food she'd eaten, but her body just wouldn't let up. Even after she finished, her muscles continued to convulse.

"Rum or water?"

Emilia forced herself to look up at the owner of the bucket. Her head continued to spin, but even through the blur, she recognized those beautiful, brown eyes.

Oh, good work, Em, she thought. *She's really going to like you now that you've puked in front of her.*

"I'm getting you something to drink," Maria said. "Do you want rum or water?"

Emilia shook her head—and then, immediately closed her eyes, as that sent her vision swirling again.

"Either," she said hoarsely.

Maria pulled out her leather pocket-flask and gave it to Emilia. "Drink that, while I get you some water."

Emilia pulled herself into a sitting position, the bed creaking beneath her. Only when she brushed her hand over the bedclothes that she'd nearly puked on, did she realize that she wasn't in her own bed.

She glanced around, noting the sheer size of the space and the number of blurred objects around her that were vaguely shaped like spools of rope.

She was in the captain's quarters.

She was in the captain's *bed*.

She took a small sip of Maria's rum, wincing a little, when it burned her sore throat.

Maria returned with another bucket and dropped it in front of Emilia. Water swished around the bucket, splashing from the sides and soaking Emilia's shoes.

Maria knelt and dipped a rag into the bucket. She then wrung out the water and lifted the wet rag to Emilia's face. "Close your eyes," she said. "It's sea water."

Emilia barely had time to register Maria's warning, before the wet cloth touched her forehead. The water soothed her, instantly, cooling her feverish skin and clearing the muddled haze in her mind.

When she heard a second splash, Emilia opened her eyes. "What are you doing?"

Maria ignored the question. Instead, she climbed to her feet and wiped her wet hands across her leather-clad thighs. "Drink," she repeated.

Emilia took another sip from the flask.

Not because Maria demanded it, mind you—but because her throat was still sore.

"Why am I in your quarters?"

Maria took a flagon of drinking water from the table. She glanced at Emilia, as she filled a tankard with water. "You passed out on the deck," she said—as if that were the only explanation needed.

Emilia stared at the floorboards, trying to think past the haze in her mind. The intense, searing ache in her hip jogged her memory. "I was stabbed."

"Yes," Maria said.

Emilia's eyes widened, as the memories came rushing back. "Oh, no! Rat-Slayer—"

Maria didn't even let her finish the panicked thought, before saying, "Behind you."

Emilia turned. She breathed a sigh of relief as soon as she saw the silver, cat-shaped blur that was curled up in the bed, next to her.

"I've never seen anything like it," Maria said, as she set the flagon on the table. "He led me right to you."

With a grateful smile, Emilia dragged her fingers through the cat's silver fur.

"I've never seen him that upset, either." Maria strode toward Emilia. She took a small sip and then held out the tankard. "Fresh water."

Emilia took the tankard and returned Maria's flask.

Emilia hadn't even realized how dehydrated she was—until she'd nearly finished her water and was still feeling parched. "Thank you."

Maria's eyes shifted toward Emilia, a hint of surprise in their dark depths. "You can have as much as you need," she told Emilia. She turned up her flask, drinking whatever rum remained. "You need the water more than I do today."

Emilia frowned, confused by this side of Maria. She glanced

toward the windows, squinting at the sunlight that slanted through. "It's morning already."

Maria searched her cupboards for more rum. "Yes," she muttered. "Sunrise *does* mean it's morning." She peered over her shoulder, offering Emilia a taunting smile. "Do they teach you that in surgeon training?"

Emilia smiled at the sarcasm, but she managed to hide her amusement behind her cup. After all, their perfectly balanced hate-relationship might unravel, if they started laughing at each other's jokes.

She couldn't have that.

"Where did you sleep?" Emilia asked curiously.

Maria refilled her flask, her gaze so narrowed on the rum that Emilia thought she hadn't heard her.

But then, under her breath, Maria said, "I didn't."

Emilia's brows furrowed. "You didn't sleep at all?"

Maria glanced at her. "How was I to protect you if I slept?" She returned the bottle of rum to its place in the cabinet and turned to face Emilia. "Someone stabbed you last night, Em. I wasn't going to leave you unguarded."

Emilia's frown deepened. "But...why not?"

"I'm your captain," Maria said. She spread out her arm, giving Emilia an incredulous look. "What? Are these just words to you?"

"Umm," Emilia stammered. What was the right answer to that? "Well, you could've just taken me to my cabin and locked the door."

"And then what?" Maria said. "How were you going to protect yourself, if the attacker got in, while you were unconscious? We're pirates, love. You think we can't pick locks?" She lifted the leather flask to her lips. "Honestly, Em, even if you'd managed to stay conscious, your plan was awful."

Emilia scowled at that. "Well, it's not like I had all night to think about it," she said defensively.

Maria closed her flask and pocketed it. "The cat didn't have all night to think, either, and he still did the right thing. And he's a *cat*."

Emilia sighed. Even when Maria was being strangely considerate, she somehow *still* found a way to insult Emilia. "Animals are more intelligent than you think."

Maria glanced at Rat-Slayer and muttered, "Apparently."

"The person who attacked me coated his blade with a drug," Emilia said, as her vision finally started to clear. "An Illopian drug."

"Well, that doesn't narrow it down much, does it?" Maria said. She leaned against the long, wooden table and crossed her arms.

Now that Emilia could see her clearly, she noticed that, for only the *second* time since they'd met, the captain wasn't wearing her swords.

No doublet or hat, either.

Just a pair of faded, leather trousers and a loose, linen shirt.

She didn't even have her hair tied back with a headscarf. Her soft, brown curls were loose and tousled, softening the scarred face that usually looked so fierce.

"I'm just relieved to know it wasn't poison," Maria said, interrupting Emilia's totally objective observations, "as I'm sure *Rat-Slayer* will be, as well."

Emilia suppressed a smile. If he weren't sound asleep, Rat-Slayer would no doubt be *gloating* over Maria finally using that ridiculous name she'd given him. "How did you calm him down?"

"The cat?" Maria said, her brows high. "I swore I'd kill the person who hurt you."

Emilia blinked. "You...what?"

"I swore to him that I'd kill the person who hurt you," Maria said, as if Emilia had simply not heard her. "Which brings us to the matter at hand—I need a name."

Emilia shook her head. "I didn't see the attacker. Rat-Slayer did, but I didn't."

"Then, we'll have to resort to the more dangerous plan," Maria said. "Works for me."

Emilia frowned worriedly. "I'm sorry. Are you..." she trailed off. "Your intention is to...murder this man?"

Maria shrugged her lean shoulders. "You say that like it's out of the ordinary for me."

Emilia nodded a little, acknowledging that. "But...whoever it is —they've served you longer than I have."

"So had Buchan," Maria reminded her.

"But you confessed to having old grudges with Buchan," Emilia said. "This time, you don't know who it is. You're just announcing that you're going to kill him."

"Yes," Maria said, as if that were totally rational behavior.

"But what if it's someone you need?" Emilia said.

Maria tapped her fingertips against the table behind her. "I don't like you implying that I *need* anyone."

Emilia rolled her eyes. If pride were a commodity, Maria would've been the richest woman alive.

"Drawing a weapon against you was bad enough. He broke my Code," Maria said, "but attacking you?" She straightened her shoulders. "That was a blatant challenge to my authority, and I won't have it."

Emilia couldn't explain it, but there was something very flimsy about that explanation—as if it were only a cover for the real reason that Maria was upset. "But aren't you supposed to give him a trial first?"

Maria lifted a scarred eyebrow. "Good idea, thief," she said sarcastically. "Let's put him on trial, and give him a chance to incriminate us both."

A cool wave of dread washed over Emilia. "You think he knows who I am."

"If I'd had any doubt," Maria said, "it was gone the moment you confirmed that it was a drug—and not poison."

"King Eldric wants me alive," Emilia realized.

"A public execution makes for a far better show than a private assassination," Maria said.

Emilia nodded, her throat suddenly tight. "He wants me back at the gallows."

With a cruel, jaded smile, Maria murmured, "The citizens of Regolis were promised entertainment. Their king must deliver."

A chill went down Emilia's spine. She wanted to argue that, surely, the commoners weren't *entertained* by such a thing, but she'd heard it with her own ears, hadn't she?

An entire city, cheering for her death.

"And yet, they say *we're* the evil ones," Emilia said bitterly.

"It's the richest city in the kingdom. What do you expect?" Maria said. She glanced toward her windows. "Besides, if King Eldric ever stops producing villains for them to hate, the people might just realize who the *real* villain is."

"King Eldric?" Emilia assumed.

Maria's dark gaze shifted back toward Emilia. "The entire fucking system."

Emilia's anarchist leanings were a bit less…intense than Maria's. But perhaps that was simply because she'd never lived beneath a corrupt king.

Emilia's mother, who'd been chieftess of Drakon Isle before her death, hadn't been *kind* in any sense of the word, but she'd been fair, at least.

Emilia had been sought out and captured by a corrupt king. She'd been orphaned by a corrupt king. But she'd never lived beneath one.

Perhaps it was different.

Emilia eyed the floorboards beneath her shoes, insecurity fluttering in her stomach. "I can only imagine how impressed with me you were *last night*," she muttered. "I thought the Buchan fight was bad, but I didn't even get a punch in this time."

Maria lifted a scarred eyebrow. "Hmm," she murmured with a decadent smile, "I thought you hated me."

Emilia looked up, frowning. "What?"

"That *was* the general point behind our little fight yesterday, wasn't it?" Maria said. "That you hate me?"

"I believe my exact words were that I don't *trust* you," Emilia said with a scowl, "but yes, as a matter of fact, I do hate you."

Maria leaned forward slightly. "Then, why do you care whether I'm impressed with you?"

Emilia sputtered in shock. "I—I don't."

Maria shrugged her strong shoulders. "Sounds to me like you do."

Emilia glared at her. "Well, I don't."

"No?" Maria said, her tone as taunting as ever.

"*If* I cared about impressing you—which I don't," Emilia assured her, "but *if* I did, it'd be out of spite."

Maria laughed. "Spite is a terrible reason to die, love."

"It's odd that you'd say that," Emilia said, "because I seem to remember hearing about a certain pirate captain who single-handedly went to war with the most powerful kingdom in all of Aletharia."

Maria grinned. "Your pirate captain isn't dead yet."

"Neither is her surgeon," Emilia countered.

Maria's smile deepened. She dropped her arms to her sides and strode toward the bed. The bed creaked softly, when Maria sat down next to Emilia.

Despite the aching wound in her side that should've been enough to distract her, Emilia's pulse still quickened the moment Maria's leather-clad thigh brushed against her own. She watched the captain curiously.

Maria took out her flask, before casting a sidelong glance at Emilia. "Do you really want to know?" she asked. "Whether I'm impressed with you or not?"

With a wary frown, Emilia muttered, "No."

What kind of trick was Maria playing on her now?

Maria took a drink from the leather flask. "The fact that your attacker didn't show his face is a reflection of *his* cowardice, not yours."

Emilia's brows furrowed. This conversation was growing stranger and stranger by the moment.

Maria leaned closer to Emilia—close enough to kiss. "The truth, my sweet surgeon, is that I've always been impressed with you."

"What?" Emilia said breathlessly.

"Since the moment you walked into the tavern," Maria confessed, "after Judith gave you the chance to run."

Emilia's heart fluttered frantically inside her chest. "Wait, you— you knew?"

A wicked smile curled at one corner of Maria's lips. "Do you honestly think that Judith would've given you the chance to run, if I hadn't told her to?"

Shock hollowed out Emilia's chest. "You were testing me."

Maria shrugged, clearly unashamed. "I have no use for cowards."

"You manipulated me from the start," Emilia said, her shock quickly turning to fury.

"I'm a villain, love," Maria said with a scoff. "Sometimes, I behave like one."

"Sometimes is an understatement," Emilia snarled. She shook her head in disbelief. "Everything Judith said to me—"

"Was what I told her to say," Maria finished.

Though she blamed Maria for it all, the fact that Judith had been such a willing participant—well, it stung.

Judith had called her a *friend*. Had Maria told her to do that, too?

"Why?" Emilia said.

Maria peered into Emilia's tankard. "I'll get you more water."

But Emilia held the tankard tightly, when Maria tried to take it. "Answer me. *Captain*."

The venomous snarl behind the title brought an amused smile to Maria's lips.

Even now, she had no shame.

Unbelievable.

"Surgeons don't negotiate often, do they?" Maria said. When Emilia didn't answer, Maria smiled. "No, I imagine you'd have no use of the skill in your line of work."

"Get to the point, please," Emilia said between clenched teeth.

"You look a bit unwell, love," Maria said with a laugh. "We can still talk, while I'm getting you water."

"I don't need anything from you," Emilia said stubbornly, even as her stomach rolled with nausea.

Apparently, the pirate captain had been waiting for a weak moment—because as soon as Emilia's grip loosened, Maria took the tankard from her hand. "Thank you."

Emilia did *not* reply to Maria's thanks; nor did she stop glaring at the insufferable pirate.

"As I was saying," Maria said, as she strode toward the table. "You clearly know nothing about negotiation."

Emilia's glare grew more murderous with each arrogant remark that came out of Maria's mouth.

"It's not an insult, love," Maria assured her. "It's just a fact. Just like *I* happen to know nothing about medicine—or that thing where you're gentle with injured people."

"Bedside manner," Emilia provided.

Maria pointed one of those tattooed fingers of hers. "Yes, that," she said. "Very bad at that one."

"You don't say," Emilia muttered.

Maria tipped the flagon of water, refilling Emilia's cup. "You see, when you're making a deal with someone, if the other person believes they're the one who needs something from *you*, then you have the power."

Maria carried the tankard back to Emilia. She took a quick sip of it, as she always did—to prove that she hadn't tampered with it.

Despite her anger, Emilia was *especially* grateful for that today, after last night's attack.

317

It was hard to make sense of the separate sides of Maria—deceptive and uncaring one moment, thoughtful the next.

Emilia accepted the cup and forced out a small, "Thank you."

Maria nodded. She took a seat next to Emilia, and just like before, Emilia's pulse quickened at the brush of Maria's thigh.

"If, however," Maria continued, "you think you're the one who needs something from *me*, then I have the power."

Emilia drank from her cup, the cool water soothing her uneasy stomach.

"Do you understand now," Maria said, "why it was necessary to trick you?"

"No, not at all," Emilia said. She angled her body toward Maria's. "Because the alternative was honesty! If we both wanted something, you could've just let the power fall evenly between us. But *no*! You have to manipulate things so that you're always in control."

Maria didn't even blink. "Yes."

Emilia glared at the captain and wished she had the strength to storm out of the cabin.

Unfortunately, her fatigued body wasn't quite ready for standing yet.

Or storming.

Maria spread out her hands. "I'm a pirate, Em."

"So you keep reminding me," Emilia muttered.

Maria turned up her flask. "Look," she said, after her drink, "you can be angry with me about something that happened in the past—"

"I literally found out like two minutes ago," Emilia reminded her.

"Or," Maria continued, "you can open your eyes and see what I've just given you."

Emilia frowned.

"Power," Maria said.

Emilia's confusion only grew. "What?"

"I've told you now," Maria said, "that I want you, that I always have. That means you get to set the terms. You can demand whatever you want of me."

Emilia stared blankly at her. "I'm still on your ship. What power do you think I have?"

"I don't have another surgeon," Maria said. "I don't want another surgeon. I want *you*." She leaned closer and lowered her voice to a whisper. "Demand what you want of me, and I'll give it to you."

Emilia rolled her eyes. "What I *want*," she countered, "is to go home and forget you even exist."

Maria's jaw tightened. *Goddess*, that woman did *not* like being denied what she wanted.

Well, perhaps a little disappointment would do her good.

"Fine," Maria said, "but you can't say I didn't *try* to set things right."

"Wow," Emilia said, drawing out the word. "You really like to pat yourself on the back for doing the bare minimum, don't you?"

To Emilia's surprise, Maria laughed loudly at that. This time, she didn't even ask. She just took Emilia's tankard and went to refill it.

At this point, Emilia realized that Maria must've intended to give Emilia all of her own water—on top of the rations she was already allotted.

And Emilia had no idea how to repay her.

What sense did it make for Maria to be so unabashedly self-serving one moment and so quietly selfless the next?

Was it another trick?

"Tell me about this drug he used," Maria said, as she refilled Emilia's cup. "It sounded as if you recognized it."

Emilia's throat constricted at the question.

Maria returned to the bed and offered the tankard to Emilia. "What is it, love?"

Emilia took the cup, staring at the clear liquid inside. "I think," she said uneasily, "you might be the one person who'd know why I recognized it."

Maria's dark gaze softened. "It's the same one they put in your water? In the dungeons?"

Emilia nodded, her throat too tight to speak.

"I see," Maria said softly. She sat down next to Emilia and took another drink from her flask. "You wouldn't happen to know where someone might find this drug, would you?"

"It's a dangerous drug. Just a few drops of hemlock short of a poison," Emilia said. "It's not something you'd want to make if you didn't have experience in healing."

"Are you saying your attacker had experience in healing?" Maria said with a frown. "I don't think that describes anyone on the *Wicked Fate*. Except you, of course."

Emilia shook her head. "No, what I'm saying," she explained, "is that I don't think the attacker was the one who made it."

"You think he bought it from someone?" Maria said.

"Or it was given to him," Emilia said.

"If it's that dangerous," Maria asked, "why does it even exist?"

"There are some surgeries that are best performed when the person's unconscious," Emilia explained. "On my island, we had… safer methods of inducing sleep." She carefully omitted any mention of magic. "But in Illopia, they use this one, dangerous drug."

"So, in order to get this drug," Maria assumed, "you'd need to know a surgeon?"

"Not necessarily," Emilia said. "It's one way to get it, but there is another."

"And what is that?" Maria asked.

Emilia sighed, "At this point, I'm guessing the entire Illopian Guard has been advised that, to capture me, I'll need to be unconscious."

Maria lifted both eyebrows, and a grin that looked almost…

impressed spread across her face. "You must've been a difficult prisoner."

"I put up a fight," Emilia admitted. "What's wrong with that?"

"Nothing," Maria said, shocking Emilia. She leaned closer, pride burning in those warm, brown eyes. "As a matter of fact, it makes me like you more."

Emilia's cheeks warmed beneath Maria's gaze, and her heart fluttered ever-faster inside her chest.

"Why are you saying this?" she breathed.

Maria's warm gaze left her, as abruptly as it came. "So, you think the Illopian Guard has its own supply of it?"

Emilia blinked. Was she just supposed to pretend that last remark hadn't happened?

"I assume so, yes," Emilia said.

"The Illopian Guard won't set foot in Nefala," Maria said. "They have no friends there." She took another drink from her flask. "Perhaps they bribed someone to go to Nefala for them."

"And onto your ship, too?" Emilia said skeptically.

"I imagine that was just a happy coincidence for him," Maria said, "finding out that I'd hired you."

Emilia watched her curiously.

"Well," Maria said with a dark smile, "it'll be the opposite of happy soon enough."

Emilia nearly shivered at the cold brutality in her tone.

"You really mean to kill this guy," Emilia realized.

"Of course," Maria said, her deep, brown eyes shifting toward Emilia, "and you're going to help me."

Emilia's eyes widened. "Me?"

"Yes, you," Maria said with a wicked smile. "You'll make such lovely bait, Em."

"Bait?" Emilia said.

Emilia didn't like the sound of *that* at all.

"How are you feeling, love?" Maria said, as if she hadn't just mentioned using Emilia as bait. "Did the water help at all?"

"Umm, yes? Thank you," Emilia said with a wary frown. "I'm still dizzy, but my stomach seems to have settled."

"And the headache?" Maria asked.

Emilia's frown deepened. "How did you know about the headache?"

"You spoke a little in your sleep," Maria said.

"I did not," Emilia said, mortified.

"You did," Maria said with a gentle smile. "I asked you what hurt, thinking you'd say the wound, but you said it was your head."

Emilia stared, her eyes wide. "I was asleep?"

Maria gave a languid shrug. "Seemed to be."

"I didn't say anything else, did I?" Emilia asked.

Horrifically, Maria didn't even answer that. "You need more water, don't you?"

Before Emilia could say no—that Maria should save some for herself—Maria took the tankard and carried it to her table.

Emilia could not have been more confused by Maria's behavior today.

Even as a child, Emilia had never been cared for the way Maria was caring for her, now. And even if Maria *was* doing it for her own purposes, it still seemed so...unlike her.

Maria picked up the flagon of water that she'd left on her table and refilled Emilia's cup. Again. "You can stay with me until noon," she offered, "but sick or not, I'll need you in the galley by midday. Can you handle that?"

"If Judith needs me, I'll go now," Emilia assured her. "I'm still dizzy, but there must be something I can do."

"For fuck's sake, Em, I'm not sending you back to work when you can't even walk," Maria scoffed. She returned to Emilia, offering her the water. "You'll stay with me until midday."

"What's so special about midday?" Emilia asked.

Maria's smile tilted wickedly. "That's when we set our trap."

Emilia frowned. "So, you won't send me back to work when I'm sick, but you *will* dangle me in front of the dangerous pirate who stabbed me last night?"

Maria lifted her lean shoulders in an uncaring shrug. "That part's unavoidable, I'm afraid."

"Somehow, I doubt that," Emilia muttered.

Maria's gaze shifted downward, lingering on the tear in Emilia's shirt. She pocketed her flask and knelt in the floor, in front of Emilia.

Reaching a hand toward Emilia's shirt, Maria murmured, "May I see it?"

Surprised by Maria's hesitation, Emilia nodded.

Emilia couldn't help but shudder, when Maria's thumb brushed her hip. She looked down, watching as the pirate captain lifted the hem of Emilia's shirt—checking the blood-soaked fabric beneath it.

"I'm no surgeon," Maria said hesitantly, "but I splashed some rum over the wound and wrapped it." She lifted her gaze to meet Emilia's. "Was that enough, or will you need some sort of antidote?"

"It wasn't a poison," Emilia reminded her, "and the drug usually only lasts about twelve hours. Give me a bit, and I'll be as good as new."

At this angle, Maria's dark, silken eyelashes cast shadows over her beautiful, brown eyes.

It was cruel—for a dangerous woman to be that beautiful.

How was Emilia supposed to make rational decisions when the woman who might kill her looked like *that*?

"Does it hurt?" Maria said softly.

For the sake of her pride, Emilia wanted to say no, but something about Maria's expression drew the honest answer from her lips.

"Yes."

Maria's thumb traced the fabric. "Ask me for his head, and I'll give it to you."

Emilia's eyes widened. She didn't know whether to feel appalled by that offer—or amused by it.

Maria was like Emilia's dragons—bringing her some strange, gory gift and expecting her to appreciate it.

It was cute—in a murderous sort of way.

"I don't want his head," Emilia assured the captain. "My cabin's too small for it. I don't think I could handle the stench."

With no warning whatsoever, Maria folded forward, bursting into a fit of hysterical laughter.

Emilia smiled at the sight.

So much for their perfectly balanced hate-relationship.

Maria must've laughed for a good minute or two, before she finally climbed to her feet.

She didn't mention the joke—or why she'd laughed so gleefully about it. She simply returned to her table.

"Helen and Pelt will probably tease you about getting so drunk last night," Maria said, as she refilled her flask. "Let them tease. I promise they'll only like you more."

"But," Emilia said with a frown, "I *wasn't* drunk last night."

"Yeah, definitely don't say *that*," Maria muttered.

Emilia's frown deepened. "I don't understand."

Maria turned toward her. "I had to tell them something. I need you to *not* contradict my story."

"Oh," Emilia said.

"Pelt said you drank your *'rum'* very fast," Maria said with raised eyebrows, "so that lie sort of dropped into my lap."

"Yeah," Emilia said with a nervous smile. "I didn't know if you'd want them to know about the wine…"

"Why wouldn't I?" Maria asked.

Emilia shrugged. "Because of the rumors?"

Maria smiled. "I thought you said it wasn't *your* job to make sure my crew respected me."

Emilia swallowed uneasily. "That's not—"

"That's exactly what you did," Maria argued. "You lied to protect my reputation."

Emilia looked away, blushing. "Maybe I *was* drunk, then."

"And after a fight, no less," Maria said.

"Clearly, I wasn't in my right mind," Emilia grumbled.

Maria crossed her arms, grinning at that. "We drink a lot more than landsmen do, so it's practically tradition for new sailors to get drunk." She laughed, "You may have unintentionally improved your own reputation, as well."

Emilia gave her a bemused look. "So, your crew likes me best when I'm punching huge men and getting drunk?"

Maria's smile faded. "They're your crew, too, Em."

"For now," Emilia said.

Maria narrowed her eyes at that.

Emilia couldn't help but think the pirate captain behaved a little like a sullen child, when she didn't get her way.

Well, perhaps a little more *murderous* than a sullen child.

But the glare was similar.

Maria tilted her head, her silky, brown curls falling to one side. She studied Emilia with a thoughtful frown, before tucking a hand behind her back.

A bit unnerved by her scrutiny, Emilia shifted her gaze toward the windows, instead. From her place on the bed, Emilia saw nothing but blue—with the occasional seagull flying overhead.

Wood creaked beneath Maria's boots, and the sweet scent of hibiscus and oranges enticed Emilia's senses.

Emilia cast a curious glance at the pirate captain, who now stood directly in front of her.

Was she waiting for something?

"Em," Maria said with a devious smile. "Would you mind picking up that bucket of water for me?"

"Oh," Emilia said. She looked down at the bucket of sea water that Maria had left by the bed and knelt to pick it up.

The moment she bent forward, however, Maria wrapped one

hand around her shoulder and shoved Emilia backward with her thigh.

The bucket fell from Emilia's hands, and the sea water spilled out of it, soaking the floor.

Maria didn't even stop to look. She shoved Emilia back and swung her thigh over Emilia's waist.

Emilia froze the moment Maria pressed a knife to her throat.

So, even when Maria wasn't wearing her swords, she was still armed?

Figures.

None of it had hurt, surprisingly enough. It was more pressure than pain, when Maria pinned her to the bed.

Emilia had no doubt that it *would've* hurt, if Maria had kicked with her knee, but she'd used her thigh, instead—controlling Emilia's body without bruising it.

Beside Emilia's head, Rat-Slayer opened one frosty, blue eye and peeked at them—before settling back into a deep sleep.

Apparently, her heroic, feline protector didn't care, as long as it was Maria attacking her.

Little traitor.

Maria's hair hung around her face in dark, silky ringlets, and the scent of the sea itself surrounded them.

"What," Emilia forced out, even as the blade pressed into her throat, "are you doing?"

"Testing you," Maria murmured, "and you, my sweet surgeon, have failed spectacularly."

Emilia narrowed her eyes at that.

As always, Maria was much too arrogant. She hadn't even pinned Emilia's hands yet.

The fight was far from over.

Emilia grasped Maria's wrist with one hand and with her other arm, she pressed into the bend of Maria's elbow.

She tried to turn her body away from the knife, but Maria's thighs restricted the movement of her hips.

So, she turned her head, instead.

Maria must've been more concerned with watching Emilia's reactions than actually putting up a fight—because she didn't even *try* to stop Emilia from pushing the knife away.

As a matter of fact, as soon as Emilia twisted Maria's wrist away from her, Maria dropped the knife.

Emilia reached for it, but Maria grabbed her by the throat and pushed her back down.

When Emilia froze in surprise, Maria pinned Emilia's wrists above her head, as well.

Maria pressed her thumb and forefinger into Emilia's throat, and Emilia's head spun in a way that wasn't...*totally* unpleasant.

Maria leaned closer, tilting her face, as if she were going to kiss Emilia again. "Yield," she whispered.

Emilia pulled at her wrists, but Maria's grip was steadfast and strong—positively unyielding. Giving up, Emilia pinned her captain with an expectant glare.

When she'd gone a moment too long without breathing, Maria chuckled. "Breathe, love," she murmured. "I'm not actually choking you."

"What?" Emilia said, and indeed, breath spilled from her lungs.

Maria pressed down again, and though she *could* still breathe, Emilia grew lightheaded.

"It's only a bit of pressure," Maria whispered, her lips curving, "to make a point."

Emilia squeezed her eyes shut, desperately trying to ignore the hollow ache between her legs.

Why did Maria have to straddle her in a bed, of all places?

And this was the second time she'd done it, too!

She *had* to know what she was doing. She just had to!

"And what point is that?" Emilia asked.

"That if I were trying to kill you," Maria said, tilting her face closer, "you'd be dead."

Emilia's core tightened with desire, as Maria's rum-scented breath fell against Emilia's lips. "I'm injured," she said breathlessly.

Emilia's body rebelled against every rational thought she'd ever had about Maria.

With Maria's thighs around her waist and Maria's mouth only inches from her own, Emilia's entire *being* ached for another kiss.

"I know you're injured," Maria assured her. "Why do you think I attacked you on the bed, rather than on the floorboards?"

Because you wanted to torture me with these thoughts I shouldn't be having? Emilia assumed.

Not willing to admit defeat yet, Emilia told the pirate captain, "You had an unfair advantage."

"Will you be fully healed by midday?" Maria said.

Emilia's brows furrowed. "No."

Maria shifted her weight slightly, and her thighs pressed harder against Emilia's waist. "Then, your attacker will have an unfair advantage, as well," she explained. "You'll need to prepare for that."

Emilia watched, as Maria's large, brown eyes dilated with lust.

Perhaps she wasn't the only one struggling with this...position.

"Are you going to let me go?" Emilia asked.

Maria pressed harder against her. "Do you *want* me to let you go?"

Emilia's pulse raced at the question. "Why wouldn't I?"

"Say it," Maria whispered against her lips. "Tell me you don't want this, and I'll get off of you now."

Desire pulsed throughout Emilia's body, and she just couldn't bring herself to lie—not while she ached with the desperation she felt now.

So, just like she'd done the day of their sword fight, Emilia gave in to it.

She leaned forward, pushing against Maria's hand, and then, she pressed her mouth against those soft, warm lips of Maria's.

With a surprised groan, Maria released Emilia's throat and sank her fingers into Emilia's hair, instead.

The taste and scent of Maria surrounded Emilia, drowning out her fears and reservations.

Maria tasted of the sea itself. She tasted of courage and adventure—and of an untapped sweetness beneath.

Maria deepened the kiss, pressing her tongue into Emilia's mouth. She was as soft as flower petals and as powerful as a deep ocean current.

And Emilia aligned oh-so-easily to her strength, like a drowning sailor caught in the undertow.

Maria's hips gave a small arch, and she breathed out a deep, sensual moan against Emilia's mouth.

Emilia's entire body burned at the sound.

"Fuck," Maria said, turning her face away. She rested her head against Emilia's shoulder, panting for breath.

Maria sat up much too soon, and Emilia desperately wanted to pull her back down. "You feel a bit clammy," the captain said breathlessly. "I'll get you something to eat."

Emilia nearly whimpered the moment Maria's strong thighs left her waist.

Even after Maria climbed out of bed, Emilia lay still, waiting for the pulsing between her legs to fade.

Emilia couldn't believe she'd just kissed the pirate captain.

Again.

When she heard the quiet thud of Maria's boots again, Emilia forced herself into a sitting position. She winced a little, her muscles still sore.

Maria returned to the bed with a shiny, red apple and offered it to Emilia. "Eat that."

Emilia accepted the apple—not arguing, for once. She grimaced, when she noticed the puddle of water around Maria's boots.

"Sorry about your bucket," Emilia said.

"Don't be," Maria laughed. "It was my fault."

Emilia cracked a small smile at that. "That's true."

Maria's gaze softened. "I didn't hurt you, did I?" she said—with what sounded like genuine concern. "I tried to stay off the wound."

Emilia swallowed uneasily. "Yeah," she said without thinking, but she quickly backtracked, "I mean, yes, you stayed off of it. Not, yes, it hurt."

Maria smiled. "I'm relieved to hear it."

Emilia had no idea how to interact with this side of Maria, so she saved herself the trouble—by choosing that moment to bite into her apple.

"If you can keep a table between you and your attacker," Maria suggested, "that would be best. It'd render his knife almost useless."

"And if he has a pistol?" Emilia asked.

"Judith will intervene if he pulls out a pistol," Maria assured her. "He won't have a chance to use it on you. I swear."

That didn't comfort Emilia as much as Maria meant for it to.

"And is there a reason this trap of yours can't wait until I'm healed," Emilia asked, "at least?"

"There is," Maria assured her. "Can you walk?" she said gently. "I'll show you."

The honest answer was probably no. Emilia's head still spun like a waterwheel any time she moved. But she was too stubborn to admit that. So, Emilia said, "Yeah," and climbed to her feet—with her half-eaten apple still in hand.

She wobbled only once, before Maria came to her aide. Emilia found herself blinking up at the pirate captain for the second time in one day. A slow rush of desire unfurled through her, as Maria pressed a hand against Emilia's back.

"I've got you," Maria said. "Come on."

With more gentleness than Emilia ever would've assumed her capable of, Maria helped Emilia to the table and then into the chair. "Where do you think we are, Em?"

Maria circled the table and picked up a roll of parchment.

She spread it out, revealing a map of the Azure Sea.

As Emilia watched Maria's tattooed fingers smooth out the map, the memory of those fingers in her hair came rushing back to the forefront of her mind. Her skin burned, and her breath grew shallow.

Was this just...*normal* for Maria? Did she often kiss women she hated and then pretend it didn't happen?

Emilia wasn't sure how she managed it.

Apparently unaware of Emilia's distracting thoughts, Maria tapped the map. "Show me."

Emilia studied the map with a frown. "I'm not sure where we are today," she admitted, "but I know we were here yesterday." She pointed at a part of the Azure Sea that bordered the Illopian forest.

"Yes," Maria said. She trailed her finger west, nearing the part of the sea that bordered the Illopian mountains. "This is where we are now." She moved her finger toward the rocky shores of the Illopian mountains, where the map bore the warning: *Beware of sirens.* "And this is where we'll be tomorrow. Do you know what that means, surgeon?"

Emilia looked up at the captain. "That you're not taking my advice about avoiding siren territory?"

"It means that if he waits even one more day, he won't be able to take you," Maria explained. "It'd be suicidal to take a longboat through siren territory. If he waited until tomorrow and tried it then, you'd both be eaten."

Little did Maria know, Emilia had a friend among the sirens. They'd eat her attacker, for sure—but they'd likely leave Emilia alone.

Then again, it *had* been nearly a decade since she'd seen Nerissa.

Who knew if the beautiful, cannibalistic siren would still honor their friendship?

"So, he'll want to do it today," Emilia said. "Is that what you're saying?"

Maria leaned forward, bracing her hands against the table. "He'll be *desperate* to do it today."

Emilia took another bite of her apple. "Why don't we just survive the night, then?" she asked. "Wouldn't he just give up?"

"Well, first," Maria said, her eyes dark, "because he'd get away with what he's done, and I refuse to let that happen."

Emilia sighed in frustration. "You'd rather risk my life than just let everyone walk away from this?"

"Yes," Maria said—without a hint of shame.

Emilia set the apple on the table, too agitated to eat. "And second?"

"Second," Maria said, her voice gentler now, "the only reason your attacker has kept your secret this long is that he wants the bounty." She shrugged. "Perhaps he plans to buy himself a pardon. Perhaps the Illopian Guard has already promised him one." She lifted both eyebrows. "Once that's no longer an option, do you think he's just going to keep your secret for the hell of it? No. He'll tell his shipmates."

A fresh wave of anxiety fluttered in Emilia's stomach.

"I've told you before," Maria reminded her, "if the crew finds out before I do, I can't help you."

Emilia dug her fingers into her thighs, fighting back another wave of nausea. "Where do you keep prisoners?"

Maria watched Emilia's hands, her brows creasing. "In the brig," she said softly. "It's below deck. You haven't been down there yet, but the cat has." She glanced at Rat-Slayer. "It's where the rats like to hide."

Emilia shivered at the thought. "Are the bars iron?"

Maria looked at her, and the softness of her gaze suggested that, perhaps, she knew why Emilia was asking. "It'll be smaller than your cell in Regolis—and wetter," she sighed. "But otherwise, the same."

Emilia's chest tightened. "Shackles?"

"We don't shackle people to the wall on this ship," Maria

assured her. "That serves no purpose, besides degradation." She sighed, "But yes, we do usually shackle the wrists."

Fear crushed Emilia's chest, like an anvil, and she gasped for breath.

Maria must've noticed—because she immediately circled the table and knelt in front of Emilia. She grasped Emilia's hands to stop her from scratching up her thighs any worse than she already had.

"Em," Maria said, the crease of her brows deeper than usual, "I don't want that fate for you. Tell me who you are, and we'll come up with a solution together."

Emilia shook her head, panic buzzing through her veins. "I don't trust you," she said breathlessly. "I won't."

Maria released her hands. "Have it your way, then," she said, and she returned to her own chair. "But you should know: by the end of this day, I'm going to know who you are, whether you tell me or not."

Emilia cast a wary glance in Maria's direction.

"And when I have you arrested," Maria snarled, "don't say I didn't warn you."

Well, Emilia decided, *at least the cruel side of Maria wouldn't evoke the cataclysmic whirlwind of feelings that her kiss had.*

Hate was easy.

Feelings were not.

CHAPTER 16

A Betrayal

" I can take you back to bed, if you're tired."

Startled awake, Emilia dropped her face from her hand and nearly bashed it against the table.

She blinked drowsily and straightened in her chair. "I'm awake."

Maria snorted at that.

Aside from Maria's occasional offer of food and water, neither of them had spoken since early that morning.

And with nothing to occupy her attention, Emilia had quickly succumbed to the sedative in her system.

The quiet scratch of quill against parchment resumed, as Maria returned to writing in that leather-bound book of hers.

"What are you writing?" Emilia asked.

"Captain's log," Maria said, without looking up. "I was too preoccupied to do it last night."

Emilia leaned forward in her chair, squinting at the book.

A smile quirked at one corner of Maria's lips, but she continued to write. "You shouldn't read my log, love. You might see something you don't like."

Emilia shrugged. "I can't read your handwriting, anyway."

Maria laughed. "It's interesting how your ability to read my handwriting increases or decreases, depending on how angry you are with me, at any given moment."

Emilia's lips twitched at that. "Wait. Are you under the delusion that there's ever been a moment when I *wasn't* angry with you?"

That remark earned an even louder laugh from the pirate captain.

"And how much do you hate me at this *exact* moment?" Maria said with a grin. "Need to know for the log."

Emilia's brows furrowed. "Why would you write about *that*?"

Maria's smile widened. "Answer the question, surgeon."

"Immensely," Emilia said.

Maria gave another short laugh. "Perfect."

Emilia rolled her eyes. She couldn't imagine what kind of nonsense Maria must've been writing in that log. Had Maria written about everything she'd ever done?

Emilia cringed as she wondered what Maria had written on the day of their sword fight. The thought of her self-destructive rage being immortalized in a captain's log was almost worse than living through it.

Emilia made a mental note to tear out a few pages before she left the ship for good.

After a few moments of surprisingly comfortable silence, Maria said, "What do surgeons do for fun?" She turned to the next page of her log. "Read?"

Emilia stared blankly at the captain. "I'm trying to decide whether to take that as a compliment or an insult," she muttered, but then, she added, "Yes, I like to read."

Though she didn't look up from her log, the deep, lovely curve of Maria's lips suggested that she was quite proud of herself for guessing correctly.

"I also like spending time with animals," Emilia said—again, carefully omitting the word '*dragons.*'

"Why?" Maria said curiously.

Emilia shrugged. "They're easier to understand than people."

Maria tilted her head slightly, intrigued. "What do you mean?"

"Well," Emilia said, "they don't lie or trick you. They don't play these strange word games because of some arbitrary, societal rule." With another shy shrug, she said, "They just say what they mean."

Maria frowned. "Em, I don't know if anyone's told you this, but," she paused, "they're animals. They shouldn't be *saying* anything."

Emilia winced. Perhaps she should've worded that in a way that was a bit less…witchy.

"Reading," Emilia mumbled. "Yes, I like reading."

Maria laughed and returned her attention to the log. "I do have a few books, if you'd like to read—all written in Illopian, of course."

Emilia smiled. "I've been reading in Illopian ever since I was old enough to steal a book of medicine from a shipwreck."

"Stealing from shipwrecks," Maria said in a tone that was playfully chiding. "Sounds like you've always been on the road to piracy."

Emilia scowled at that. "There's a difference in taking a book from a ship and being the one who sunk it."

"And yet, we both have books we've taken from ships," Maria countered.

Emilia rolled her eyes at the oversimplification.

Maria gestured vaguely with her quill—so vaguely, in fact, that Emilia had no idea what she was pointing at. "My books are in that wooden chest back there. You're welcome to take any you like."

Emilia counted at least four wooden chests in the captain's quarters, and all of them were identical.

"I'm surprised you don't have a proper library," Emilia said. "Navy captains have libraries, don't they?"

Maria turned another page in her leather-bound book. "Did Catherine tell you that?"

Emilia froze, her blood cooling in her veins. She tried not to let the pain show, as she looked up at the captain. "Why do you keep mentioning Catherine?" She realized her mistake a little too late and quickly said, "I mean…Admiral Rochester."

That clearly wasn't the right answer, either, because Maria's dark knuckles whitened around the quill.

Maria looked up, sparks of fiery rage burning in those large, brown eyes of hers.

"Just say Catherine."

Emilia frowned. Was that jealousy she'd heard underneath Maria's words?

Considering Maria's current hatred of the Royal Navy, it seemed strange to think she might be jealous of Catherine's title.

But if not that, then what?

"I take it you're, umm," Emilia hazarded, "not happy about her promotion?"

Maria leaned back in her chair. Her hand naturally went to her hip, but there was no sword there, this time, for her to clutch. "The navy's the same, no matter who's admiral. They're all just puppets for their king."

Though her words sounded dismissive enough, the dark fury in her eyes conveyed a very different message.

"I do wonder, though," Maria said, her eyes dark, "who she had to capture to earn this promotion."

Emilia shifted uneasily in her chair.

"Her first prestigious promotion happened after she captured me. By my estimates, this last promotion must've happened several months ago," Maria said. She leaned forward. "Remind me, thief," she growled. "How long ago were you captured?"

Emilia looked away, her heart racing.

How did she know? How had she figured it out so easily?

Emilia decided to appeal to the captain's ego. "Surely, you don't think I'm important enough to earn her a promotion as prestigious as the one you earned her?"

"Perhaps not," Maria said.

Emilia didn't know if Maria had actually fallen for that or if she were simply dropping the subject, but she was grateful for the brief respite, either way.

Maria set her quill aside and closed the leather-bound book. Her nostrils flared slightly, and her breasts rose and fell beneath her thin shirt.

By the time she stood, she looked significantly calmer.

"Do you have any preferences on books?"

Emilia stared at her, stunned by her abrupt change in attitude. Curious about what sort of books Maria enjoyed, Emilia said, "Surprise me."

Maria's lips curved. "Oh, Em," she teased. "You're such a pirate, and you don't even know it."

Emilia didn't quite understand that—nor did she particularly *like* it—but she was too enamored by Maria's smile to argue.

Maria knelt in front of one of the wooden chests and opened it.

Emilia looked away, trying *not* to notice the way Maria's leather trousers stretched around her strong thighs, when she knelt.

Maria rifled through the chest, books and paper rustling inside.

She pulled out a heavy book and dusted off the cover. She then carried it to the table and dropped it in front of Emilia. "That one's banned in Illopia."

The leather cover of the book bore no title. Instead, it depicted a burning castle, embroidered into the brown, leather cover with golden thread.

Emilia traced the symbol with her finger and then opened the book to read the title.

"A book about anarchy," Emilia said with an amused smile. "Why am I not surprised?"

"I have another banned book you might enjoy," Maria said with an enticing grin, "but it's a bit...*salacious*."

Emilia's brows furrowed. "You can't mean that," she assumed. "I've *never* come across such a book."

"But you're interested now, aren't you?" Maria teased.

Emilia placed the anarchist book in her lap, freeing her hands. "Please. Show me."

Maria's smile widened. She returned to the chest and knelt to pick up this supposedly obscene book of hers. This one's cover was embroidered with blue thread, instead.

Maria returned to the table, her hands tight around the book. "On your island," she asked, "which gods did you worship?"

Emilia hesitated. The topic of religion veered dangerously close to Emilia's secret.

"The islands depend on the sea for their livelihood," Emilia explained, "much like sailors do, I assume."

"Is that so?" Maria said.

"Your ship happens to bear the image of the goddess we loved most," Emilia said. "Aletha."

"In that case," Maria said with a deep smile, "you're *really* going to love this."

Emilia peered curiously at the book, but Maria kept it pressed against her chest, hiding the symbol.

"I don't know how much islanders know about Illopian law," Maria said, "but I assume you know that worship of Aletha is outlawed in the kingdom?"

Emilia nodded. "They think she's evil, but they're wrong."

"She sent her sea monsters after the monarchy," Maria reminded her. "Your people don't consider that evil?"

"The Whispering Abyss is the *home* of sea monsters!" Emilia said defensively. "They had every right to defend it." She knew arguing about gods and goddesses would get her nowhere with Illopians, but she loved Aletha far too much to ignore the blasphemy. "They had the Westerly Sea already. It's not Aletha's fault that your monarchy was too greedy to accept that."

Maria lifted a scarred eyebrow. "*My* monarchy?"

Emilia shrugged. "You're Illopian, aren't you?"

"I'm a pirate," Maria stated. "I claim no home but the sea."

Emilia fell silent, actually impressed, for once, by Maria's witty remark. "Their monarchy, then."

Maria grinned. "Better."

Emilia regretted her outburst, just as she'd regretted it after her argument with Zain, but what none of them could possibly understand was that Aletha wasn't *just* Emilia's goddess.

She was the person who'd decided Emilia deserved to live— after Emilia's mother had decided otherwise.

"Well," Maria continued, "after the sea serpents dragged the royal ship down to the bottom of the sea, taking most of the royal family with it, the next in line for the throne—a great-great-great-great grandfather of King Eldric—ordered that all books and images of Aletha be destroyed." With a sly smirk, Maria tapped the book in her hand. "This is a *very* old book."

Emilia lifted her eyebrows. "It's about Aletha?"

"Not *just* Aletha," Maria said, stepping forward. She placed the book in front of Emilia and waited for her to read the cover.

"The Love Affair of the Wind and Sea," Emilia read aloud. She looked up, her eyes widening. "It's about Aletha and Aria?"

The two goddesses who'd given Aletharia its name, whose love for each other was only matched by their hatred for each other.

According to Aletha, it was, indeed, both at once: love and hate.

Their relationship was strange, to say the least, and when they fought, *everyone* knew.

"It is," Maria assured her. She braced a hand against the back of her chair and watched with a smile, as Emilia thumbed through the scandalous book. "Do you have *any* idea how many Illopian laws that one book breaks?"

Emilia glanced up at the pirate captain, her excitement rising. "How did you get it?"

Maria lifted her lean shoulders in a shrug that practically oozed arrogance. "I have my ways."

Emilia flipped through the book. "This is amazing!"

Maria's smile tilted wickedly. "Having second thoughts about leaving me yet?"

Emilia looked up. "You think one book is all it takes to keep me here forever?"

"Darling, I'll give you every book from every ship in the damn sea," Maria offered, "if you give me what I want first."

Emilia lifted her eyebrows. "Which is me," she assumed, "for some reason."

Maria leaned forward, resting her weight on her hand. "You fit here, Em," she murmured. "You may not realize it yet, but you do."

A hint of pain twisted at Emilia's brows. "I've never fit anywhere," she said honestly. "I doubt that'll ever change."

Maria frowned curiously at that. "I'll just have to convince you otherwise, then."

Emilia didn't know what to think of that promise. Was having a surgeon really that important to Maria, or was this simply a matter of her wanting what she'd been denied?

Emilia returned her attention to the book, scanning the chapters with interest. The first time she came across a sex scene, however, she slammed the book closed and placed it on the table.

"I don't think I should read that," Emilia said, blushing.

Did Aletha *know* about this book?

"You haven't even gotten to the best part yet," Maria said, taking the book. She flipped through, until she found the page she was looking for. Then, she dropped it in Emilia's lap. "That's my favorite part—where they fuck so hard they cause a hurricane."

Emilia stared at the graphic description, her eyes wide.

Maria slipped her lean form between the table and Emilia's chair. She hopped onto the table and curled a finger beneath Emilia's chin. "Look at you," she teased. "Pink as a sea star."

Emilia glared at the captain, but as heat gathered in her cheeks, she knew that Maria was right. She was definitely blushing.

Emilia tried her best to ignore the fact that, with Maria sitting on the table, that left Emilia seated between her thighs—but it was hard to ignore things like that when Maria looked at her like *this*.

"Promise me you'll read it?" Maria murmured.

Emilia closed the book. "I worship her."

Maria chuckled. "So, did the wind goddess, apparently."

Emilia rolled her eyes. If Aletha found out what Emilia had just read, she'd never let her live it down.

The sea goddess was playful and mischievous, and she loved to make Emilia blush.

Apparently, Maria did, too.

Maria rested her hands on her leather-clad thighs. "I take it the stories they told on your island were less…graphic?"

"A bit," Emilia said.

Maria laughed. "But it's true?" she said with a surprised smile. "The sea goddess really is into…women?"

Well, she'd definitely be into one as gorgeous as you, Emilia thought.

"Gods experience attraction in diverse ways, just as humans do," Emilia told her. "Aletha enjoys women—humans, sirens, goddesses, all of it. There's no type of woman she isn't intrigued by."

Maria's eyebrows lifted. "Sirens?" she repeated. "But they're like…fish. Right?"

Emilia's eyes widened at that. "Please, don't say that in front of them. They wouldn't hesitate to tear your flesh from your bones."

"That sounds like something you'd enjoy," Maria said.

Emilia feigned interest. "You know what? You're right! *Please*, get eaten."

Maria tilted her head back, laughing loudly.

Emilia blushed. How was she supposed to remember that she hated Maria, when the pirate captain laughed like that?

With her voice so full of joy and that gleeful, golden glow beneath her brown skin?

Maria leaned forward, precariously balanced on the edge of the table. The scent of hibiscus and citrus swirled between them, as her soft, brown hair fell forward, and she clasped her tattooed hands between her knees.

"Tell me more," she encouraged. "Tell me your island's stories."

For the second time that day, Emilia hesitated. The Drakon sorcerers had a much more intimate relationship with the gods than humans did.

If she'd lived on any other island, anywhere other than Drakon Isle, she would've learned different stories.

Maria might've been trying to trick Emilia into revealing which island was her home.

But the intrigue that burned in Maria's dark eyes looked so sincere, and Emilia had never known anyone to listen to her with such enthusiasm before.

With a smile, Emilia began, "Long ago, before ships, before anyone *dared* cross the seas, the goddesses of sea and wind hated each other."

"Is that so?" Maria said.

Emilia suddenly felt like a child again, telling stories to her dragons, as she coaxed them to sleep.

It was too bad that Maria had let Rat-Slayer out hours before. Emilia thought he would've enjoyed the tale, as well.

But as it was, Maria's captivating smile was encouragement enough.

"Oh, yes," Emilia assured her. "In those days, not only was it unsafe to cross the seas, but all of Aletharia faced treacherous danger every time Aletha and Aria fought."

"Hurricanes?" Maria assumed.

"Hurricanes, maelstroms, tsunamis!" Emilia said, excitement jittering in her fingertips. "Every deadly danger caused by the collision of wind and sea wreaked havoc on the lands of Aletharia."

Maria's smile deepened, and Emilia was so bewitched by it that she couldn't have stopped, even if she'd wanted to.

"Unfortunately, this drove humans toward the mountains,

where the *god* of mountains waited to ensnare them with greed," Emilia continued.

"Interesting," Maria said with arched eyebrows. "Your people think the god of the mountains is evil?"

Emilia froze. Perhaps she'd said too much.

"No, don't stop," Maria said worriedly. "Continue. Please."

A *please* from a woman as prideful as Maria was hard to ignore.

With a wary frown, Emilia warned, "Our beliefs about Petra differ greatly from Illopia's."

"Darling, I was taught that Aletha was evil and cruel," Maria reminded her, "only to become a sailor and find that the sea was kinder to me than land." She grinned mischievously. "I am *very* open to new ideas."

Emilia swallowed uneasily. "Illopia believes that Petra blessed them with gold. We believe he ensnared them with it."

"They're the greatest kingdom in Aletharia," Maria scoffed. "How *ensnared* can they possibly be?"

Emilia scowled at that. "You can't think that," she said in disbelief. "They're not great. They're greedy."

Maria waved a hand dismissively. "Great, as in *powerful*."

"Power isn't greatness," Emilia argued.

Maria gave her a baffled smile. "What is greatness," she laughed, "if not power?"

Of course she'd say that. Maria was practically obsessed with power.

"I don't know," Emilia said softly. She shrank back in her seat. "A younger, more naïve version of me would've said kindness, but I'm not that person anymore."

Maria's smile faded, and her scars deepened. "That beautiful sparkle has left your eyes," she murmured, more to herself than Emilia. "I've upset you."

"What? No," Emilia said dismissively, but then, her cheeks grew warm. "Wait. Did you say...beautiful?"

"I've never seen eyes as green as yours," Maria whispered, but before Emilia could wonder at that remark, she said, "Tell me more. Tell me how these two goddesses overcame their hatred for each other."

Emilia stared at the captain, her heart fluttering so fast she thought it might fly away without her. "Well," she said breathlessly, "they had a mutual enemy."

"Petra," Maria assumed. "God of the mountains."

"Yes," Emilia said softly. She stroked the leather cover of the book, letting the soft material soothe her anxiety. "Humans fell into his trap *so* easily."

"And the trap," Maria asked, "was the gold they mined from the mountains?"

"The trap was greed," Emilia said. "He convinced them that magic was the enemy and that gold was a blessing."

Maria shrugged. "You can't survive without gold. Not in this world."

"Why not?" Emilia countered. "Do you eat gold? No. It's just a tool they used to force people into a hierarchy of rich and poor."

Maria's brows furrowed.

"Petra gave the Kingdom of Illopia wealth, yes," Emilia said, "but it wasn't a reward for outlawing magic—as Illopia says it was. It was a trap—to keep them enslaved to greed forevermore."

"According to the tales of your island," Maria added.

No.

According to the goddesses themselves.

But rather than say something that would *definitely* arouse suspicion, Emilia simply said, "Yes."

"So, the goddesses united against Illopia's chosen god?" Maria said. "Against Petra?"

"Yes," Emilia said. "They tried to free humans—entice them with the sea, pull them from the mountains—but some of them just wouldn't let go of their greed."

"Entice them with the sea," Maria said thoughtfully. "I like this

345

tale of yours," she said, leaning back. "Because the sea has always felt like freedom to me."

Emilia smiled. "They say Aletha has a soft spot for anyone who heeds her call."

Maria lifted a scarred eyebrow. "You think your goddess would like me?"

"Oh, I'm sure of it," Emilia said, "but don't worry. I'm allowed to disagree with her."

Maria chuckled, and Emilia couldn't help but laugh along with her.

"A soft spot, though?" Maria said, shaking her head. "The sea goddess is supposed to be this terrible, ruthless deity, and you're telling me she has a soft spot?"

"Aletha is violent and tempestuous by nature, but she can be kind, too," Emilia assured her. Her chest lightened, as she remembered the kindness the sea goddess had once shown her. "Even the fiercest beings can have a softer side."

Maria's smile faded, and a hint of awe flickered in those dark eyes of hers. "You think so?"

The sudden uncertainty in Maria's voice caught Emilia by surprise. Maria's tone usually held so much authority, so much pride, so much humor, even. But now, there was hesitation—and doubt.

Emilia felt a bit of doubt rise in herself, as well, as she considered the question.

It was what she'd always believed about Aletha, of course, but could it be true of her vicious pirate captain, as well?

Surely, this woman, who Emilia hated, had nothing in common with the goddess she loved.

And yet, she knew, as she considered Maria's temperament, that wasn't true at all.

Maria personified the sea almost as well as the goddess herself —wild and unpredictable, violent and fierce.

Was it possible she could be as kind, too?

Surprising even herself, Emilia said, "I do."

Maria's lips parted, and a soft breath spilled out—as if Emilia's answer had knocked the breath out of her.

Several emotions flashed across her face—astonishment, fear, doubt, and...perhaps even appreciation.

But Maria wiped those emotions from her face so quickly that Emilia didn't have time to analyze them.

"That's a lovely thought," Maria said, hopping off the table. She grinned at Emilia. "But I wouldn't bet on it."

Emilia watched curiously, as Maria strolled over to the windows.

Maria rested a hand against the glass and gazed out at the sea.

Sunlight streamed in through the windows, casting Maria's long, lean form in shadow.

Maria didn't speak for a long time after that, but her brows remained creased.

Silence spread between them in a steady crescendo, and just when Emilia thought she could bear it no longer, Maria spoke.

"She betrayed you, didn't she?"

Emilia blinked, caught off-guard by the question. "What?"

Maria turned toward Emilia, her gaze dark and unyielding. "Catherine."

Like always, Emilia's pulse spiked at the mention of her ex-lover. "W-what do you mean?"

Maria's unshakable calm in the face of Emilia's panic was unbearable. It was a reminder of everything Emilia disliked about herself, a reminder of how her emotions had costed her people everything.

"Catherine," Maria stated. "She betrayed you, didn't she?"

"No," Emilia breathed. She couldn't bear to sit still—not while Maria was prying open her wounds without a touch of gentleness.

So, Emilia stumbled from her chair, her balance faltering. Her head spun, and the books hit the floor with two, soft thuds.

Despite her calm demeanor, Maria was at Emilia's side within a moment. She grasped Emilia's elbow to steady her. "Careful."

But the panic blinded Emilia.

She stumbled back, her arm falling from Maria's grasp. "Who—who told you?"

"No one," Maria assured her. "I figured it out on my own."

Emilia shook her head quickly. It was more like a spasm than a conscious gesture—her blood a deafening roar in her head. "No. You couldn't have. It's—it's—" Her stammering devolved into quick, shallow breaths.

Maria's hand gently curled around Emilia's arm. "Em," she said in a low tone. "You need to breathe."

Emilia's mind and body spiraled into a dangerous mix of panic and disorientation, and she reached out, attempting to push Maria away.

But Maria caught her arm and pulled her closer.

Holding tightly to Emilia's arm with one hand, Maria touched Emilia's face with the other.

Emilia froze.

With three fingers, Maria lifted Emilia's face, urging Emilia to meet her gaze. "Em," she said carefully. "I've seen you like this before. I didn't spare your life and cause my entire crew to question me, just for you to make the same mistake twice." She traced Emilia's jaw with her thumb. "I need you to calm down."

Emilia didn't move, trapped both by Maria's hand *and* her gaze. Her chest rose and fell with each labored breath, their bodies close enough that Emilia could feel Maria's breasts against her own. "I wouldn't have," she said breathlessly. "I wouldn't have made the same mistake."

Maria nodded slowly. "Good," she murmured. She released Emilia's face and let her fingertips trail along Emilia's cheek.

The action was so soothing that Emilia found herself closing her eyes. With her pulse racing and her head spinning, Maria's touch was all that felt steady, at the moment, and so Emilia leaned into it, like a sail against the wind.

"Take a deep breath for me, love."

For the first time since they'd met, Emilia actually obeyed—inhaling deeply, then exhaling.

"Again," Maria whispered, and Emilia did so again.

"Perfect," Maria murmured.

Emilia opened her eyes, her stomach flipping, as she met Maria's dark gaze. "Thank you," she said softly, "Captain."

Maria stepped closer. She trailed a fingertip along Emilia's cheekbone and tilted Emilia's face toward her own. Her soft, full lips curved at the corners. "So fierce," she said, her breath warm and sweet against Emilia's lips. "Yet, you melt so easily."

Warmth rushed to Emilia's cheeks. Maria was taunting her—like a cat toying with the mouse in her claws—and though Emilia had every reason to fight or flee, all she wanted, in that moment, was to kiss the soft lips that were taunting her.

A haze of desire swirled around her head, intoxicating her as effectively as rum.

And just when Emilia thought Maria might kiss her, Maria stepped back. "I realized it on my own," she said. "I swear."

Emilia swallowed uneasily. "How long have you known?"

"Since the day of our sword fight." Maria kept a steady grasp on Emilia's elbow, not letting her fall. "How do you think I beat you so easily?"

Making a valiant attempt at her usual snark, Emilia said, "So, it *wasn't* your expert swordsmanship, then?"

Maria chuckled. "It was that, too."

Emilia's smile faded as quickly as it had appeared. "I don't understand. How could you have known?"

"I take it Catherine didn't tell you about me?" Maria said.

"She told me plenty," Emilia argued. "She told me you hated her—that you were her greatest enemy."

"And before I was her enemy?" Maria said. "Did she tell you about that? Did she tell you how she betrayed me?"

"What?" Emilia breathed.

"Of course not," Maria sneered. "Yet, you believed her tales, anyway."

Maria's cruel anger strayed no further than her face, her touch still gentle, despite it.

"Why didn't she tell me about that?" Emilia asked.

Maria lifted a scarred eyebrow. "I don't know, surgeon," she scoffed. "Why do you *think* she'd leave out the part that might've warned you of what she was really like?"

Emilia nodded at the harsh reminder. "Fair point," she muttered, "but I'd ask you to remember that there *is* a mind-altering drug in my system right now."

"What's your excuse for before that?" Maria said.

Emilia narrowed her eyes. "Look, I only came to you in the first place because she hated you," she said, "and I figured the enemy of my enemy is my friend, right?"

A vicious smile curled at the corners of Maria's lips. "And how did that turn out for you?"

Emilia pursed her lips, rage simmering in her gaze. "I just gained another enemy."

Maria's smile faded. She stepped closer. "Is that what I am to you? Your enemy?"

"Well, you're definitely not my friend," Emilia said. "You've tricked me and used me at every turn. What are you, if not my enemy?"

Maria pressed a knuckle beneath Emilia's chin, lifting Emilia's face toward her own. "Your fucking captain."

Emilia leaned forward and hissed, "Not for long."

Maria dropped her hand. "Darling, you don't want me as an enemy."

"And you think you want me as one?" Emilia countered. "You don't even know who I am."

Maria stepped closer, backing Emilia toward the table. "No, but I will," she growled. "Before the end of the night, I'll know *everything*."

Emilia stepped back, squeaking in surprise, as her back hit the table. "Captain—"

Maria laughed, derision in her smile. "Oh, *now* it's Captain?"

Emilia leaned against the table behind her, suddenly wishing she had her sword.

Though, considering her tendency to act rashly when she was upset, perhaps it was good that she didn't have it.

Almost as if she knew what Emilia was thinking, Maria glanced down at Emilia's hand, noting its placement on her hip. "Your sword is with mine. Behind my table. Do you want it? I'll get it for you," she offered. "But I should remind you. Wounded or not, I won't show you mercy again."

"I don't need your mercy," Emilia said.

With a laugh as sharp as her sword, Maria said, "Oh, you weren't lying about having a good teacher. Catherine has incredible skill." She leaned in. "But don't kid yourself, love. She's nothing compared to me. And *you*?" She stepped closer—her height and proximity forcing Emilia to look up. "You sure as hell aren't."

Emilia swallowed down the insecurity that tried to rise in her throat. "Oh? Then, tell me something, Captain," she said. "If you're so much better than Catherine, who gave you those scars?"

The momentary shock and anger that flashed across the pirate captain's face was all the confirmation Emilia needed.

Emilia didn't get a chance to revel in her victory, though, because Maria suddenly muttered, "You're bleeding on my floor."

"Oh."

Emilia pressed her hand against her torn shirt, feeling the blood that had already soaked through.

"Sit," Maria said. "I'll get a new wrap."

Emilia eased herself into the chair, worried she'd open the wound more, if she moved too quickly.

Maria knelt and picked up the books that had fallen from Emilia's lap and set them on the table in front of her.

"Thank you," Emilia said softly.

"My pleasure," Maria murmured, and then, she returned to her cupboards to get more supplies.

It turned out that what Maria referred to as a 'wrap' was just an uneven strip of linen that she'd most likely cut with her sword.

"Remind me to teach you how to properly dress wounds, when I'm less...disoriented," Emilia said tiredly. "That way, you won't accidentally kill yourself or someone else, after I leave."

"Stay with me," Maria suggested, "and you can ensure we all live yourself."

"I can't," Emilia said softly.

Maria grabbed another bucket of water and a bottle of rum. "I know how to slow the bleeding," she told Emilia. "That's the important part, right?"

With a slightly amused smile, Emilia said, "It's *an* important part—not the only one."

Maria returned to Emilia's chair with her supplies. "I know that," she said, "because the *other* important part is the rum."

Emilia shook her head. "If you say so, Captain."

Maria knelt beside her chair. "Lift your shirt for me, love."

Emilia stared down at the pirate captain, bewildered by how easily she could flip from deadly to gentle.

Maria looked up at her, and from this angle, the scar over her eye looked even deeper than usual.

Emilia couldn't have said what she was thinking when she did it—or if she was thinking at all. But before she even realized what she was doing, she'd reached out to touch the scar over Maria's eye.

Maria recoiled like a startled beast, closing her eyes and turning her head, but at the last moment, she seemed to change her mind—because she stopped and waited for Emilia to touch her.

The scar dipped beneath Emilia's thumb—a deep, amaranth crevice in the pirate captain's smooth, brown skin.

Maria opened her eyes, gazing up at Emilia, through long, sooty eyelashes.

"Was it really her?" Emilia breathed.

"Yes," Maria said.

Sympathy coiled around Emilia's throat like a rope. "Why?"

"Ambition. Jealousy," Maria said. "Whatever she accused me of feeling, she felt it first."

Emilia nodded. Even before she'd realized how selfishly ambitious Catherine truly was, she'd heard a hint of jealousy in her voice—every time she'd mentioned the infamous Captain Maria Welles.

Catherine was an admiral, now. What did Maria even *have* for her to envy?

A loyal crew?

"Oh, she'll tell you it's about right and wrong—that I broke the law and she was just doing her duty," Maria said, "but I'm a few scars beyond *duty*, don't you think?"

"I'm sorry," Emilia said softly.

"Don't be," Maria said. "It was a good guess, and besides…I took some cheap shots at you first."

Emilia looked away. "I could've let her die."

Maria frowned at that. "What do you mean?"

"She was dying, when they brought her to me," Emilia said, her voice thick. "I helped her. I spent months nursing her back to health."

"Did you know who she was?" Maria said.

"Not at first," Emilia admitted, "but she told me, eventually. I was…already in love."

Maria looked down. "I see."

Perhaps it was the pain or the disorientation, but for whatever reason, the words spilled from Emilia's mouth before she could stop them.

"It's the worst thing I've ever done—loving her," she breathed. "I hurt so many people."

Maria looked up, her brows furrowed. She took Emilia's hand

from her face—and absolutely stunned her by threading her fingers through Emilia's. "Catherine's deception is...persuasive."

It felt as if time had stopped, when Maria's fingers intertwined with Emilia's—but perhaps, it was simply Emilia's heart that had stopped keeping time.

Her stomach fluttered, as she stared into those dark eyes. Maria's fingers were so warm and soft, her touch careful and gentle, and Emilia couldn't reconcile it with the aggressive demeanor she'd grown accustomed to.

"By the third swing of your sword, I'd recognized it," Maria told her. "No one has fought Catherine as often as I have. No one knows her fighting style like I do."

Emilia licked her lips nervously. "Why didn't you tell me?"

Maria shrugged. "For a moment, I thought I'd kill you," she said. "You signed the Code. You knew the consequences. If I'd killed you, you'd have only yourself to blame."

"I know," Emilia admitted.

"For all I knew, she might've sent you to betray us," Maria said. "I should've killed you. For the sake of my crew, I should have."

Emilia's voice came out as no more than a whisper. "So, why didn't you?"

Maria took Emilia's hand and turned it over. Brushing a fingertip across Emilia's scarred wrist, she said, "Because we share the same scars."

Emilia shuddered at her touch.

That one point of contact anchored her to the spot. It drew all of her senses toward Maria, like a source of gravity.

Emilia could think of nothing else but Maria's touch, Maria's scent, Maria's voice...

"Captain," Emilia whispered.

"Lift your shirt for me, love," Maria said again. "I need to see it."

Like that first night in Maria's quarters, Emilia hesitated, insecurity rising within her.

Sailing and battle had sharpened Maria's body like a whetstone. There was no part of her that wasn't strong and fit.

Emilia, on the other hand, had enough strength in her legs for dragon-riding, but her stomach was soft.

Most of her was soft.

Sure, she'd thinned a little, while starving in the Regolis dungeons, but with guaranteed meals each day, her curves had returned.

What if Maria—so strong and arrogant—saw Emilia's curves as weakness?

But with that thought, came another.

Why did she even care what Maria thought of her?

Emilia knew the answer, even if she'd never admit it.

Emilia rolled the hem of her shirt upward, revealing the blood-soaked linen beneath.

"I guess I shouldn't have stood up," Emilia said with a frown.

"Not so quickly, anyway," Maria agreed. Her dark gaze shifted upward. "Do you need some rum for the pain?"

Emilia shook her head. "I'm fine," she said, "but thank you."

Maria nodded. She leaned forward, pressing more of her weight onto her leather-clad knee.

Her tattooed fingers made quick work of the blood-soaked linen, untying the ends and pulling it free from Emilia's waist.

When Emilia winced, Maria murmured, "I'll be quick."

Emilia would've thanked her for that promise, but the pain was so intense, at the moment, that she couldn't seem to unclench her jaw.

Maria poured some rum onto a small rag. "Are you ready?"

Emilia gave her a look that she *hoped* conveyed the message: *'Just do it.'*

She must've succeeded because Maria nodded and pressed the rag against Emilia's stab wound.

Emilia squeezed her eyes shut at the pain, but she didn't make a sound.

"You're a lot tougher than you look, aren't you?" Maria muttered.

Emilia opened her eyes, half-convinced she'd misheard that.

Maria dropped the rag into the bucket and unfolded her strip of linen. "Are you sure it wasn't poison?" she asked. "It doesn't look good."

"I'm sure," Emilia assured her. "I'll make a salve for it later. It should heal up nicely, after that."

Maria nodded. "I was talking to Judith a few days ago. She said you made one for her, after she cut her finger. A salve, I mean."

"Did she tell you it worked?" Emilia said.

Maria leaned forward and wrapped the strip of clean linen around Emilia's waist. "She did."

Emilia smiled at that.

Maria tied the strip around Emilia's waist. "Judith will be in the galley with you, but she'll be hidden." She leaned back, resting her weight on her heels. "I want him alive—so that I can question him —but I'm not playing with your life *quite* as recklessly as I implied."

"Really?" Emilia said skeptically.

"I told her to shoot first and ask questions later, if he has a pistol," Maria told her. "I don't want you hurt any worse, love—not even for something as important as this."

Emilia lifted her eyebrows at that. "You have a strange way of showing it."

Maria's lips twitched. "Yes, I do."

So, they agreed on something, after all.

Who would've thought?

Maria wiped the blood on her leather trousers and climbed to her feet. "Now, let's get *you* ready to be the perfect bait."

Emilia pinned her with a peeved look. "Yes, Captain," she sneered.

Maria laughed. "Just look at how quickly you've caught on!"

Emilia rolled her eyes.

CHAPTER 17
A Trap

When it came time for her ever-so-kind captain to put her to *use,* Emilia followed Maria below deck.

At Maria's urging, Emilia had left her sword in Maria's quarters. Apparently, the lack of sword made her more appealing bait.

It also left her mostly defenseless.

Emilia doubted anyone was foolish enough to attack her above deck, in broad daylight, but that didn't stop Maria from keeping a protective hold on Emilia's arm the entire walk.

Emilia couldn't exactly complain, though—because she hadn't quite recovered her equilibrium and likely would've fallen several times without the captain to help her stay upright.

Judith met Emilia at the bottom step. She took hold of Emilia's arms and looked her up and down, her gaze lingering on the tear in Emilia's shirt. "How're you feeling, mate?" she said with genuine concern. "Captain says you were attacked last night."

Emilia scowled at the aforementioned captain, as she stepped past them. "Did she also tell you that she barely gave me five

357

minutes to recover, before demanding I put myself in danger again?" she asked Judith.

"I gave you hours, not minutes," Maria muttered, as if she actually needed to defend herself.

Judith gave Emilia's arms a reassuring squeeze. "Don't you worry about a thing, Em," she said. "I'll be here, looking out for you the entire time."

Emilia smiled, comforted by the promise. "Thank you, Judith."

Maria watched Emilia's reaction with a frown. "You trust her?"

Emilia flashed a bitter smile at the pirate captain. "She might be the *only* person on this ship I trust."

"Interesting," Maria murmured.

Emilia glanced back and forth between Maria and Judith. A sense of dread coiled deep in her stomach.

Was she imagining things, or had Judith just glared at Maria?

The look that the two pirates seemed to exchange, now—it was as if they were having a silent conversation amongst themselves.

And Emilia found her anxiety increasing by the moment.

"Judes," Maria said with a beguiling smile, "fetch some oranges for Em, won't you?"

Emilia's brows furrowed. "I'm not hungry."

But Judith just muttered, "Yes, Captain," and trudged off toward the back.

Maria waited until Judith disappeared behind a stack of barrels to approach Emilia.

Though her posture was languid and calm, Emilia couldn't help but notice that Maria had her hand hidden.

She knew of only one other time that Maria had kept her hand out of sight.

In her quarters.

Early that morning.

So, this time, when the knife came rushing toward her, Emilia was ready.

Protecting her chest with her forearm, Emilia dove straight for the knife-wielding hand. With her right hand, she pressed into Maria's thumb, twisting the pirate captain's wrist inward.

Maria still didn't drop the knife. So, Emilia used her forearm to flatten the blade and push it inward, pressing with her entire body and forcing Maria's hand to press the knife into her stomach, instead.

Though the knife was still in Maria's hand, it was Emilia who had full control of it now.

A soft gasp escaped Maria's lips, as the blade cut her shirt—and possibly her skin, as well.

In her current position, Emilia could feel the soft brush of Maria's breasts against her shoulder and the warmth of Maria's breath on her ear.

Maria's warm, wet lips touched the shell of Emilia's ear, as she whispered, "Much better."

Emilia couldn't help but smile, her cheeks warming at the praise.

With a soft laugh, Maria said, "You can let go of me now, love."

Emilia released Maria's wrist and straightened. Pain radiated through her hip—the wound once again aggravated by her movement.

Maria must've seen the pain in her expression—because her smile faltered. "Are you all right?"

Emilia would need to heal the wound before facing her attacker, but she needed Maria to leave first.

Hiding her pain behind a smile, Emilia said, "More than all right—now that I've finally beaten you."

She expected Maria to argue, but instead, Maria grinned and presented the knife to Emilia.

The grey blade glistened, when the firelight fell upon it.

The knife appeared to be made from some sort of stone.

Flint, perhaps?

And it was sharp enough to cleave meat from bone.

But what made Emilia gasp in surprise was the thin coating of blood on the tip of the blade.

"I did get you!" Emilia realized.

"Only a little," Maria said with that unfazed smirk of hers. If the cut hurt her at all, she didn't show it. "Here. Keep the knife. I don't want you defenseless." She flipped it, offering the cool, stone handle to Emilia. "But keep it hidden. He's more likely to bite the bait if he thinks you're unarmed."

Emilia took the knife with a frown. "I prefer for men *not* to bite me, thank you very much."

"And women?" Maria said with a quirked eyebrow.

Emilia's entire body clenched at the thought. She swallowed, trying her best to suppress the desire that coursed through her at the captain's words.

The soft thud of Judith's boots signaled the cook's return. She came out from behind the barrels with a sack of fruit in her hand.

Emilia looked away, willing her flushed cheeks to cool.

When Judith reached the two of them, she offered the bag to Maria. "Found the oranges for *Em*," she said, rolling her eyes.

Maria grinned at Judith's tone. She took the bag, peeking inside. "I'm only going to take a few."

Judith scoffed at that. "You're so full of shit."

In reality, Maria took the *few* oranges and handed those to Emilia, while keeping the rest for herself.

That woman clearly loved her fruit.

Before Maria left with the bag of oranges, she offered Emilia a final piece of encouragement. "Fight like you did just now, and he won't stand a chance."

Emilia gripped the knife that Maria had given her, feeling the cool stone against her skin. "You say that, but you don't even know who he is."

"I have a hunch," Maria assured her.

"Oh," Emilia said.

Why hadn't Maria mentioned this before?

"If it's who I think it is," Maria said, "he typically fights with knives." She nodded toward the flint knife in Emilia's hand. "Hence our practice."

Emilia nodded.

"And if he brings a pistol, instead, Judith knows to act quickly," Maria told her.

Judith patted the pistol on her hip, as if to confirm the captain's words.

"And," Emilia said nervously, "is this 'hunch' of yours any good in a fight?"

"He's no Buchan," Maria assured her, "but he's decent."

"Oh," Emilia said, her shoulders falling.

Maria leaned in and whispered in her ear, "But you, Em, are *much* better than decent."

Emilia suppressed a shudder—and then blushed, when Maria seemed to notice. "I thought I was *'nothing compared to you.'*"

"Everyone's nothing compared to me," Maria said, arrogant as ever. "Doesn't mean I'm not impressed."

A bewildering warmth unfurled in Emilia's chest.

Maria glanced at Judith. "He'll never walk into the trap, if I'm here," she said, "so I'll need to leave."

"She'll be safe with me, Captain," Judith promised.

Maria nodded. She then turned to Emilia and tried—one, final time—to persuade her.

"There's still time, Em," she said. "Come clean to me now, and I'll do what I can to help you."

Emilia's smile faded. Bitterness rose in her throat. She suddenly doubted that Maria's compliment had been sincere at all.

It was just *another* trick, Emilia figured, just like everything else Maria had said and done.

"No," Emilia said.

"You'd rather me arrest you," Maria said in disbelief, "than tell me what I'll soon know, anyway?"

For all Emilia knew, this wasn't a trap for her attacker—and was one for her, instead.

Everything Maria had said to her could've been a lie.

Emilia refused to make the mistake she'd made with Catherine.

She refused to prove her mother right.

"I can't," Emilia said—for the last time.

Maria gave an uncaring shrug. "Have it your way, then."

She then turned and strode up the steps.

When Emilia turned away with a sigh, she found Judith staring at her. "What?"

"Em," Judith said, gesturing toward the steps, "she offered to help you, and you refused."

"You don't understand," Emilia said—because how could she? "If I were to trust her…it'd mean I'd learned nothing."

"Or," Judith argued, "it'd mean that you don't want to be arrested."

Emilia shook her head. "I don't trust her, Judith. I can't," she tried to explain. "I know you do, and I honestly don't understand why. But I don't."

Judith leaned her hip against the table and sighed. After a quick glance at the steps—to ensure that Maria had already left—she said, "You're right. You *don't* know why I trust her. You couldn't possibly know, and perhaps that's the problem."

Emilia frowned. "What do you mean?"

"If there's a chance it could change your mind," Judith said, "I'll tell you why I trust her."

After a moment of hesitation, Emilia nodded.

Judith pulled a coin from her pocket. She held out her hand, the thin, silver coin resting in the center of her palm. "Do you know what this is?"

Emilia recognized it easily. "It's the coin the captain told me to give you."

"Yes," Judith said, "but do you know what kind of coin it is?"

Emilia squinted at the unfamiliar face of the coin, the thin, dented silver shining in the firelight. "No," she admitted. "I've never seen it before."

"I'd assume not," Judith said, turning the coin in her hand. "I'd bet no one but an Aevarian, who lived through the Great Drought, would recognize it now."

"Aevarian?" Emilia repeated. "Wait, are you trying to say the captain's Aevarian?" Her frown deepened. "But her accent sounds Illopian."

"But she looks Aevarian, doesn't she?" Judith said.

"That doesn't mean anything," Emilia said with a shrug. "People immigrate. The races are all diverse these days."

"These days," Judith repeated, "as in...since the drought, right? That's when most of the immigration began."

Emilia was only twenty-five years old. Most of the immigration had already taken place before her birth. "The Great Drought was over thirty years ago."

Judith lifted an eyebrow. "The captain's thirty-two."

It shouldn't have surprised Emilia. The legends of Captain Maria Welles—the most feared villainess of the high seas—had existed for at least a decade.

But still, it had never occurred to her that Maria might've lived through the drought.

Judith held out the coin yet again. "This coin is the only possession the captain has left that belonged to her mother."

Emilia immediately thought of her own enchanted dagger—the one that was so precious to her, despite it being a gift from a mother who'd never even liked her.

Her chest tightened. "You said she was Adda's orphan girl," Emilia remembered.

Judith nodded. "Her mother died during the drought," she confirmed, "but before she died, she gave Adda all she had left— this one, single coin—and asked Adda to save her daughter."

Emilia swallowed. "Was that enough?"

"No," Judith said. "By that point, Aevaria's trade had collapsed.

Their currency was practically useless. It could barely buy a bag of rice—much less passage on a ship." She sighed, "But Adda didn't have the heart to tell a dying woman that her only possession wasn't enough to save her child."

"So, what did she do?" Emilia asked.

"She took the coin as payment," Judith said, "and smuggled herself and the child—illegally—onto a ship."

Emilia's heart pounded inside her chest. All of this time, she'd thought of Maria as an Illopian, but Maria was born outside the wealthy kingdom, just like Emilia was.

"Adda was a fencer. So, she took the child to Nefala—where she knew she'd be able to make a lucrative career, off of the pirates," Judith said, "which would allow her to feed the child that was now in her care."

Emilia frowned. "So, the captain grew up around pirates. She had all of the connections already," she realized. "That's what she meant when she said she was born for it."

Judith nodded. "But Adda wanted better for her," she explained. "The captain had the wits and swordsmanship to make a life outside of crime—a life that, Adda assumed, no one could take from her."

Emilia frowned at the way she'd said that. "What happened?"

Judith sighed, "You know Illopia has a bit of prejudice when it comes to gender. It's not always as easy for women as it is for men." When Emilia nodded, Judith said, "Still, no one could deny the captain's skill. She joined the navy when she came of age and soared through the ranks. No one could beat her. Not even her sparring partner and closest friend." She paused for a moment, before saying the name. "Catherine."

Emilia's stomach flipped.

Judith looked down at the coin, turning it over, once more. "She gave this to me, during our first voyage together. She knew the guards would take it when they arrested her, and she didn't want to lose it."

Emilia's frown deepened. "*When* they arrested her?"

Judith looked up. "The official story is that she stole from the Crown, isn't it?"

Emilia nodded. That was what Catherine had told *her*, anyway.

With a solemn nod, Judith said, "Many Illopians are aware that the king isn't the kindest person," she assured Emilia, "especially those of us who grew up in the places he abandoned—like Nefala." She sighed, "But I don't think any of us were aware of just how corrupt he truly was."

Emilia's brows furrowed. "What are you saying?"

"I'm saying," Judith said, "that we assumed the cargo we'd been asked to transport was gold or spices." Her brows creased. "Not...human."

"Slave trade," Emilia said.

Judith nodded. "We were taught that our wealth, as a kingdom, came from Petra, the god of the mountains. In exchange for eradicating magic from our lands, he'd blessed us with gold and plentiful resources." She shrugged. "But it was corruption all along."

"You never knew?" Emilia said.

"No one did," Judith said, "until we joined the navy." She looked away. "When the captain found out what we were transporting, she made a quick and easy decision—that would change all of our lives forever."

Emilia blinked in surprise. "She freed them."

Judith nodded. "We all helped, but," she sighed, "she took the fall."

Emilia's mouth fell open. Could it be true?

Could the infamous pirate captain that the entire world had been taught to fear be someone who had simply done the halfway decent thing, when faced with an atrocity?

Judith was a pirate, too. She was just as likely to lie as any pirate, and yet, Emilia trusted her.

Judith was her friend.

The one friend she'd ever had.

"Those scars the captain has," Judith said softly. "That could've been me. It could've been Pelt. It could've been every member of her crew—if she hadn't taken the fall for us. When she was betrayed, instead of keeping us on the ship to fight alongside her, she helped us escape—and then fought the battle alone."

"When she was betrayed," Emilia repeated. She considered their conversation in the captain's quarters. Maria had said that Catherine betrayed her.

"By her First Mate," Judith confirmed, "Catherine Rochester."

Another wave of nausea washed over Emilia.

"She led a mutiny against the captain," Judith explained, "and when she won, she placed the captain under arrest and took her to Regolis to be hanged for piracy."

"Why?" Emilia breathed.

"Because we committed a crime?" Judith assumed. "Or perhaps, she just saw it as her one chance to rise above the legendary Captain Maria Welles." She shrugged. "It matters little now. It resulted in the same fate, regardless."

Emilia swallowed uneasily. She thought about the way Catherine had bragged about capturing Maria, and now, knowing the truth of it, the memory turned her stomach.

"We chose to break the law," Judith assured Emilia, "but what was done to our captain—that should've never happened." She stepped toward Emilia. "That's why I trust her—because when it was us or her, she took the fall."

Emilia looked away, her heart fluttering. "She's admitted to manipulating me."

"I know," Judith sighed, "and look, I'm not saying she's a good person. The legends didn't come from nowhere. She's as vengeful and bloodthirsty as they come."

Emilia glanced at her curiously.

"I'm not saying she won't use you," Judith added. "I'm not even saying she won't kill you." She held out the coin. "All I'm saying is," she said, "she told you to give me this coin for a reason. It's a message that only I understand." She lifted her eyebrows. "It means she wants you kept safe."

Emilia blinked in shock. "What?"

"Until she takes this coin back," Judith said, "you should assume that she still intends to help you." She closed her fingers around it. "But once she asks for it back..." She shrugged. "You'll be on your own."

Emilia stared in disbelief at Judith's closed hand. Was it possible that Maria actually wanted to help her? Was it possible that trusting her *wouldn't* be a mistake?

Emilia's chest ached, and she just couldn't hold it back any longer. "I want to trust her, Judith, but," she gasped, anxiety crushing her lungs, "you—you don't understand." She kept her gaze on the floor, shame rising inside her. "I trusted someone before, and it—it turned out so badly." Her eyes burned with unshed tears. "If you even knew the horror I was responsible for..."

Judith stepped closer. "Em," she said with a worried frown, "what is it?" When Emilia's breath came faster, Judith told her, "I won't judge you, Em. I swear."

A lump of emotion welled up in Emilia's throat.

Could she?

Could she trust Judith?

She wanted to.

Oh, how she wanted to.

She hadn't talked to anyone about it. Well, besides her dead mother, that is—who certainly hadn't made Emilia feel any better about it.

Judith took another step forward. "I swear, Em," she whispered again. "You can trust me."

Emilia had promised herself she'd never trust anyone again.

But Judith had called her a friend. No one else had ever done that.

Surely, that meant something.

Above them, wood creaked.

"Shit," Judith hissed, and without another word, she fled to the back of the galley, ducking behind the crates and barrels.

Emilia quickly swiped her fingers under her eyes, wiping away any tears that had tried to escape. She heard another creak of wood —on the steps, now—and she quickly hid her knife, too.

She tucked it into her belt and pulled her shirt down over it.

Then, with her heart hammering inside her chest, she turned to face the person descending the steps.

Her brows furrowed, when she caught sight of the tightly-bound braid of orange hair.

Helen?

No.

Maria had said 'he.' Multiple times, she'd used masculine pronouns. She couldn't have possibly thought it was Helen.

And even if she had, she was wrong. Helen had the height and strength of any man on Maria's ship, sure, but she didn't have the low voice. The voice Emilia had heard the night before was low.

It couldn't have been Helen.

Yet, it was Helen, who descended the steps, now.

"Em!"

Emilia forced a smile. "Hi, Helen."

The gunner's smile was just as delighted as Maria said it'd be. Helen spread out her arms. "Word on the ship is that you and the captain got drunk last night!"

How had that story spread so fast?

And why was Helen so *excited* about it?

Pirates were a strange bunch, Emilia decided.

"I told Pelt last night—I said, 'She might look uptight, but she's got adventure in her soul,'" Helen said.

Emilia barely understood half the stuff that came out of Helen's mouth. "I, uh—I look uptight?"

Helen waved a hand. "Well, not today."

Emilia frowned. The only difference in this day and previous days was that blood was currently oozing from her hip.

368

Helen pulled her long, red braid over her shoulder and plucked a splinter of wood from it.

Surely, she hadn't blown up something *already*?

It was barely noon.

"So," Helen said with a knowing grin, "is it true?"

Emilia's frown deepened. "Is what true?" she asked. "That I drank too much?"

"No, no," Helen scoffed. "I know that part's true." At Emilia's raised brows, Helen added, "Pelt saw you passed out. He told us all about it."

Us?

Emilia wondered if Maria had thanked Pelt for spreading her lie so diligently.

Helen nudged Emilia's shoulder so hard that Emilia nearly fell backward.

Apparently, being any lighter than a cannon around Helen was a safety hazard.

"Come on, Em," Helen whined. "Did you do it or not?"

"Do *what*?" Emilia said, her eyes wide.

With a meaningful look, Helen whispered, "You and the captain."

"Got drunk," Emilia assumed.

Hadn't they just done this?

Helen sighed, apparently disappointed with Emilia's inability to read her mind. "The captain doesn't let anyone sleep in her quarters."

"I was passed out," Emilia reminded her.

"Yes, but when you *weren't* passed out," Helen said, wriggling her hips playfully, "did you..." She lifted those red eyebrows of hers.

For Aletha's sake.

Emilia's dragons communicated better than this.

Helen threw up her hands in defeat. "I'm trying to find out if she fucked you, Em!"

369

Emilia's eyes widened. "What? No!" she squeaked. "Why would you think that?"

Helen crossed her arms, her stained, white shirt stretching to accommodate her muscles. "Have you *seen* you two together?"

"That would be impossible," Emilia said with a frown. "Well, if I had a mirror, maybe. But I don't."

Helen snorted, "All right, all right." She dropped her arms and gave a playful huff. "I'll go tell everyone the bad news."

Emilia watched her, as she headed toward the steps. "Bad news?"

"A bit of gambling. Don't worry," Helen said with a dismissive wave. "Fulke will be happy."

Emilia squinted in confusion. "Okay," she said, drawing out the word. "Bye, Helen."

Emilia was still lost in thought—when Helen came to a stop on the bottom step.

What did Helen mean by, *'Have you seen you two together?'*

All Maria and Emilia did, when they were together, was fight.

Okay, fine. So, there was that *one* kiss.

And then, that other kiss.

But Emilia refused to speak of those—which meant they didn't count.

Right?

"Well, hey, Jonas," Helen said, suddenly.

Jonas?

Emilia glanced toward the steps, her heart racing, as the carpenter descended them.

The steps were too narrow for two people, at once. So, Helen waited at the bottom.

"What are you doing down here, Helen?" the carpenter asked.

"Just having a chat with our naughty, little surgeon," Helen said.

Emilia rolled her eyes. Why couldn't Maria have chosen a lie

370

that *wouldn't* result in Helen, of all people, thinking she'd done something *naughty*?

"And are you finished with your chat?" Jonas said.

"You're not trying to get rid of me, are you, Jonas?" Helen said with a playful smile.

Jonas returned the smile. "Of course not."

It couldn't have been Jonas, could it?

He'd testified in her defense, after her fight with Buchan.

He'd been kind to her every time they'd spoken.

'One moment of kindness is all it takes for you,' her mother had said.

Emilia swallowed the lump of guilt in her throat, and she inched toward the table. Maria had warned Emilia to keep a table between them.

Jonas's blue-grey eyes shifted toward her, and Emilia froze.

The last thing she wanted to do was alarm him enough that he'd hurt Helen, too.

Emilia deserved this.

Helen didn't.

Jonas stepped into the galley, his cool, blue gaze settling on Emilia.

His blonde hair fell around his face, messier than usual, and dark circles lined his light blue eyes.

He clearly hadn't slept well the night before.

Apparently, Helen hadn't noticed anything off about his smile, though—because she followed him now, energetic as ever.

"Did you know our little surgeon here got drunk last night?" Helen asked—with a ridiculous amount of enthusiasm.

Jonas made eye-contact with Emilia, but she quickly looked down, unsettled.

It wasn't Jonas who unsettled her, really. It was just eye-contact in general.

It was difficult enough when she *wasn't* nervous, and right now, she was definitely nervous.

"I heard," Jonas assured Helen. "I also heard that the captain watched over her all night."

Had there been some resentment in that?

Emilia wasn't sure.

"Rare, don't you think?" Jonas said to Helen.

"I know!" Helen said with a laugh. "Which is why I assumed that they'd…you know. But nope! I lost *that* bet."

Emilia shook her head in disbelief.

What on earth had she missed last night?

"Hey!" Helen said, shoving Jonas so hard he nearly fell over.

The woman was like a grizzly bear who'd been raised by mice.

"*You* didn't make any bets last night, did you?" Helen accused. "Where were you?"

"I wasn't feeling well," Jonas muttered.

"I thought you said you were on watch last night," Emilia said with a suspicious look.

"You were drunk," Jonas said. "You probably misheard."

Helen fell silent, her brows furrowing.

Helen had mentioned talking to Pelt the night before. Perhaps Pelt had told her that Jonas was on watch.

Perhaps Helen was starting to notice that something was off about her shipmate.

Jonas strode casually to the table, reaching for a tankard.

That was when Emilia saw it. From his elbow to his wrist were deep, festering claw marks.

Rat-Slayer.

"Are those cat scratches?" Emilia asked.

Jonas immediately looked at her, his blue eyes as cold as ice.

Emilia tried to keep any suspicion from coloring her tone. "That might be why you felt sick," she told him. "They're infected. I can take a look at them, if you want."

Jonas narrowed his eyes, clearly not falling for the innocent offer.

Helen, on the other hand, relaxed. "Jonas," she said, nudging him playfully, "you messed with the cats? You know they don't like you!"

Emilia's dragons had never liked Catherine, either. Animals were good judges of people, when Emilia often wasn't.

Jonas shrugged. "I was just offering them some food."

Liar, Emilia thought.

Those were Rat-Slayer's scratches.

He was the only one with paws that large.

Holding up the empty tankard, Jonas said, "I didn't eat during the midday meal. You don't think Judith would mind if I grabbed a bit of ale, do you?"

Emilia knew already what he intended to do. There was a barrel of ale behind the table.

Forcing a smile, Emilia said, "I'm sure it'd be fine."

Helen picked up a potato, turning it over in her hand, as if she'd never seen an uncooked one before.

With a bemused frown, Emilia wondered if the master gunner had inhaled a little too much gunpowder today.

Meanwhile, Jonas circled around the table to—supposedly—grab some ale.

Emilia stiffened, when he pressed a knife to her back.

"Make her leave," Jonas hissed in her ear.

Emilia carefully kept her hands by her sides. She wouldn't pull out her own knife until Helen was gone.

She wouldn't do anything that would put Helen at risk.

"Helen," Emilia said.

The master gunner dropped the potato and looked up at her.

Helen's hazel eyes shifted from Emilia to Jonas—and then narrowed.

She knew.

Even though she'd been friends with Jonas for years, even though she had only just met Emilia, she'd taken one look at the anxiety in Emilia's face, and she'd known.

Emilia couldn't let Helen act on the knowledge, though—not if she wanted to protect her. "I, umm… I haven't seen Judith in a while," she lied. "Do you think you could…find her for me?"

"Of course," Helen said, but she said it like a threat. "I think I saw her heading to the captain's quarters, actually."

Helen was lying for her. One nervous look, and Helen had lied for her.

A strange warmth fluttered in Emilia's stomach.

Why would Helen look out for her like that?

Why would Judith?

Why would Maria?

Why was this crew so full of people who looked out for her?

Even after all of the mistakes she'd made.

Sending a glare Jonas's way, Helen said, "I'll go to the captain now."

Emilia waited until Helen had made it up the steps, before speaking to Jonas. "There. She's gone."

"Did you have to make it so fucking obvious?" Jonas snarled at her.

"You have a knife against my back," Emilia muttered. "You're the one being obvious."

Jonas growled in frustration. "We have to go now. If she sends the captain after me, I'm dead."

"You really think you can get me to shore, before the captain catches you?" Emilia said with a laugh of disbelief. "You're already dead."

Enraged, Jonas spun her around, and Emilia smiled—because that was exactly what she'd wanted him to do.

Before he could put the knife against her neck, Emilia took her knife from her belt and thrust it into his wrist.

The blade that Maria had clearly kept *very* sharp impaled not just his wrist, but the table, too, pinning his wrist to its wooden edge.

His knife fell to the floor, the metal clanging against wood, and he screamed out in pain.

He grasped for the hilt of the flint knife, preparing to pull it out, but Emilia spoke up, before he could.

"I wouldn't do that, if I were you."

Jonas froze, his gaze darting toward her. "Why not?"

"I put that through the arteries," Emilia explained. "If you remove it, you'll begin to bleed out."

Jonas glared at her, his nostrils flaring.

Whatever friendliness she'd seen in those blue eyes before was gone now.

"I can heal you, of course," Emilia offered, "but—"

"Don't even think about touching me, you fucking witch!" Jonas snarled.

Emilia cringed.

Judith would've heard that. There was no hiding it now.

Jonas shook with pain, as he, once again, reached for the knife.

"I hate to break it to you, but I don't think you can row the boat, while you're bleeding out," Emilia warned.

"Then, you can row," Jonas said.

Emilia lifted her eyebrows in disbelief. "So you can take me back to the gallows?" she scoffed. "I don't think that's much incentive for me to cooperate."

Jonas reached behind him and snatched a pistol from its holster. He aimed the pistol at Emilia's head. "How's this for incentive, Emilia Drakon?"

Emilia's stomach turned with dread.

Not because of the pistol—but because he'd said it: *Drakon*.

If only he'd crossed that line *before* he'd said her people's name...

No. Maria still would've figured it out. She was always going to figure it out.

Emilia had merely been delaying the inevitable.

Judith emerged from the back with her pistol already pointed at Jonas. "Put it down."

Jonas glanced at Judith—and then back at Emilia. "You lied!"

"So did you," Emilia said, but there was no victory in it now.

"Drop the pistol," Judith snarled, "or this shot goes into your head."

"The captain'll kill me, anyway," Jonas muttered, but still, he placed the pistol on the table.

Judith held out her free hand, and Emilia took the pistol from the table and gave it to her. Judith tucked that pistol into her belt and then grabbed a pair of shackles.

When had she gotten those?

Judith tossed them at Emilia, and Emilia caught them with a pained look.

"Shackle him to the post. By the fire."

Emilia barely heard Judith's instructions. She stared at the heavy, iron shackles, terrible memories whirling in her head.

Her heart raced, and her head spun.

Emilia tried to ground herself. She tried to remind herself that she wasn't in those dungeons anymore—that it was over.

But the memories lingered, still.

Suddenly, she found herself thinking of all the times Maria had spared her from this feeling—taking sips of her drink to prove it was safe, pleading with Emilia to trust her, rather than face the shackles.

Emilia hadn't been able to make sense of the kind actions before. They'd seemed so at odds with the woman Maria appeared to be now.

But after the story Judith told her, Emilia started to wonder if, perhaps, Maria had always had a hint of kindness beneath her anger and ambition.

Maria had never even questioned her about her fears. She'd behaved as if Emilia's post-traumatic fears were normal.

She'd made Emilia *feel* normal.

But this realization came a little too late.

Judith likely already hated Emilia, and once Maria heard the truth, she would, as well.

Emilia's mistrust had been logical. It'd made sense, but now, she felt a pang of regret.

"Now, witch," Judith demanded.

Emilia flinched.

Judith had never spoken to her like that.

Emilia removed the knife from Jonas's wrist, and then, since the truth was already out anyway, Emilia lay her hand over his mangled wrist, while he screamed in pain, and healed it.

Fatigue pulled at her muscles—the price heavy for two healing spells in one day.

Tiredly, she led the anguished carpenter to the support beam by the fire.

"At least let me sit down first," Jonas said, his voice hoarse from screaming. "Who knows how long she'll leave me here?"

Emilia tried to help him, but he shoved her away and sunk to the floor himself.

Emilia wasn't sure why she felt bad for the person who'd tried to sell her to the Illopian Guard, but she did feel a stab of sympathy for him, when she saw the look on his face.

Emilia knelt behind the beam. She didn't have to pull his arms back—because he placed them behind the wooden beam himself.

"I'll tell her everything I know before she kills me," Jonas said. "If I'm dying for this, I'm taking you down with me."

Emilia cast a wary look at Judith, whose expression was colder than she'd ever seen it.

"I think you've already succeeded in that," she said softly.

"Good," Jonas said.

Emilia locked the shackles around his wrists. "Was it worth it?"

"It would've been," Jonas muttered. "For that much gold *and* a pardon? I'd give them my own mother for that."

"Well," Emilia said, her sympathy fading slightly, "at least your mother will be safer."

She climbed to her feet, doing her best to ignore the carpenter's glare. "What now?" she asked Judith, who aimed the pistol at her now.

"Gag him," Judith said. She tossed a headscarf at Emilia.

Jonas quirked a blonde eyebrow. "You want to hide me from Zain," he realized.

Judith didn't confirm or deny it, but she did turn the pistol back toward Jonas. "Do it now," she told Emilia.

With a sigh, Emilia circled around the post again and knelt to wrap the headscarf around his face.

The carpenter didn't even resist. Maybe he still hoped to negotiate his freedom—offer his silence in exchange for his life.

Emilia wished him luck with that.

After all, it seemed absolutely random—when Maria showed mercy and when she didn't.

Emilia, on the other hand, had less hope. She was sure that, by now, she'd used up all of her own chances of mercy.

Emilia straightened, and even though she didn't flinch, this time, when Judith pointed the pistol at her, her chest still ached.

"Captain's quarters," Judith demanded. "Now."

CHAPTER 18
Oh Captain, My Captain

When they reached the captain's door, Emilia lifted her hand to knock, but Judith waved her back.

To prevent her from running—though Emilia wasn't sure *where* Judith expected her to run—Judith pressed the pistol against her head and then, with her free hand, slid a heavy, brass key into the lock.

She pushed the door open and waved the pistol toward the captain's quarters. "In."

Emilia stepped into the captain's quarters.

Though there were no candles burning, this afternoon, Maria's cabin was brighter than ever, illuminated by the warm rays of sunlight slanting in through the windows.

Maria leaned against the table, her right hand curled around the hilt of her sword, as it so often was.

She was fully dressed, now—all except for her tricorn.

She wore that black, leather doublet and the double-belted scabbard she'd always worn. She'd braided and beaded two, thin locks of brown hair and left the rest loose and curly, beneath her blue headscarf.

Her softer look from earlier was gone. She looked—very firmly —like Captain Maria Welles, now.

With a tired sigh, she said, "You have *no* idea how much self-control it took for me to not come down there."

"I had it all under control, Captain," Judith assured her.

Maria lifted a scarred eyebrow. "Not according to Helen," she said, her voice tinged in disapproval. Her dark gaze shifted toward Emilia. "She was worried about you."

"I needed her to leave," Emilia explained. "I was afraid he'd hurt her, if she didn't."

"Were you?" Maria said with a thoughtful frown.

Emilia just nodded.

After ignoring Judith's pistol for nearly a minute, Maria asked, "Was she not compliant?"

"She was plenty compliant," Judith assured her, "but she's also a lot more dangerous than she led us to believe."

Emilia's brows furrowed. "I don't think I led anyone to believe *anything*."

Maria crossed her arms, her thin shirt clinging to those strong shoulders of hers. "What do you mean?"

"She's not a surgeon, Captain," Judith told her. "She's a witch."

Emilia rolled her eyes. "Those two things aren't mutually exclusive," she grumbled. "I'm a surgeon *and* a witch."

Maria's dark gaze shifted toward her. "You confess to witchcraft, then?"

Emilia spread out her arms and flashed a bitter smile. "Might as well."

"Not just any witch, either," Judith added. "He called her Emilia Drakon."

Maria's brows lifted. "The Dragon Child?"

Emilia cringed at the title. She didn't realize the prophecy had made it *off* the island, too.

Much like the unique talents of nonmagical humans, witches also often excelled in a unique type of magic.

A warrior sorceress, like Emilia's mother, excelled in curses and offensive magic. They were often the bravest of their age—and also, often the most cruel.

Healers, like Emilia, were the opposite of that—in almost every way. They excelled in healing magic and often had a gift for empathy.

It was one of the many reasons Emilia's mother had hated her.

Emilia had never wanted to be chieftess, but that didn't stop her mother from *constantly* reminding her that she couldn't be.

'*Healers can barely protect themselves,*' her mother had so often told her, '*much less their entire tribe.*'

That was the reason Emilia had asked Catherine to teach her to use a sword. She wanted to prove her mother wrong.

But she'd trusted the wrong human and proved her mother right, instead.

That wasn't the only reason her mother hated her, though. The other reason was…the prophecy.

Emilia's uncle had been an oracle, which was what her people called witches who excelled in divination.

Before Emilia's birth, he'd seen a future, in which Emilia was the last dragon sorceress.

They called her the Dragon Child because it was said that she'd be an outcast among her own kind—but a beloved companion of the dragons.

Thanks to her mother's hatred of her and the kindness of the dragons, that prophecy had fulfilled itself.

But the last of her kind? Her mother had assumed that meant Emilia would get her entire tribe killed.

She'd been right about that, too.

With her throat tight, Emilia said, "It's been a while since I was called a child, Captain."

Maria studied her with a frown, and Emilia shifted uneasily beneath her scrutiny.

Maria then turned her attention to Judith, as if she *hadn't* just learned that Emilia was an infamous witch.

"Was it him?"

Judith nodded. "You were right. It was our master carpenter," she sighed. "Jonas."

Maria looked away, wincing. "Zain's really going to give me hell about *this* murder."

Yet, she apparently wasn't having any second thoughts about it.

Maria pushed away from the table and strode toward them.

She kept her warm, brown gaze on Emilia the entire time, but when she reached them, she curled her hand around Judith's pistol and pushed it down.

"She's not going to run," Maria told the cook, who was clearly more than a cook. She made eye-contact with Emilia. "Are you?"

Emilia looked down, nervousness fluttering in her chest. She felt a bit of fear, still, but for some reason, the desire to fight or run had just...left her.

"No, Captain," Emilia said. "I won't."

Maria's gaze seemed to soften at that.

"Captain," Judith warned, "if the crew finds out you brought a witch aboard—"

"I know," Maria interrupted.

Worry twisted at Judith's brows. "I don't want to see you lose your ship."

Maria offered Judith a gentle smile. "I know."

With a sigh of defeat, Judith returned her pistol to its holster. "I used the shackles on Jonas. Should I get more for her?"

Emilia squeezed her eyes shut, her chest tightening at the thought.

Maria's voice was softer than Emilia had ever heard it. "*No one will touch her with shackles*," she stated. "You can use rope."

Emilia opened her eyes, stunned. She briefly met Maria's gaze and found those lovely, brown eyes of hers soft with under-standing.

"She's a witch, Captain," Judith reminded her.

Maria shrugged. "If she is, then shackles won't hold her, either."

With a worried frown, Judith said, "Then, what will?"

Emilia tensed. Maria would say it now. There was no stopping it. Emilia had revealed too much already.

Maria *knew* the weakness that Catherine had used against her.

The Illopian drug.

The drug that Maria could so easily take from Jonas—the one he'd probably give her willingly, just so that he could take Emilia down with him.

But instead, Maria said, "Loyalty."

Emilia looked up, her eyes wide.

What sort of trick was this?

Emilia was sure she'd made it clear, by now, that she was the *least* loyal person on this ship. What was Maria playing at?

"Tie her to the support beam," Maria told Judith, "and then, leave us."

With a look of pure terror, Judith said, "You want me to leave you alone with the most dangerous witch in Aletharia?"

See? That was loyalty.

Judith was loyal.

Emilia had tried to kill Maria before! What was she thinking?

"I'll be fine," Maria said, her arrogance rearing its big head, as it always did. "All I need from you, Judes, is secrecy. Hide our carpenter for a few hours, and I'll handle everything else."

Judith gave a reluctant nod. "Where do you want me to hide him?"

"The bilge," Maria said. "No one goes down there, unless forced." Her lips quirked at the edges. "Well, the cats do, but Rat-Slayer hates him. So, I think it'll be fine."

Judith frowned. "Rat-Slayer?"

Despite the danger of their situation—and the fact that Emilia was literally being arrested—Maria and Emilia still shared a brief, amused look.

"The captain named him," Emilia said.

Judith looked skeptical.

Maria returned to her table, shuffling through some maps.

She must've found the one she was looking for—because she soon picked up a quill, dipped it in ink, and circled something.

Judith picked up a spool of rope and took Emilia by the arm, leading her to one of the wooden posts in the middle of Maria's quarters.

"I don't usually kill people. I leave that to my captain," Judith whispered, "but if you kill her, I'll kill you."

Emilia nodded at the threat, a lump forming in her throat.

When Judith pulled Emilia's arms behind the post and began to tie her wrists, Emilia couldn't help but mumble, "I thought we were friends."

Judith hesitated, her fingers cool against Emilia's wrists. "You were supposed to."

Emilia's chest ached.

"Don't tie it too tightly," Maria said distractedly. "She's a surgeon. She needs her hands."

Judith blew out an annoyed sigh and then went to work loosening the ropes she'd just tightened. "I swear to god, Captain…"

Meanwhile, Emilia watched Maria with a frown. Why did she care if Emilia could do her duties as a surgeon after this?

Unless she planned on setting her free?

When Judith finished, she said, "Anything else, Captain?"

Maria looked up from her map. "Yes," she said softly. "Be careful, Judes."

Judith smiled. "You, too."

Judith locked the door behind her when she left, and a heavy silence settled over the captain's quarters.

Maria continued flipping through her maps, and Emilia quickly grew bored with standing against a wooden beam.

"What are you going to do to me?" Emilia asked impatiently.

Maria didn't even look up. "Haven't decided yet."

"Well," Emilia said, wriggling her tied wrists in frustration, "no rush or anything."

Maria stuck the end of the quill in her mouth, like some sort of animal, and reached over the table to grab another handful of maps.

Emilia lifted her eyebrows. "If you need extra hands, I have two that I'd *love* to have back."

Maria dropped the armful of maps and started quickly sorting through them, before finally pulling that quill out of her mouth.

"Thanks for the offer, love, but I'm fine," Maria said, as she circled something else.

"Well, I'm not," Emilia grumbled.

Maria spread out a second map. "Maybe I'll just leave you there," she said, after a few moments. "You'd make a lovely view from my bed, don't you think?"

Emilia scowled at that. "You're not funny, Captain."

Maria chuckled. "I think I am."

"Of course you do," Emilia muttered.

They must've passed another half hour in silence, and Emilia grew more and more annoyed by it.

Eventually, Maria must've grown tired of the silence, as well—because she suddenly said, "What, exactly, was your plan?" She *still* didn't look up from her maps. "When we reached the Azure Islands, what would your people have done to us?"

Caught off-guard by the question, Emilia looked away, and her stomach twisted with grief.

"Em," Maria said, when she didn't answer, "this is the part where you answer my questions."

Emilia glared at Maria, her pain and anger blending into one, terrible burn. "What people?" she snarled at the oblivious pirate captain. "I'm the only one left."

Maria froze, her quill still hovering above the map. She looked at Emilia, her brows furrowed. "What?"

"Am I not speaking clearly enough for you, Captain?" Emilia

said, her voice rising in tangent with her emotions. "They're dead. They're all dead."

Maria's frown deepened. "How?"

"You wanted to know what Catherine did to earn such a prestigious promotion?" Emilia said. "Well, now you know."

Maria set down her quill and pressed her hand to the table, leaning against it. "How?" she said again.

"Just a few months after she recovered from the fatal injuries that *I* healed," Emilia said, her jaw tight, "she came by my tent and asked me to have a meal in the mountains with her."

"She drugged you," Maria assumed.

"Her ships came while I was unconscious—and too far away to help," Emilia said, her voice strained. "By the time I awoke, it was all gone."

"The cannons?" Maria assumed.

"Half the island was nothing but smoke," Emilia said, her voice cracking. "I was so far away, but I could smell it. Even from there." Her chest rose and fell, as she sucked in a harsh breath. "Burning flesh."

Every time Maria's brows creased, her scars would deepen, and in the brief span of time that Emilia had known her, she'd come to understand that expression as well as she understood words.

It was pain.

This terrible, infuriating pirate was...*hurting* for her.

How was Emilia supposed to hold on to her anger, when Maria looked at her like that?

"Did they kill the dragons, too?" Maria asked.

"I imagine, if they had," Emilia said, "I'd already be dead." She sighed, "The dragons escaped in time."

Maria nodded. "That's why they took you to the Regolis dungeons—to interrogate you."

"I gave them nothing," Emilia assured the captain. "I may have failed my people, but I won't fail my dragons."

There was a flicker of something in Maria's dark eyes, but she hid it before Emilia could make sense of it. "You wanted me to sail through dragon territory," she accused. "Did you intend for them to kill us?"

"Only if necessary," Emilia confessed. She offered a bitter smile. "Your death or mine, right?"

Maria narrowed her eyes. "Do you think that answer's going to get you set free?"

"No," Emilia said.

At that, Maria leaned back on her heels and crossed her arms. "Em, I can't endanger my crew. If I have to kill you to protect them," she said, shrugging, "it must be done."

Emilia sighed. She didn't want to confess her secrets to anyone, much less to Maria, but she'd chosen not to run. For some, foolish reason, she'd chosen to let Maria arrest her.

Despite all of the logic and rationality that told her *not* to trust Maria, Emilia had trusted her.

"I can call them off," she admitted. "The sirens listen to no one, but the dragons listen to me. That's why I told you to sail through dragon territory."

"How do these fire-breathing beasts listen to you?" Maria said.

"They're not beasts," Emilia snapped, irritated on their behalf. "They're intelligent. They're practically demigods."

"They've burned entire cities to the ground," Maria reminded her.

"Yes," Emilia said, "when their chieftains asked it of them. They fight for my people, and my people have been at war with the Kingdom of Illopia for centuries—much longer than you have." She tilted her head back against the support beam. "The dragons protect us, and we protect them."

"How?" Maria asked again. "I want to know how you communicate with them."

Emilia sighed. She couldn't think of anything terrible that Maria could do with *that* information, so she told Maria, "Dragon sorcerers are born of dragon magic. We share a telepathic link with the species that gave us life."

"Interesting," Maria said. She was quiet for a moment, but then, a playful grin tugged at one corner of her mouth. "You know... they have some *sordid* tales about your kind in Illopia."

Enraged beyond belief, Emilia glared at her. "Yes! Tales that were born out of prejudice," she snarled, "and their belief that we're less civilized than them!"

Maria's smile widened. Clearly, her love for antagonizing Emilia had not faded. "I assumed as much," she assured Emilia, "of course." A playful gleam flashed in her large, brown eyes. "But you *did* say you were born of dragons."

Emilia rolled her eyes. "I was born of dragon magic, not dragon...*body*!" she snapped. "My mother did not have sex with a dragon, Captain!"

"Well," Maria said, obviously enjoying Emilia's outburst, "I guess that explains your lack of scales."

"You're not funny," Emilia said again, but she had to suppress a laugh, as she said it.

Scales! Really?

The nerve of this woman.

"Hypothetically," Maria said slowly, "if I were to take you to your *real* home—to Drakon Isle—could you fix my maps?"

Emilia blinked at the question. She didn't want to set her hopes high, but it was really beginning to sound like Maria intended to free her. "What's wrong with them?"

"I have the flight routes of three dragons," Maria said, "but there are more than three, aren't there?"

Emilia nodded—but didn't dare give her any more information than that.

"Well?" Maria asked. "Would you show me the routes of the others?"

With a surprising amount of regret, Emilia said, "I can't put them in danger, Captain."

"I'm offering you freedom, Em," Maria said, "in exchange for a bit of harmless information."

"The Royal Navy offered me the same," Emilia reminded her. "I turned them down, too."

"Why?" Maria asked curiously.

"If there's a chance, at all, that it could make the dragons vulnerable, I can't do it," Emilia explained. "I'm the only protector they have left. If I don't keep them safe, no one will."

"You just called them demigods a moment ago," Maria scoffed. "Surely, you don't think they need *your* protection?"

Emilia refused to look at Maria, staring straight ahead, instead. "Do what you have to do to me," she sighed, "but I won't betray my dragons."

Maria didn't respond to that. Silence spread between them once again, but this time, Emilia could *feel* the warmth of Maria's gaze on her.

It wasn't like before—when Maria had ignored her, in favor of her maps. This was a calculated silence.

Maria was thinking.

Choosing.

Parchment rustled, as Maria pushed her maps aside, and then, she strolled toward her bed, floorboards creaking beneath her boots.

She didn't ask Emilia to look at her. She simply placed herself in Emilia's line of sight.

She spoke quietly, now—her voice a mere murmur, really. "Do you want me to free you, Emilia Drakon?"

A steady warmth unfurled beneath Emilia's skin. It was the first time Maria had ever said her real name, and the way she'd murmured it, as if it were something secret, something *sensual*—it stoked the sparks of desire in Emilia's middle, awakening flames where there should've been only fear.

Unable to keep the breathlessness from her voice, Emilia said, "Obviously."

A smirk pulled at one corner of Maria's lips. She closed the space between them in a few, long strides, and Emilia tilted her head back, looking up at the tall pirate captain.

Maria's fingers seared her like a flame, when they brushed Emilia's stomach.

Emilia froze in shock, when Maria tugged Emilia's shirt from her trousers.

Practically gasping for breath, Emilia said, "What are you doing?"

Maria didn't answer. She simply untied the blood-stained strip of linen. Those dark, scarred eyebrows of hers lifted, when she saw the smooth, pinkish skin beneath.

"It's gone," Maria muttered. "The wound's gone."

Emilia watched the astonishment pass over Maria's face. She'd barely reacted to the news that Emilia was a witch, but seeing the evidence of it—*that* had affected her.

"Well," Maria said, blinking, "at least, now, I know how your bruises healed so quickly."

"I told you I'd be fine," Emilia said.

Maria looked up. "So, you did."

Emilia pressed more of her weight against the beam. It wasn't her sore muscles or her weary mind that made her curl away from Maria's touch.

It was the intense burn of desire in her core—the one that flared hotter each time Maria's warm fingertips brushed her hip.

"Were there any other times that you used magic on my ship?" Maria asked.

"Your oil," Emilia confessed. "I added a...health charm."

Maria's brows furrowed. "A what?"

Emilia looked away, her cheeks warming. "It won't heal major injuries or anything, but it might make you feel better, any time you're feeling sore or...less than well."

Confusion twisted at Maria's scars. "Why would you do that?"

"I don't know," Emilia said, her blush deepening. "You were kind to me that day. I wanted to repay you."

Maria stared at her in disbelief.

Emilia stole a small glance at Maria, wary of her reaction. "It's not a powerful spell or anything!" she said defensively. "You'll just feel a little better after you use the oil. I can still fatally wound you, if I want to!"

Maria lifted a scarred eyebrow. "Em," she said slowly. "Are you apologizing to me for doing something nice—by assuring me that you can still kill me?"

Emilia frowned. It did sound a bit odd, when she said it like that. "Yes?"

Maria's lips twitched at that. She took a step backward. "Those bright green eyes of yours *would* be lovely to see each morning," she paused, trailing her gaze downward, "along with a few other parts of you."

Emilia blinked. Her body—traitorous as it was—warmed at the insinuation that Maria found any part of her *lovely*.

Fortunately, her mouth listened to her mind, instead, which was a little more rational. "You would never do something so... *ridiculous*."

Maria's dark eyes gleamed at the challenge. "Ridiculous?" she repeated. "Wouldn't you rather me leave you here than kill you?"

"Why would you kill me?" Emilia said. "I've been cooperative. For Aletha's sake, I even let you arrest me!" She narrowed her eyes. "You have no reason to kill me."

"No reason?" Maria said with a look of disbelief. "Do you have *any* idea how much risk you pose to my position here?"

Emilia glared at her. "If you'd kill me to protect your power, you're no different than Catherine."

All traces of humor faded from Maria's face. She stepped forward, her footstep heavy against the floorboards. "Do *not* compare me to Catherine," she snarled, "witch."

Emilia lifted her chin. "If the boot fits."

Rage burned in her eyes, like flecks of golden fire. "Perhaps I'll kill you for no reason whatsoever," she said. "I'm Captain Maria Welles. I don't need a reason."

A hint of empathy pricked at Emilia's chest. "No," she said gently. "That isn't you."

Maria's brows furrowed. "What?"

"Killing for no reason," Emilia said. "It isn't you." Her voice softened. "You kill, yes—but not without reason."

Maria's frown deepened. "What are you talking about?"

"It's about power," Emilia said. She understood it now—in a way she'd never expected to. "Your reputation gives you power, so you play into it—even the parts that are untrue."

"And pray tell, my sweet surgeon," Maria said, venom in her voice, "what part do you think is untrue?"

Emilia studied her curiously. "You're not driven by greed or madness," she said. "You're angry and vengeful, yes—but who wouldn't be?"

Maria let out a soft, disbelieving laugh. "You're telling me you don't believe the tales?"

"Not all of them," Emilia said.

"Look at me," Maria said, spreading out her arms. "I am exactly what they say I am."

Emilia kept her gaze steady, showing no fear. "No. You're not."

"I'm a madwoman," Maria said, her voice edged with bitterness, "prone to murderous bouts of rage and starting rebellions for no fucking reason."

Emilia might've believed her, if she'd insisted on that before, but she knew better, now. "You had a reason. Judith told me your reason."

Maria froze, and the wild anger that had raged within her dark brown eyes dissipated in an instant.

The facade was gone.

And for the first time ever, Maria seemed to be at a loss for words.

"She shouldn't have done that," Maria said softly.

Emilia leaned forward, ignoring the way the ropes burned her wrists, when she did. "Don't be angry with her," she pleaded. "She was just trying to convince me to trust you."

Maria's brows furrowed. "Clearly, she failed."

Emilia tried to shrug, but lifting her shoulders in this position was harder than she'd anticipated. "Captain, you know I—" She hesitated. "I trusted a human once, and I'll never forgive myself for it." She sighed, "Even if I wanted to trust you, I—I can't make the same mistake twice. I just can't."

She saw it again—that crease of Maria's brows, that deepness of her scars, that flicker of pain in her dark brown eyes.

Empathy.

"Then," Maria said, her voice quiet now, "I won't ask you to."

Emilia stammered in shock, "You—you won't?"

Maria shook her head slowly. "I won't ask you to do something you're not ready to do," she promised, "and I'm sorry I ever did."

Emilia stared at the captain, absolutely speechless. Emilia's thoughts shifted once again to the way Maria had tasted her drinks for her—as if Emilia's hesitation was normal.

"You'll find a way past what they did to you," Maria said, "but it's something that shouldn't be rushed."

Emilia sagged against the support beam, her heartbeat pounding loudly in her head.

How was she supposed to reconcile these two contrasting sides of Maria? The side that would kill someone without a second thought and the side that promised not to rush Emilia's recovery?

"The ropes aren't bothering you, are they?" Maria asked. "Not in the way that…iron would?"

"They're fine," Emilia whispered. She tilted her head. "Well, not fine, but— I still expect you to untie me!"

Maria snorted. "Of course you do."

"Are you going to get around to that soon?" Emilia said. "Because I've been waiting for a *while*."

"Nearly an hour," Maria said with a smile. "You were very patient, while I marked my maps."

With a growl of frustration, Emilia said, "Well, you've used up all of my patience now. So, untie me!"

Maria lifted a scarred eyebrow. "First, I'll need some sort of assurance that you won't kill me as soon as I untie you."

"The only assurance you're getting, *Captain*," Emilia snarled, "is that I'll kill you, if you don't."

Emilia wasn't sure what she'd expected from the most dangerous pirate in Aletharia, but the alluring smile Maria gave her, in response, wasn't it.

Maria held up a finger, nautical tattoos swathing her skin, like a tentacle. "Before I free you, I need you to answer one question for me, *Emilia Drakon*."

Now, why did she have to say it like that?

Like Emilia's name was some rare wine that she needed a moment to savor?

"I drew this out for quite a while," Maria reminded her. "What kept you here?"

Emilia blinked slowly. "Rope," she said, disbelief accenting her words. "Did you...forget about the rope?"

She'd just mentioned the rope, hadn't she?

Maybe Maria had hit her head. As well as she could, without the use of her hands, Emilia checked the captain for signs of a concussion.

"You're a witch," Maria said, interrupting Emilia's very important medical examination. "Surely, you could've freed yourself."

Emilia frowned. "Well, yes, obviously," she muttered, "but—"

"But what?" Maria interrupted. "Why didn't you free yourself, Em?"

"You," Emilia stammered, "you had me arrested!" She frowned, suddenly unsure. "Didn't you?"

"King Eldric had you arrested, too," Maria reminded her. "You didn't stay put for him."

"Well, that's because he's not my..." Emilia trailed off.

"Go on, love," Maria said, her voice low and breathy. "Say it."

Emilia shook her head, denial whirling within her.

"Say it," Maria said, "and I *swear* I'll protect you with my life."

Emilia's heart raced inside her chest. "You misunderstood. That's not what I was going to say."

"Oh, I think it was," Maria murmured. She leaned closer. "There are only three things that might've kept you here." She lowered her voice to a whisper, "One is fear. Are you afraid of me, Em?"

Emilia narrowed her eyes at that. "No."

Maria circled the wooden beam, prowling around Emilia the way Emilia's dragons so often prowled around their prey.

Maria curled her fingers into the knot—perhaps to point out how loose it truly was. "The second is...*lust*."

Emilia's brows furrowed. "Wait, what?"

Maria took a handful of Emilia's shortened, black hair and tugged it backward—gently.

The moan that escaped Emilia's lips surprised *her* more than it did Maria.

Maria's lips curved against Emilia's ear. "Maybe," she whispered, "you *like* being tied up."

Emilia shuddered, chill bumps rising on the back of her neck. "No," she said breathlessly. "No, I do not."

Well...she hadn't until now, anyway.

What the hell was Maria doing to her?

Maria's warm, wet mouth brushed lightly against Emilia's neck, and another moan spilled from Emilia's mouth.

Maria chuckled, her breath warm against Emilia's skin. She let go of Emilia's hair and finished her circle, bringing herself face-to-face with Emilia yet again.

Emilia sagged heavily against the beam, her knees weak.

Maria's brown eyes darkened with lust—pure, visible lust that burned at the fringes of her iris, like a ring of fire. "Are you sure you don't like it?"

Emilia glared at her. "I think you're projecting, Captain," she said, as if they hadn't *both* just heard her moan. "You're the one who keeps saying it'd be a lovely view!"

Emilia had hoped that would get under Maria's skin—just as Maria had gotten under hers—but Maria just laughed.

She stepped closer, her leather doublet cool against Emilia's chest. "Darling," Maria said with a ridiculously sexy smile, "I wasn't the one who denied it."

Another wave of heat poured through Emilia's body, pooling between her legs.

"It wasn't," Emilia said, her voice not much louder than a gasp. "It wasn't that."

"Then, that leaves only one possibility," Maria said. "Say it."

Emilia's pulse raced.

With a gentle brush of her knuckle, Maria lifted Emilia's face. "What am I to you?"

Emilia recalled Judith's remark from the week before.

"That woman could take one look at you and know whether you respect her or not."

Maria had known this was coming. She'd seen it—the moment Emilia stepped into her quarters.

That was why she'd urged Judith to put away the pistol.

She'd *known.*

Emilia rolled her eyes, begrudgingly accepting defeat. "You're my self-serving, infuriating, arrogant, murderous, power-hungry, and...*occasionally* kind," she paused to take a breath, "captain."

Maria's smile was its own sort of magic, enthralling Emilia as effectively as a spell. "So, I'm not your enemy anymore?"

"Oh, for the love of the goddess, Captain!" Emilia snapped. "Didn't I just say that?"

With a delighted laugh, Maria kissed her. It took Emilia by surprise, but luckily, Maria curled her hand behind Emilia's head to stop it from hitting the wood behind her.

Emilia smiled into the kiss, when she tasted the hint of orange on Maria's lips.

Of course Maria had already gotten into that sack of oranges.

The woman was as obsessed with fruit as the ship cats were with chin rubs.

When Maria stopped to catch her breath, Emilia said, "I feel like you're misunderstanding me. I still hate you, and I still might kill you."

"No, I got it," Maria said—and then, she kissed Emilia again.

This time, Emilia couldn't help but melt against her.

Maria brushed her thumb along the curve of Emilia's jaw, tilting her head back, and she flattened her lean form against Emilia's curves.

The wood was rough against Emilia's back, and the curved, steel handles of Maria's swords pressed into her stomach, but Emilia couldn't bring herself to care.

Because no matter how rough any other part of this kiss was, Maria's tongue was as soft as silk.

Emilia tugged at her wrists, aching to run her fingers through Maria's thick, brown curls—to pull the headscarf free and let them spill around her shoulders, the way they had that morning.

Maria stepped back, and Emilia fell back against the beam, a whimper of frustration escaping her mouth.

Maria unbuckled the scabbard and removed it, draping it over a nearby spool of rope.

She returned to Emilia. "You really are lovely," she murmured, "and I'm not just making a joke this time."

Emilia blushed, and her stomach fluttered. "Lovely?"

When Maria insulted her, Emilia's brain pumped out a gazillion responses, but when Maria complimented her, it apparently couldn't manage to do anything but repeat a single, two-syllable word.

Maria laughed softly. "Yes, Em. Lovely."

For the briefest moment, Emilia wanted to tell Maria that she was lovely, too—that her eyes were dark and deep and held an enticing fire that Emilia just couldn't resist, that her mouth was warm and sweet, that her tongue was sinfully soft.

But it'd be strange to say those things to someone she supposedly hated.

Wouldn't it?

Maria brushed her fingers along one side of Emilia's face, gently tracing her cheekbone, and then, she leaned in close and pressed her mouth to Emilia's ear.

"Do you want me to untie you," she whispered, "before we…"

Feverish heat flooded Emilia's cheeks, and Emilia was sure Maria had felt it in her fingertips.

Maria leaned back on her heels, searching Emilia's face for any fear or reluctance.

She hadn't finished her sentence, but the implication was clear.

Intoxicated by the visceral lust she saw in Maria's eyes, Emilia shook her head.

Maria smiled, and a strange sort of hunger flashed in those dark brown eyes of hers.

Maria stepped closer, wood creaking beneath her boots. "You'll tell me if I do something you don't like."

If Maria had meant that as a request, she'd said it totally wrong.

It sounded more like a demand.

An ultimatum—that this would end, immediately, if Emilia didn't agree.

Emilia nodded.

"I mean it, Em," Maria said softly. "Anything at all—I need you to tell me."

Desire filled Emilia's body like smoke, making it nearly impossible to speak—or even breathe.

So, again, Emilia nodded.

But Maria shook her head. She lifted Emilia's face with her finger. "It's important to me, love," she said gently, "that you give me something clearer than a nod."

Emilia forced that strange heat from her lungs—enough so for her to speak, anyway. "Yes," she said breathlessly, "I'll tell you." Then, as an afterthought, she tacked on a very awkward, "Captain."

The pirate captain snorted at that. She tilted her face closer to Emilia's, as if she were going to kiss her, and whispered, "Maria."

Emilia's cheeks grew warm, as she repeated, "Maria."

Maria closed her eyes and breathed out a small, shuddery sigh —as if she'd enjoyed Emilia saying her name, as much as Emilia had enjoyed saying it. "Perfect."

Maria cupped her warm hands around Emilia's face and kissed her deeply.

Maria pressed her harder against the wooden post, and without the swords there to keep them separated, Emilia felt the muscles in Maria's stomach, as they pressed against her.

When Emilia's lips parted, just for a moment, Maria slipped her tongue into Emilia's mouth.

Gods, she tasted so sweet.

As Maria's tongue coaxed a moan from Emilia's mouth, her hand slid downward.

Maria unfastened Emilia's trousers and slipped her fingers between the fabric and Emilia's soft stomach.

Emilia gasped the moment Maria's fingers slid between her thighs.

Maria smiled against her lips. "You do like it, don't you?" she murmured. Her fingers teased Emilia's wet, aching center, driving her mad. "How long have you been this wet?"

Emilia tilted her head back against the beam, gasping at Maria's touch. "Do not," she said breathlessly, "make me stab you."

Maria laughed, and the sound was far too sweet.

Emilia didn't *want* to adore it, but she did.

Maria's muscles flattened against Emilia, and her fingers continued to tease—until Emilia was trembling and arching against the beam.

"Maria," Emilia said, struggling to keep the whine out of her voice.

Maria brushed her mouth against Emilia's and whispered, "Beg."

Emilia melted against the support beam behind her, a desperate moan spilling from her lips.

She'd find a way to win back the upper-hand some other time, but right now, she'd flown far too close to pleasure.

"Please," Emilia gasped. "Maria, *please.*"

Maria buried her face in the curve of Emilia's neck and groaned.

It was the first time she'd heard a crack in Maria's self-control, and Emilia found she adored that sound, too.

Maria slid a finger inside and smiled into the sensitive skin of Emilia's neck, when Emilia arched against her.

Maria moved her finger slowly, at first, giving Emilia's body time to respond.

Perhaps she was afraid Emilia wouldn't like it—or that it'd hurt her—but Emilia moaned deeply at her touch.

Emilia's breath came faster with each movement of Maria's fingers, and when Maria's thumb circled her clit, she barely held back a cry.

Emilia vaguely realized that Maria wasn't totally unaffected, either. Her breasts—soft against Emilia's—rose and fell with each quick, desperate breath she took.

Maria watched the way Emilia's body arched at her touch. She watched Emilia with this deep, decadent smile that made Emilia feel like a fly caught in her web.

Maria had caught her so thoroughly, trapped her in this climb of pleasure, and Emilia couldn't help but admire a woman who could trap a creature like her.

Maria's soft, warm mouth covered Emilia's, muffling the gasps and moans that spilled from her lips.

Maria quickened her pace, pushing Emilia closer to the edge.

"So beautiful," Maria murmured, but Emilia could barely hear her over the roar of her own blood.

Desire and pleasure pushed and pulled at Emilia's muscles, like ocean waves, and Emilia drifted closer and closer to the edge.

Maria leaned back, watching Emilia with eyes so dark and dilated that they were almost black.

When tremors of pleasure began to ripple through Emilia's body, Maria murmured, "There you are." She leaned closer, her smile deepening. "Come, love."

Pleasure crashed over Emilia, like a tsunami—devastating and cataclysmic, drowning out every rational thought or fear and leaving only pleasure.

Only them.

Every muscle pulled tight, and every nerve seemed to burst. Her back arched, and Maria's name spilled from her lips.

Emilia vaguely realized that Maria was holding her, keeping her body steady in the midst of these euphoric waves.

"Careful, love," Maria said against her lips. "Don't hurt your wrists."

Emilia sagged heavily against her, as every muscle in her body decided to relax, at once.

She blinked wearily, far too relaxed to hate the arrogant smirk that curved at Maria's lips.

Emilia would let her have her arrogance for now. She'd...sort of earned it.

Maria pulled her hand from Emilia's trousers and, with an irresistibly sexy smile, she held her fingers in front of Emilia's mouth—an unspoken request.

Emilia immediately took the two fingers into her mouth, licking away the wetness, as Maria watched.

"Fuck," Maria breathed.

Now, where had her arrogance gone?

Emilia tilted her head back against the wooden beam, Maria's fingers slipping out of her mouth. Her chest heaved, as she tried to catch her breath, her vision still blurry.

But Maria seemed just as breathless, when she leaned in and slipped her fingers into Emilia's hair.

"Now, let me taste," she whispered—before sliding her tongue into Emilia's open mouth.

The pirate captain kissed Emilia deeply, and a soft, almost *pained* moan escaped her mouth. She pressed herself as close to Emilia as possible, her leather-clad waist pressing against Emilia's stomach, her soft, small breasts pressing against Emilia's chest.

Every inch of Maria was warm and firm, as she clung tightly to Emilia.

The sound of wood creaking outside Maria's door startled them. Maria stepped back, suddenly, leaving Emilia to slouch against the post. "Someone's here," she muttered, and then, she circled around Emilia.

Emilia's brows furrowed, as she felt Maria's fingers against her wrists, loosening the ropes. "Maria?"

Maria froze. "Captain," she corrected. "It was fun, but it's over."

"Oh," Emilia said, as cold reality splashed over her.

Maria returned to loosening the rope, but her touch, at least, was gentler than her voice. "Look," she said with a sigh, "I don't mean to be harsh. It's just…Em, if someone hears you—"

"I get it," Emilia interrupted.

Maria finished freeing her wrists. "I'm risking a lot."

With her muscles still fatigued from that intense orgasm, Emilia nearly collapsed the moment the rope wasn't holding her in place. Fortunately, Maria must have anticipated it—because she came around, just in time to catch her.

Maria held Emilia's arms gently, the rope still dangling from her hand. Her warm, brown eyes searched Emilia's face, and her brows furrowed.

"Thank you," Emilia mumbled, desperately trying not to respond to Maria's soothing touch, "Captain."

Maria's frown deepened. "Can you stand?"

Emilia nodded, her face warm. "I'm fine, Captain."

Maria flinched a little, as if Emilia's persistent use of the word *Captain* had actually stung.

Emilia hoped it had.

Maria released her—and then, with a small shrug, handed the rope back to Emilia, as if Emilia had *any* idea what to do with it. She turned to walk away.

"What am I supposed to do with this?" Emilia said, frowning at the rope. "Keep it as a souvenir?"

Maria snorted at that. But then, the wood creaked outside her door, and her harshness returned. She quickly returned to Emilia, pointing a tattooed finger at her. "I will keep your secret and protect you," she whispered, "but only for as long as you're part of my crew. If that changes—if you leave us or betray us—you're on your own, then. Do you understand?"

Emilia nodded slowly. "Thank you, Captain."

"Don't thank me. Just," Maria sighed, "don't make me regret it."

"Yes, Captain," Emilia recited—with a good deal of bitterness.

Maria's brows creased, and she opened her mouth, as if she wanted to say something else—but the door burst open before she could. The pirate captain and Emilia both turned to see who it was.

Thank the goddess, it was just Judith.

Judith pulled up short, her brows furrowing, as she glanced back and forth between them. "I came to warn you that Zain was coming," she said, "and to tell you that you needed to decide what to do with her quickly." Her bright blue eyes narrowed, when they shifted in Emilia's direction. "But it seems you already have."

Emilia shrank back. Somehow, Judith's reaction stung even worse than Maria's harsh warnings.

But Maria just waved a hand dismissively, as she strode back to her table. "Take her with you," she told Judith, "and keep an eye on her at all times."

Emilia spun toward her. "What sort of freedom is that?"

Maria picked up a map, not even sparing a glance for Emilia's complaints. With an annoyed sigh, she told Judith, "Right. Obviously not when she goes to piss or whatever, but…any other time."

Emilia scoffed in disbelief. "You can't be serious."

Maria glanced at her, one scarred eyebrow raised. With a shrug, she added, "She can sleep alone, too."

"Ah! Thank you, Captain," Emilia snarled, "for that tiny, little leash you've given me!"

A small, almost unnoticeable smile twitched at one corner of Maria's mouth. "It's a rope, darling."

With a growl of frustration, Emilia threw the rope—her irritation only growing when Maria caught it, instead of letting it smack her in her smirking face.

Maria held up the rope. "I'll save it for next time."

"Fuck you, Captain," Emilia snarled. She spun on her heels and stormed toward the door, not wanting to spend another moment in the captain's presence.

Judith held up both hands, as Emilia stormed past, clearly not wanting to get involved. But then, she met the captain's narrowed gaze and sighed, "I'm going."

EMILIA TRIED TO GO OFF ON HER OWN, AS SOON AS THEY WERE OUTSIDE —just as a challenge, really—but Judith caught her by the arm, before she could.

"You heard the captain, witch," Judith reminded her. "You have to come with me." Without waiting for Emilia to agree, Judith began to tug her along.

"So, you're both calling me that, now?" Emilia said.

Judith glanced back at her. "Witch?" she said with a frown. "That's not an offensive word for you, is it?"

Emilia blinked in shock. Despite the fact that she'd aimed a pistol at Emilia's head, despite the fact that she was *literally* dragging Emilia down the steps, Judith was still concerned about... offending Emilia, strangely enough. "*Witch* is fine," Emilia assured her, "but until today, you were fine with using my name."

"A fake name," Judith reminded her.

"It's close enough," Emilia said. "I've come to like being called *Em*, actually."

Judith let go of her the moment they reached the galley. "Good for you," she said under her breath.

Emilia frowned, as Judith walked toward the table. "Why do I get the feeling that you're angrier than the captain?"

Judith tossed a pot on the table more forcefully than usual. "Because, apparently," she muttered, picking up a knife, "the captain's anger disappeared the moment you let her fuck you." She didn't even wait for Emilia to stammer out a reply, before she said, "Yes, I can tell."

Emilia held out her hands, not sure what to say. "*If* that happened—which I'm not confirming—why would you care?"

"She's risking a lot for you, Em," Judith told her.

A twinge of guilt turned in Emilia's stomach. "Were you hoping she would kill me, instead?"

"Of course not," Judith said easily. "I just...worry about her. That's all." She set down the knife, her brows creased. "I don't like that you've put her in this position, but that doesn't mean I want you dead."

Emilia looked away. "I'm sorry for any trouble I've caused," she confessed. "I really am." She looked at Judith. "I don't want her—either of you, really—to risk anything for me."

Judith looked up, blinking in surprise.

Emilia stepped closer. "If you have to incriminate me to save yourself—or her—please, do it."

"Why would you say that?" Judith breathed.

Emilia shrugged, and though her mother's taunts echoed in her head, she spoke the truth, anyway. "Because even if I was never really your friend, you really were mine."

A small smile tugged at Judith's lips, and her blue eyes softened. She held up the bulb of garlic in her hand and asked, "Can witches eat garlic?"

Emilia crossed her arms and lifted her eyebrows. "I've eaten garlic in front of you before, Judith."

Judith nodded. "Fair point." She returned it to the table and began to chop it up. "So, are there any witchy weaknesses I *should* know about?"

"It's easy to haunt us," Emilia offered.

"Oh, good," Judith said with a laugh. "I'll keep that in mind, if you ever kill me."

A hesitant smile curled at the corners of Emilia's lips. "So, does that mean... Can you forgive me?"

"Forgive *you*?" Judith said.

Emilia shrank back, worry twisting in her stomach.

"You just found out that I've been spying for her all this time, and you're asking me to forgive *you*?" Judith said with an incredulous laugh.

Emilia frowned, her fear morphing into confusion. "But you said—"

"That I care about her and worry about her," Judith said, "but it seems you do, too. So, we're good!"

"Wait, no," Emilia said with a frown. "I never said I cared about her. I still hate her. I definitely hate her."

"Of course you do," Judith said with a wink.

Emilia blanched. "What is the wink?" she squeaked. "Why are you winking?!"

Judith threw her head back and laughed loudly, and Emilia watched, growing more confused by the moment. Judith set down her knife and circled the table. "Look. I'm not sorry for doing my job, but I *am* sorry you felt like you lost a friend because of it."

"Felt?" Emilia repeated.

Judith rustled Emilia's shortened, black hair playfully. "I cut your hair, remember? You think I'd do that for someone I didn't like?"

Emilia wasn't sure how to answer that. "Maybe?"

"No, Em," Judith said with a playful smile. "I'm not going to risk someone punching me over a terrible haircut, unless I *really* like them."

Emilia touched her hair worriedly. "Terrible?"

"Shhh. Forget I said that," Judith teased. She slung her arm around Emilia's shoulders and pulled her closer. "I cannot believe the Wicked Witch of the Azure Sea is just a pretty girl in need of a friend."

Emilia scowled at the overly-affectionate pirate. "I don't *need* a friend," she said defensively. "I was just...surprised to have one—until I realized it was a lie." She sighed, "Then, it all made sense."

"Em," Judith said. "You're still my friend. If you can look past the fact that I've lied to you all this time, then...I absolutely still want to be your friend."

A cold, numbing wave of shock poured through Emilia's veins. "Really?"

Judith lifted her eyebrows in disbelief. "We're really going to have to do something about that sad, witchy heart of yours."

"Witchy?" Emilia repeated.

"Dragon heart. Whatever. I don't know the anatomy," Judith said with a shrug. "I don't judge."

Emilia's frown deepened.

"The point is," Judith said, turning toward her, "we're still friends—for as long as you want to be." She held out her hand, as if they were brokering an official agreement of some kind. "Deal?"

Judith was back to being her playfully friendly self, and Emilia knew Judith was waiting for her to laugh along with her—but Emilia's throat was too tight, too full of emotion. She didn't know what to think of this gesture. It was just...too good to be true.

"Come on, Em," Judith laughed. "Shake my hand."

Emilia hesitantly placed her hand in Judith's.

Judith offered her a baffled smile, clearly confused by Emilia's seriousness. She gripped Emilia's hand tightly and glanced down. Her smile faded, and she turned Emilia's wrist, studying the thin lines on her wrist.

"Em," Judith said, her brows furrowing. "Did the captain have sex with you while you were tied up?"

Emilia jerked her hand away. "Why do you keep insisting that we had sex?"

Judith shot a pointed look at Emilia's trousers, and Emilia blushed as she realized that they were still undone. She quickly fastened them, her face burning.

"There's also this," Judith said, playfully ruffling Emilia's messy, black hair. "It was obvious, Em."

Emilia's blush deepened. "And you waited until now to tell me?"

Judith flashed a small smile—but didn't laugh. "I'm going to need you to answer my question," she told Emilia. "I trust the captain. I know she wouldn't do anything without consent. But... I'm still going to need to hear it from you."

"She asked. I agreed," Emilia assured her. "We both wanted..." Her cheeks reddened. "I told her yes."

Judith laughed—and then immediately held up her hands. "No judgement here," she assured Emilia. "I just needed to know things were...communicated."

"Yes," Emilia said, her face still hot. "Can we talk about something else, now?"

Judith stepped back. "Of course. Let me get you a drink," she said, as she went to grab a flagon of rum. "Then, I'll need to make sure all of the ropes are hidden. Wouldn't want you to get the wrong idea."

Emilia glared at her. "You're not funny."

Judith poured two tankards of rum and brought one to Emilia. "Oh, you know I am."

In Judith's mind, there apparently weren't any occasions that didn't warrant rum.

Emilia took the tankard. "How does she expect me to survive, spending every moment with you and your teasing?"

"Not every moment!" Judith said with a laugh. She sipped her rum, before offering a teasing grin. "Don't forget. You get to sleep and piss on your own."

Emilia rolled her eyes. "Is she always such an—"

"Asshole?" Judith said. She took another drink of her rum. "No, not really. Occasionally, she's…"

"Kind?" Emilia assumed.

Judith frowned thoughtfully. "Herself."

Emilia cast a curious look at the ship cook.

"But hey, don't worry," Judith said, never one to let a serious moment linger. "We're going to have so much fun together in the coming weeks! You know, whenever you're not sleeping or—"

"Yes, I got it," Emilia groaned.

CHAPTER 19

Buckets and Blushes

E milia mixed a burn salve for Helen, which had become her
weekly routine, at this point.

"How did you manage this one?" Emilia asked.

Helen hopped onto the surgery table and waited. "Unless you
want to lie to the captain for me," she said, "I think it's best if we
just pretend it was spontaneous."

Emilia laughed.

Honestly, there was no reason for Helen to worry. Maria mostly
avoided Emilia these days.

Ever since they'd…

Emilia's entire body warmed at the memory, and she ground
the stone pestle a bit harder.

Occasionally, she'd find Maria watching her in the galley, while
she served meals to the sailors, or on deck, while Emilia laughed
with Judith or Fulke or Pelt…

But Maria always walked away before Emilia could approach
her.

It annoyed Emilia—like many things Maria did.

Like being a total asshole after sex.

410

With a playful smile, Emilia said, "How you manage to keep your job is a mystery to me."

Helen winked at her. "The first time you see me in battle, you'll understand."

"I bet," Emilia said, and she meant that sincerely.

Helen was clearly passionate about cannons—and explosions in general, for that matter—and if there was anything you could count on passionate people to be, it was skilled.

"The captain has a knack for finding people who are *really* good at what they do but not well-behaved enough for the navy," Helen explained.

"Solid strategy," Emilia admitted.

She could admire Maria's wits without liking her, couldn't she?

"She remembered me from training," Helen told her, "but she also knew I'd been discharged during my first year for...*appalling* behavior." Helen rolled her eyes, as if she thought that description were an exaggeration.

Knowing Helen, Emilia doubted it was.

"At first, I was like, *'Do I really want to become a pirate and face the danger of the noose for the rest of my life?'*" Helen continued to chatter, as Emilia worked on the salve. "And then, I was like, *'Yeah, I do, actually.'*"

Emilia had no idea how Helen remained so calm, while missing nearly an entire layer of skin on one finger.

Helen's fair, freckled hands *were* covered in thick callouses, but surely, she could feel that.

"Have you visited the mines in the Illopian Mountains?" Helen asked. When Emilia shook her head, she said, "That's what they sent me to do, after I got discharged. Might've been fun, if they'd let me blow things up more often. But no! They wanted to do everything the *safe* way."

Emilia lifted her eyebrows at that.

Emilia's favorite thing about spending time around Judith or

Helen was that neither of them stopped talking long enough for an awkward silence to even *think* about existing.

It was a relief, really—because Emilia never felt any pressure to talk.

She'd always felt pressured to make conversation around the people of her own island, and she'd always failed spectacularly at it.

"Thing is," Helen said, adoration bleeding into her tone, "I wouldn't have made shit in the mines. My mother was in so much debt. I was just trying to keep her out of debtor's prison, but I was failing. But then, the captain paid her debts. She saved my mum."

Emilia froze, her hand poised over the stone mortar.

See, that was the problem with listening to the crew's stories.

It was easy to hate Maria for her bloodlust and power-lust, but then, that bravery or compassion of hers would come sneaking up on you again and send you into a confusing state of admiration.

"Have you punched anyone lately?" Helen said, jolting Emilia from her reverie.

Emilia blinked at the question. "I've been practicing...patience."

"Well, that's boring," Helen complained, "though I'm sure your face is grateful."

Emilia sighed at that. It didn't matter how quickly she'd healed the bruises. Helen would never let Emilia live down losing a fight that badly.

"I can teach you to throw a better punch, if you'd like," Helen offered. Her hazel eyes shifted downward. "We'll have to do something about those little arms first, though."

"My arms are a normal size!" Emilia said.

They even had a bit of fat on them—now that Emilia was eating regularly.

Emilia placed the stone mortar on the table and went to grab the bucket of water.

"You should try kicking next time," Helen suggested. "Your thighs look surprisingly strong."

Emilia chose *not* to ask Helen how she'd noticed the strength of her thighs—and instead, gave her the easiest, dragon-less response she could think of.

"I ride."

Hopefully, Helen would assume she meant horseback and not... *dragons*.

But instead, Helen's eloquent response was, "Face or cock?"

With a squeak of surprise, Emilia dropped the bucket.

"Oops," Helen said, as sea water flowed across the floor. "That wasn't important, was it?"

Emilia ran her hand through her shortened, wavy hair, willing her flushed cheeks to cool.

"Partial to face myself," Helen continued, as if nothing had ever happened. "Not very picky about man or woman, though."

Emilia blew out a shaky breath, her eyes wide. "Helen," she said slowly, "has it ever occurred to you that there are things I don't need to know about you?"

"Like what?" Helen said.

Emilia shook her head in disbelief. "Never mind."

She picked up the bucket and peered down at the tiny puddle of sea water that had managed *not* to spill out. "I guess this is enough for now," Emilia sighed.

At that moment, Emilia's door flung open, and the last person Emilia had expected to see in her cabin that day...stepped into her cabin.

Captain Maria Welles crossed her arms, a linen shirt clinging to the strong slopes of her shoulders. "I was looking for Helen," she explained to Emilia, "so that I could murder her."

Helen winced at that. "Do you think she saw it?" she whispered to Emilia.

"Saw what?" Emilia said.

"The thing I blew up," Helen whispered.

"Yes, Helen," Maria growled. "I fucking saw it." Her brown

eyes shifted toward Emilia. "And what have you done to my surgeon? I've never seen her turn that many shades of red."

Helen waved her uninjured hand. "She's just embarrassed about dropping her bucket."

Emilia stared blankly at the master gunner.

Yes, that was totally what it was. She was blushing about a bucket. It had nothing to do with the *very* graphic image that Helen had so gleefully put in her head.

A small smile quirked at the corner of Maria's mouth. "She wasn't even that red when Jane put her tits in her face."

Emilia glared at the captain, who hadn't spoken to her in weeks but was apparently absolutely fine with bringing *that* up again.

"When Jane did what?" Helen said, suddenly interested.

"Helen," Emilia said with a long sigh, "I need to treat that burn." She glanced at Maria and added, "*Before* any murdering occurs."

Maria rolled her eyes. "Fine," she said, turning to leave. "I'll be waiting on the gun deck."

Helen cringed at the warning. "Please, feel free to take a very, *very* long time treating me."

Emilia laughed at that. "I'll try."

AFTER MARIA HAD NO DOUBT YELLED AT HELEN TO HER HEART'S content, she found Emilia on the deck, removing a splinter from Fulke's massive hand.

This mountain of a man could laugh off a blow to the head but was terrified of removing his own splinters.

"There," Emilia said, holding up the small piece of wood. "Now, just keep it clean, and you'll be fine."

Fulke signed his gratitude to her and went back to work.

Emilia smiled to herself, already endeared to the gentle giant.

"I told you, didn't I," Maria said, startling Emilia, "all those weeks ago? You belong with us."

Emilia turned to the captain, her chest fluttering at the thought. She'd always longed to belong somewhere, but she also knew the captain would say whatever it took to make her stay.

"Fulke likes everyone," Emilia reminded Maria. "Being accepted by him doesn't mean I'm accepted by the crew."

Maria shrugged. "Zain's a bit suspicious of you, still, but I'd say the rest of them like you well enough."

Emilia squinted skeptically at that. "So, are you...*talking* to me again?"

An amused smile tugged at Maria's lips. "What was it I told you that night?" she said softly. "That you, erm, weren't to leave Judith's sight unless you were..."

Emilia rolled her eyes. "Sleeping or peeing," she provided. "Obviously, I'm doing one of those right now."

Maria, shameless as she was, looked down at Emilia's trousers. "Well, I hope it's not pissing."

Emilia glared at her. "Have a nice day, Captain," she said—and tried to step past her.

But Maria caught her by the arm and tugged her back.

Warm, potent desire flooded Emilia's body the moment Maria's right breast pressed against her back.

All of the sudden, it wasn't the tropical sun burning Emilia's skin but *Maria*—the memory of her fingers as clear as the night it happened.

"What if I let you fight me?" Maria murmured in her ear.

Emilia turned to frown at her. "What?"

"You must be dying to use your sword by now," Maria said with an enticing smile. "It's been weeks and still no battles. I'm getting a bit antsy myself." She leaned closer—close enough for Emilia to smell the hibiscus and orange on her skin. "Fight me, and I'll show you how to kill Catherine."

Emilia tried to hide her interest, but a spark of enthusiasm was already rising in her chest. "I already know how to kill her."

"With magic, perhaps," Maria whispered, careful not to let anyone overhear.

Maria brushed her fingers over Emilia's cheek, and suddenly, Emilia could think of nothing, except for the way her own pleasure had tasted on them weeks before.

"Trust me, my sweet surgeon," Maria said, her voice lilting and seductive. "It's *so* much more satisfying to kill with a sword."

Breathlessly, Emilia said, "Don't you want to be the one to strike the killing blow?"

"I do," Maria admitted, "but I intend to give you everything you want, Emilia Drakon, and I think vengeance is at the top of your list."

The arousal intoxicated Emilia like rum, warming her skin and swirling around in her head.

Maria whispered the next words against her lips. "Am I wrong?"

Emilia needed to escape to the galley as soon as possible—if she wanted to avoid kissing the captain right there in front of the whole crew.

"When and where?" Emilia breathed.

"Here," Maria told her, "at nightfall."

Emilia lifted her chin boldly. "See you then, Captain."

Maria chuckled, when Emilia turned to leave. "Save some energy for me, Em."

Emilia blushed. Did she *mean* that as an innuendo or…?

Emilia chose to assume she hadn't. "Yes, Captain."

"One of these days, Em," Maria called after her, "you're going to learn to stop making deals with pirates."

～

416

That night, Emilia found her captain exactly where she said she'd be—leaning against the taffrail, waiting for her.

Up near the helm, Henry caught Emilia's eye and gave her a friendly nod.

With an affectionate smile, Emilia waved back at him.

Before his liver failed him a few weeks back, Emilia had never even held a conversation with the helmsman before. Now, he spoke to her every time he saw her.

"It's almost unfair," Maria said, her voice soft enough that only Emilia heard her, "that he'll never know how close he came to death."

Emilia glanced at Maria, her eyes wide and curious. Maria had overseen the surgery. She knew what no one else knew—that Emilia had used magic to save him.

Maria hadn't spoken of it, at the time, so to hear her say it, now, made Emilia's stomach flip in surprise.

"I didn't even know if *you'd* realized," Emilia admitted.

"I've been quiet these past few weeks," Maria said, "but that doesn't mean I haven't noticed all you've done for my crew."

Emilia shied away from Maria's praise. It always left her feeling a little too warm and fluttery, and it was hard to remember why she hated Maria, when Maria made her feel like that. "I haven't done much," Emilia argued. "I just treated a few cuts and burns."

"And brought my helmsman back from certain death," Maria reminded her.

Emilia nodded, her shoulders stiff.

Maria lifted that leather flask of hers to her lips, taking a long drink of rum. "The more I watch you, the less I want to see you go."

Emilia looked away. She'd assumed Maria's silence had meant she'd given up on that goal.

Clearly, she'd assumed wrong.

"You can't make me stay," Emilia said—though a part of her *did* ache at the thought of leaving.

Had she really grown so attached to these people already?

"I know that," Maria assured her, "but for the sake of my crew, if there's a chance I can change your mind, I'm going to try."

For the sake of her crew.

It was so rare to hear Maria actually admit what Emilia had come to realize in all of these weeks at sea—that Maria would do almost anything for the people who called her captain.

Ironically enough, she'd also *kill* them, every now and then.

Consistency wasn't really her strong point, was it?

Emilia had never known anyone who somehow managed to be both merciless and kind.

In a world of dragons, gods, sea monsters, and sirens, this human pirate captain was somehow the most enigmatic creature Emilia had ever known.

Maria drew her right sword. Emilia still hadn't seen her use the left.

"I let Zain know that I'd be sparring with you tonight," Maria told her. "As long as you don't kill me, you shouldn't face any consequences."

"Aww," Emilia said with a disappointed whine. "Killing you was the part I was looking forward to!"

Maria laughed. She gave a small nod, as if she understood that. "I was, erm, a little unpleasant after our...time together, wasn't I?"

Emilia thought that *'our time together'* was an odd way to say unforgettable sex, but she nodded, anyway.

"You were a complete and total asshole," Emilia informed her.

Again, Maria nodded. "I'm not good with it—the stuff that comes afterward."

Emilia squinted bewilderedly. "What comes afterward?" she muttered. "Washing your hands?" Under her breath, she added, "Or your face."

Maria laughed loudly at that. "That's not what I was referring to, no."

Warmth fluttered in Emilia's stomach. She'd forgotten how lovely Maria's laugh was. "What, then?"

Maria's smile faded. "Vulnerability."

"The captain doesn't linger," Judith had said—that first night, at the tavern.

Emilia looked away. She hadn't expected an apology—nor had Maria given one—but somehow, honesty was even more shocking than an apology would've been.

"I thought..." Emilia trailed off. Maria had given her honesty, but Emilia feared giving it back.

But she'd already said too much. Maria would never let her cower away now.

"You thought what?"

Emilia's gaze darted back toward Maria, and her face warmed. "That you'd," she said, searching for the right words, "gotten what you wanted out of me and lost interest."

Maria stepped closer. "What I *wanted*?"

Emilia stepped back, floundering. "Wait, no. I wasn't trying to say you wanted me," she stammered, "just that you wanted the truth."

Maria continued to pursue her with heavy, purposeful steps. "So, you think I *didn't* want you?"

Emilia stumbled backward. "Uh? Well, no?" She frowned. What had she been trying to say again?

Maria followed every step she made. "You think I haven't thought about you every night since?"

"Uh," Emilia said, taking another step back, "every night?"

Maria prowled toward her, like a predator stalking its prey. "You think I haven't thought about the way you felt?"

Emilia squeaked in surprise, as her back collided with the rail.

Behind her, strong waves—spurred on by the night wind—lashed against the hull of the ship.

Still, Maria closed the space between them. She whispered the next words against Emilia's lips. "You think I haven't touched myself to the thought of you?"

Emilia gasped. Every inch of her skin burned, and a sudden rush of desire ached and pulsed between her thighs.

But Maria had her trapped now, and she pressed the sword against Emilia's neck.

The blade pressed into the right side of Emilia's neck—slanted from the front of her shoulder to the back of her ear, the steel cold and sharp against her carotid artery.

"You'd be dead," Maria said, as if Emilia hadn't already realized that. She lowered her sword. "Don't let your guard down again."

Emilia might've glared at the arrogant pirate, if she hadn't been clamoring to get her body back under control.

Maria stepped back. "Draw your sword, Em."

Emilia stared at her in disbelief. Here Emilia was, halfway to hyperventilating, and Maria was acting like she hadn't said a word.

See? Asshole!

Total asshole.

With an annoyed glare, Emilia stepped forward and drew her sword.

"If you let me control the footwork, I've already won," Maria told her.

"Yeah, yeah, I got it," Emilia grumbled.

Somehow, Emilia doubted her real enemies would be speaking so casually of self-pleasure, though.

Catherine had never been quite so...*indelicate.*

"I hate to be the bearer of bad news, love," Maria said, "but Catherine didn't teach you to wield a sword out of the kindness of her own heart."

Emilia's brows furrowed. "What do you mean?"

Maria lifted that scarred eyebrow of hers. "I assume you had no other tutor?"

Emilia shook her head. "Using weapons on our island is sort of...embarrassing."

Maria rocked back on her heels, her dark brown eyes wide. "What?"

Out of all of the things that had happened in the last few minutes, *that* was what shocked Maria?

Emilia glanced around, checking to make sure that none of the night watch were close enough to hear. "We have…warrior sorcerers. My mother was one."

Maria nodded slowly. "But you weren't."

"Curses are difficult for me," Emilia said with a shameful shrug. "I didn't inherit my mother's talent for them."

"So, you learned to protect yourself with a sword, instead," Maria assumed.

Emilia nodded.

"And that was supposed to embarrass you?" Maria said with a look of disbelief.

"My mother thinks so," Emilia told her.

Maria gave her a look that seemed a little…*worried.* "Thinks?" she said slowly. "But I thought your whole tribe was…"

As a witch, Emilia was so nonchalant about hauntings that she'd totally forgotten that humans weren't. "Oh!" she said, blinking. "Her ghost."

Maria's eyes widened. "Her *what*?"

"The line between life and death is thinner for my kind," Emilia explained. "We can still communicate—in a sense."

Maria stared, clearly disturbed by the thing Emilia thought of as so ordinary. "Well, that explains a lot."

"Hmm," Emilia said with a frown, "like what?"

Maria shook her head. "Never mind," she muttered. She looked away, tilting her head slightly, as if she were trying to decide whether to say something or not. "Well, regardless of what your… dead mother says," she said with a shudder, "I happen to admire your resourcefulness."

Emilia nearly dropped her sword. "What?!"

"Right," Maria said, changing the subject quicker than Emilia could blink. "Catherine's a brilliant swordsman." She spread out her arms. "Well…she was my sparring partner. So, obviously, my skill rubbed off on her."

Emilia rolled her eyes. Humility was clearly a foreign concept for Maria.

"But *being* a brilliant swordsman means she knew that if she meant to betray you," Maria said, "she'd need to leave herself a way out—just in case her *other* plan fell through."

"You mean if I'd been smart enough *not* to accept a drink from her?" Emilia said.

Maria scowled at her word choice. "Did you sleep next to her?"

Emilia blanched at the question. "I don't see how that's any of your business."

"I'll take that as a yes," Maria muttered.

The wind was cool and strong that night, and it rustled those beautiful, little curls of Maria's. Only her beaded braids were heavy enough to hold steady.

Emilia looked away, blinking, as she tried to remember what she'd been irritated about.

"If you trusted her enough to sleep next to her," Maria said, oblivious to Emilia's distracted thoughts, "I would say accepting a drink is minor in comparison."

Sleeping.

Was that what she'd meant by *'what comes afterward?'* Helen had mentioned that Maria didn't let anyone sleep in her quarters, hadn't she?

Maria had even waited for Judith to leave before she'd removed her swords.

And Judith was the one person Maria trusted.

Perhaps the reason Maria understood Emilia's issues so well was that she had plenty of her own that she'd never worked through.

"The point is," Maria said dismissively, "she didn't just teach you to wield a sword. She left gaps in your technique—gaps that *she* could exploit."

Emilia frowned worriedly at that. "She taught me to lose?"

Maria shook her head. "No, she would've known you were too smart for that. She taught you to win," Maria assured her, "against anyone *except* her."

"But you won against me, too," Emilia reminded her.

Maria nodded. "Yes, because I know Catherine," she said, "and because I know exactly what sort of snake she is."

Aiming for a bit of levity, Emilia guessed, "A basilisk?"

Maria snorted.

That not-laughing-at-each-other's-jokes plan seemed to have fallen through somewhere.

"If I'm going to give you your vengeance," Maria said, "I need to close those gaps."

Gratitude crackled inside Emilia's chest, like a warm, soothing fire, and just a few more of those negative feelings she'd harbored toward Maria began to melt away.

"I won't have you face her until you're ready," Maria told her. "I hope you'll trust my judgement on that."

Emilia surprised herself by saying, "I do."

"Good," Maria said with a wicked smile, "then, let's see how fast you lose this time."

"One question," Emilia said, holding up a finger, "since I'm a healer and can undo any damage I do, am I allowed to stab you?"

Maria scoffed, as if that were the most absurd thing she'd ever heard. "You can *try*."

Emilia smiled at the prospect.

MARIA HADN'T FOUGHT LIKE THIS IN NEARLY A DECADE. IT WAS ALMOST like having her old sparring partner back—except where Catherine had been ambitious and jealous, Emilia Drakon was curious and clever.

And lovely.

So lovely.

In the moonlight, she looked almost ethereal—with her hair as black as shadows and her fair skin like lilacs in the pale blue light.

Em had Catherine's technique—but not her skill. Not yet.

After all, Catherine would've never let Maria beat her three times in a row, and she'd already beaten Emilia six times.

Soon to be seven.

But even if she didn't have the skill yet, she had the potential of an unblossomed rose.

They'd been fighting for hours, at this point, and though Maria could see the flush of exhaustion in Emilia's cheeks, the witch had yet to ask for a break.

For the seventh time that night, Maria knocked the sword from Emilia's hand and pressed the tip of her own sword against Emilia's neck.

"Any last wishes?"

Emilia laughed, despite the sword against her throat. "You shouldn't count your victories so early, Captain."

Maria didn't lower her sword, but the certainty in her smile wavered—just a little. "You're unarmed."

Emilia shook her head slowly, and an adorable, impish smile pulled at one side of her mouth.

Which was...admittedly, a bad thing for Maria to focus on during a sword fight.

In that one, distracted moment, Emilia ducked past Maria's sword and shoved that strange dagger of hers into Maria's stomach.

Metal clanged against wood, as Maria's sword fell to the deck.

Maria looked down, staring in mute shock at the long, shining dagger in her stomach.

Emilia leaned forward and lifted her chin, and on her toes, like that, she was almost tall enough to whisper the words against Maria's lips.

"Do you yield, Captain?"

Even with a blade in her stomach, the faint urge to kiss Emilia still flared up inside of her.

This woman was more addictive than rum.

As the initial shock faded, the pain spread slowly through Maria's abdomen.

"You stabbed me."

"Of course I stabbed you," Emilia said with a soft laugh. "You told me I could."

Maria glared at the strange surgeon. "Em—"

"Oh, don't worry!" Emilia assured her. "The good thing about being a surgeon is that I know how to cut without damaging organs. You'll be fine."

Maria stared blankly at her. "You stabbed me!"

Emilia's enchanting, green eyes sparkled in the moonlight. "I gave you the chance to tell me no," she reminded Maria. "It's not my fault you were too arrogant to take it."

"Em," Maria said.

She'd be lying if she said she wasn't a little impressed, but it also fucking *hurt*.

Emilia gripped the dagger's engraved hilt. "I need you to stand very still, while I remove it," she told Maria. "It'll hurt worse, if you don't."

"Remove?" Maria repeated, her eyes wide. "Wait, no—"

But it was already done. The blade slid from her abdomen, as if it were merely water.

Apparently noticing Maria's surprise, Emilia said, "I have a steady hand, Captain."

Of course she did.

She was a surgeon.

Still...Maria had barely even felt it.

Emilia examined the blood that glistened on the blade. "Did you know enchanted daggers take in the essence of the blood?" she said. "I can use your blood now, if we ever need a summon."

Great. The witch was speaking gibberish now.

"Em!" Maria said.

Emilia looked up, her bright green eyes shining like emeralds.

"I am bleeding," Maria reminded her.

"I need fire for the spell," Emilia said. "Is anyone in the galley?"

Maria shook her head. "Judith's on the gun deck with Helen and Pelt."

Emilia cast a puzzled look at the starry sky. "This late at night?"

"They're gambling," Maria said, "not working."

"How long will she be gone?" Emilia asked.

"All night," Maria said. She pressed a hand to her stomach. "I can't believe you fucking stabbed me."

Emilia laughed. "You're such a sore loser," she teased. She hooked her fingers through the gold chain that Maria wore around her neck and tugged. "Come here."

Maria followed the pull, stepping closer to the strange surgeon.

Emilia pressed her palm against Maria's stomach, and the pain seeped out of her, like water spiraling through a drain.

Maria nearly gasped in relief. "I thought you needed fire."

"To heal it, I do," Em said. "You're not healed yet. I just took your pain—so you'd lose the sour attitude."

Maria scowled at her teasing. "What do you mean *you took my pain*?"

Emilia shrugged. "It's a bit like empathy—except with magic."

"That doesn't make sense at all," Maria informed her.

Emilia rolled her eyes. "You're such a human sometimes."

Maria blinked. Out of all the insults she'd ever heard, that had to have been the strangest.

"At least I don't talk to the ship cats like they're people," Maria muttered.

"Might I remind you of the time you killed your carpenter, simply because you told Rat-Slayer you would?" Emilia countered.

Maria sighed. She did have a point there.

She wouldn't say that was the *only* reason she'd killed him, though.

Just as Emilia turned to head toward the galley, Maria noticed the tremor in her right hand. Maria reached out and grasped Emilia's wrist, watching as her fingers trembled.

She said she took the pain. Did that mean…

"Em," Maria gasped. "What did you do?"

Emilia glanced from her wrist to Maria. "I told you," she said with a frown. "I took it."

"Why?" Maria said, frustration sparking within her. "Give it back!"

Emilia looked at her like *she* was the crazy one. "Captain, that's not how this works."

Maria wanted to shake some sense into her. "Why would you do that?" she snarled. "What sort of vengeance is it, if you're the one feeling the pain?"

Emilia's brows furrowed. "Who said anything about vengeance?" she scoffed. "I stabbed you to prove I could, not for vengeance."

Maria released her wrist, blinking.

A slow smile spread across Emilia's face, and a surprised laugh fell from her lips. "Wait. You—you thought I stabbed you because you were rude? After we," she lowered her voice to a whisper, "had sex?"

Well, this was just *all* wrong. Maria wasn't the one who was supposed to feel embarrassed.

That was the blushing surgeon's job.

"Even if that wasn't the reason," Maria said, trying to regain control of this situation somehow, "I still think it was a foolish thing to do."

Emilia frowned. "The stabbing or the—"

"The magic, Em. The magic," Maria said.

Emilia shrugged. "Well, you'll just have to get over it, then.

There's nothing *you* can do about it."

"I'm your captain," Maria reminded her. "I could increase your workload. Or have you whipped!"

Maria would obviously do neither of those, but it was fun to say it, anyway.

Emilia laughed at the threat. "Yeah, I'd love to see you try to explain that to Zain."

Maria narrowed her eyes at that.

"Come on," Emilia said, as if she were coaxing a hissing cat from his corner. "Let me get you healed before someone thinks I tried to kill you again."

With the sourest look she could muster, Maria sneered, "Yes, surgeon."

The laughter Emilia gave her in return was absolutely frustrating.

And...adorable.

CHAPTER 20

Dragon Magic

"Captain!"

Maria turned so quickly she nearly knocked over the barrel of apples. "Hmm?"

"Would you get your hand out of the apples and put some pressure on your wound?" Emilia said. "You're bleeding on the floor!"

Maria glanced down at the floor, blinking at the small puddle of blood. "Well, it's your own fault," she said defensively. "I keep forgetting about it because I can't feel it anymore."

Emilia rolled her eyes, as she hung a pot of water over the fire.

Maria had to be the only person in the world who would complain about *not* feeling pain.

A *crunch* behind her let Emilia know that Maria had chosen the damn apples over her bleeding wound.

"I swear to the goddess…" Emilia grumbled.

"What's that for?" Maria said with a mouthful of apple.

Startled by the sudden closeness of Maria's voice, Emilia nearly dropped the jar of honey into the floor. She spun around, glaring at her fruit-obsessed captain. "Have I not told you to sit down seventeen times already?"

"Don't know," Maria said, taking another bite of that shiny, red apple. "I haven't been keeping count."

Emilia gave her an exasperated sigh. "The next time I think about taking your pain," she complained, "remind me that you're an imbecile without it!"

Maria laughed at the insult. "I told you that you shouldn't have done it."

Emilia shook her head in disbelief. "Captain, would you, *please*, sit down so I can do my job?"

Emilia tried to return her attention to her work, scooping out a spoonful of honey, but she stiffened when she felt Maria's warm breath against her ear.

"I love it when you beg," Maria whispered.

Emilia nearly dropped the jar.

Again.

She turned, her eyes wide. "Captain!"

Maria took another bite of her apple. "What?" she said with an innocent smile.

Emilia narrowed her eyes. "I should've stabbed you a *lot* deeper."

Maria snorted. "If you're going to heal me, anyway, what's the harm, right?"

At this point, Emilia was about ready to throw the entire jar of honey at her. "Captain Maria Welles, if you don't sit down *right* now," she snarled, "I'm telling the entire crew that you lost a sword fight."

Maria stopped chewing.

Pleased with her reaction, Emilia flashed a vicious smile. "Well?"

Maria's nostrils flared slightly, as she huffed out a defeated sigh. "Fine."

Emilia watched victoriously, as Maria trudged toward the table. She hopped onto its rough, wooden surface and bit into her apple, chewing indignantly.

"Thank you," Emilia said politely.

"Fuck you," Maria said—*less* politely.

Emilia laughed and returned her attention to the honey. She could definitely see her new blackmail material proving *very* useful for the foreseeable future.

"You're the one who wanted to make me a pirate," Emilia reminded her.

"And what a fine one you make," Maria murmured.

Emilia glanced back at her, blushing at the dark smile she saw on Maria's face.

Between the sex, the several weeks of silence, and the sword fight tonight, Emilia wasn't sure where the two of them stood anymore.

She only knew that their animosity felt flimsy now, like an old strip of fabric, stretched thin and ready to tear through.

What hid beneath it was as much a mystery to her as the darkest, deepest depths of the sea.

"Do you need me undressed?" Maria asked.

Emilia swallowed. After the way her body had reacted to seeing Maria in a thin shirt, without her doublet, she feared how it'd react to seeing her in *less*.

"Not necessarily," Emilia said nervously. "I need access to the wound, so…you'll need to lose the doublet. But you can just roll up the shirt, if you like."

"And if I prefer to remove both?" Maria said, her gaze dark and calculative. "Would that bother you?"

Heat rushed to Emilia's face. Did Maria *know* how strong Emilia's attraction to her was?

"Em. If it will bother you, I need you to tell me," Maria repeated.

"Why would it bother me?" Emilia said, blushing. "I'm a healer. I can handle…" she trailed off.

Maria lifted a scarred eyebrow. "You can handle what?"

Emilia turned away, feigning indifference. "Do what you want."

The soft crunch of the apple was Maria's only response.

When Emilia finished making the mixture she'd need to use to dress the wound, she turned to tell Maria it was ready.

But the words died on her lips.

Maria stood, facing away from Emilia, as she undressed. She'd already removed her leather doublet and scabbard, and she tugged her bloodstained shirt over her head, now.

While Maria was long and lean—with smaller muscles than someone like Helen or Buchan—the strength in her shoulders and back was clear.

Tattoos ran down both of her arms, as dark as shadows against her radiant, brown skin.

But aside from the strip of cloth that held her breasts close to her chest, her back had been left bare.

And it was what Emilia saw on her back that took Emilia's breath now.

Raised lines crossed at all angles across her back—almost like intricate latticework.

Except it was her skin, not fabric.

Emilia couldn't have counted the scars any easier than she could've counted grains of sand.

The scars were far too numerous, and they formed terrible, asymmetrical webs on both sides of her spine.

Emilia couldn't help herself. She gasped at the sight.

Maria stiffened, but she didn't turn around.

Did she know how painful it looked? Had she ever seen it herself?

Emilia crossed the space between them in a few, frantic steps, as if she thought the scars might look less terrible from a closer angle.

Unable to keep the pain from her voice, Emilia breathed, "Captain."

"Did you think you'd seen the worst of it already?" Maria said, but still, she didn't turn around.

Had Emilia thought that?

The scar over Maria's eye was a terrible one, after all. From the looks of it, Maria was lucky to have recovered her eyesight in that eye.

But it wasn't really that Emilia hadn't anticipated any worse scars.

It was that she couldn't possibly have anticipated *this*.

"Catherine did this?" Emilia said breathlessly.

Maria gave a bitter laugh at that. "She didn't swing the whip herself, no—but do I blame her for it?" She paused to think about it. "I suppose so."

Emilia reached out and traced her finger along one small corner of the intricate web of scars, and Maria shuddered at her touch.

Usually, Maria's skin felt smooth and warm beneath her fingers, but there was nothing smooth about Maria's back.

Out of all of the things she could've said, only one word came readily. "Why?"

"I wasn't an ordinary prisoner," Maria reminded her. "Public flogging is the standard form of punishment in the King's Navy."

Emilia had known that, of course, but this was much worse than any ordinary flogging.

"How many lashes?"

Goddess, it looked like hundreds.

"Twenty a day," Maria said. She folded her shirt and placed it on the table, "but I couldn't tell you how many days. It all bleeds together in my mind."

Emilia knew the feeling. "How did you even survive?" she said breathlessly. "The chances of infection, alone, are…"

Maria turned to face Emilia, and that thin strip of white linen that held Maria's breasts close to her chest was the only thing that hid them from Emilia's gaze.

"They made sure I survived—for the same reason you're wanted alive and not dead," Maria said. "Because the citizens of Regolis *love* a show."

The thought sickened Emilia. How could anyone enjoy watching such a thing?

Her mother had often watched justice with an uncaring eye.

Back then, Emilia had turned her head to all but mercy.

She liked to think she was tougher than that now, but the empathy inside of her still writhed in agony at the thought.

But it made sense, now—why Maria was often so merciless in her judgements. She'd had the mercy literally beaten out of her.

And perhaps, to someone who'd experienced this sort of punishment, death *was* the merciful choice.

Still, for reasons Emilia would never understand, the pirate captain had shown *her* mercy.

Emilia glanced down at the narrow incision in Maria's stomach —that Maria had so carelessly left to bleed freely. "Let me get that healed," she sighed.

Maria sat down on the table, watching as Emilia walked away. "Is there anything you *can't* heal with magic?"

Emilia returned with a small bowl. "There's plenty," she assured her. She scooped her fingers into the bowl, coating them in a salve that smelled strongly of honey. "Healing spells are good for mending—not as good for reconstruction."

When Emilia began to smear the sticky salve onto Maria's skin, Maria frowned. "I still can't feel it."

Emilia, on the other hand, winced at the pressure. "Don't worry. I can."

Maria stared at her in disbelief. "I still don't understand why you did that."

Emilia didn't know how to explain it, either, so she ignored the remark. "With magic, I can heal some things but not all. With surgery, I can treat some things but not all. But by learning from everyone— and not just my own culture—I've learned to treat almost anything."

"Almost?" Maria repeated.

"Anything but death," Emilia confirmed.

Maria gave her a taunting smile. "So, the great dragon sorceress is incapable of necromancy."

Emilia rolled her eyes. "Necromancy is a myth. It exists only to take gold from the pockets of fools."

"I've heard village witches can perform it," Maria said.

"Of course you have," Emilia scoffed. "They're the ones who need the gold."

"What do you mean?" Maria said curiously.

Emilia set the bowl on the table and wiped her hand clean with a rag. "I mean," she explained, "if you want me to make a corpse dance for you, I can, but if you want me to revive the dead, that's impossible."

Maria's brows furrowed.

"It's a trick," Emilia said with a shrug. "A cheap puppet show; that's all." She set down the rag. "No one who looks like you or me can give life. That's divine magic."

Maria watched Emilia with a puzzled frown. The woman didn't even seem to notice her own state of undress.

Emilia wished *she* hadn't noticed. It made it just a bit harder to concentrate.

And it hadn't been easy to start with.

"What is divine magic?" Maria said.

Emilia's brows furrowed. "You don't know the source of magic?"

On Drakon Isle, it was the foundation of everything they were taught. Emilia couldn't imagine reaching the age of thirty-two without hearing of it.

"I was raised in a country where even the mention of magic is outlawed," Maria reminded her.

Emilia nodded, though she still didn't understand it.

Where was their curiosity? How could a whole multitude of people believe that something was evil, if they didn't even know its origin?

Then again, the worship of Aletha was also outlawed in Illopia, and yet, the captain had those books about her.

Maria *did* have some curiosity in her.

Emilia grabbed a handful of rice from a sack on the table and took one apple from the barrel.

Maria held out her hand for the apple, and Emilia scowled at her.

"Do you want to learn this or not," Emilia said, "you greedy fruit-hoarder?"

Maria snorted at that and dropped her hand to her leather-clad lap.

"Life and death, creation and destruction," Emilia said, holding out the apple, "is what we call divine magic. It runs only in the blood of the gods."

Amusement danced in Maria's large, brown eyes. "The apple is a god?"

"Shut up and listen," Emilia grumbled.

Again, Maria laughed.

Beside Maria, on the table, Emilia set down the apple and then scattered a handful of rice into a small circle.

Emilia took a knife and chopped the apple into four slices.

"Why are you dismembering a god?" Maria interrupted.

Emilia shot a peeved look at her—before arranging the apple slices into their own circle. "For the sake of this illustration, these apple slices represent the gods," she explained.

"What is the rice, then?" Maria asked.

"That's worldly creation," Emilia told her, "like you."

"No, no," Maria said, shuffling the food into a totally wrong arrangement, "I don't like rice. I'm the apple slice. The gods can be the rice."

Emilia slapped the pirate captain's hand. "Don't touch!" she snarled—as she went back to work, rearranging what Maria had just messed up.

Maria just laughed.

When Emilia finally had it fixed again, she pointed to the apple slices and said, "Gods!" She then pointed at the rice. "Worldly creation!"

When Maria opened her mouth to object, Emilia brandished the knife at her.

"No touching!"

Only half-dressed and apparently unfazed by the threat of another stab wound, Maria just grinned.

"The gods' first creation was dragons," Emilia said. She took two apple slices and part of the circle of rice and arranged them into their own, smaller circle. "Dragons are demigods—half godly, half worldly."

Maria tried to snatch one of the apple slices from the old circle, but she jerked her hand back, just in time to avoid the fruit knife that Emilia stabbed into the table.

"So, as you can see," Emilia continued, as if she hadn't just tried to stab her captain again, "dragon magic is only half divine."

"And half rice," Maria said.

Emilia rolled her eyes. "What that means," she said, "is that dragons can do some of what gods can do—but not all."

Maria made another attempt at stealing one of Emilia's apple slices, so Emilia just grabbed another apple from the barrel and shoved it into Maria's hands.

With a satisfied smile, Maria took a bite.

This time, Emilia took only one of the apple slices. "Drakon sorcerers are born of dragon magic, but we also have a bit of human in us." She took another handful of rice and scattered it around the one, lonely apple slice. "Which means our magic is only dragon magic in *part*—which results in the *divine* magic in our blood being reduced to an even smaller portion."

Maria took another bite of her apple, but her dark gaze didn't leave Emilia.

"Which means," Emilia added, "we can do some of what dragons can do—but not all."

Maria nodded slowly. "And the other witches in the world?"

Emilia took another handful of rice. "The people you refer to as village witches are mostly human." She dropped the rice onto the table, and then, she reached out and plucked the small stem from Maria's apple. She buried it in the rice, and it easily disappeared from sight. "They still have a tiny spark of dragon magic in their blood, somewhere, but it's so diluted that they likely will never master it."

Maria lowered the apple. "So, they're related to you?"

Emilia tilted her head and squinted thoughtfully. "Possibly," she admitted. "A descendent of one of the original families of the Drakon tribe would've needed to mingle with their bloodline somewhere for them to have even a spark."

Maria nodded slowly. "So, not necessarily related to you, but related to *someone* from your tribe?"

"Yes," Emilia said. "As the magic trickles down, it becomes less divine and less powerful. So, if *my* people can't revive the dead, I can guarantee you the village witches can't either."

Maria took another bite of her apple.

"All they're doing is reanimating a corpse," Emilia said, "which would be the equivalent of me changing the color of that apple. It might look different, but it's still an apple."

Maria cast a puzzled look at the shiny, red apple in her hand. "You can do that?"

Emilia snapped her fingers, and the red apple skin instantly transformed into a lustrous shade of purple.

Maria dropped the purple apple.

Emilia rolled her eyes. "Now, why did you do that? I just told you it's still an apple."

Maria stared, her eyes wide.

Emilia returned to the fire and held out her hands, and—much like her dragons had taught her to do—she channeled the fire's energy into her own body.

Maria watched in stunned silence, as Emilia's hands took on the glow of the fire.

"Only the gods can give life," Emilia said, in conclusion.

Maria continued to watch Emilia's hands, even after Emilia returned to the table. "Is that just the lore of your island or something you've seen with your own eyes?"

"It's something you've seen with *your* own eyes," Emilia said, "Captain."

Maria's brows furrowed. "What do you mean?"

Emilia gave her a sad smile. "You knew the term *Dragon Child*," she said. "Do you know the prophecy it was taken from?"

"Prophecy?" Maria repeated. "I suppose that might be what it was." Her gaze followed Emilia's strange, burning hands. "The mountain priests teach that the Dragon Child will one day come to Illopia, riding on dragons, to rain down fire upon the kingdom."

Emilia shrugged. "It's possible, I guess," she admitted. "I am a dragon rider."

"Rider?" Maria said. "People can do that?"

"*People* can't," Emilia informed her. "Some Drakon sorcerers can, but even we can't just *choose* to ride a dragon. The dragons have to trust us first."

Maria lifted those scarred eyebrows of hers. "And they trust you?"

Emilia nodded. "I lived among them as a child. So, I suppose it was a little easier for them to trust me."

"You lived among whom?" Maria said. "The dragons?"

Emilia swallowed uneasily. "I'll need to touch you to heal you."

Maria's gaze softened at that. "I know," she assured Emilia. "I remember you having to touch Henry." When she realized Emilia was waiting for permission, she said, "Go ahead, love."

Emilia pressed a fiery hand against Maria's stomach, and Maria flinched.

"Your hands are hot!" Maria complained.

Emilia looked up at her. "I'm channeling energy from a *fire*," she reminded Maria. "Did you expect them to be cold?"

Maria watched her with raised eyebrows. "You know I don't even know what those words mean, don't you?"

"Well, Captain," Emilia said. She pressed harder against the unyielding muscles of Maria's stomach. Where was she even *putting* all of that fruit she ate? "I learned nautical terms for you. Perhaps you should learn some witchy terms for me."

Maria's lips quirked up. "I'd love to," she said, much to Emilia's surprise. "Tell me everything, love." She brushed a finger beneath Emilia's chin, gently urging her to look up. "Starting with why a child was living amongst dragons."

Emilia blushed under her warm gaze. She'd expected snark, not interest. She cast another concerned glance at Maria's stomach, feeling the skin slowly mend beneath her hand. Then, she stepped closer, standing between Maria's spread thighs.

Maria's eyes grew wide and dark.

"The prophecy I mentioned," Emilia said uneasily, "it was given before my birth. It's tradition, you see, for our oracles to look into a child's future before their birth."

"Why?" Maria said.

Her voice was low and breathy, just like it had been weeks ago, when her fingers were between Emilia's thighs.

"Multiple reasons, I suppose," Emilia said. "Some happy, others...not." She watched her own hand, instead of Maria's face, afraid she'd drown in those eyes, if she looked into them now. "There's no need for a mother to risk her life in childbirth, if the child won't survive, anyway—for instance."

"I take it your reason wasn't happy, either?" Maria assumed.

With a sad sigh, Emilia said, "My uncle foresaw that I'd be the last dragon sorcerer."

Maria gave an understanding nod. "They assumed you'd be responsible for their deaths."

"I *was* responsible," Emilia said, guilt churning in her stomach. "So, my mother—who was chieftess of the Drakon people—judged me and sentenced me." She sighed. "Before my birth."

"Sentenced?" Maria repeated.

"To death," Emilia said. "On the day of my birth, my sentence was carried out."

Maria stared at her in disbelief. "What the fuck does that mean?"

Emilia couldn't meet the captain's gaze. Was it sadness or shame she felt? She couldn't say. "They tied me to a stone and dropped me in the ocean."

Maria was quiet for a while—before she finally muttered, "I'm waiting for you to tell me you're joking, Em."

"I'm not," she said.

Maria looked away, stunned. "The more you tell me of your mother, the less I regret not having one."

Emilia winced at that. "It sounded like your mother really cared for you," she said with a gentle smile. "I'm sure she would've been wonderful."

Maria's dark gaze darted toward Emilia, and her lips parted.

"And my mother wasn't that terrible, either!" Emilia added.

Maria lifted a scarred eyebrow, clearly questioning Emilia's sanity, at this point.

"She was doing what was right for our people," Emilia tried to explain. "She was protecting them."

"She was drowning a fucking infant," Maria corrected.

"The decisions leaders have to make for the sake of their people aren't always easy," Emilia said defensively.

"Em," Maria said slowly, both brows arched. "I am an evil pirate captain, who's murdered more people than I can count, and even I wouldn't look at a baby, and say, 'Let's fucking drown it.'"

Emilia sighed and looked away. "I don't think you're evil," she confessed. "Not totally."

Maria opened her mouth and then closed it, apparently not sure how to respond to that. "How did you even survive?"

"I didn't," Emilia said, glancing up at her. "That's what I meant—when I said you'd seen it with your own eyes." She watched the confusion twist at Maria's scars. "Aletha pulled my corpse from the sea—and gave me back what they'd taken from me." She shrugged. "Life."

"Aletha?" Maria said breathlessly. "You've *met* the goddess of the sea?"

Emilia laughed at the question. "Many times."

Maria blinked in shock.

"Aletha's the most beloved goddess of my people," Emilia explained. "Her judgement overruled my mother's."

"I would imagine so," Maria muttered.

"But to ensure my mother wouldn't try to hide what had happened," Emilia added, "Aletha let the dragons raise me for a few years."

Maria squinted at that.

"It honestly wasn't her best decision," Emilia whispered. "The dragons are wonderful, but they just...*really* aren't any good at feeding witch babies."

Maria stared at her.

Realizing that Maria apparently expected more, Emilia added, "They kept trying to feed me things that would rather eat *me*."

Shaking her head in disbelief, Maria said, "You weren't kidding about being feral, were you?"

A surprised laugh escaped Emilia's lips, and then, she let her hand slip away from Maria's stomach and folded forward, dissolving into a gleeful fit of laughter.

The story of her childhood had always been such a source of sadness for Emilia. It was like a breath of fresh air to find herself laughing about it, instead.

Maria watched her with an affectionate smile. Her warm voice cut through the laughter.

"You're beautiful."

Emilia froze. She looked up, certain she'd misheard that.

"And your mother's quite the unfeeling bitch," Maria said, lest she say too many nice words in a row, "whether you want to admit it or not."

Emilia didn't know how to respond. She grasped for words and found nothing useful.

"Her ghost isn't very nice, either," was what she finally settled on.

Maria snorted at that. She cast a curious glance down at her stomach, frowning at the smooth, brown skin. "It's gone."

"Yes," Emilia said.

Maria looked up, her brown eyes wide.

She'd watched Emilia heal a failing liver weeks ago, and she was surprised by mended *skin*?

Emilia took the rag from the table and offered it to Maria. "It might be a little sticky, still."

With a baffled frown, Maria took the wet cloth and rubbed it across her lean stomach, wiping away the honey-like salve.

When she finished, her dark gaze shifted up, meeting Emilia's.

Emilia swallowed. "I should, um," she said, taking a step back, "clean this up before Judith gets back."

Maria slid off of the table and took a step toward Emilia. "She'll be gone all night."

Emilia took another step back, trying her best to keep her gaze on Maria's face, rather than on that thin strip of linen that was just *barely* covering Maria's small, rounded breasts.

She must've failed a few too many times—because Maria laughed and said, "You didn't see a lot of breasts on that island of yours, did you?"

Emilia scowled at that assumption, but the heat that rushed to her cheeks gave her away.

Why did Maria like to goad her so?

"Not…really," Emilia said begrudgingly.

That'd been how, as a young witch, Emilia had realized that she loved women the way some women loved men.

She'd gone utterly speechless at the sight of a siren's breasts.

Nerissa.

Her first kiss.

Her first infatuation.

Emilia had never told her mother exactly *how* she'd brokered a friendship with the sirens.

Her cold, calculating mother wouldn't have approved.

Emilia's eyes widened, when she saw Maria's hand stray toward the linen. "You don't have to do that!" she blurted out. Her face warmed. "I—I've already healed you, so, you know, I don't n —need...you to remove...it."

Why was she stammering?

Why was Maria smiling about it?

"Do you want me to stop?" Maria asked.

No.

Emilia looked away, attempting to protect her traitorous body from itself.

Maria stepped closer and with those warm, tattooed fingers of hers, she took Emilia's face and turned it toward her own.

"Yes or no?" Maria said in a stunningly gentle tone.

The firelight reflected beautifully in Maria's large, brown eyes, and Emilia melted at the sight.

"No," she whispered. "No, please, don't stop."

A quiet hum—not quite a moan but...*so* close—escaped Maria's lips, and she took Emilia's face in her hands. Maria kissed her deeply, her tongue warm and soft—and tasting very obviously of apple.

Emilia nearly giggled at the thought.

"What?" Maria murmured against her lips.

"Nothing," Emilia said with a smile. She tugged the navy blue headscarf from Maria's head, freeing her soft, brown curls.

Emilia traced her fingers along Maria's gentle jawline and entangled them in the dark, silky curls behind her ear.

Maria watched her with an almost...tender smile, as Emilia leaned forward, onto her toes.

Maria looped her fingers through Emilia's scabbard, tugging her close, and her lips—plump and rosy-brown in the firelight—brushed lightly over Emilia's.

One of the advantages of channeling magic from fire, instead of from her own energy, was that Emilia still had some left over, after healing.

And like kindling tossed into a flame, Maria's kiss relit it.

"You're warmer than usual," Maria murmured.

Emilia's lips curved against Maria's. "Would you like to see what else magic can do, Captain?"

"Maria," the captain whispered.

Affection fluttered in Emilia's stomach, as she repeated, "Maria."

Maria traced Emilia's cheekbone with the side of her thumb. "Show me."

Emilia pressed a glowing hand against Maria's bare stomach and let the heat pour through her.

Maria gasped. The gold undertone that shimmered beneath her dark skin seemed to catch fire, and her breath quickened.

She grasped Emilia's wrist, her eyes dark. "What are you," she breathed, "doing?"

Emilia's smile tilted impishly. "I told you," she said. "Magic."

With a half-hearted glare, Maria muttered, "Fucking witch."

Emilia laughed. She tugged the strip of linen from Maria's chest, and her own breath quickened at the sight of Maria's bare breasts.

More muscle than curves, Maria's breasts were small and rounded, her nipples a deep umber, rather than the rosy-pink shade of Catherine's.

"You're turning red again, love," Maria teased.

Which only resulted in Emilia blushing harder. "Shut up," she grumbled, as she tossed the linen onto the table.

Maria's skin was bare from the waist up, while Emilia hadn't even bothered to remove her sword yet.

For a woman who feared vulnerability, Maria didn't seem too

bothered by *this.*

Perhaps it was because Emilia was the one who turned into a stammering fool at the sight of breasts.

Maria kissed her, and Emilia responded by pressing her hand against Maria's lean stomach and unleashing another wave of magic.

Maria twisted her fingers into Emilia's thick, black hair and moaned into her mouth. Her bare skin brushed against the front of Emilia's shirt, and her lips pressed harder into Emilia's.

Heat coursed through Emilia's veins, and when Maria loosened her grip, Emilia trailed her lips downward—kissing the scar across Maria's throat, kissing her collarbone, kissing her soft, rounded breast…

When Emilia's mouth lingered over Maria's nipple, Maria twisted her fingers into Emilia's hair again.

Emilia licked, feeling Maria's nipple harden beneath her tongue, and Maria tilted her head back, a desperate moan spilling from her lips.

Emilia shifted her attention to Maria's other breast, kissing it, as well.

But she could already see Maria's muscles tightening, desperation writhing within her.

Emilia tugged at the front of Maria's trousers, unfastening them, but Maria grasped her wrists, stilling them.

"Boots, love," Maria reminded her.

Too lost in the whirlwind of desire to fully process the logic, Emilia cast a puzzled look at Maria's boots.

With an amused smile, Maria stepped away from her and went to sit in the closest chair. She tugged off her leather boots and tossed them aside, and Emilia sank to her knees in front of the chair.

When Maria had her trousers tugged down to her thighs, Emilia took over, peeling the dark, leather trousers down Maria's legs.

Each time Emilia's fingers brushed the silky skin of Maria's thighs or calves, Maria's eyes grew darker.

Emilia set the trousers aside and glanced up at her now fully undressed captain.

She was absolutely beautiful in the firelight, the gold undertones of her skin glowing as warm as the tropical sun itself.

Emilia glanced at the dark curls between Maria's thighs, and with a curious smile, she brushed a finger against her, feeling the wetness that gathered between Maria's thighs.

Maria gasped at her touch, and the muscles in her thighs tightened.

Emilia noticed the wetness glisten on her fingertip, and her entire body pulsed at the sight.

Maria *wanted* her.

Somehow, Emilia had remained in doubt until that moment.

Despite the kisses or the stares, despite even the sex itself, Emilia had convinced herself that it was impossible—that Maria could feel the same longing Emilia felt.

As impatient as ever, Maria sank her fingers into Emilia's hair and pulled her closer.

When Maria pressed Emilia's face between her legs, Emilia looked up at her.

Maria hesitated, her chest heaving. "Is this all right?" she said softly.

Heat pulsed through Emilia's entire body, confirming exactly how *all right* it was, and she nodded.

Delight burned in Maria's dark eyes, and she twisted her fingers tighter into Emilia's hair, pressing her closer. "Then, eat me, witch."

Emilia licked lightly, relishing the bittersweet arousal that coated her tongue, and Maria arched against her, breathing out what was clearly her favorite word in the entire language.

"*Fuck.*"

Emilia slid her hands beneath Maria's legs, feeling Maria's calf muscles flex against her fingers, and she lifted—more as a hint than with actual intention.

Maria leaned back in the chair. She placed her legs on Emilia's shoulders and crossed her ankles against Emilia's back, holding her close.

Emilia swept her tongue against Maria's clit, and Maria arched harder against her. She sank both hands into Emilia's hair, as if she were afraid of falling.

Emilia moaned against her, and with each lick, Maria's back arched in a lovely motion—a motion that was so beautiful and surprisingly...*delicate.*

Emilia licked faster, and the moans Maria gave in response grew longer and sweeter.

As Maria drew closer to climax, she eventually took control, grinding mercilessly against Emilia's mouth, and Emilia held tightly to her thighs, delighting in it.

Maria's blood roared in Emilia's ears, as her thighs tightened, and finally, her body gave one last, beautiful arch, and just a bit more wetness coated Emilia's tongue.

Maria breathed out Emilia's name the moment she fell apart.

Not 'Em.'

Not 'surgeon.'

Not 'witch.'

Emilia.

When the pleasure was spent, Maria said, "Fuck," again.

Because of course she did.

What was this warmth Emilia felt now? When had she grown so fond of Maria's quirks?

Maria leaned back in the chair, gasping for breath, and Emilia, suddenly alarmed by her own emotions, climbed to her feet.

She took off in the direction of the water, intending to wash her face, but Maria caught her by the hand.

Maria looked up at Emilia, her eyes wide and dark. "Kiss me?" she said breathlessly. "Please?"

Emilia's heart seemed to sputter to a stop. That sound in Maria's voice—that strange, foreign sound—was that vulnerability?

Caving to that sound, Emilia folded herself into Maria's lap and kissed her.

She'd analyze her feelings later. Right now, she'd let herself feel them—for one more moment.

A sudden creak on the steps jolted them apart. Judith stood there, blinking those bright blue eyes at them.

"I have so many questions," Judith said slowly, "but first... who's bleeding?"

"THE CAPTAIN SAID YOU'D BE GONE ALL NIGHT," EMILIA SAID.

Besides getting dressed, which Emilia wouldn't exactly call a *contribution*, Maria had offered nothing to the conversation.

And if Emilia—whose face was on fire at the moment—had to do all of the explaining herself, she certainly wasn't going to waste her breath defending her unrepentant captain.

"Clearly, she lied," Emilia added.

Maria folded her arms across her chest, but still, not a shred of guilt crossed her face.

"No, no," Judith said, waving her hand in a strange, wobbly motion, "I normally do stay out all night."

Maria gave Emilia a tight smile, as if to say, *'Told you so.'*

Judith walked into a chair, knocking it over, and then, she turned and glared at it, as if it had walked into *her*.

Emilia squinted bewilderedly at her.

"Did you knock that over, or did I knock it over?" Judith said.

Emilia's frown deepened. "Umm..."

"Don't worry about it," Judith muttered. "I'll get it tomorrow."

"Judith," Emilia said worriedly, "are you all right?"

"A bit drunk. That's all," Judith slurred. She pointed at the small puddle of Maria's blood. "I'm still waiting to hear who was murdered."

"No one was murdered," Emilia assured her—for the third time.

"The captain murdered someone," Judith said. She tried to brace her hand on the chair she'd already knocked over and nearly fell sideways. "See? She's got the blood on her shirt."

When Judith tried to lean on the missing chair *again*, Emilia snatched it up and set it in front of her.

Judith fell into the chair. She propped her elbow on the table and her face in her hand.

"I hope you don't need my help tossing the body," Judith told Maria, "because I am...a *little* drunk."

Maria lifted her eyebrows at that.

"Judith, I swear we didn't murder anyone!" Emilia tried to tell her. "The captain was bleeding because I stabbed her."

Judith gave her a patronizing laugh. "Sure you did, Em."

Emilia spread out her arms. Spinning toward Maria, she said, "Tell her!"

Maria, choosing her pride over everything, shook her head.

"If you don't tell her, I will," Emilia warned.

Maria held out her hand, gesturing for her to go ahead.

Did she think Emilia wouldn't call her bluff?

Emilia spun back toward Judith. "We fought. With swords!"

Maria glared at her, and Emilia, feeling suddenly very petty, stuck out her tongue.

Maria looked down, trying to hide it, but Emilia caught the slight curve of her lips.

"Swords," Judith repeated, shaking her head. "Is that some sort of euphemism?"

Emilia's brows furrowed. "What sort of euphemism could that be?"

"I don't know," Judith mumbled, and then, as if she hadn't already said it thirty times, she told them, "I'm a little drunk."

Maria gave Emilia a look of warning, and that was all the encouragement Emilia needed.

"It was a real sword fight," Emilia insisted.

Judith nodded. "Between...the two of you?"

"Yes," Emilia said, ignoring Maria's glare. "The captain challenged me to a sword fight, and I won."

Maria—who hadn't uttered a *word* since Judith caught them—suddenly said, "Only because you stabbed me!"

Emilia turned toward her. "Well, that's what you're supposed to do during a sword fight, Captain. I assumed you knew that—considering how renowned you are for your swordsmanship."

Judith watched them with raised eyebrows. "This is all…great," she cut in, "and certainly explains the blood. But there's one part of all of this that I still find strange." When they both turned to look at her, she said, "Why was the captain naked?"

A long, awkward silence followed that question.

When Emilia could stand it no longer, she whispered, "Captain?"

Maria lifted a scarred eyebrow. "No, you go ahead. You were doing so well by yourself."

Emilia scowled at that.

Judith raked her fingers through her short, brown hair—and then frowned, when she found a chip of wood in her hair.

Emilia frowned curiously.

How exactly did a gambling game lead to wood chips ending up in Judith's hair?

Judith noticed Emilia watching, and with an alarmed look, she tried to shoo them out. "You know what?" she laughed. "How about we just agree not to speak of this night ever again?"

Helen was always blowing things up. So, Emilia knew that the gun deck was covered in splinters of wood.

She'd picked them from her own clothes for weeks, after she'd spent the afternoon with the ship cats.

If someone were to lie down on the gun deck—for whatever reason—they might just end up with a few in their hair.

Maria pinned Judith with a suspicious look. "Are you trying to get rid of us?"

Apparently realizing that Emilia had already figured it out,

Judith shot a frantic look in her direction.

With an amused smile, Emilia reached out and took Maria's arm. "Come on, Captain," she said. "Judith needs some sleep."

Maria turned her suspicious glare on Emilia. "Are you trying to *help* her?"

"Help her with what, Captain?" Emilia said with an innocent smile.

Maria narrowed her eyes. "She fucked Helen, didn't she?"

Emilia tugged on Maria's arm, dragging her toward the steps. "Goodnight, Judith!"

"Goodnight, Em," Judith said, wincing.

"We're not done talking about this!" Maria yelled, even as Emilia dragged her from the galley.

WHEN THEY REACHED THE MOONLIT DECK, EMILIA ASSUMED THEY'D GO their separate ways, but Maria caught her by the arm and pulled her back.

Emilia turned, looking up at her captain. Moonlight reflected in Maria's dark eyes, and Emilia drew closer to her.

"Come to my quarters," Maria said.

Emilia shook her head, confused. "I thought you weren't good with," and then, she quoted, "*'the stuff that comes afterward?'*"

Maria shrugged, and a mischievous smile tugged at one corner of her mouth. "Who says it has to be afterward yet?" She stepped closer and brushed a tattooed finger along Emilia's cheek. "After all, I still haven't gotten a chance to taste you."

"Umm," Emilia said, her eyes wide. Her skin warmed beneath Maria's touch, and another rush of desire poured through her.

Maria leaned closer, and then, as if she were sharing some secret part of herself, she whispered, "I only ask that you leave before I fall asleep."

Emilia nodded easily. "Of course."

CHAPTER 21
A Suspicion

T
hat had been the plan, anyway.

Which was why Emilia found herself very confused, when she awoke in Maria's bed the next morning.

She sat up in bed, clutching the blanket to her bare chest, and she blinked wearily at the man who'd just shaken her awake.

"Zain?"

The quartermaster wrinkled his nose in distaste. "Damn, you're a mess."

Emilia gave another weary blink. She cast a puzzled look around the cabin, squinting at the rays of sunlight that poured in through the windows. "Where is the captain?"

"I was hoping you could tell me," Zain said, his dark brows high, "seeing as you're in her bed."

Emilia glanced at him. The last thing she remembered was Maria pressing her into the bed and…

Emilia blushed.

Zain rolled his eyes at her silence. "Tell her I need to talk to her," he muttered. "And here." He tossed a comb that appeared to be carved from some sort of white stone on the bed. "You need that more than I do."

Emilia pressed a hand to her head, self-consciously checking her hair. She cringed, as she felt the tangles Maria had left in it.

What were the chances that Zain would assume her nakedness, her hair, and her presence in Maria's bed *didn't* have anything to do with sex?

Based on the force with which he slammed Maria's door, Emilia didn't think they were too good.

EMILIA WAS FULLY DRESSED BY THE TIME MARIA RETURNED TO HER quarters, but she hadn't gotten around to using the comb yet.

"Judith sent food," Maria said, holding up a sackful of oranges, "in exchange for me not punishing her for breaking my Code."

Emilia suppressed a smile. The Helen law wasn't even a real law, but leave it to Maria to find a way to wield it to her advantage.

And of course, out of all of the things Maria could've black-mailed Judith for, she'd used it for fruit.

"Captain," Emilia said with a wince.

Maria took one look at her expression and laughed. "I wore you out. It's fine," she said. "If I wanted you gone that much, I would've carried you to your cabin."

Emilia blushed at the thought. "No. I mean, I *am* sorry for falling asleep in here, but that's not..." she trailed off. "There's something you should know."

Maria set the sack of oranges on her table and started counting them. "There's ten. So, eight for me, and two for you. That's even, isn't it?"

Emilia frowned at her math. "Two's fine," she muttered. "Cap-tain, I need to tell you something."

"You drive a hard bargain, surgeon," Maria said with a sigh. "Fine. You can have three."

"Captain!" Emilia said, exasperated.

Maria turned to look at her. She blinked those large, brown eyes at Emilia, and Emilia felt herself melting beneath them again.

Emilia picked up the stone comb and held it out. "Zain came by."

Maria glanced down at the comb, and a hint of worry flickered across her face. But she quickly returned her attention to the fruit.

"Four, then?"

"Captain," Emilia said with a frown, "did you hear what I said?"

"Of course I did," Maria said. "Three oranges or four, Em?"

Emilia didn't understand why Maria was being so dismissive about this. "I said two was fine."

Maria rolled her eyes. "Three, then."

"Captain," Emilia began.

"Em, you're not the first woman I've fucked. Not even close," Maria scoffed. She continued to set out her oranges. "I assure you: he wasn't that surprised."

"Captain," Emilia tried again.

"He'll tell me not to let my feelings cloud my judgement, and I'll tell him that I haven't. Then, he'll push me a little too much, and I'll tell him to fuck off," Maria said. "It's really not that serious, love."

Emilia sighed, "Captain." When Maria still ignored her, she said, "Maria."

Maria stiffened. "I'm your fucking captain."

Emilia narrowed her eyes at that. "Right," she muttered, and she headed for the door. "Goodbye, Captain."

"Em…"

Emilia ignored her.

Maria dropped the sack of oranges and turned toward her. "Em," she breathed, "I'm sorry, all right?"

Emilia stopped. She turned to face Maria, her brows high.

"Either stick to what you say, or deal with your issues enough that you're not snapping at me every time we have sex."

"I'm trying," Maria said, much to Emilia's surprise. She looked away, her scars deep and twisted. "Last night—that was me trying."

Emilia's gaze softened at that.

Maria held out an orange. "Eat with me. We'll have a drink, and we can…face our fears together," she said, "if you want."

Emilia had never heard the captain speak so transparently. "You mean it?"

Maria nodded. "And I can still take the first drink," she offered, "if you're not ready."

Emilia smiled at the offer. She crossed the space between them and took the orange from Maria's hand. "Like I'd ever let you outdo me in anything," she teased.

The smile that curved at Maria's lips, then, was the most beautiful one Emilia had ever seen.

Maria waited until Emilia left to call Zain to her quarters. The last thing she wanted was for her kind-hearted surgeon to realize how much danger she was in.

Maria had promised to protect her—and so she would.

She wrote in her daily log, keeping her attention elsewhere, as Zain sat in the chair across from her. She would show him no sign of concern.

"Do you know why I wanted to talk?" Zain asked.

Maria flipped the page in her leather-bound book. "Is it to tell me that my trousers are faded?"

Zain scowled. "No."

Of course not.

Zain did like to give her advice on her state of dress every now and then. He took much better care of his own clothes than she did of hers.

But no, this wasn't a friendly visit.

Not today.

"I finished reading through the letters," Zain explained, "from the mainland."

Maria kept her hand steady, continuing to write. "How's your mother?"

"She's fine," Zain told her. "She says hi."

Maria chuckled. Zain's mother had to be the only law-abiding woman in Aletharia who would send well wishes to her son's villainous pirate captain.

She was a lovely lady.

A bit vain sometimes, but otherwise, sweet.

"You know she's staying with her sister in Regolis, right?" Zain added.

Maria's fingers tightened around her quill. "I remember you mentioning it."

"Her most recent letter," Zain said, "was about this...chaos that broke out at the gallows a few months back." He paused to watch her reaction. "When she wrote to me, it, of course, had just happened."

Maria didn't look at him. "She is quite the gossip, isn't she?"

"Captain," Zain said, his eyes dark and burning with accusation, "did you know?"

"Did I know what?" Maria said.

Zain narrowed his eyes. "Don't play this game with me, Captain," he warned. "I know you too well."

Maria sighed. She set down her quill and looked up at him. "She's a fugitive, yes," she admitted. "So am I. So is everyone who calls me captain. Including you."

Zain laughed in disbelief. "So, that's the story you're going with? That she's just a fugitive. A normal, *human* fugitive."

Maria frowned. "Does she look inhuman to you?"

Zain looked away, disappointment twisting at his thick, black brows. "I've earned better than this from you, Captain," he sighed, and Maria felt a small stab of regret. "But fine. If this is how you want to do it...fine." He looked at her. "How long have you been aware that you hired a fugitive?"

"Since the day I saw her," Maria said honestly.

"You saw her," Zain repeated, "not Judith?"

"Yes," Maria admitted.

Zain shook his head in disapproval. "And you maintain that she's human?"

Maria spread out her arms. "What else could she be?"

"I see," Zain said darkly, as if she'd just signed her death warrant. "Then, can you explain to me, Captain, how a woman in chains not only escapes her own execution, but also sets fire to the gallows and the entire town square?"

Maria leaned forward, giving him a forced smile. "What are you suggesting, quartermaster?"

"I'm suggesting that your new...fascination," he paused, lowering his voice, "is a witch."

Maria gave him a baffled laugh. "My fascination?"

"Well, I'm not sure what else to call her, Captain," he said, his eyebrows high. "A few months ago, I was certain you two would kill each other, but today..." His eyes narrowed. "Today, Captain, I found her in your bed."

Maria crossed her arms. He might've been able to pull a shred of regret from her for lying to him, but for this, she'd apologize to no one. "We're both consenting adults. Can I not fuck who I want to fuck?"

"Of course you can," Zain assured her. "It's just that when you begin to look at these two things together—your fascination with her and the way you're choosing her over your crew—it paints a very alarming picture."

Maria rolled her eyes. "Do you have any idea how much a woman in my position has to bury her emotions just so that people will trust her judgement?" she snarled. "Just so that people won't accuse her of what you're accusing me of now?"

"I do, Captain," Zain assured her, "which is why I was hoping I was wrong."

Maria leaned back, sighing. "She saved Henry. Does that mean nothing to you?"

"*How* did she save him?" Zain said, his brows high. "It looked to me like he was on the cusp of death that night, and then, the next day, he's fine?"

"She's a good surgeon," Maria said.

"She's a witch," Zain snarled back.

Maria narrowed her eyes. "As far as I can tell, you have no proof."

Zain leaned toward her, his sleek, black hair falling over his red waistcoat. He said it quietly, but the accusation was clear. "Only because you're protecting her."

Maria stood, and Zain leaned back, his eyes dark. "Bring me proof, or get out of my fucking face."

Zain shook his head. He climbed to his feet and shoved his chair back toward the table. "You could've come clean to me, you know?" he said sadly. "I stood by you. Even when you were impulsive, even when you murdered in bloodlust like the madwoman they said you were, I told you my feelings in private and stood by you in front of them."

Maria looked away, a small stab of guilt twisting at her stomach. "I'd like to know, if you intend to mutiny."

"Why?" Zain asked. "So you can kill me before I tell them?"

Maria didn't meet his gaze.

"Goodbye, Captain."

Maria had chosen a side. What happened now was beyond her control.

～

"DID SHE SLEEP?"

Emilia brought Judith a bowl of dry, freshly chopped cabbage, and Judith added it to the stew.

"I don't know," Emilia admitted. "She was awake when I fell asleep and gone when I woke up."

"Probably not, then," Judith said. She handed the ladle to Emilia. "Stir that for me, will you?"

"Sure," Emilia said, taking her place in front of the pot.

Judith headed to the back to grab another barrel of vegetables. "It's still a huge step for her, though!"

Emilia stirred the simmering stew, Maria's words ringing loudly in her head.

"Last night," she'd said, *"that was me trying."*

Why would Maria even bother to try?

And for Emilia, no less?

Judith returned with a barrel that was almost half her size. It hit the floorboards with a loud crash. "Even if she stayed up all night," she reiterated, "the fact that she was willing to risk it—falling asleep around you—is huge."

Emilia's brows furrowed. "Is there a reason," she said curiously, "that the captain fears this particular thing?"

Judith shrugged. "I assume so, but we've never discussed it."

Emilia glanced back at her. "I assumed you two talked about everything."

Judith gathered up the tools she used to open the barrels. "Not everything," she said, a hint of sadness in her voice. "There are some things the captain doesn't talk to anyone about."

Emilia's chest ached with sympathy. Maria wore her scars without shame. What could they have done to her that she wouldn't even talk to Judith about?

Emilia cleared her throat and turned to face Judith. "Enough about my night," she said with a forced smile. "Why don't we talk about yours?"

Judith chuckled. "It ended terribly—with far too much vomit."

Emilia wrinkled her nose. "You did mention a few times that you were drunk."

Judith snorted. "We drank my brother's rum."

Emilia cringed at the thought. She'd only tried it that once, and she still remembered the taste.

Now that Emilia was acquainted with the taste of good rum, it was much clearer to her that Judith's brother's rum was...*not*.

With a concerned frown, Emilia said, "So, did the forbidden sex happen when you were drunk? Or..."

"Forbidden sex!" Judith said with an amused laugh. "We'll have to call it that from now on."

Emilia smiled. "You two do this a lot, don't you?"

"Not a lot, but," Judith paused, grinning at her, "occasionally. Pelt covers for us, when we do."

Emilia's eyes widened. "The gambling games!"

Judith laughed. "The captain pretends not to know, but I know she does."

"What makes you think that?" Emilia asked.

"Well, she told you I stay out all night," Judith reminded Emilia. "You don't think she honestly thinks we're gambling that long, do you?"

Emilia nodded in understanding.

"I only came back early last night because I couldn't stop puking," Judith muttered. "We drank way too much of that shit."

With a mischievous smile, Emilia said, "So, does that mean the rat may not have been *'just resting?'*"

"Oh, no," Judith said, waving the hammer in a threatening manner, "you can fuck her all you like, but you're not taking her side in the rat debate. You were *my* friend first!"

Emilia dissolved into a fit of gleeful laughter.

It really *did* feel good to have someone call her a friend.

They both fell silent, as a yell rung out somewhere above them.

Emilia couldn't understand what was being said, but she could tell it wasn't just a sea shanty.

"Is it a fight?" Emilia guessed.

Judith stared at the wood above them, as if she could see straight through it. She shook her head slowly. "Douse the fire."

Using a thin cloth, Emilia took the pot and moved it to the table and then hurried to grab a bucket of water.

Judith set aside her tools and rushed over to the steps. She stepped onto the second one and tilted her head, her short, brown hair falling to the side, as she listened.

The galley went dark, when Emilia doused the fire. The only light they had left was the rays of sunlight that poured through the portholes.

"What is it?" Emilia whispered.

"I think a ship was spotted," Judith said. "I don't hear any swords yet."

Emilia's brows furrowed. "Why would you hear swords?"

Judith glanced at her. "The captain and I are concealing a witch, Em," she reminded her. "Mutiny's always a possibility."

Emilia's stomach turned with guilt. She didn't want *that*. Was Maria really risking that for her?

Judith grabbed a pistol from the table and tucked it into her belt. "Stay down here for a moment. Just in case."

"No," Emilia said, certain of this one thing, at least. "You're not going up there without me."

Judith sighed, "I appreciate your concern, mate, but if it *is* a mutiny—"

Emilia didn't let her finish. "If it's a mutiny, then I'll defend my captain," she informed the person who had quickly become her closest friend, "and my friend."

A surprised smile curved at Judith's lips. "She was right about you, Em."

CHAPTER 22
A Black Flag

"What will you need, if we're hit with cannon fire?"

Maria lifted a long, brass spyglass to her eye and peered at the ship in the distance.

Emilia had never seen the *Wicked Fate* in this much of a frenzy—nor had she ever expected to. Sailors ran from one side of the ship to the other, shouting orders and readying the ship for battle.

Maria, however, was calm in the face of battle—calmer, even, than she usually was. Whether that was an act, meant to calm the crew, or genuine confidence on Maria's part, Emilia couldn't have said, but she suspected that it was a bit of both.

"My cabin only has enough space for two people," Emilia told her. "I'll need to set up a temporary space that can hold a lot more."

Maria nodded. "You can use the hold." She held up a hand, which must've been some sort of signal—because Henry immediately turned the wheel. Maria glanced at Emilia. "What else?"

"I'll get what I need for salves and tinctures from the galley," Emilia said, "but I'll also need plenty of bandages and hammocks."

Maria nodded at that, too. "I'll send whatever we have."

"And captain?"

Maria glanced at her, concern flickering in her large, brown eyes. "What is it, love?"

Emilia stepped closer and pressed a small bottle into Maria's hand. "I need you to drink this?" she said—unable to keep the uncertainty from her tone.

Maria looked down, her brows furrowing at the small bottle in her hand. "What is it?"

Emilia kept her voice soft enough that no one would hear. "It'll protect you."

Maria looked up, blinking. "Like what you put in my oil?"

Emilia blushed. "A bit stronger than that." She shrugged. "It's the best I could do on such short notice."

"Why?" Maria said softly.

Emilia gave another nervous shrug. "I can heal anything that happens to you, except death. This will—*hopefully*—prevent you from dying."

Maria shook her head and tried to give the bottle back. "I don't need it."

"Oh, for Aletha's sake, Captain!" Emilia said. "Drop the arrogance for just *one* moment, and drink it!"

Maria lifted a scarred eyebrow at Emilia's reaction. "Give it to someone else."

"Captain, please," Emilia said, desperation twisting in her throat. She grasped Maria's hand, before she could drop the bottle. "Please. For me."

For me?

Why had she said that?

Why, in the name of the goddess, would Maria ever do anything for *her*?

Out of all of the things that could've come out of Emilia's mouth, in that moment, that was, by far, the most ridiculous.

What had she been thinking?

But surprisingly enough, Maria didn't pull away. "Why?"

Why?

Why did she keep asking that? Emilia didn't know *why!* She'd been acting on a sudden impulse—a sudden fear that she'd lose this person she supposedly hated. It didn't make any more sense to her than it did to Maria.

"Wouldn't you say, Captain," Emilia said, her voice steady, despite the chaos bouncing around in her head, "that your crew needs you alive?"

Maria's brows furrowed. "For this battle, yes."

"Then, drink it," Emilia said softly.

There.

That was what she should've said the first time. Maria would do it for her crew.

Not for Emilia—but for her crew.

"I'll drink from it, too," Emilia offered, "if you don't trust me."

Maria tilted her head slightly, a strange confusion twisting at her brows. She took the bottle and opened it. She then tilted it up, and, to Emilia's surprise, drank every drop.

When she was done, she held out the empty bottle.

Emilia stared up at her lovely, infuriating pirate captain, and emotions she couldn't even *hope* to identify welled up in her throat.

"We're going into battle together," Maria said, quiet enough that only Emilia heard. "Today, of all days, we *must* trust each other."

Emilia nodded slowly, her heart rattling in her chest.

"I've given you my trust, surgeon," Maria said, stepping closer. "May I have yours?"

Emilia surprised even *herself* with the response that came so naturally from within her. "You have it, Captain."

Maria brushed a tattooed thumb against Emilia's cheek, and her soft, full lips curved into a grateful smile. "Keep my crew alive for me," she said, "my sweet surgeon."

Emilia's stomach fluttered. Maria had never said those words in that...*way* before. It was just a taunt, usually.

There was always that patronizing bite in her tone—that taunting glint in her dark brown eyes.

But this time, she'd said it differently. This time, she'd said it like a term of endearment.

What did *that* mean?

"I will," Emilia promised her.

Maria lifted a scarred eyebrow. "That means you, too, Em. Stay safe."

Emilia frowned. "Me?"

Not her most eloquent response, admittedly.

"Just make out with her in front of the entire crew, why don't you?" came a sudden grumble nearby.

Maria glared at her quartermaster, as he passed them on the way to the quarterdeck.

Emilia glanced warily at Zain, who didn't even look her way. His scowl was more sour than usual. "What's his problem?"

Maria glanced at Emilia, her dark eyes unreadable. "Nothing that concerns you."

"It *sounds* like it concerns me," Emilia pointed out.

That gentle, golden-brown jawline of Maria's seemed to shift, as if she were grinding her teeth. "Zain and I are having a bit of a spat," she said with a forced smile. "That's all."

Judith's warning about mutiny echoed in Emilia's head. "How serious is it?"

"Not serious enough to matter during a battle," Maria said.

That didn't comfort Emilia much.

"Captain!"

The yell came from somewhere up above them—a sailor in the rigging, perhaps.

Maria dropped her hand and looked up, squinting at the sunlit sails. "I have to go, love," she said gently. She glanced back at Emilia. "Stay safe."

Anxiety fluttered in Emilia's chest. "Wait!" When Maria stopped, Emilia asked—with a bit of hesitation, "Is it her?"

Maria didn't ask who Emilia meant. She didn't need to. "It's too soon to tell," she said quietly. "From this distance, I can't even make out the name of the ship." She drummed her fingers against the hilt of her sword. "I can only tell you that she's flying King Eldric's colors."

Emilia nodded. "And what colors are we flying?"

A cruel smile curled at one corner of Maria's mouth. "Black, as always."

"Oh," Emilia said.

Maria's smile widened. "The *Wicked Fate* hides from no one, love."

"HOLD HIM STEADY," EMILIA TOLD JUDITH—AS THE SHIP ROCKED WITH another cannon blast.

"Easier said than done, Em," Judith said, but she held down the sailor's arms, anyway.

Emilia was literally up to her elbows in blood, but her confidence held stronger now than it had in months. Emilia loved healing the way Maria loved a battle and the way Helen loved explosions.

Really, everyone was in their element today.

Except for Judith.

"Tell me those aren't his entrails," Judith groaned.

Emilia frowned at the request. "What should I tell you they are, instead? Blood-soaked eels?"

Judith wrinkled her nose in disgust.

"They've been perforated," Emilia explained. "I can mend them, but I have to remove the shrapnel first."

Judith looked away, cringing. "That's a lot of blood, Em."

Emilia risked a quick glance at her. "Are you all right?"

"Mm-hmm," Judith said, though she looked a bit pale. "Just remind me to drink *a lot* more rum next time."

Emilia suppressed a smile. "The rum is for the injured sailors, Judith."

"Well, *I* say," Judith said, "it's for the injured sailors *and* the cook who's having to help her friend dig through fucking entrails."

Emilia laughed at that. She picked up a small set of forceps and leaned forward to remove a piece of metal.

The sailor was far too drunk to know his own predicament, by this point, but every now and then, he'd open his eyes, see Emilia's blood-soaked arms, and panic.

Hence the need for Judith's assistance.

Under any other circumstances, Emilia would use magic to keep him asleep, but after healing at least seven sailors already, she didn't have much magic left.

She'd need to recover her energy soon—but there was no time for it now.

Judith kept her head turned to the side, but she peeked at Emilia out of one eye. "Are you done?"

Emilia dropped the shrapnel in the bowl beside her, metal clanging against metal. "Not quite."

Judith groaned miserably. "You know, I've always said I have a stomach of steel—because I can handle my rum—but if you're not queasy right *now*, then you, my friend, are the one with the stomach of steel."

Emilia laughed. "You get used to it."

The hatch opened, and the boisterous chaos outside grew louder. The wooden steps creaked under their feet, as Fulke and Pelt came down into the hold, carrying another injured sailor.

Well, Fulke was doing most of the carrying. Pelt was just sort of...daintily holding the feet, as if he weren't sure what else to do.

"Got another one for you, Em!" Pelt yelled, over the cannon fire.

Emilia didn't look up from her work. "Give him some rum, and tell him to drink until the pain dulls," she called. "I'll be there as soon as I'm done with this one."

Again, Judith gave her a miserable groan.

Emilia offered Judith a quick, amused smile. "I can make you a tincture for the queasiness, if you'd like."

Judith stared blankly at her. "There are literal organs spread out in front of me. I don't think a tincture is going to help."

Emilia laughed. "You'd be surprised."

Judith squinted at that, but Emilia could tell she was considering it.

"I need to make a run to the galley, anyway," Emilia added. She threaded a needle. Normally, she used magic for mending, but she needed a temporary, nonmagical solution—at least until she could recover her energy. "I can have you a tincture made in a matter of minutes."

Judith frowned worriedly. "You're leaving me with the bloody eels?"

"Don't worry," Emilia said with a laugh. "I'm sewing him up first."

"Don't worry?" Judith scoffed. "Easy for you to say."

Emilia couldn't help but laugh. She'd always thought of Judith as someone who wasn't fazed by anything.

Apparently, *anything* didn't include intestines.

With a desperate whine, Judith said, "Will you at least bring back more rum?"

"Of course," Emilia assured her.

CHAPTER 23
A Ghost from the Past

Emilia took a quick detour on her way to the galley. A little distracted that morning, she'd remembered to arm herself with a sword, but she'd forgotten her enchanted dagger in Maria's quarters.

If she retrieved it now, she could use its reserve of magic to restore her own.

Just like she'd done the day of her escape.

Despite the warship she did battle with, the *Wicked Fate* had taken on a lot less cannon fire than the naval ship.

Flames coiled into the sky, burning the navy ship's sails and hull and filling the air with thick, black smoke.

The *Wicked Fate*, on the other hand, needed only a few repairs, before it'd be back on its way.

Maria was quick and clever, and whoever captained the other ship just couldn't compete.

Emilia could admire Maria for her brilliance without liking her, couldn't she?

Just like she could feel these strange, warm feelings inside her and still insist she hated Maria.

Right?

She certainly wasn't in denial or anything.

The sea rumbled beneath the ship, and Emilia had to grasp the wall to keep herself from falling.

Emilia avoided the chaos as well as she could on her way to Maria's quarters.

She carried a rag in her hands that she used to wipe the blood from her arms. She'd scrub them properly when she returned to the hold.

She unlocked Maria's door with a simple spell—one that required less energy than the healing spells she'd been using for the last hour.

Somewhere above, Maria shouted orders at the gunners. Emilia couldn't understand them, exactly, but she recognized her captain's voice.

If Maria was up there, she couldn't be in her cabin. So, Emilia assumed, of course, that the captain's quarters would be empty.

She stepped inside and immediately veered toward the bed, where she'd left her dagger.

"Emilia?"

She froze.

Time slowed to a halt, as she turned in the direction of that soft, familiar voice.

Emilia's skin cooled, and she blinked quickly, hoping this terrible hallucination would dissolve before her eyes.

The woman in front of her now felt more like a ghost than her mother's *actual* ghost had.

Her blonde hair didn't fall loosely around her shoulders, like it had during their time together on the island. She wore it in a tight braid now, bound behind her head.

And she wore that fitted, blue waistcoat that Emilia had come to hate.

The one that confirmed her *true* loyalties.

"Catherine," Emilia whispered.

The naval admiral cast an alarmed glance at Emilia's blood-stained arms and clothes. "What have they done to you?"

Emilia looked down, frowning. "It's...not mine."

It wasn't her most eloquent response, but at least she'd managed to say *something*.

Did Maria know they'd been boarded?

Emilia needed to warn her, somehow.

She noticed a window cracked open behind Catherine—and realized that she'd caught it early.

Perhaps, no one else had boarded yet.

The sea rumbled again, and Emilia grasped the beam beside her to prevent herself from falling.

"Don't worry," Catherine said, as if Emilia had *any* idea what she was talking about. "I have more ships. I meant for this one to sink."

So, that's why the sea was rumbling like an unsettled stomach.

It was swallowing a whole damn ship.

But what did Catherine mean by *'don't worry?'* More ships was definitely a reason to worry.

Emilia stepped back, and her hand strayed to her sword.

Catherine noticed, and she narrowed those light blue eyes that Emilia had once adored.

"You're armed," Catherine said with a frown. "Why would she arm a prisoner?"

Prisoner?

Catherine thought Emilia was a prisoner?

So, that was why she hadn't attacked. It wasn't shock, like Emilia had assumed. It was a mistake.

She'd assumed Emilia was on her side.

Oh, how the tables had turned.

Emilia didn't have the manipulative skills of Catherine, but perhaps, just *perhaps*, she could use this.

Emilia took a step forward, and despite the hatred seething inside her, she forced a smile. "How are you here?"

Catherine's gaze softened at the sight of her smile. "I came to rescue you."

A fresh wave of hatred rose in Emilia's throat. Did Catherine really think she was that gullible?

Emilia took another step forward, but still, Catherine's boots didn't budge.

She'd seen Emilia's sword, but apparently, she still thought Emilia was on her side.

"How did you know you'd find me here?" Emilia asked softly.

Catherine floundered a little at that. Perhaps Emilia had called Catherine's bluff a little too soon.

Emilia prepared to draw her sword.

But Catherine pulled a brass spyglass from her belt and held it up. "I saw you."

It looked similar to the one Maria used—but without the tarnish. If Maria hadn't been able to see Catherine from that distance, Catherine definitely couldn't have seen Emilia.

And Emilia had spent the last hour in the hold—not that Catherine would ever guess *that*.

"I don't understand," Emilia said. "The last time we saw each other, you were going to kill me."

"What?" Catherine said with a sickeningly innocent smile. "I would never kill *you*, Emilia."

It was weird to hear her full name, after being called *Em* for months. It felt as if Catherine were talking about a person who no longer existed.

Only Maria called her *Emilia* now—and she'd only done so under a very...specific circumstance.

Emilia's skin warmed at the memory.

"You wouldn't kill me with your own hand, perhaps," Emilia said, though she doubted even *that* was true, "but you were plenty willing to lead me to the gallows."

"No," Catherine said, and now, it was her, who stepped closer. One more step, and Emilia would have her. "I sent the guards away, remember?" She took one more step and then cupped Emilia's face in her hands. "I let you escape, remember?"

Emilia's chest ached at the familiar touch, and she had to force herself to not cringe away from it.

How did Catherine's cool hands still feel so familiar? After all of these months?

"You *let* me escape," Emilia repeated, pure venom on her tongue.

She'd outsmarted Catherine, used her vanity against her, and now, Catherine wanted credit for it?

Catherine hesitated. She'd heard the anger in Emilia's voice. She dropped her hands and reached for her sword.

But Emilia already had her fingers around her own. Using a close range tactic that Maria had taught her just one night earlier, Emilia drew her sword and twirled it in a swift, controlled wave.

'Control is key,' Maria had said.

She hit Catherine's wrist in the upswing, knocking the sword from her hand, then turned her wrist to let the blade land against the left side of Catherine's neck.

Catherine froze, when the sharp steel pressed into her skin. "Where did you learn that?" she breathed.

Emilia smiled. "Not from you."

The dark shadow of disbelief and betrayal passed over Catherine's face.

As if she knew *anything* of betrayal...

"That's her move. *She* uses that," Catherine said. She still didn't say Maria's name. Was she afraid of it? "Why would someone who kidnapped you teach you that?"

Emilia lifted her eyebrows. "Did I *say* she kidnapped me?" When Catherine's light blue eyes widened in horror, Emilia said, "I don't think I did."

"But if she didn't, then—" Catherine tried to step back, but Emilia kept the blade against her throat. "That would make you a pirate."

"A pirate *and* a witch," Emilia said, her smile absolutely vicious. "What are you going to do? Hang me twice?"

Catherine's eyes darkened. "I thought you were different, Em."

"*Different* got my people killed," Emilia reminded her. "Now, I'll be whatever I have to be."

"A villain?" Catherine sneered.

Emilia ignored the insult. She'd once defended her use of magic. She'd once fretted at the thought of anyone calling her a villain.

But those days were over. If Catherine wanted to make her the villain of this story, Emilia would let her.

"Has anyone else boarded the ship?" Emilia asked.

Defiance gleamed in Catherine's light blue eyes. "I am the Admiral of the King's Navy, and you think *you* can get answers out of me?"

Emilia shrugged one shoulder. "If I can't, I'm sure the captain can."

For the first time, Emilia recognized the dark glint of jealousy in Catherine's light blue eyes. "Captain?"

A smile came naturally to Emilia's lips. "My captain."

ON THE DECK, CHEERS ROARED ACROSS THE SHIP, AS THE CREW celebrated their victory. Another naval ship swallowed by the sea, thanks to Captain Maria Welles and her unquenchable thirst for naval blood.

Emilia hated to ruin the celebration, but...Maria needed to know.

Gradually, the cheers quietened—a slow and steady decrescendo, as one sailor after another recognized the woman Emilia held at the point of her sword.

Maria was one of the last people to notice, but when she did, a hatred unlike anything Emilia had ever seen darkened those large, brown eyes of hers.

Catherine stiffened at the sight, but Emilia urged her up the steps.

Maria curled her fingers around the hilt of her right sword—something that seemed almost like a reflex of hers—but she waited patiently by the helm, as they made their way up the steps.

When they reached her, Catherine snarled, "Maria."

Maria narrowed her eyes. "I guess the captain *doesn't* go down with her ship."

Catherine laughed at that. "I'm much more than a captain these days, Maria Welles."

Irritation flickered in Emilia's chest. She knew Catherine's use of Maria's name was intentional—a cruel reminder of the title and power Catherine had stripped from her—and Emilia didn't like it one bit.

Catherine gave a small squeak of pain, when Emilia pressed her sword closer.

Maria's dark gaze flickered toward Emilia, but if she'd noticed Emilia's reaction, she said nothing of it.

"How the hell did you turn Emilia Drakon against *me*?" Catherine snarled at Maria.

A soft murmur traveled across the ship at the mention of Emilia's real name.

Only Zain seemed unsurprised by the revelation. He simply crossed his arms and looked away.

Maria forced a smile. "You did that yourself, Cat."

It was strange to hear Maria use a nickname for the navy admiral—as if Catherine were a ghost to her, too.

How close had the two of them been, and how had Catherine turned against her so easily?

"It's Admiral Rochester to you, *pirate*." Catherine spat the word, as if it were the vilest insult in the Illopian language, but Maria simply smiled.

After all, Maria had never hesitated to call herself a pirate. She'd never felt a shred of shame about it.

Maria stepped closer. "It must've taken a lot of self-control to not kill her, Em," she said. "Why haven't you?"

Catherine froze, a tiny spark of fear flickering in her light blue eyes.

"She won't tell me if she was the only one who boarded," Emilia explained. "I thought you might get more out of her."

Catherine glared at Maria, anger and disbelief radiating from her strong frame. "What did you *do* to her?"

Emilia had never known anyone so shocked by the consequences of her own actions—nor anyone so quick to blame it on some random pirate captain.

Emilia had hated Catherine long before she'd met Maria. The scars Catherine had left on Maria were just kindling added to an already blazing fire.

"She also mentioned other ships," Emilia added.

Catherine's jaw tightened.

Maria looked at Catherine. "Of course. An admiral wouldn't be wandering the seas without her fleet." She glanced around at the miles and miles of empty, azure-blue waves. If Catherine did have more ships, she'd hidden them well. Maria's dark brown eyes returned to Catherine. "Where are they?"

"I'll never tell you," Catherine sneered. "Just know they're close enough to attack, if I give the signal."

With a worried frown, Zain said, "What signal?"

Maria cast her eyes downward, and alarm flickered within them. "Let her go, Em."

"What?" Emilia said.

But before Maria could explain, Catherine pressed the end of a flintlock pistol to Emilia's chin.

"You're a better witch than pirate, darling," Catherine said with a laugh. "You didn't even bother to tie my wrists or check me for other weapons."

Humiliation rose in Emilia's throat. She'd never taken a prisoner before, but still, Catherine was right.

She should've thought of that.

"It can't be the pistol," Zain muttered to Maria. "If her ships were close enough to hear her pistol, we'd be able to see them."

"Do you want to test that theory, Officer Amari?" Catherine said.

Zain's jaw tightened.

"He's quartermaster now, Cat," Maria said.

Catherine ignored the correction. "Drop your sword, darling," she warned Emilia, "or you'll die." With a cruel laugh that cut like a blade, she added, "And that'd be a tragedy, wouldn't it? For you to miss your own execution? Again?"

The blade twisted deeper into Emilia's heart. How had she been *so* wrong about Catherine?

Again, Zain murmured his advice to Maria. "She needs to drop it, Captain," he said. "Catherine's most likely bluffing, but just in case she isn't..."

Maria nodded. "Em," she said softly.

Emilia gripped her sword tightly, her chest fluttering, as she met Maria's dark gaze.

"Do you trust me?"

Catherine laughed. "You're a pirate. She'd have to be a fool to trust *you*!"

Emilia swallowed. She'd been a fool to trust Catherine. She didn't want to be one again.

But...

But Maria had asked for Emilia's trust.

'*Today, of all days, we must trust each other.*'

Emilia nodded slowly.

A stunningly soft smile curled at the corners of Maria's lips.

"Then, drop your sword, and step back."

Maria wanted her to willingly disarm herself? Emilia wasn't sure about that.

Maria stepped closer. "Trust me, Em. *Please.*"

Emilia had never heard Maria say *please* in front of her crew before. It was a vulnerable word—one she'd only ever used in private.

Catherine frowned, apparently just as confused as Emilia.

Emilia thought of all the times Maria had drunk for her, never asking for her trust—because she knew Emilia wasn't ready to give it—and she dropped the sword.

Catherine dove for it, but Maria drew both of hers.

Maria had drawn her left sword only once the night before, and even then, it was only after Emilia had disarmed her of her right sword. She knew Maria was comfortable using both hands, but she'd never seen her use both at once.

Catherine, however, clearly had. She took a step back, her long, fair-skinned fingers wrapped loosely around Emilia's sword.

Emilia knew, as well as Maria did, that the sword Catherine preferred to use was heavier than Emilia's.

Already, she was at a disadvantage, but that wasn't enough to discourage her.

Zain tapped Henry's shoulder, and the helmsman released the wheel. It spun, and the ship shifted slightly—before steadying.

Zain and Henry both took several steps back, giving their captain space to fight.

Catherine lunged forward, aggressive as ever.

In what looked like one, fluid motion, Maria parried with her left hand and thrust with her right, nearly piercing Catherine through the stomach.

But Catherine leapt back, just in time.

Maria stepped to the side, crossing one boot over the other, and Catherine mirrored her movement.

Like vicious sharks waiting for their moment to strike, the two circled each other.

But even after all of these years, they knew each other's fighting patterns far too well.

Catherine knew how to counter every move Maria made, and

even with a sword that wasn't hers, Catherine held her own against her former captain.

Catherine had once told Emilia that sword-fighting was like a dance, but Emilia had never fully understood it until she watched the two of them.

If sword-fighting was a dance, the two of them were expert dancers—light on their feet, heavy on their swords.

Two steps, *strike*.

Four steps, *strike*.

Even an ambidextrous fighter like Maria had a hand she favored —the right, as Emilia had learned in her own fights with the captain—and Catherine clearly knew this, too, because she focused her attention on Maria's weaker hand, until, finally, the smaller sword fell from Maria's left hand.

Now, they were both down to one sword.

They clashed again—a steady rhythm of steel clanging against steel, until…finally, one gained the upper hand.

In a very similar move to the one Emilia had used against Catherine earlier, Maria knocked the sword from Catherine's hand and then winded the blade with the precision of a serpent—to rest against Catherine's throat.

Catherine had lost.

Emilia hadn't expected to feel so much satisfaction from someone *else* beating Catherine, but she decided, in that moment, that if anyone deserved to beat Catherine, it was Maria.

But the moment of true vindication—the moment of Catherine's death—didn't come.

The pirate captain, who'd killed so mercilessly, *so* many times, hesitated to kill Catherine.

Why?

"Yield," Maria said.

"Never," Catherine snarled back.

Maria tilted her head slightly, her curls falling to the side. "Yield, or I'll kill you."

Catherine laughed, and her long fingers brushed the back of her belt—where she'd stowed the...

"Pistol!" Emilia said.

But it was too late.

Catherine straightened her arm, pointing the flintlock pistol directly at Maria's head.

Maria flashed a bitter smile. "Cat," she said in a low, chiding tone, "using a pistol in a sword fight is beneath you."

"You're a *pirate!*" Catherine spat with a venom unlike anything Emilia had ever heard. "I'll kill you by whatever means necessary, and none of it is beneath me!"

All those months of loving Catherine, and Emilia had never heard her talk like that.

Had this venomous hatred existed all along? Had it been hiding beneath every kind word Catherine had ever spoken?

This was the Catherine who had so callously ordered the slaughter of Emilia's people. This was the Catherine that Emilia had been so unable to see, beneath her well-constructed mask.

"Do you *want* me to kill you?" Catherine yelled. "Is that what you're waiting for?"

Maria simply lifted a scarred eyebrow. She was a steady current, where Catherine was a breaking wave, bashing itself against the rocks.

Catherine cocked the pistol and curled a finger around the trigger.

Maria would've survived the shot, most likely. Catherine had probably been ordered to keep her alive.

And even if she hadn't, Emilia had given Maria a potion that would help her cling to life, even after a fatal injury.

But none of that was enough to slow the surge of panic that rose in Emilia's throat and spilled out in a sudden cry.

"No!"

Catherine froze.

Maria blinked in surprise, as well, and her warm, brown eyes shifted toward Emilia.

Catherine didn't lower the pistol, but in her shock, she let go of the trigger. She cast an incredulous look over her shoulder.

Emilia clamped her mouth shut, her pulse racing.

"You can't be serious," Catherine muttered.

Emilia didn't know how to respond to that. "About?"

Catherine's lip curled, and venomous jealousy darkened her blue eyes.

"You fall really fucking easily, don't you?"

Emilia squinted in confusion. Yes, she'd fallen in love with Catherine fairly quickly, but...was Catherine trying to imply that Emilia had fallen for Maria, too?

That was nonsense.

She hated Maria.

She'd panicked at the thought of her being hurt, yes, but...that didn't mean anything.

Right?

Catherine shook her head and let out a bitter laugh. "I broke your heart, so you flung yourself into the arms of my greatest enemy?"

"I didn't fling myself at anyone," Emilia muttered.

Catherine scoffed at that. She glanced from Maria to Emilia, her brows furrowing in thought, and then, her lips curved slowly.

Before anyone could stop her, she dashed backward and grabbed Emilia. She wrapped her left arm tightly around Emilia's chest to hold her still, and with her right, she pressed the pistol against Emilia's head.

Emilia definitely regretted not grabbing her enchanted dagger *now*.

The color seemed to fade from Maria's hand, as she gripped her sword tightly. "What are you doing?"

"I'm offering you a deal you can't refuse, Maria Welles," Catherine said with an arrogant smile. "I didn't expect to find the witch here, but now that I have, my choices have become a little more...*varied*."

Maria made brief eye-contact with Emilia, and something about the ferocity in Maria's dark eyes kept Emilia frozen to the spot. "King Eldric is disappointed with you, isn't he?" she murmured to Catherine. "You lost me. You lost her. You have a *very* hard time holding onto your prisoners, don't you?"

Emilia couldn't see Catherine's face, at the moment, but she could feel the anger that pulled her muscles tight.

"He'll be satisfied if I return with either of you," Catherine said, her soft, lilting voice practically vibrating with rage, "and out of the two of you, the witch is obviously the easier target."

Maria's eyes darkened. "Are you sure about that?"

Somehow, the fact that her ex-lover kept calling her '*the witch*,' rather than her name, rattled Emilia more than her implication that Emilia was an easy target.

When Maria or Judith called her that, there was a touch of teasing beneath it. When Catherine said it, there was only revulsion.

"If I return her to the gallows," Catherine said, "the entire fleet of warships that I have, waiting to drag you all to the bottom of the Azure Sea, will accompany me. Which means you and your crew of pirates, Maria, will live another day."

It didn't *sound* like a bluff.

Could their salvation be that simple?

Just a simple trade of a witch that none of them had even known long, anyway?

Catherine was right.

It was too good an offer to refuse.

But just when Emilia was *sure* Maria would accept, Maria said, "No."

Catherine laughed, as if she couldn't believe her ears. "No?"

"No," Maria said again, her voice as cold as ice. "I don't make deals with your king." Disgust darkened her large, brown eyes. "Or his glory-starved puppet."

The muscles in Catherine's arm flexed against Emilia's chest. "You'd choose a witch over your own crew?"

Maria stepped closer. "No," she said with a dark glare. "I'd choose a witch, who *is* my crew."

Emilia stared at her captain, her heart racing. What was Maria thinking? Why would a pirate captain risk her ship and crew for Emilia?

Why would *anyone*?

"And how does the rest of your crew feel about that?" Catherine challenged. She shifted her icy blue gaze toward Zain. "What do you think, Amari? Was defending a witch in the job description?"

Maria glanced at her quartermaster, and a hint of worry flickered across her face.

But Zain just lifted that dark eyebrow of his and said, "If my captain says it is, yes."

A smile twitched at one corner of Maria's mouth.

Whatever *spat* the two of them had—it hadn't torn them apart.

Catherine cast an alarmed glance around the ship, as if she expected to find a mutiny breaking out at that very moment.

But no one moved.

A puzzling warmth unfurled in Emilia's stomach. Why wasn't anyone taking Catherine up on the offer?

They knew what Emilia was, now. They knew she'd lied. What were they doing?

Somewhere behind them, someone said, "Let her go."

Was that Pelt?

A few voices joined with him, and that familiar, *lovely* glow of pride kindled in Maria's eyes.

Emilia could barely breathe.

"You'd rather me bring an entire fleet to attack you," Catherine said, just as shocked as Emilia, "than give up one witch?"

Maria stepped forward. "The woman you're threatening is my

surgeon, and I'll fight for her, just as I'd fight for anyone under my command."

Panic fluttered in Emilia's chest.

This wasn't right. They were pirates.

They were *supposed* to make deals like this one.

They weren't *supposed* to risk their lives for her.

"Admiral Rochester," Maria said, a dark warning in her eyes, "you'll unhand my surgeon. Now."

"Or what?" Catherine snarled back.

"Or you'll die," Maria said without a moment's hesitation, "in the most painful way I can imagine."

"Captain," Emilia breathed.

Why was she doing this? This was madness.

Emilia had joined this crew with the intent of leaving them—even *betraying* them, if necessary.

She wouldn't let them die for her.

She wouldn't let anyone *else* die for her.

"Can I take the deal on their behalf?" Emilia blurted out.

Maria's brown eyes shifted toward Emilia. "Em."

"You want to," Catherine stammered, apparently not expecting this, "trade their lives for yours?"

"What? No," Emilia said. "No, of course not."

The eyes of her shipmates seared her, like rays of sunlight.

"I'm offering my own freedom in exchange for theirs," Emilia explained. "If I let you take me back to the gallows, like you want, will you let them live?"

Zain gave her a curious frown, which was what Emilia chose to focus on—because Maria's glare, at the moment, was absolutely murderous.

Apparently, she didn't approve of Emilia's plan.

"You'd willingly give up your life to save some pirates?" Catherine said, her voice full of disbelief.

Emilia struggled to ignore the anger radiating from Maria. She didn't *want* to ignore it. She wanted to analyze it. She wanted to know why Maria even *cared* whether Catherine took her, but Emilia needed to focus on the cold pistol pressed to her head—and the woman who held it. "I would," she breathed.

It was strange that Catherine acted so appalled by this deal now, when she was the one who'd proposed it. "I...suppose," she muttered, "if you're foolish enough to do that."

"You're not doing that, Em," Maria said, as if she could actually stop her.

Emilia did her best to ignore it.

Just a few more moments, and the crew would be safe.

A few more moments, and *Maria* would be safe.

Emilia noticed movement in the corner of her eye—and she looked, just in time to see Maria take Henry's pistol. She tried to yell no, but it was too late.

Like the enraged madwoman everyone believed her to be, Captain Maria Welles fired the first shot.

And doomed them all.

The scent of gun-smoke burned Emilia's nose, somehow stronger, in that moment, than any other scent—stronger, even, than the scent of cannon fire and burnt flesh, which still singed the salted, sea air.

It was the smell of anger.

The smell of war.

Silence settled over the ship.

Catherine's grip on her loosened, and Emilia could practically feel the shock radiating through her body.

"There's your fucking signal," Maria snarled, and then, she aimed the pistol at Catherine. "Now, unhand my surgeon, and get off of my fucking ship."

"Have you lost your mind?" Catherine breathed.

An odd question, considering how many times Catherine called Maria a 'madwoman' to Emilia.

To the entire world.

"You can't possibly think that you can take on an entire fleet with one ship," Catherine scoffed.

Maria shrugged those strong shoulders of hers. "I'll suppose we'll see," she muttered. "Now, unless you want me to strap you to the side of my ship, so your own cannon fire can blow right through you," she paused, giving that threat time to sink in, "run."

Without another moment of hesitation, Catherine shoved Emilia away from her, and Maria caught her with one arm.

And while Maria was occupied with Emilia, Catherine bolted toward the side of the ship, climbed onto the rail, and then leapt into the sea.

Yells of alarms rung out, and nearly every pirate on the ship rushed to the rail to search for the navy admiral. But Emilia's head was spinning too fast to make sense of any of it.

"What have you done?" Emilia breathed.

Maria pulled Emilia into her arms and, though she still held her weapons, she held Emilia tight. The scent of hibiscus, orange, leather, and smoke filled Emilia's lungs, and Maria's lips brushed against her.

"If she wants war, she can have it," Maria said into Emilia's thick, black hair, "but she's not getting you."

With her face pressed against Maria's dark, leather doublet, Emilia breathed slowly, too stunned to react.

Maria had never embraced her like this.

Not when they'd kissed.

Not when they'd had sex.

Never.

Adjusting her weapons to one arm, Maria freed her hand and slipped a tattooed finger beneath Emilia's chin. She lifted Emilia's face, and Emilia couldn't help but sink deeply into those lovely, brown eyes.

"And the next time you're tempted to risk your life for me or my crew," Maria said, her brows high, "don't."

CHAPTER 24
Here Be Dragons

"Land, ho!"

With a mix of excitement and astonishment, Emilia rushed to the quarterdeck, where Maria stood with her spyglass, peering at the land in the distance—to see which island the sailor on lookout had spotted.

"Is it…" Emilia couldn't even bring herself to say the words—but she didn't have to.

With a smile, Maria offered her the tarnished, brass spyglass. "Take a look for yourself, love."

Emilia took it and peered into it, gasping as she saw the familiar shape of Drakon Isle on the horizon. It'd been so long since she'd seen her homeland, and yet, she recognized it, as if it'd been only yesterday.

"Welcome home, love," Maria murmured.

Emilia pulled the spyglass away from her face and glanced at Maria. She'd waited so long to hear those words, but now, they just…sounded wrong.

The *Wicked Fate* was her home, too, wasn't it?

Emilia wasn't sure when she'd started to feel that way. Was it during the battle—when Maria had declared war on an entire fleet of ships, just to stop Catherine from taking Emilia?

Or was it during the trial?

Trial was a strange word for it, really.

If Emilia had been surprised by Maria's refusal to send Emilia back to the gallows, it was nothing compared to the surprise she'd faced at the trial itself.

Maria had begrudgingly allowed the trial to take place, but she'd guarded Emilia like a viper throughout the entire ordeal, striking at anyone who dared to even *think* about shackles.

Once the smoke had cleared, Rat-Slayer had slinked onto the deck and perched himself at Maria's side, like some sort of guard dog.

Or guard cat.

But Maria's protection had been almost entirely unnecessary. Surprising no one more than Emilia herself, Zain had agreed that— after Emilia's attempted sacrifice—neither the shackles nor the imprisonment were needed.

He'd also rushed along the trial itself—because, as Judith had so vehemently pointed out, *someone* had to deal with the perforated intestines in the hold, and there apparently weren't any other volunteers.

In the end, only a few sailors had been unwilling to trust the witch who'd offered her own freedom in exchange for the crew. Despite the hatred of magic that was taught to all Illopians, this crew had set that prejudice aside and accepted Emilia for who she was.

Even now, emotion welled up in Emilia's throat, as she remembered the way one shipmate after another had spoken in her defense.

They'd told of times she'd helped them and treated their wounds. Somehow, in just a few months, Emilia had gone from the woman they all wanted to see killed...to the one they'd defend in front of the crew.

Emilia didn't understand it at all.

It still felt like a dream, really, and each day Emilia awoke on the *Wicked Fate* and realized it wasn't, she found herself more and more astonished by it.

They'd declared her innocent of endangering the crew and sent her back to work within the hour—mostly because Judith was threatening to drag them all down into the hold with her, if they didn't send Emilia to heal the injured sailors soon.

"What is it, Em?" Maria said. Her palm brushed against the curve of Emilia's back, and despite the sadness swirling inside of Emilia now, a tiny spark of desire still flared to life at Maria's touch. "This *is* what you want, isn't it? To return to your home?"

"Of course," Emilia said, but her voice cracked as she said it.

Maria studied Emilia with a concerned frown, but she didn't press her. "I'd like to go ashore with you, if that's all right?" she said with a surprising hesitancy. "The rest of the crew will remain aboard the ship."

Emilia nodded. Maria couldn't get the gold Emilia had promised her without coming ashore, and Emilia was secretly relieved by that fact—because it pushed their goodbye just a bit further away.

Why did her chest ache so much at the thought of saying goodbye to this pirate that she'd supposedly hated? What was this...*feeling* between them now?

"Has there been any sign of her?" Emilia asked.

Maria didn't ask who she meant. "Not yet."

Worry twisted deeper in Emilia's stomach. The last thing she wanted was for Catherine and her fleet to find the *Wicked Fate* after Emilia had left the ship—when she wasn't there to help.

She was so close to her home, and yet, she'd never felt more homesick than when she thought of leaving this crew—than when she thought of leaving Maria or Judith, Helen or Pelt, Fulke or the ship cats...

Even *Zain*.

He might've been suspicious of her, at first, but after her attempted sacrifice, he'd softened to her quicker than she'd ever thought possible.

Emilia swallowed against another lump of emotion that welled up in her throat.

Almost as if she'd seen the pain in Emilia's face, Maria suddenly curled an arm around Emilia and pulled her close. The scent of hibiscus and oranges filled her lungs, and Emilia ached at the thought of never smelling that scent again.

"There's a lot I want to say to you," Maria whispered into Emilia's hair, "but I'd rather say it on the island—when we're alone."

Emilia couldn't imagine *why*. Maria hadn't hidden their relationship in weeks. Even now, she embraced Emilia with no concern for the sailors who watched.

"There's something I need to say to you, too," Emilia murmured against Maria's neck—even though she wasn't sure she had the courage to say it.

DESPITE THE FACT THAT, OUT OF THE TWO OF THEM, EMILIA WAS THE one who'd climbed this mountain before, somehow Maria was less winded than Emilia, when they reached the cliffside.

"What is it you're expecting to find up here?" Maria asked.

Emilia suppressed a smile. "You'll see."

Maria grasped her hand and tugged her backward, and Emilia laughed as her back collided with Maria's leather-clad front. "You really know how to entice a pirate, don't you, love?" she said in Emilia's ear.

Emilia suppressed a shudder. "We're almost there."

After all, Emilia could already hear the roar of the waterfall.

With an annoyed sigh, Maria released her hand.

Emilia laughed. So much had changed between them since that

first night at the tavern, but the one thing that hadn't was Maria's impatience.

She was like a petulant child, sometimes.

Just…with a penchant for murder.

"I think Judith's still hoping I'll drag you back to the ship," Maria said, as they neared the cliff. With a roll of her eyes, she added, "Helen offered to help if I wasn't strong enough—which was just insulting."

Emilia laughed at that. "Captain, I'm not exactly the *lightest* woman on your ship."

The lightest was probably Judith—with her narrow hips and shoulders.

Or one of the cats.

Winter, maybe.

The moment Emilia stopped to peer over the edge of the cliff, Maria came up behind her, and—with no warning whatsoever—scooped Emilia up into her arms.

Maria lifted that scarred eyebrow of hers. "You were saying?"

Emilia slapped her hand against Maria's shoulder. "Put me down, you arrogant pirate," she said, barely able to catch her breath, "before we fall off this cliff!"

Maria chuckled and set her back on her feet.

Shaking her head in disbelief, Emilia gazed over the edge of the cliff. She watched the spray of the waterfall rise into the air, and she closed her eyes, calling telepathically for her dragons.

Whether they'd hear her or not depended on where they'd gone after the attack. She'd assumed they'd come back, but she had no way to know for sure.

"You know, Captain," Emilia said, as she waited for a response from her dragons, "with so few people living here now, there will be plenty of extra resources." She turned to Maria, offering her a hopeful smile. "Perhaps, the island would be a good place to stop to restock supplies, whenever you're in the Azure Sea."

The corners of Maria's lips curved upward. "You'd let us do that?"

"Of course," Emilia said, "as long as the dragons don't mind." She stepped closer to the pirate captain. "And I don't think they will—not once they find out that you're someone I...care about."

Those dark brown eyes of Maria's widened. "Em."

Emilia looked away, her heart racing. "I just mean—"

But before she could back out in shame, Maria took Emilia's face into her hands and kissed her.

She tasted of rum and fruit, and her hands were as warm as always.

"Em," Maria gasped. She rested her forehead against Emilia's, her curls soft and silky against Emilia's skin. "There's something I need to tell you, something I should've said weeks ago."

Emilia rested her hand against Maria's doublet, curling her fingers around the captain's narrow, leather-clad waist. There was so much left unsaid between them, and Emilia could only imagine that Maria's confession would be less terrifying than her own.

"What is it, Captain?" Emilia whispered.

A strange part of her hoped Maria would say she'd changed her mind—that she'd never release Emilia from her service. It was an insane thing to hope for, but at the moment, her desperate heart was willing to cling to anything that wasn't a goodbye.

But Maria didn't say that. What she said, instead, was, "I'm not asking you to stay." She leaned closer, her breath warm against Emilia's mouth. "I said you have my blessing to leave, and I meant it. But Em...I need you to know," she paused, and another pained gasp spilled from her lips, "I've fallen for you."

Emilia was almost one-hundred percent positive that she'd heard that last part wrong, but she didn't have time to ask.

Because at that moment, a powerful gust of wind blew them both backward.

Maria's tricorn flew off her head before she could catch it, and she stumbled back, her dark eyes wide.

No less than five dragons soared into the air, their wings outstretched, their scales glimmering like diamonds in the sunlight.

"Captain Maria Welles," Emilia said, grasping onto the pirate captain so that she wouldn't fall, "I'd like for you to meet the most fearsome creatures of Aletharia."

Maria gazed up at the dragons, her brown curls blowing in the wind, her breath spilling from her lungs in quick, uneven pants.

To Emilia's amusement, the arrogant pirate, who'd never blinked in face of death or battle, looked anything *but* arrogant now.

Wonder glowed in Maria's beautiful, brown eyes, and suddenly, Emilia was far too enthralled with that beauty to *not* say the strange, impossible words that had taken up residence in her heart.

"And...I think I might love you, too."

Maria looked down at Emilia, her eyes wide.

"He's not going to hurt you, Captain," Emilia said—for what must've been the twentieth time in the last hour. She sat, cross-legged, in the grass with a dragon leaning its massive head against her shoulder.

Maria couldn't think of a single thing to say, except: "There is a massive, fire-breathing beast, trying to...snuggle with you."

"Yes," Emilia said with an amused smile, "I can see him."

Maria just stared.

And she'd thought the cat situation was bizarre.

"Does it...do this often?"

"Of course," Emilia said. She stroked the dragon's green scales, ignoring the burst of smoke that puffed from his snout. "Especially when I bring him treats."

Maria eyed the dragon warily. "But we didn't bring any treats," she said with a frown, "did we?"

"Well, I did bring a certain pirate captain," Emilia said with a devious smile. She looked up at the green dragon. "What do you think, Emryn? Do you like the taste of fried pirate?"

Two, quick puffs of smoke poured from his snout, almost as if the enormous, fire-breathing beast were laughing at Emilia's joke.

Could dragons laugh?

A sudden explosion echoed in the distance, and the ground quaked beneath them.

Maria glanced toward the sea, and her heart stopped at the sight of the black smoke that coiled into the sky.

"What was that?" Emilia asked.

Cold, numbing shock poured through Maria's veins. "Cannons," she mumbled. "She's here."

Emilia climbed to her feet and turned toward the large, green dragon. "Get the other dragons," she said, and then, as if he'd understood her clearly, the dragon huffed out another puff of smoke and took to the air.

His incredible wings unleashed a gust of wind that nearly knocked them both into the grass.

Emilia grasped Maria's arms to get her attention. "Captain," she said, her beautiful voice cutting through Maria's shock, "we have to go."

The horror that wrapped around Maria's throat had left her barely able to speak. "I won't make it in time."

"I've lived here all my life, Captain," Emilia reminded her. "I promise you: I can get us there in time to save them."

Maria blinked slowly, convinced—for the second time that day—that she'd hallucinated. "Us?"

"Yes, Captain. Us," Emilia said. "What did you think Emryn and I were talking about all of that time?"

Maria hadn't thought they were talking at all—especially considering Emryn was a dragon, who...*didn't* talk. "What are you saying, Em?"

With an adorable, mischievous smile, Emilia said, "I've decided the pirate's life *is* for me." She plucked a blade of grass from Maria's curly hair. "If you'll still have me."

Maria could barely breathe. "I'll always have you."

Emilia let go of her and stepped back. "In that case, Captain," she said with an absolutely dazzling smile, "I think it's *finally* time for me to summon the goddess of the sea. Don't you?"

TO BE CONTINUED...

Book 2

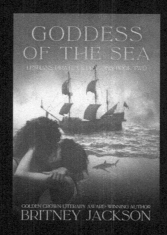

T he story of Emilia Drakon and Captain Maria Welles
continues in *Goddess of the Sea* (*Lesbians, Pirates, & Dragons*:
Book 2).

Author's Note

This book has been a *long* time in the making. Many of you know this—because you were such a wonderful source of encouragement to me, while I was writing it (and rewriting it... and rewriting it again... and then rewriting it again). It was such a fun story to write—because what's more fun than pirates, right? But it was also terrifying—because I put so much pressure on myself to get everything right.

I started world-building for it several years ago, when I was still working on my queer vampire series, and I've been writing (and rewriting) it steadily for the last two years.

And hey, if we're being totally honest, it's the book I've been dreaming of writing since I was clueless, young lesbian, crushing hard on Elizabeth Swann in *Pirates of the Caribbean*.

It's changed a lot since its initial outline. I originally meant for it to be a standalone, but I was only a few chapters deep when I realized that Maria, Emilia, and Judith would never let me go so soon.

This book has seen me through the grief of losing my mother and through so many ups and downs in both my mental and physical health. It's been a source of comfort on my darkest days.

That's what I love so much about stories. They pull me through, even when I don't have the strength to do it without them.

I hope this book has offered you some comfort, as well, and I hope you've come to love these lesbian pirates as much as I have.

And I hope you'll join me for Maria and Emilia's next adventure.

Thank you all so much—both for reading and for wanting to read. I couldn't have done it without you. Your excitement and encouragement has meant the world to me.

I love and appreciate you all, and please, remember: you deserve love and happy endings, no matter what sort of cruel lies your brain likes to tell you.

Love,
Britney Jackson

Also by Britney Jackson

Lesbians, Pirates, and Dragons:

Pirates of Aletharia

Goddess of the Sea

The Dragon Child
(Coming Soon)

Creatures of Darkness Series:

The Stone of the Eklektos

The Tomb of Blood

The Assassins of Light

The Reign of Darkness

About the Author

Britney Jackson is an award-winning author of LGBTQ speculative fiction. She's adored books for as long as she can remember and has loved writing for almost as long.

She has a passion for creating the kind of heroes she needed when she was younger: heroines with mental illness, flaws, and traumatic pasts. She centers her books around strong, lesbian and bisexual women who find courage, love, and happy endings.

She resides in Alabama with her two kids and the snuggliest cat you'll ever meet. She has a Bachelor of Science in Fine Arts and Religion and did her graduate work in English.

Learn more at britneyjackson.com.

Milton Keynes UK
Ingram Content Group UK Ltd.
UKHW041523190724
26UKWH00047B/585